"Alessandro, what are you doing here?"

"Trying to get you to walk faster?"

My brain finally regained the ability to form complete sentences. "Why did you kill Conway? He was a lead in my investigation and now he's dead."

"He was a very bad man. You were chasing him with a knife."

"I needed to ask him some questions."

He smiled like a wolf baring its fangs in a dark forest. "Were you going to stab him if he didn't answer?"

"I don't need to stab people to get answers."

He sighed. "Collect your friend and go home, Catalina. There are no answers for you here."

What?

Runa rounded the corner at full speed, saw us, and froze.

"I'm so sorry," Alessandro said. "I have to leave now. Go home, stay safe, and forget all about this."

Ahead the elevator chimed.

"I'll see you around." Alessandro raised his hand. Somehow there was a gun in it. I didn't see him draw one. The gun barked, spitting bullets, the window to our right shattered, and Alessandro jumped out of it.

10/19

By Ilona Andrews

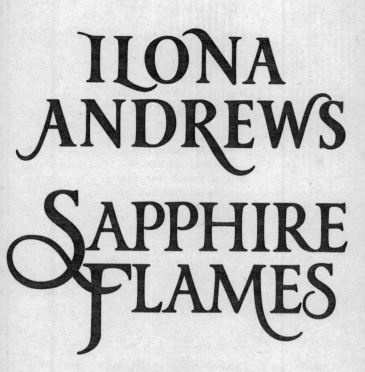

ILONA ANDREWS

SAPPHIRE FLAMES

A Hidden Legacy Novel

AVON BOOKS

An Imprint of HarperCollinsPublishers

SAPPHIRE FLAMES. Copyright © 2019 by Ilona Gordon and Andrew Gordon. All rights reserved. Printed in the United States of America. No part of this book may be used or reproduced in any manner whatsoever without written permission except in the case of brief quotations embodied in critical articles and reviews. For information, address HarperCollins Publishers, 195 Broadway, New York, NY 10007.

First Avon Books mass market printing: September 2019
First Avon Books hardcover printing: August 2019

Print Edition ISBN: 978-0-06-287834-2
Digital Edition ISBN: 978-0-06-287833-5

Cover art by Gene Mollica

FIRST EDITION

3 1559 00282 9057

19 20 21 22 23 QGM 10 9 8 7 6 5 4 3 2 1

To Anastasia and Helen

 **Chapter 1**

I was swimming through the warm water of the Gulf when someone knocked on the sky. The bright little fishes following me scattered, the crystal-clear water vanished, and I landed on the sand.

The sky above me shuddered. *Boom, boom, boom.*

The dream tore like wet tissue, and for a disorienting moment I didn't know where I was. Slowly the familiar contours of my bedroom came into focus through the gloom. The alarm clock on my nightstand glowed with bright red. 2:07 a.m.

Someone was pounding on my door.

"Catalina!" my sister yelled. "Get up!"

Panic pierced me. I jumped out of the bed, sprinted across the bedroom, and flung the door open. "Did the plane go down?"

"What? No!"

I sagged against the door frame in relief. Our older sister, Nevada; her husband; and her mother-in-law were flying to Spain for a funeral. Over the ocean. It caused me no end of anxiety.

"The plane is fine," Arabella told me.

"Then what is it?"

Arabella's face was flushed, and her blond hair stuck out from her head in weird directions. She wore an old, stained Sailor Moon T-shirt, and her basketball shorts were on backward.

"Augustine is downstairs."

"Augustine who? Augustine Montgomery?"

"Yes!"

I snapped out of my relief back to full alert. "Why?" Why in the world would the Head of House Montgomery be downstairs, in the middle of the night?

"He wants to see you. He says it's an emergency. Hurry up before Mom shoots him."

She turned around and ran down the stairs leading from my loft suite to the rest of the warehouse we used as our home and place of business.

Augustine was absolutely the last person I expected at two o'clock in the morning. Something terrible had happened.

I looked at myself. I wore an oversize grey T-shirt that came to my knees and said "I ♥ Sleep." No time to change. I took the stairs barefoot and followed my sister into a wide hallway. The light in the media room was on, casting a warm electric glow and illuminating the way just enough to see.

The hallway led to a door on the left where a small section of the warehouse was designated as the Baylor Agency's office. The entire family congregated in front of the door, all except Mom.

Grandma Frida, thin, tan, with a halo of platinum curls, looked worried. Bern, my oldest cousin, resembled a bear awakened halfway through his hibernation—big, muscular, his light brown hair disheveled, holding a tablet that looked too small for his hands. Next to him, Leon, his younger half brother and complete opposite, leaned on the wall, totally awake. Lean and dark-haired, Leon was a ball of wiry energy. And he still wore the jeans and T-shirt I had seen him in last night. Either he fell asleep in his clothes, or he felt the need to be fully dressed at two o'clock in the morning for some nefarious reason. Leon didn't have any other kind of reasons.

Ahead of me, Arabella darted up the stairs and into her bedroom and emerged with a huge Texas A&M sweatshirt. She threw it at me. "Boobs."

Bern woke up enough to roll his eyes.

"Thanks." I pulled the sweatshirt on, hiding the fact that I wasn't wearing a bra. "How did Augustine get here?"

At night, access to the warehouse was blocked by concrete barriers. Only one road remained open, guarded by a checkpoint staffed with our security people, who were supposed to prevent exactly this sort of thing from happening. Augustine was ruthless. He could have killed us all in our sleep.

"Did our guards let him in? Did anyone call and say he was coming?"

"Funny thing," Leon said. "We have this lovely footage."

Bern turned the tablet toward me. A view from the surveillance camera inside the security booth showed two guards, a Hispanic female in her forties and a white man in his mid-twenties with dark hair. Lopez and Walton. A silver Bentley Bentayga pulled up to the booth. The passenger window of the car rolled down, revealing me.

"Hello, Ms. Baylor," Walton said.

The fake Catalina nodded.

"Check the log, check the log . . ." Leon sang out.

The log of arrivals and departures lay right there, on the counter. It would show that I was already home.

The guard reached over, and his hand passed above the log to the switch attached to the barrier mechanism.

"Epic fail!" Leon announced.

Walton flipped the switch and a heavy metal clang announced the spiked barrier retracting. The window rolled back up and the armored vehicle slid forward and out of view.

I couldn't even. My ability to *even* was severely compromised.

Lopez frowned. "When did they get a Bentley?"

The male guard shrugged. "Who knows? Maybe it was a birthday present."

"Dumbass," Arabella said.

Augustine Montgomery was an Illusion Prime. He could look like anyone, he could sound like anyone, and he could pass both fingerprint and retinal scanners. And he'd just breezed past our security like it was nothing.

"We're in trouble," I said.

"No shit," Leon said.

"Catalina," Grandma Frida said, "your mother is in the conference room with that ass and a Desert Eagle. Get in there before she puts a .50 round between his eyes."

I opened the door, walked into the office hallway, and shut the door behind me. This part of the warehouse with its high-traffic beige carpet, a drop ceiling, and glass walls looked just like any regular work space. The three offices on my right and the break room with a kitchenette on my left lay shrouded in gloom. Only the conference room, just past the break room, was brightly lit, and the electric light shone through the glass into the hallway.

I took a step and stopped. As of three days ago, when I officially turned twenty-one, I also became the Head of House Baylor. We were a brand-new House, formed only three years ago. Our grace period, a reprieve which shielded us from attacks by other Houses, was about to expire. I had dealt with magical heavy hitters before in the course of our business, but this would be my first interaction with another Prime as the Head of a House. And Augustine was a shark in a four-thousand-dollar suit; a sleek, deadly great white with razor-sharp teeth.

I had to do this right. I couldn't just barge in there. Emergency or not, I had to act the part.

My stomach fluttered.

Think Prime, Head of the House, Victoria Tremaine's granddaughter, confident, dangerous, not afraid, woken up in the middle of the night . . . annoyed. Definitely annoyed.

I walked into the conference room with a slightly irritated expression.

Augustine pivoted toward me in his chair. Louis Auchincloss, who wrote novels about polite society and old money, once famously said, "Perfection irritates as well as it attracts, in fiction as in life." Augustine was deeply irritating.

Being an Illusion Prime, Augustine crafted his appearance the way one would paint a masterpiece. His face was beautifully sculpted with defined cheekbones, a square jaw that communicated masculinity without implying brutishness, a straight nose, and a broad forehead. His cheeks were slightly concave, just enough to communicate maturity. A virtuoso barber had turned his blond, nearly platinum hair into a masterpiece. A thin pair of glasses was the only imperfection Augustine allowed himself and it wasn't enough. There was something ageless and cold about him. He was about as alive as a marble statue.

At the other end of the table my mother sat watching him like a coiled cobra. Her right hand stayed under the table, most likely touching the Desert Eagle .50, the largest legal caliber for a handgun in the US. It was the closest thing to handheld artillery Mom could conceal under the table. It could send a round through a full refrigerator and kill a person on the other side.

My mother had spent almost ten years as a sniper and her magic guaranteed that she didn't miss. If she killed Augustine, Montgomery International Investigations, the firm Augustine owned, would crush us. If he miraculously survived, he would kill her. As happened often in life, there were no good options. I had to get him out of here.

I made my tone cold and annoyed. "Mr. Montgomery, while you're always welcome in our home, it's the middle of the night."

"I apologize," he said. "It's an emergency." He reached into his pocket, pulled out a phone, and showed it to me.

On the screen, an adolescent boy smiled into the camera. Bright red hair cut short, grey eyes, pale skin, and the smug grin of a teenage boy who has just gotten away with mischief. He looked vaguely familiar, but I couldn't for the life of me remember where I'd seen him before.

"This is Ragnar," Augustine said. "He's fifteen. He has a dog named Tank. He likes detective books and the Sherlock Holmes show. He plays a Ranger in Hero Tournament. Two days ago, his mother and sister died in a fire."

"Why are you telling me this?"

"Right now he's standing on the roof of Memorial Hermann Hospital. He's thinking of jumping and he's a Prime, so nobody can get to him. If we don't hurry, his broken body will be the leading story on the morning news."

Alarm rolled through me in an electric rush.

"Augustine, you know that's not what I do. I've never pulled someone off a roof before. If I fail, I'll be responsible for his death . . ."

"But you can do it. It's within your power." He looked straight at me. "Your sister asked me for a favor once. I'm now asking you for assistance, one Head of House to another. He has one sister left. Right now, she's at the hospital praying he doesn't fall to his death."

And if I tried and failed, there would be a grief-stricken Prime who could turn all of her agony and rage onto me. This was beyond reckless.

"I don't know if I can help you. I may make this worse."

Augustine's composure cracked, and a human being looked back at me through his eyes. "He's just a child, Catalina. He already lost so much. He's in the worst pain of his short life and he has no idea how to contain it. He just wants to stop hurting. Please try."

I opened my mouth to tell him no and thought of a boy standing on a ledge, all alone in the dark. So desperate and hurt that he was willing to end it in the most painful way possible.

My father had stood on a ledge like that, except his ledge was cancer. We had tried so hard to pull him from it. We fought for every minute. We sold the house and moved here, into the warehouse, to pay for his medical bills. Then we mortgaged our business to Augustine to pay for experimental treatments. My dad had built Baylor Investigative Agency from the ground up. He'd viewed it as his legacy, a business that would feed and clothe us, and we had used it as collateral to borrow money. It felt like a betrayal, and we hid it from my father, because it would have killed him faster than any cancer. In the end we only delayed the inevitable by a few months, but it was worth it. I would give anything for one more day with my dad. Anything.

Ragnar was only fifteen years old.

"Yes. I'll try."

"Are you sure?" my mother asked.

"Yes."

"Take Leon with you," she said.

"No." If this situation turned ugly, I didn't want him getting hurt.

"I'll bring her back safe and sound," Augustine promised.

My mother gave him her sniper stare. "You do that."

Augustine's silver Bentley sped south on Gessner Road. It was after 2:00 a.m. and even Houston's roads lay empty. The chauffeur squeezed every drop of speed out of the heavy armored car. Normally, the trip to Memorial Hermann would've taken at least fifteen minutes. We would make it in less than half of that. Augustine rode in the front passenger seat, presenting me with a view of his blond head. I really wanted to reach over and smack it. If someone told me this yesterday that I would end up in the backseat of Augustine's car in the middle of the night wearing a sweatshirt over my sleep T-shirt and a pair of sneakers without socks, I would've asked them what they were smoking and told them to seek professional help.

I missed my weapons. It made me feel naked.

Augustine was right though. Nevada did owe him a favor.

My father was born into House Tremaine, a small House consisting only of him and my grandmother Victoria. A truthseeker like Nevada, Victoria could wrench information from a person's mind against their will. My father had no magic and Victoria was a terrible mother, so when he turned eighteen, he had escaped and started a new life under an assumed name. In her search for him, my grandmother had rampaged through the Houses all across the continent. Just mentioning her name made powerful Primes back off.

Three years ago, before we became a House, Victoria came looking for us. Augustine knew Nevada's identity. He could've shared it with my grandmother and benefited from it, but instead he had allowed Nevada to mess with his mind, so Victoria left empty-handed. I hated debts of any kind. It would be good to get this one over with.

It didn't change the fact that I had no idea what I was doing.

"How do you know the family?" I asked.

"Ragnar's sister contacted MII in regard to her mother's and sister's deaths. She doesn't think the fire was an accident."

"Was it?"

"I'm not at liberty to discuss the details."

Right. "Did you take the case?"

"She knows our rates."

"You turned her down. Augustine! She came to you and you turned her down, and now her brother is going to kill himself."

He looked in the rearview mirror, his expression iced over. "If I'm going to put my people in danger, I have to properly compensate them. I'm not running a charity, Catalina. You of all people should know how much can be at stake when one looks into a Prime's death."

Oh, I knew. When a team of hired killers stormed your home, sending tornados of fire and summoning monsters into the slaughter, it tended to leave a lasting impression.

I glanced out the windshield and saw the futuristic crown on top of the Memorial Hermann Tower, outlined with glowing red, white, and blue triangles shining against the ink-black sky from the height of thirty-three floors. Almost there.

"Did you at least tell his sister what to expect if I have to use my magic?"

"I told her the boy would have to be sedated."

The car pulled into the parking lot. A Hispanic man, his face frantic, ran to the car and swung my door open. A blast of January air hit me. Winter in Houston tended to be mild, but a cold front had come through and the temperature had dropped to below thirty. My bare knees shook.

"Did he jump?" Augustine barked.

"No, sir."

"Come on." Augustine jumped out of the car.

I scrambled out of the vehicle. Wind tore at me with icy teeth.

Augustine and I hurried at a near run to the doorway. The glass doors slid open, letting us pass, and the warm air of the hallway bathed me. A group of people waited by the bank of elevators, some in scrubs, others in professional clothes, and all wearing the same panicked expression. They saw us and scurried out of the way, leaving behind a young woman with red hair. She turned. Recognition punched me.

"Runa? Runa Etterson?"

Her tearstained eyes widened in recognition. "Catalina?"

Three years ago, at Nevada's wedding, an enemy

of House Rogan poisoned the wedding cake. The only reason any of us were alive now, Augustine included, was because Runa purged the toxins before the cake was served. She was a Prime Venenata, a poison mage. She could kill everyone in this room in seconds. And the boy on the roof was her brother. Oh my God.

Augustine strode past me into the open elevator. "Catalina, there is no time."

I had come this far. Poison mage or no, Ragnar was still a fifteen-year-old boy on the edge of a skyscraper's roof. If I didn't try to save him, I wouldn't be able to sleep at night.

I hurried into the elevator. The doors slid shut. The last thing I saw was Runa looking at me like I was the answer to all her problems.

The elevator hummed, carrying us upward, brightly lit and perfectly normal. I caught my reflection in the mirrored wall. I looked like I had just rolled out of bed. There was a touch of surreal in it all: me in my sweatshirt, standing next to impossibly perfect Augustine in an elevator of mirrors and electric lights and soft music. Maybe I was dreaming.

Runa's mother and sister were dead. And Augustine must have quoted her an impossible price. I had planned to simply walk away if I managed to get the boy to safety, but this changed everything.

"You didn't tell me he was a Prime Venenata."

"I told you he wouldn't let anybody get to him."

Dread washed over me. "Did he kill anyone?"

Augustine sighed. "He's a gentle child. He made them sick enough to turn back, but he didn't inflict permanent damage."

"What did he do?"

"Don't worry. You'll smell it."

The numbers in the elevator's digital display crawled up.

"When the doors open, turn left," Augustine said. "Go to the door marked exit, and up one flight of stairs. There will be a metal door that will give you access to the roof."

"That's a terrible plan," I told him.

"Ragnar will hesitate to hurt you. If he does, I'll be there, and I'll help."

"If he sees you . . ."

"He won't see me."

The elevator doors swung open with a soft chime. I made a left and followed the hallway to the exit door and up the stairs. My hands shook.

The air stank like acid and vomit. A trail of chunky stains marked the steps. I didn't want to look too closely at it.

The ice-cold metal door handle burned my fingertips. I pushed it and stepped onto the roof. The dark sky unfolded above me, impossibly huge and black, with the crown glowing against it. The frigid wind pierced my body, going straight through me all the way to the bone.

Ragnar stood on the very edge of the roof, a thin figure in faded jeans and a hoodie, balancing on a concrete ledge. He seemed so very small against the night, like an ant on a skyscraper.

He turned and looked at me, his face lit by the neon glow of the crown. I saw certainty and relief in his eyes. He wasn't relieved to see me. He was relieved because he'd made up his mind and decided to jump. I had no time.

"Tell Runa I'm sorry—"

I hit him with everything I had.

When the Keeper of Records named my magic, he called me a siren, which fit me well, because like the sirens of legend, I called people to me and they couldn't resist. And like ancient sirens, I had wings, beautiful magic wings nobody could see unless I let them. They snapped open behind my back now, as the focused torrent of magic drenched Ragnar.

He froze. His heels protruded an inch over the ledge. One slip and he would die.

"Ragnar," I called him, turning his name into a sing-song lure.

He licked his lips nervously. "Hi."

"Hello. I'm Catalina." Magic stretched from me to him and I wove more and more of it around him with every syllable.

"You're so pretty," he said.

"Thank you. It's cold and dark. Do you think we could go inside?"

He nodded, fascinated.

I held out my hand. "It's scary up here. Will you hold my hand?"

He moved, stumbled, teetering on the edge, his arms waving . . . My heart jerked, trying to leap out of my chest.

Augustine materialized out of thin air next to Ragnar, grabbed a handful of his hoodie, and yanked him back. Runa's brother landed on the concrete roof.

Holy crap. My knees almost gave out.

Ragnar righted himself, walked over, took my hand, and offered me a shy smile.

I smiled back. "Let's go inside."

We went through the door and down the stairs with Augustine bringing up the rear. I scanned him. Clean.

None of my magic had hit him. I had focused all of it in a laser-tight beam on Ragnar. Augustine could turn himself invisible. Nevada would lose her mind when I told her.

We boarded the elevator. Sweat glistened on Augustine's flawless forehead. He was breathing like he'd run up all thirty-three floors to the roof. Ragnar held my hand very gently, as if my fingers were made of glass. It wouldn't last.

Most magic users had to put some effort into doing magic. I was the opposite. I had to hold mine in. When I was born, a nurse tried to kidnap me. She paid for it with her career. In the years that followed, before I learned to control my power, perfectly normal people did insane things to hold on to me. My elementary teacher attempted to smuggle me out of her classroom and into her car. My classmates tore out chunks of my hair so they could keep a piece of me.

Other kids were encouraged to be cute, to perform for adults. If I smiled, the adults became mesmerized, and if I wanted them to like me, they would love me with obsessive intensity. Their children would cry hysterically when I left the playground.

Right now, Ragnar loved me, madly, beyond all reason. Soon touching me wouldn't be enough. He would want to hold me, crush me to him, rip out a lock of my hair to smell and taste. He'd want a piece of me to stroke and to bite.

The Keeper might as well have called me Orpheus. Sooner or later those who tasted my magic would want to tear me apart and they would love and worship every precious drop of my blood and shred of my flesh as they killed me. Only my doctor was immune; we didn't know why. And my family. I didn't need to magic them. They already loved me.

The elevator stopped. The doors swung open and Runa lunged to hug her brother. Her arms closed around him, breaking Ragnar's hold on me.

Ragnar screamed as if cut. It was a raw, animal sound. His sister let go, stunned, and he dived at me and clamped my hand in his.

A man shouldered his way through the crowd, carrying a small medical case.

"Ragnar," I called.

He gazed at me with adoration in his eyes. I knew it was temporary, but even so, it made me cringe.

"That gentleman is going to give you a shot. I'm scared of shots. Are you?"

"No." He shook his head. "No, I'm brave."

"Will you show me how to be brave, Ragnar?"

He held his arm out, his gaze fixed on me. Runa hugged him. I watched the needle go in. "You'll feel a little sleepy in a minute. It's okay to fall asleep."

"Don't leave!"

"I won't leave," I promised. "I'll stay here and hold your hand."

Ragnar's hold on my hand slipped. He sighed happily, closed his eyes, and sagged in his sister's arms.

I turned to Augustine. "I need you to transport him back to the warehouse."

"He needs to be under observation," Augustine said.

"No, he needs to be back at the warehouse, so I can purge my magic from him. If he wakes up and I'm not there, he may escape and try to find me. And this time, people will die."

Augustine turned to Runa. "It's your call."

I met her gaze. "You know me. You've seen what I can do. Please trust me on this."

"Let's go," she said.

The trip home was taking considerably longer than the trip to get to the hospital. The chauffeur seemed in no hurry, and the Bentley all but crawled up the dark street. Runa's rented Nissan Rogue had no trouble keeping up. She had insisted on following us with Ragnar in her car.

I sat in the backseat next to Augustine. The adrenaline had worn off, leaving behind a soft fatigue. If I hadn't been in the vehicle of a dangerous Prime, I would have closed my eyes and gone to sleep.

"Well done," Augustine said.

I didn't need his approval. "Nevada's debt to you is paid in full. We're even."

"Agreed. Although technically it was a favor to House Etterson."

"Your dealings with House Etterson are between you and Runa. I'm surprised you cared enough to get involved tonight."

"I know what it's like to be responsible for a younger brother."

Oh. Humanity from Augustine. Unexpected.

Augustine tilted his head. "House Etterson may prove a valuable ally for you, if they survive. They now owe you a favor they can't refuse. You need allies, Catalina. The reprieve granted to your House is about to expire. People will be coming for you and yours. You're powerful but inexperienced, and because of your sealed records, you are an unknown. Unfortunately, being an unknown isn't enough of a deterrent."

"What are the terms?" I asked.

Augustine raised his eyebrows.

I counted off on my fingers. "You separated me from

my family. You're aware that my older sister and my brother-in-law are out of the country and are unable to advise me at the moment. It's the middle of the night and I'm tired from expending magic. You've complimented me, you've mentioned the danger facing my House, and we are driving at barely fifty miles per hour. You have an offer for me. Let's hear it."

Augustine cleared his throat. "Good. Skipping extended explanations and hand-holding makes things easier."

I waited.

"I offer a strategic alliance between House Montgomery and House Baylor. Occasionally, cases which are uniquely suited to the talents of your family cross my desk. I'd like you to handle them. In return, I offer generous financial compensation, access to MII's resources within the scope of those particular investigations, and the benefits of an association with my House."

He was offering protection and guaranteed income. More, he offered contacts and data. MII maintained an extensive network of informants and observers. Very little took place in Houston without Augustine knowing about it. He hoarded sensitive information, holding on to it until someone paid or threatened him. Access to that database was truly priceless.

Augustine was also a master at determining precisely what people needed most. It didn't take a genius to recognize that our most urgent need was security.

I had to make a decision.

"House Baylor is flattered by your generosity. However, at this time, we must regretfully decline."

Augustine chewed on it for half a minute.

"Why?"

"You have made a similar offer to Nevada three times. I'm aware that she declined, and I share her reasons for it."

"Indulge me," Augustine said.

"Very well. The real value of this partnership for us wouldn't be in money." Although we could certainly use it. "It would be in the connections and the elevated profile that comes from working with Prime clientele. A way for us to enter Prime society and forge relationships and alliances that would anchor our House."

And of course, the database and access to MII surveillance agents, who were legendary. We both understood that, so there was no need to mention it.

I kept going. "I want to underscore that I fully understand the value of your offer. However, currently there is a massive power imbalance between House Montgomery and House Baylor. I have seen how MII operates. If we agree to your proposal, you'll expect us to abide by your contract, which may require us to compromise our ethics. We're a family business. All we have is our name and our reputation. We follow only three rules. First, once bought, we stay loyal to the client. Second, we try not to do anything illegal. And third, at the end of the day we have to be able to look our reflection in the eye. Those are the principles my father laid out for us, they are the rules my older sister followed, and I will follow them as well. If we form an alliance with House Montgomery, we'll enter as equals, not as vassals or subcontractors, and we will adhere to our own norms of behavior."

The silence stretched out between us.

Augustine opened his mouth. "We're not equals."

"Exactly. House Montgomery is a behemoth and we're small and new. As you have said, we may or may not survive. But we must stand on our own. We worked very hard to move out of House Rogan's shadow and I won't trade that independence for an easy paycheck."

Augustine's face was impassive. "Thank you for your honesty."

"There may be a time I'll come to ask for your help," I told him. "If I do that, I'll be sure to bring information of equal or greater value."

The Bentley turned onto our street.

"Then I'll leave you with this piece of advice," Augustine said. "It's free. Do not become involved in the Etterson case. I know exactly what you're up against, and the price I quoted her was a gift. Sometimes when you search the night, you'll find monsters in the dark. You're not ready."

"I'll keep it in mind," I told him.

Chapter 2

I had texted Mom while en route, and the family met us at the door. Bern took Ragnar from Augustine and carried him into my office; Grandma Frida wrapped a blanket around Runa, Arabella thrust a cup of hot cocoa into her hands, Leon told her she was safe now, and Mom thanked Augustine and shut the door in his face.

Then everybody left, abandoning us in my office. Runa blinked at me from the client chair, her hands wrapped around the mug of hot chocolate, looking a little shell-shocked.

I walked over to where Ragnar lay on the floor, to the left of my desk. Someone had already moved the rug, exposing the arcane circle underneath, and Bern had placed the boy inside it. Drawn in chalk by hand, arcane circles served various purposes. Some refined the mage's power, some amplified or channeled it. This one drained excess magic. I had drawn it for just such an emergency and redrew it every week, for practice. From above, it resembled a complex double ring, encircled by glyphs. Straight lines of various lengths pierced the rings, radiating out like the sun's corona.

I took a piece of chalk from the shelf and drew two lines connecting the second circle under my chair to the one with Ragnar in it. I sat in the chair and sank a burst of magic into the smaller ring under my feet. The chalk lines flashed with silver and faded to a weak white glow as the circle began to sap my magic from Ragnar. Eventually I would get tired and have to quit, but I had a lot of power and I was willing to bet Ragnar would be purged first.

"He'll be fine," I told Runa. "There is no way to keep his magic from being drained as well, so he might be groggy, powerless, and kind of flat emotionally for the next few days."

"That might be for the best," she said.

I felt pressure to say something, but my brain refused to come up with anything appropriate. Asking her if she was okay was pointless. Her mother and sister had just died. In her place I would be catatonic.

Runa looked away from me to the corner of my desk. Her eyes widened. I glanced to the right to see what she was looking at.

A framed picture of Alessandro Sagredo sat on my desk. The frame itself was square, but the photograph cutout was shaped like a heart, its edge studded with rhinestones seated in the small pools of the glue from the hot glue gun. The left half of the frame was a hideous Pepto-Bismol pink; the other was covered in pink glitter. Massive plastic jewels decorated both. The image of Alessandro was black and white, and on it in pink glittery marker someone had written, "My smoochie poo."

I would recognize that cursive anywhere. My twenty-eight-year-old sister took the time out of her busy schedule of wrenching the truth from terrorists and murderers and preparing for an extended trip overseas to make this monstrosity, and then conspired with my other sister to troll me with it.

Why, Nevada? Why . . .

He was tall and broad-shouldered. He stood with an easy, natural grace. I used to stalk his Instagram and I knew every line of his face, but he hadn't posted for a while and usually his pics were posed. Alessandro against a Maserati. Alessandro on a yacht. Alessandro riding an elegant Andalusian horse like he was born in the saddle. Alessandro the Prime. Count Sagredo. The heir to one of the oldest noble families in Italy. Wealthy, powerful, handsome, once a teen heartthrob with millions of followers on Herald and Instagram and now a man who weaponized his influence and beauty. He could make the photograph communicate whatever he wanted.

But this, with the sun in his eyes and wind messing with his brown hair, this was real. And his smile was magic. I looked at it and was eighteen again, standing across from him in a trial room, waiting to match my magic against his and prove that I was a Prime. He had spoken to me, impossibly handsome, with amber eyes and that slightly lopsided grin, and I couldn't even make noises come out of my mouth.

I thought I was over this.

"Boyfriend?" Runa asked.

"No." And that didn't hurt at all.

Whenever I looked at Alessandro, in pictures or in person, he made me think of duels and courting, of a time when men carried swords and women concealed daggers. There was a dangerous edge to him, hidden deep in his eyes, and it drew me to him like a magnet. But that Alessandro was a fantasy, born from reading too many books set in medieval Italy with all its wars, glamour, art, and poison. He was a fantasy the way imagining being a secret princess was a fantasy. I knew it wasn't real, but it was so seductive, I couldn't let it go.

The real Alessandro didn't carry a sword. He was an Antistasi Prime. His magic nullified other mental magic. The Keeper of Records had chosen him to test my power during the trials. To be recognized as a Prime, I had to make Alessandro step over the line drawn on the floor. He took the full brunt of my power and resisted it for several minutes, but in the end I won.

With that type of talent, there were only two paths open to Alessandro: military service or private protection. He chose neither. Instead, he did what many young Primes with too much money and freedom chose to do. He indulged. He sailed yachts, raced fast cars, and dated stunning women.

He and I were worlds apart. He would never be what I imagined him to be and it was probably for the best.

I slapped the frame facedown on the desk. The back of the frame was covered in pink hearts and small pictures of Alessandro printed from his Instagram.

If the world had any compassion in it at all, I would teleport a thousand miles away.

Runa squinted at the back of the frame. "Is that Alessandro Sagredo?"

I picked up the frame to throw it in the trash, changed my mind halfway there, and dropped it into the desk's top drawer instead. Putting him in the garbage was beyond me. "My sisters have a weird sense of humor."

"Sisters do that," she said, her voice dull.

And hers was dead. "I'm so, so sorry."

She looked at me with haunted eyes. "Thank you. You're the only person who's been nice to me since this happened."

Who wouldn't be nice to her? She just lost most of her family. "What do you mean?"

"I was at UCLA. I'm working on my master's, molecular toxicology."

Her tone was flat, her expression detached. She had to be barely keeping it together. I'd been there before, in a place where you're so freaked out that you hold yourself supertight, because any splash of emotion could break the dam and you would fall to pieces.

"On Monday I got a call from the Houston PD. They said, 'The residence in Piney Point Village burned down and we believe your mother and sister died in the fire.' Just like that. I understood that sentence, but also kind of didn't. I knew what the words meant, I just couldn't put them together to make sense. I must've stood there with the phone in my hand for ten minutes, just trying to process, you know?"

I didn't, but I could imagine it in vivid detail.

Runa sighed. "I took the first flight."

It was Wednesday now. She'd been in town for two days.

"I came back to a burned-out husk of a house and two dead bodies. Ragnar was on a school trip to Colorado at an astronomy camp. No cell reception. I had to call the local police station and get them to notify him. That first day, after I viewed the bodies, I just didn't know what to do with myself. I mean, what do you do when your mom and sister are lying on a table so burned, the ME has to use dental records to identify them?"

That was odd. Why dental records? Everything Primes did was dictated by the need to strengthen and preserve their magic. Parenthood was no exception. The Houses based marriages on calculated DNA matches most likely to result in powerful offspring. Because of this, every magically significant bloodline registered with a genetic database. It would take at most twenty-four hours to compare DNA from the bodies to their genetic profiles, and unlike dental records, DNA match was error-proof.

Runa looked into her cup. "I didn't want to be by myself, so I called Michelle. We've been friends since middle school. She wouldn't take my call. Then I called Felicity, my other friend. She picked up, made all the right noises, and then when I asked her if I could stay with her for one night, she told me she would call me back in five minutes."

Runa looked at me. Her eyes looked dead. My heart cracked. When I met her three years ago, Runa was larger than life. She made jokes, she ate poisoned fondant, she flirted with Rogan's security detail. She was strong and confident and alive. This Runa wasn't even a shadow of herself. She was a ghost.

"Felicity never called back?" I guessed.

"No. I've known these people for years. They were my squad. We've lost touch since we all went to college, but we got together on holidays. We follow each other's accounts on Herald. These were my friends, Catalina." A little life came back into her gaze. "I expected them to have my back."

That didn't surprise me. Houses entered alliances based on family ties and mutual benefit. Runa wanted to hire Augustine, which meant she suspected that her family was murdered. If she was right, both she and Ragnar could be targeted. Runa was alone and inexperienced, which made her vulnerable. Sheltering her, aiding her, or associating with her brought no advantages. It only put you in danger.

"I spent the night in a hotel," she said. "Ragnar flew in the next day. I met him at the airport and his face just fell. He must've expected me to tell him that it wasn't true, but it is, and then he shut down. He went limp on me right there, and he was too heavy for me to carry. Then airport security called the first responders, and I let them take him to the hospital. I didn't know what else to do. I was late to my appointment with Montgomery, but he agreed to meet me at Memorial. You know the rest. When Montgomery offered to see me at the hospital at one o'clock in the morning, I really thought he would help. I should've known better."

"What did he quote you?" I asked.

"Twenty million. Even if I sold every financial asset the estate has, I couldn't raise enough money." Runa shook her head.

Even for MII, that was a high price tag. But then Augustine came and got me to help her. He had a moment of compassion. Unfortunately, telling her that wouldn't make anything better.

Runa looked down at her hot chocolate. "Thank you again. I'll be out of your life as soon as Ragnar wakes up."

The responsible thing to do, the Head of the House thing to do, would be to send her on her way. This wasn't our fight and there was no profit to be made here. We were an emerging House, and we had neither the financial resources nor the manpower of MII. If I helped her, I would be putting all of us in danger.

But she was a friend. She'd kept us all from dying at Nevada's wedding, and when I looked at her, my chest hurt.

"You're not going anywhere," I told her. "We have more than enough guest bedrooms and if you don't want to be alone, you can crash on the media room couch. Someone's always in the media room."

She stared at me.

"It's a very special couch," I told her. "Mad Rogan once fell asleep on it. We're thinking of having it gold-plated and donated to a museum . . ."

Runa's composure broke like a glass mask and she cried.

I got up, took away her hot chocolate before she sloshed it all over herself, and hugged her.

Morning came far too fast. Normally I got up at 7:00 a.m., but Ragnar didn't finish draining until a little past 4:00 a.m., and when my alarm blared, I turned it off and slept for another hour. That proved to be a mistake. I had a nightmare and woke up scared out of my mind. When I finally made it downstairs, bleary-eyed and carrying my laptop, Mom, Grandma Frida, and Bern were already there, finishing their breakfast. Grandma gave me a zombie look from above the rim of her coffee mug. Neither one of us did well with little sleep.

I landed in my chair. Mom put a cup of tea in front of me and I drank it. It was so hot, it made the roof of my mouth wrinkle, but I didn't care.

"Easy there," Bern said.

"Let me have my drug." I drank more tea. "Mmm, caffeine. So delicious. Where is everybody?"

"Leon left last night to close the Yarrow case," Bern said. "Arabella has an appointment with Winter, Ltd."

"Let me guess, they still haven't paid us?"

"Yep."

Occasionally, clients were slow to pay. We reminded them once, then a second time, and then we sent my sister in an Armani suit, armed with her laptop. None of us had any idea what she said, but the payment usually arrived within twenty-four hours.

My phone chimed. A text message from Nevada. **Landed safe. Everything ok?**

I texted back. **Everything is great. Selfie or it didn't happen.**

"They landed in Barcelona. They're okay." I couldn't keep the relief out of my voice.

Bern raised his tawny eyebrows. "You do realize that you're more likely to die in a car going to the airport than to get into a plane crash?"

"Yes, but I can influence the outcome of my car ride. I can drive myself or hire a driver. I can choose the type of car and the route. I can't influence the plane."

When Bern boarded a plane, he relaxed in his seat and looked out the window, because "Woo, technology." When I got on a plane, I calculated my odds.

My phone chimed again. My sister stood against a backdrop of green mountains, smiling, her big brown eyes laughing. She was beautiful, with a golden tan and blond hair the color of light honey. Next to her Connor Rogan loomed; huge, muscular, dark-haired, his blue eyes piercing in contrast to his bronze skin. He was smiling too, a genuine warm smile. Looking at them made me so happy. I could almost feel Spain's sunshine.

"About the Ettersons," Bern said.

I sighed and opened my laptop. Bern had sent me an email titled "Etterson." I clicked it.

House Etterson:
- Sigourney Etterson, Prime Venenata, 50, single;
- Runa Etterson, Prime Venenata, 22, single;
- Halle Etterson, Prime Venenata, 17, single;
- Ragnar Etterson, Prime Venenata, 15, single.
- James Tolbert, Significant, purifier, 52, ex-husband and father of the children; whereabouts unknown.

As I thought. Both Runa's mother and her siblings were Primes.

No known House alliances. Estimated worth: $8 million.

In the sea of Houston's elite, the Ettersons were a relatively small fish and they swam by themselves. No strong ties to other Houses, no patrons of great influence. It wasn't unusual. Many smaller Houses preferred to operate independently, unattached to a larger family. Powerful Houses had powerful enemies, and when you allied yourself to one, you inherited their friends and their rivals.

Bern took a slow swallow of his coffee. "Are you sure about this?"

"Yes."

He looked at me. "Our grace period runs out tomorrow. I don't need to remind you of the statistics."

He didn't. I could rattle the numbers off the top of my head. Ever since the invention of the Osiris serum over a century ago, magic and power became synonymous and intrinsically linked. Arcane talent was hereditary; those who had it bred to keep it, and bloodlines and families became the new power units of society. When a family produced two Primes in three generations, it could petition for and be formally recognized as a House; an honor that came with life-changing benefits and drawbacks.

On average, seventeen new Houses emerged every year nationwide. Of those, a quarter survived the first eighteen months after their grace period was over, and only a third of the survivors made it to the five-year mark as an independent entity. As soon as they were fair game, their competitors killed them off or the more powerful families dismantled them, scavenging their Primes for their own uses. Some voluntarily entered alliances, like the one Augustine had offered me, and became vassals, eventually absorbed by their patron House or killed, used as the first line of defense in House warfare. A grand total of 1.42 families lived through the melee.

The next year would be crucial. Our first case with me as the Head of the House would be equally important.

This morning, sometime between turning off the alarm and jerking awake, I had dreamed that Arabella burned to death. In my nightmare, I was holding her charred corpse to me, looking at her picture on my cell phone, and crying. I woke up with my face wet. For Runa, it wasn't a nightmare, it was reality.

"Venenatas are combat mages. Runa Etterson would make a formidable ally," I said. "I've looked at our schedule, and if Leon closes the Yarrow case today, we're wide open."

We were wide open because for the first time in the last three years we had decided to lighten our load for the holidays. We had mostly succeeded, except for the Yarrow fraud and the Chen case. The Chen case was a nightmare. Someone had stolen a van with three prize-winning boxer dogs in it on Christmas Eve. The van was found abandoned the next day, all three dogs missing, and the breeder was beside himself. Cornelius, an animal mage and our only nonfamily investigator, had taken that one, and we hadn't seen him or Matilda, his daughter, since the day after Christmas. He'd emailed me yesterday to inform me he was still alive and working.

Bern smiled. "That's a solid argument, and if I wasn't your cousin, I would totally believe it. You're making an emotional decision. You would help her if her magic consisted of conjuring up cute garden gnomes."

"Bernard," my mom said in her Mom voice.

"I want to help her as much as anyone," Bern said, "but my job in this family of Care Bears is to provide logical analysis, so humor me."

"I understand your point. It's valid." I sipped my tea to buy time. Bern could be swayed, but you had to present your arguments in a methodical fashion. "You're right; the grace period is almost over, and I'm an unknown commodity. It would be different if Nevada was the Head of the House."

"If Nevada was here, I would give her the same assessment," he said.

"Either way, we'll be watched and our first case with me in charge will be scrutinized. I considered it carefully and I like the message this case is sending."

"What message?" Grandma Frida asked. The coffee must have finally kicked in.

"We stand by our friends," I said. "We aren't a House who abandons allies out of convenience. If you earn our trust, we'll honor it."

Bern nodded. "Very well. As long as we're all clear on what we're walking into. Two Prime Venenatas may have been burned to death in their home, on their own turf. We all know what that means."

"What does it mean?" Runa asked from the doorway. She wore a big T-shirt and a pair of leggings. Her hair was a mess, dark circles clutched at her eyes, but some of the stiffness in her posture had eased off.

"House warfare," Mom said.

House warfare had its own rules. When people who could incinerate entire city blocks and throw buses around fought to the death, the government turned a blind eye, as long as all reasonable precautions against civilian casualties had been made. You went to the courthouse, filed some paperwork, and walked out with carte blanche to murder your enemies as you saw fit. If your House was in a feud and people with guns and magic were storming your home, 911 wouldn't take your call. If you were running down the street with a pack of summoned monsters on your heels, the cops wouldn't stop to help you. That was one of the many costs of being a Prime. You weren't above the law, but, in many cases, you existed outside of it.

"We don't know for sure that it's House warfare," I said. "Let's get all the facts and then make a decision."

"I don't want to put anyone in danger," Runa said.

"Danger is our middle name," Grandma Frida said.

Mom stopped what she was doing and looked at Grandma Frida.

"What?" Grandma Frida shrugged. "It's been too quiet around here. I'm ready for some action."

"The last time you got some action, you drove Romeo through a storm mage's compound, while Nevada rode shotgun and fired a grenade launcher at the giant animated constructs chasing you," Mom said. "Your tank had to be rebuilt from the tracks up, and you had four broken ribs and a gash on your head that needed thirty stitches."

"Don't you worry about me getting action, Penelope." Grandma Frida grabbed a handful of her white curls and pulled them back, exposing the edge of a scar. "It adds character." She paused. "And an air of mystery. A woman can always use more mystery."

"God help me," Mom said.

"Thank you for inviting me into your home," Runa said. "But this is my problem. I don't want any of you getting hurt because of us."

Mom pointed at the chair next to Bern and said, "Sit."

Runa sat. The combination of mom and sergeant always worked.

"You've helped our family," Mom said. "Now you're in danger and you're responsible for your brother, who also might be a target. His safety should be your first priority. We're offering you a protected base and assistance. We may not have the resources and the manpower of larger firms, but we close our cases. You are the Head of your House now, Runa. Do what's right for your House."

"Yes, ma'am," Runa said.

I turned to Runa. "Do you have a dollar?"

She gave me an odd look and dug through her pockets. "I have a five."

"If you give me that five-dollar bill, I'll consider us officially hired. Your choice." I held my hand out.

"I don't expect you to work for free . . ."

"Have no fear, we'll bill you for all of the expenses that will come up. If you still feel that you need to adequately compensate us, we can trade you for poison-detecting services."

Runa took a deep breath and put the money in my hand. "House Etterson is honored to accept help from House Baylor."

"Good." Mom put a plate of pancakes and sausage in front of her.

"Tell us about the fire," I said.

"It's bullshit," Runa said.

"Eat your pancakes," Mom said.

Runa dug into a pancake with her fork. "The house was four thousand square feet, two stories, and every bedroom had an exit. Mom's bedroom was on the first floor, Halle's bedroom on the second, and it opened to the backyard balcony. When she was little, she used to jump off that balcony into our pool. Drove Mom crazy.

The house had six smoke detectors and a high-tech alarm that should have sensed the rising temperature and alerted the fire department."

"Did the alarm go off?" Bern asked.

Anger sparked in her eyes. "I don't know. It should have though. Somehow, despite the alarm, and the smoke detectors, and the easy access to outside, my mother and my seventeen-year-old sister ended up dying together in the study at three in the morning. My mother could kill an intruder from thirty feet away. Halle could probably do the same, although she mostly specialized in purging toxins. None of this makes any sense. Especially the part where everyone I talked to insists on referring to this as 'a tragic accident' as if they're all reading from the same script."

She was right. Nothing about this story made any sense so far.

I opened a new case file on my laptop and hit record. "January 5th, Runa Etterson interview. I'm going to ask you some unpleasant questions. The more honest you are, the better we can help you."

Runa's expression hardened. "Let's do it."

"Your House includes your mother, your sister, your brother, and you, correct?"

"Only me and my brother now."

"What about your father?"

Runa gave a jerky, one-shoulder shrug. "When I was ten, my 'dad' gave up all pretense of being a father and a husband. He'd already had a string of affairs. Everybody knew it. I knew it. I was nine years old and I walked in on him having sex with some random woman on our dining table. For my birthday, he cleaned out our accounts and disappeared. My mother had to start from scratch. Nobody knows where he is, and nobody wants to know. He can die for all I care."

"So, you don't think there's any way he could be involved?"

Runa shook her head. "No."

"Does he have any financial claim on the estate? Life insurance, ownership of the house?"

"No. Mom removed him from everything after he left. He never paid child support and he stole from my mother. There is a police report and a paper trail, so if he showed up, he would be arrested."

I would have Bern check on it, but we probably could scratch James Tolbert off the suspect list.

"Are you aware of any feuds or problems with other Houses?"

"No."

"Did your mother ever tell you that she had a problem with anyone?"

Runa shook her head. "If she'd thought we were in danger, she would've warned me."

"Was she seeing anyone? Did she have a significant other or others?"

"No. Her last relationship ended about a year ago and it was amicable. She wasn't seeing anyone, because when we talked last week, she mentioned Halle pushing her to join a dating network on Herald. She said she wasn't interested in another relationship. Men were a sore point with Mom. I don't think she ever really trusted anyone after Dad."

"What about Halle? Any recent problems, drugs, obsessive boyfriend or girlfriend, hanging out with the wrong crowd?"

Runa sighed. "Catalina, she was seventeen. Her life was school, volleyball, and college prep. No drugs, no weird boyfriends. She tried shrooms one time and hid in my room because she was scared the couch would eat her. She was a sheltered kid."

"Are you now the Head of the House?" I asked.

Runa nodded. Her voice was bitter. "Yes, I'm the Head of all of me and Ragnar." She held her arms out to her side. "The House of two."

"Have members of any of the other Houses contacted you to make any claims or to ask you to make any financial decisions?"

"No."

"Did your mother owe anybody money? Was the House having financial problems?"

Runa tapped her phone and showed it to me. A bank interface listing four accounts totaling $3.6 million.

I met her gaze. "This is the part where I'm ethically bound to inform you that you have other options. We're a small firm. We don't usually do murder investigations. The police and the Texas DPS both have more experience and greater resources. If you want a private option, there is MII. Do you understand that you have other choices available to you?"

"Yes."

"Are you entering the contract with Baylor Investigative Agency of your own free will?"

"Yes."

"To find your mother's and sister's killers, I'll have to tear your life apart. You may learn things about your family that you won't like. If you are hiding secrets and they have bearing on this case, they will come to light. If at any point during the investigation, I find out that you have deceived or misled me, I'll immediately terminate our contract. You have my promise that when I deliver results to you, I'll have proof. However, I don't guarantee results. I swear that I'll do everything in my power and within the law to solve this case, but not all murders are solved. Do you understand?"

Runa didn't hesitate. "Yes."

I shut off the recording. "I have a small pile of paperwork for you. Once you're done with it, we'll start."

"*Where* do we start?"

"At the medical examiner's office. You said that the ME used dental records to identify your mother and sister."

"Yes?"

"You are a House, which means your DNA profile is in some genetic database somewhere. Which genetic firm are you using?"

Runa frowned. "I don't know. Mom handled all of that."

I pulled up the Scroll website. Scroll was the largest DNA database in the US and the one we also used. I logged into our account, typed "House Etterson" into the search window, and the website spat the result at me.

"You are registered with Scroll. They will have all four of you in their database. We're going to give them a call and have a representative meet us at the morgue. They should be able to confirm the identity of the bodies within twenty-four hours."

Runa stared at me. "Why?"

I had to be really careful not to get her hopes up. "Because DNA identification is foolproof and dental records are not. Genetic testing is the established way to identify dead Primes. If it wasn't done, I want to know why, and I want it done properly. That's where we're going to start."

Chapter 3

$\mathcal{T}$he Harris County Institute of Forensic Sciences occupied a nine-story building on Old Spanish Trail. Its blocky lines, rectangular windows, and orange brick practically screamed government agency.

I maneuvered our Honda Element into the parking lot. It used to be our surveillance vehicle, because it blended with traffic, but last year Grandma Frida decided to rebuild it from wheels up. Now the Element sported a new engine, bulletproof windows, B5 armor, and run-flat tires among other fun modifications, which struck a perfect balance between protecting us and letting us get away fast. Unfortunately, even Grandma Frida had her limits, and steering was a bit sluggish. I aimed for a parking spot in the middle row.

"So, what's with you and Alessandro Sagredo?" Runa asked.

The steering was sluggish, but the brakes worked perfectly. I jerked forward, and my seat belt slammed me back.

"Nothing."

"Aha." Runa pulled on her own seat belt. "That's why we screeched to a stop halfway into the parking space?"

"My foot slipped." I gently eased forward and brought the Element to a smooth stop.

"So you're just going to go with 'nothing'?" Runa asked.

"That's right."

"Your sister said you met during your trials."

Sistercide was not a word, but it would be after today. Well, technically, *sororicide* was a word, but most people wouldn't recognize it. When did Runa even have a chance to talk to Arabella?

"Yes," I said.

"Yes what? Is there a story behind that?"

No. He didn't follow me on Instagram, and he didn't take my breath away during the trials. And he definitely didn't show up under my window trying to convince me to go for a drive.

"We met during the trials, and my sisters haven't stopped teasing me about it for the last three years. There is absolutely nothing between me and Alessandro Sagredo."

Strictly speaking, there were 5,561 miles between our warehouse and the Sagredo estate near Venice, Italy. A commercial flight with one connection could get me to Venice in thirteen hours. I could be under Alessandro's window tomorrow, asking him if he would like to go for a drive.

"You zoned out there for a second," Runa observed. "Are you imagining there being nothing between you and Alessandro?"

She was trying to distract herself from the horror of

never seeing her mother and sister again, but I had to put a stop to it, or I would never get out of the car.

I used my logical, reasonable voice. "Runa, do you see Alessandro in this car? No. He isn't in this parking lot or in that building either, so he's a non-issue. Let's go."

We started across the parking lot. Cold wind buffeted us.

Runa hugged her arms to herself. She wore a light windbreaker over a green sweater dress. "I should get a coat like yours. Is that Burberry?"

"Yes. I got it on sale last year at half off."

"Lucky."

I was wearing a beige mid-length trench coat over a grey sweater and blue jeans tucked into soft boots. The coat had a double-breasted front closure with a row of black buttons on each side. I had left it open. It flattered my figure and looked stylish and expensive enough to belong to a Prime, but most importantly, it hid my knife resting in a special sheath sewn into the lining on the left side.

There were only a handful of ways to conceal a blade long enough to be effective in a fight. You could wear it on your thigh under a loose skirt, which would have you pawing at your skirt to draw it and was impractical in cold weather. You could wear it in a shoulder sheath, but if you took the outer garment off, it was no longer concealed. Hiding it in the coat lining was the best option. Even if I took the coat off out of politeness or necessity, I could carry it so I could draw in an instant. It was highly unlikely that the Forensic Institute would require me to check my coat.

We entered the lobby. The designers of the institute must have been great fans of modern industry, and monochromatic colors. The floor gleamed with white tile, the walls highlighted with pale grey; the ceiling featured stainless-steel beams with long fluorescent lights, and the counters practically glowed with pristine white. Even the visitor furniture, upholstered soft chairs, were a greyish off-white. The place begged for a plant or a Gustav Klimt print.

I walked up to the receptionist behind the counter. I had checked the case status on the institute's website. The case was listed as pending, so I called ahead and warned them that the two of us would be coming.

"Catalina Baylor and Runa Etterson," I told the woman behind the counter. "We're here about the Etterson case."

The receptionist, an older Latina woman, gave me an apologetic smile. "I've spoken to AME Conway and he says that you can't view the bodies."

"Can't?" Runa asked. "What do you mean by can't?"

"They're not available."

The air around Runa shimmered with a faint trace of green. Her voice went cold. "Make them available."

The lobby went completely silent, as the three admins behind the counter held very still.

I had to defuse this standoff before someone panicked and escalated it. Luckily, bureaucracy was made of rules, and rules and I were friends.

I smiled at the receptionist. "As the next of kin and Head of her House, Prime Etterson has a right to view the remains of her family members at will. If you deny her access, I'll be forced to notify her House counsel and you will have to show cause for failing to comply with your own regulations, in court, before a judge. I'll wait while you check the validity of our claim with your in-house attorney."

The receptionist reached for the phone. "One moment

please." She turned away from me and spoke into the phone in an urgent whisper.

I stepped away and steered Runa toward the window. Minutes ticked by.

"What is taking so long?" Runa ground out.

"They'll sort it out."

The admin hung up. "Our apologies." She motioned to a young white man with longish, dark hair who had been hovering by the copier behind her. "This is Victor."

Victor, who had been trying very hard to be invisible up to this point, performed an award-winning impersonation of a deer in headlights.

"Victor will take you to the correct autopsy suite."

"Thank you," I said. "We're also expecting a Scroll representative. Please have him join us when he arrives."

We followed Victor to the elevator. It took us to the third floor, which was just as gleaming as the lobby. We walked through a white hallway to a large room, where six autopsy tables waited in a row against the wall. Four stood empty. The other two held bodies covered with white fabric.

A white man in his late thirties waited by the nearest table with his arms crossed. He wore a pristine white lab coat, which gave a glimpse of a striped grey dress shirt and yellow tie. His dark hair was cut so short, it was barely there. You would expect him to be clean shaven, but the stubble sheathing his face and neck was about the same length as his hair. It looked like he had gotten up a couple of mornings ago, shaved everything from the neck up, and now was letting it grow out. The effect was rather unsettling.

Victor beat a hasty retreat without saying a word. The man in the lab coat showed no signs of coming forward to greet us, so I headed for him. Runa followed. Two security cameras, one on the right wall and the other directly above the door, watched our every move.

The man lifted his badge, showing it to us. "Silas Conway, MD, assistant medical examiner."

I waited. Nothing else came out. That was the totality of the introductions. Great start.

"Catalina Baylor and Runa Etterson. Thank you for meeting with us on such short notice, Dr. Conway."

"What are you doing here?"

"What do you think we're doing here?" Runa asked.

"Wasting my time."

He did not just say that. "We're here to view the bodies."

Conway fixed me with his stare. "Why?"

"It doesn't matter why." Runa took a step toward him. "You have no right to block my access to the remains of my family."

"I wasn't blocking your access. I was otherwise occupied. I had to drop everything and come down here to accommodate you. The bodies are not in any state to be viewed, and it is the policy of this office to spare the family members the unnecessary trauma. I was trying to be considerate, but clearly my efforts and concern were wasted."

Clearly. He was a veritable fountain of consideration and sympathy. He couldn't even manage a "sorry for your loss."

This felt wrong. First, I had called ahead, so he knew we would be arriving. Second, he wasn't just irritated but borderline hostile, as if he were trying to antagonize Runa. This was a routine procedure and he was in breach of protocol. What possible reason could there be for that hostility? If he acted like this with everybody, let alone Primes, he would be fired. He had to know everything he said was being recorded on the security feed.

I should've come by myself, but I needed Runa to cut through the bureaucracy. Still, Runa was traumatized and fragile, and she swung from jokes to anger in half a second. I had to be very careful with her, and now this guy was pushing for a confrontation for no apparent reason. Controlling this situation was getting more and more complicated, and using my magic on a city employee was a felony. Starting this investigation by breaking the law wasn't on my agenda.

Conway marched over to the two tables and stood between them. "You wanted to view the bodies, here they are."

He jerked back the two sheets covering the remains.

I had read about burn victims in forensic textbooks. Several years ago, Nevada was forced into tracking down a pyrokinetic Prime. None of us could help her, so I sat at home, worried out of my mind, and read every book on fire and burn victims that I could get my hands on. At the time, Arabella had pointed out that I was just driving myself crazy, but somehow that was my way of coping with the stress. A kind of self-imposed exposure therapy.

Reading about someone burning to death and seeing an actual body were two different things.

The two charred figures on the tables couldn't have weighed more than sixty pounds each. The heat of the blaze had desiccated them, and as the muscles and ligaments dehydrated, the bodies contracted, bending their knees and elbows and curling their fingers into fists. Textbooks called it the pugilistic pose because it was similar to the defense stance of a boxer. The facial features were gone. The skin and subcutaneous layer of fat were gone as well. It was impossible to guess at gender, race, or age of the bodies. I was looking at the two vaguely human-shaped objects sheathed in blackened, shriveled flesh.

A hint of a sickening odor spread through the room. Bitter, nauseating, sweet, and coppery, it was like nothing I had smelled before; a greasy, burned pork roast mixed with charred leather. Bile rose to my throat.

I turned away and saw Runa, standing statue-still behind me, her face so pale she looked dead herself. And in a sense, she was. Losing my mother and sister would've killed a part of me. It must have hurt so much. All we could do was hope that they'd died before the fire reached them. Nobody deserved to burn to death.

"Satisfied?" Conway asked. "Wouldn't it have been better to remember them the way they were?"

"No," Runa said. "I want to remember them just like this. I'll never forget this, and I'll make whoever did this pay."

"This was a tragic but accidental fire," Conway said. "It's natural to look for someone to blame, but we've found no signs of violence. My estimate is that the arson investigation will uncover the source of the fire and the final finding will demonstrate a terrible turn of events but not a criminal one. Go home, Miss Etterson. You'll find no answers here."

"Was there particulate found in the lungs?" I asked.

He glared at me and took a step forward. Trying to intimidate me with his age and size.

All my life I worked at being overlooked. Drawing any attention to myself meant putting others in danger. I didn't just avoid conflict, I made sure I would never be anywhere near it. My natural inclination was to flee; out of the institute, to my car, and then to the safety of the warehouse and my family where everybody loved me, so I could recover from being glared at by this jerk.

However, there were two bodies on the tables and Runa needed answers. I took the job and I had to do it. Besides, I was right, and he was wrong.

I channeled my best impression of a displeased Arrosa Rogan, fixed Conway with a frigid stare, and held it. Eye contact and derision didn't come naturally to me, but Rogan's mother had been adamant that I learn how to do both. I practiced this expression in the mirror for weeks until I got it just right. It was like firing an emotional shotgun loaded with cold disgust.

Conway halted in mid-move.

"I assume they keep you around because you're good at your job, since your manner and conduct are appalling. That you would meet a survivor with aggression and arrogance is beyond any guidelines of the ME's office or common human decency."

Conway's face turned purple.

"So, I'll ask again. Was there smoke in their lungs? If you can't answer my question, find someone who can."

Conway drew in a deep, rage-filled breath. I braced myself.

Victor appeared in the doorway.

"What?" Conway roared at him.

Victor stepped aside, letting a man in a severe black suit into the room.

"Hello, Mr. Fullerton," I said.

The Scroll representative walked into the room. He was in his forties, trim, neat, with skin tanned by the sun, and dark hair combed back from his face. His eyes were an unexpected, very light shade of blue. They were also the only spot of color. Everything else—the Wolf & Shepherd oxfords, the tailored suit, the crisp shirt, the impeccable tie, and the glasses—was black.

"Ms. Baylor, it's always a pleasure." He offered his

hand to Runa and she shook it. "Ms. Etterson, my deepest condolences."

"Who is this?" Conway demanded.

Fullerton looked at him for a full second. "I'm here on behalf of Scroll, Inc., to perform genetic identification at House Etterson's request."

Conway's eyes went glassy and wide. Panic shivered in his brown irises. He took a jerky step back and threw his arms out to his sides, touching each corpse. A wave of revulsion slammed into me, sudden and overwhelming, a terrible feeling that things had just gone horribly, horribly wrong.

The desiccated body on the table next to me lunged up. I saw it coming but my mind had half a second to react, and it refused to accept what it was seeing. The corpse leaped at me. Cold, hard fingers locked on my throat.

Panic slapped me. The air vanished. Pain clamped my throat in a steel vise and squeezed.

Conway sprinted to the door. Fullerton stepped aside, letting Conway pass, his face perfectly calm as if we were at a society lunch. Runa spun, aiming at Conway with her hand. If she poisoned him, whatever he knew would die with him.

I clamped my hands together and drove them up between the corpse's arms. Its hands fell off my neck and I rammed my heel into its midsection. It stumbled back.

"No!" I croaked.

A burst of green shot from Runa like a striking viper and lashed Conway's shoulders, just before the other corpse jumped over me and landed on her back. Conway dove through the doorway and vanished from sight.

Crap.

The first corpse righted itself. I sucked in a breath—my

throat was on fire—and pulled my knife out. The reanimated bodies didn't act like zombies; they were simply vessels for the reanimator's magic, like puppets on invisible strings. Stabbing it in the heart or the head would get me nowhere. I had to disable it.

My magic sparked, pulling me, and I let it guide my strike. My siren talent came from my father, but this I inherited from my mother. It made her a deadly sniper, it allowed Leon to make impossible shots, and it never steered me wrong.

The desiccated husk of a human charged at me with its arms open wide. I caught its right wrist, stabbed my blade into its armpit, and twisted. The seven-inch CPM-3V high-carbon steel sliced through the shriveled gristle of the tendons and cartilage like it was old, dry leather. The arm fell from the shoulder, hanging by a thin strip of flesh.

I let go of its wrist, jerked the blade free, and slashed across the back of the corpse's neck. Its head rolled off its shoulders. I stabbed my knife into its other shoulder, wrenched the bone out of the socket, cut across the body's lower back, severing the vertebrae, and hammered a kick to the back of its knee. The corpse collapsed, falling apart. Pieces of the body writhed on the floor, no longer a threat.

The second corpse had sunk its fingers into Runa's hair, hanging off her. Green mist wrapped around both, turning the body's charred flesh green.

"Don't touch!" Runa screamed. "I've got this. Go!"

I dashed past Fullerton and out of the room. The hallway on the right lay empty. On the left, Conway staggered forward, bent over and grabbing the wall for support. Yep, she poisoned him.

Never again. Runa Etterson wasn't coming with me

to interrogate any more leads. I had minutes, maybe seconds, to squeeze answers out of him.

I ran.

Conway glanced over his shoulder and sped up. He was nearly to the corner. I had to get to him before her poison finished him off.

He stumbled, clutched at the wall, and pulled himself up. I was almost to him.

A tall, lean man in an expensive black suit rounded the corner and stalked toward us. He moved with grace, not like a dancer but like a swordsman, swift and supple, and carried himself with complete assurance as if he owned the whole building and his mere presence was an honor to behold. His longish brown hair had fallen over one side of his face.

Conway lunged to the left, trying to avoid him.

The man's hand snapped out. He caught the AME's shoulder, steadying him, pulled a long, narrow dagger out of his jacket, and stabbed Silas Conway in the heart.

It was a breathtaking strike. Smooth, fast, flawless. My magic sparked, as if acknowledging the beauty of it. He didn't even aim. He did it all in a single offhanded motion, as if he had taken his car keys out of his pocket and tossed them to a friend. This wasn't expertise, this was mastery, born of pure muscle memory and superior reflexes.

The man raised his head. Alessandro Sagredo looked at me over Conway's shoulder, smiled, and smoothly withdrew his knife from the AME's chest.

My brain short-circuited. I tried to stop, but I was sprinting on a polished concrete floor, and the laws of physics conspired against me. I slid. The floor squeaked under my boots, and I skidded past the two men at full speed. Alessandro tilted his head and watched me slowly come to a stop.

How was this possible? Alessandro Sagredo was a playboy. He took pictures in the Caribbean with his shirt off. He surfed in Fiji and shopped in London. He didn't stab random government workers in the heart with surgical precision.

Alessandro was looking at me. Right at me. Like I was the only thing in the world. A hot, predatory fire played in his amber eyes. He looked at me like I was a delicious steak and he was a hungry wolf.

Say something smart, say something smart . . . "Hey!" *Oh my God.*

Without saying a word, Alessandro stepped over Conway's body and walked toward me. I should have turned around and run the other way, or at least raised my knife. Instead, I just stood there, like a complete idiot.

Alessandro reached over and offered me his bent arm. I rested my fingers on his forearm. The muscle under the suit's fabric felt like steel. Alessandro moved, and we strolled around the corner.

I was hallucinating. I had to be.

"I . . ."

"Shh," he said in a slightly accented voice. "Just keep walking. Building security will be here soon, and we need to not be here."

He had killed Conway. It didn't bother him. It didn't disturb him any more than swatting a fly. Alessandro had stabbed a human being in the heart before. Many, many, many times before.

I'd made a serious error in judgment.

"I like your knife," he said. "You might want to put it away though, before someone gets excited."

I slid the blade back into its sheath in my coat. Wait. He'd shushed me. Like I was five. He told me to put my knife away and I did. And now I was letting him walk me away.

What the hell am I doing?

"Why are we walking?"

He glanced at me, his tawny eyes amused. "Because I've just knifed someone. Security will want to ask me a lot of boring questions. I hate boring questions. And there will be paperwork. I hate that too."

Oh yeah, well, in that case. "You killed Conway."

"Yes, I did."

I stopped. He stopped too and looked at me.

"Alessandro, what are you doing here?"

"Trying to get you to walk faster?"

My brain finally regained the ability to form complete sentences. "Why did you kill Conway? He was a lead in my investigation and now he's dead."

"He was a very bad man. You were chasing him with a knife."

"I needed to ask him some questions."

He smiled like a wolf baring its fangs in a dark forest. "Were you going to stab him if he didn't answer?"

"I don't need to stab people to get answers."

He sighed. "Collect your friend and go home, Catalina. There are no answers for you here."

What?

Runa rounded the corner at full speed, saw us, and froze.

"I'm so sorry," Alessandro said. "I have to leave now. Go home, stay safe, and forget all about this."

Ahead the elevator chimed.

"I'll see you around." Alessandro raised his hand. Somehow there was a gun in it. I didn't see him draw one. The gun barked, spitting bullets, the window to our right shattered, and Alessandro jumped out of it.

The elevator doors slid open, and guards in grey uniforms poured out, guns drawn.

"Put your hands up!" the leading guard roared.

I put my hands on my head and let them handcuff me.

Ten minutes after the building security apprehended me, the Houston PD House Response Unit arrived at the scene in a blaze of glory. They released Fullerton, who was clearly a neutral third party, detained Runa and me, and asked us questions for forty-five minutes. The way they concentrated on the description of the mysterious male who stabbed Conway made me think Alessandro had tampered with the hallway cameras. After the third round of the same questions, I dug my heels in, gave them the name of our attorney, and pointed out that my client was traumatized by having her family reanimated and that she had enemies powerful enough to corrupt an AME and that I could see at least three spots from which one could line up a long-range shot and snipe her. After that I answered every question with "Are we free to go?" They gave up and released us. I grabbed Runa and all but shoved her into the elevator.

The moment the elevator doors closed, Runa spun toward me. "You lied to me!"

"Not here," I warned her. "When we get out of the elevator, walk next to me. Stop when I stop and if I tell you to run, run."

Runa's face hardened. "You think they'll try to kill me."

"Yes."

"I hope they try."

Right. Runa's emotions had clubbed her rational thinking over the head, dumped its body on the side of the road, and took my friend for a joy ride. Just what we needed.

Client. Not friend; client. Friends were for other people. You wanted your friends to like you, and when I wanted someone to like me, the chances of my magic leaking out and enthralling them was much higher. I'd spent twenty-one years avoiding making friends. It was irresponsible to start now.

I did like Runa. I liked her when I first met her, and I wished I could be more like her, funny and charming and comfortable in her skin. Seeing her now broke my heart. I wanted to fix all the shitty things for her, and I had to watch myself very carefully. Besides, she didn't need a friend right now; she needed a professional investigator.

The elevator opened. I took a second to scan the lobby. No visible threats. I walked out and headed for the door, my head held high. Next to me Runa marched like she was daring someone to block her way.

We exited the building, and I accelerated, almost breaking into a jog. The space between my shoulder blades itched, as if someone was aiming at me through a rifle scope.

Get to the car, get to the car . . .

I popped the locks, and we jumped into the Element. I started the engine, reversed out of the parking spot, and sped out onto the street.

"Alessandro was in that building. I saw him, Catalina, with my eyes."

"I had no idea he would be there." I concentrated on driving. The car shot down the road. Nobody followed us.

"What was he doing there?"

"Killing our suspect."

"Why?"

"I don't know," I said. "Call Bern."

The sound of my phone dialing came from the car's speakers and Bern picked up. "Yes."

"You were right." I took a turn a little too fast and accelerated up the access road, shifting to the left to enter the highway ramp. "It's House warfare. We're coming back to the warehouse. Lock us down."

"On it," Bern said. "Are you coming in hot?"

"Not that I can see." I merged into the traffic.

"Is my brother awake?" Runa asked.

"No," Bern said. "I'll call if there is any change."

"I need everything you can dig up on AME Silas Conway. In particular, sudden large payments to his accounts in the last month or so and where they came from."

"What did he do?"

"He tried to prevent us from viewing the bodies, and when the Scroll rep showed up, he reanimated the corpses of Runa's mother and sister and tried to kill us with them. The cops are digging into Conway's past as we speak."

"Are you okay?" my cousin asked.

"Yes. Fullerton got the samples, but Conway died before I could question him."

"What happened?"

"Alessandro Sagredo."

The phone fell silent.

"I'm sorry, say again?"

"Alessandro Sagredo happened. He showed up in the Harris County IFS and stabbed my suspect in the heart. He did it as if he had a lot of practice. Then he told me to collect my friend, go home, and not to worry my pretty little head about it."

And when I found him, he would regret every word. He'd surprised me this time, but he wouldn't again.

"He said what?" Runa asked.

The car speaker remained silent.

"Bern, are you there?" I asked.

"Yes," he said. "You've had a pretty big morning."

"See you soon." I hung up.

"How is Sagredo involved in all this?" Runa asked.

"No idea. Do you know him? Do you know his family? Did your mom have any contact with him?"

"No."

"But you recognized his picture," I reminded her.

"I recognized him because I had a giant crush on him in high school, like every other girl my age. When he got engaged for the first time, Felicity, Michelle, and I had a pity party with cheesecake and whipped cream."

When I heard about his first engagement, I locked myself in my room and cried alone. I had cried the next two times too, because I was a moron.

Runa shook her head. "Trust me, if anyone has any connection to Sagredo, it's you. He doesn't even know I exist."

If House Etterson had no connection to House Sagredo, then why was Alessandro at the morgue, and why had he killed Conway and told me to go home? He was involved in this somehow. He had to be.

I needed to find Alessandro, and for that I would need Bug.

Bug served as Rogan's surveillance specialist. Magically altered, he processed visual information at an astonishing rate. He could sift through the simultaneous feed from dozens of CCTV cameras and track a person across the entire city. If anybody could find Alessandro, Bug could.

He was also fanatically loyal to Rogan. The moment we involved Bug, Rogan would know every detail of what we asked, real and imagined, because Bug wouldn't just report the facts, he would embellish them with his conclusions delivered with his particular flair.

I could just imagine the way that report would go. *Hey, so you'll never believe this dick fart thing: they want me to find Alessandro Sagredo. The gnome molester apparently stabbed somebody, and your sister wants to marry him. She's paying me a fortune to find him before he kills again and ruins the romance. She believes the dimwit shit-for-brains can be redeemed, I guess, by the love of a good woman. Isn't that just reindeer balls?*

Nevada would then drop everything and fly back here to help and fix things which would jeopardize Mrs. Rogan's claim. Rogan's grandfather was difficult in life and he saw no reason to change in death. His will specified that unless Rogan and Nevada were present for the entire duration of his funeral and the mourning period, Mrs. Rogan would be cut out of her father's will.

Mrs. Rogan wanted to inherit only one thing from her late father: the family's summer house on the coast where her late mother had planted a beautiful garden. When Mrs. Rogan was a little girl, before her mother's death, the family would vacation there. It was the place of her happiest memories.

For the past three years Mrs. Rogan educated and trained me. She found tutors for my magic, she arranged for etiquette lessons, she took me to museums and art galleries trying to hone my taste. She did it all never expecting anything in return, except a thank-you. Nevada and I wanted her to get that house more than she did.

I loved my brother-in-law, but to say that he was paranoid when it came to safety was like saying a typhoon was a gentle breeze. I had no doubt Connor had us watched. He couldn't help himself. That meant he already knew that Augustine showed up at our place in the middle of the night and that I left with him and came back with Runa and her unconscious brother. Whether he shared it with my sister was another question, but sooner or later Nevada would find out that we took a dangerous case. The likelihood of her rushing back home was already high, and Bug's litany of curses could push her over the edge.

The only way to stop this from happening was to level with her. It was too late to call her now. She would be in bed.

We needed Bug now. It was vital that we got a handle on where Alessandro was and why he was here. I couldn't wait till tomorrow.

"Call Bug."

The phone barely had a chance to ring before Bug snatched it up. "What do you want?"

"I need to hire you to find somebody, but you can't tell my sister. I'll tell her myself first thing in the morning. Can you wait that long?"

"Depends on who it is."

Nice try. I wasn't born yesterday. "Promise first."

"Fine. I promise."

"Alessandro Sagredo."

Bug's voice spiked. "Your virgin girl crush? The Italian Stallion?"

"Does everybody know that I had a thing for Alessandro?"

"Anybody who knows you. What did he do? Have you given up on pining from afar and decided to sweep him off his expensive cordovan leather loafers?"

I ground my teeth. "He killed my prime suspect."

Silence.

"How?"

"He stabbed him in the heart. Less than five feet away from me."

"Ohhh. That's good. That's too good. I've got to tell the Major."

"Bug! Think way back, about two milliseconds ago, when you promised me that you wouldn't tell?"

"You tricked me. I don't know if I can hold it in. It's too good."

Argh. "Okay, you can tell Connor if you swear him to secrecy. He can't tell Nevada. I'll explain it to her myself, tomorrow morning. Can you do that?"

"I'll try."

"They're asleep, anyway."

Bug snorted. "The Major never sleeps. Sometimes he rests his eyes while thinking deep thoughts."

"Connor is at his grandfather's funeral trying not to murder his obnoxious family. He's dealing with a lot right now, Bug. You don't want to add to that, do you?"

"You always ruin things with your logic. Fine. Where was the fancy boy last seen?"

"Jumping out of a third-story window of the IFS."

"Okay, I'll give it to him, that's pretty badass. I'm on it."

"We haven't discussed your fee."

Bug moaned. "Catalina, I'm so fucking bored. Nothing is happening. Another day and I'll pay you to hire me. At least this is something to do. With a face like that, he'll be easy to find. I'll call you when I learn more."

He hung up.

"You know some weird people," Runa said.

"It comes with the job. Are you okay?" I asked her.

"No, I'm pretty far from okay. My mother's dead body tried to rip my hair out."

There was nothing I could do or say to take that away from her.

"She loved us so much. I could go to my mom with anything, and she would make me feel better. He used her like she was a thing. Like she wasn't even a person."

"I'm sorry."

"Why?" she ground out. "I want to know why this happened."

"We'll figure out why. We learned two things already: your family was murdered, and their killer is powerful enough to compromise an AME."

"Yeah, no shit," Runa said. "It started weird and it keeps getting weirder, Catalina."

"I told you this could get ugly when we started. Do you want to walk away, Runa? You still can, but there will be a point when we can't stop what we started, and it's coming up fast."

"We didn't start anything. Whoever killed my mom and my sister started it." Runa swiped a tear from her eyes. Her teeth were clenched, her expression hard and angry. "But I'll finish it. You have my word."

 **Chapter 4**

Houston traffic was murder. It took us twenty-five minutes to cover the distance we could have driven in fifteen if the streets were empty. Nobody tailed us, but still I couldn't breathe right until we turned onto the road leading to the warehouse.

The security checkpoint, a squat armored building, was an eyesore, but when I finally saw it up ahead, I wanted to run out and hug it. Almost home.

"Catalina!" Runa yelled.

A truck horn blared. I nearly jumped up out of the seat. A delivery truck screeched to a halt on our right, from the access road. Another foot and it would have plowed into us. The driver waved his arms, his face skewed by anger.

I had run a stop sign. I knew the stop sign was there and I ignored it, because we were on high alert. There should have been a two-foot-high steel barrier obstructing that access road.

This was beyond ridiculous.

I stepped on the gas, drove up to the security booth, and rolled down my window. Kelly, a white man in his forties, with dark blond hair and a farmer's tan, slid open the window and grinned at me. "Stop signs are there for a reason, Ms. Baylor."

There should have been two people in the booth.

I had two choices. I could either chew him out in front of Runa and highlight exactly how incompetent we were, or I could let my mother, who oversaw our security, chew out his superior in private. I settled for the latter. "Raise all security barriers. No vehicles come in."

"But what about the deliveries?"

I made my voice very calm. "No vehicles come in, Mr. Kelly. Find Mr. Abarca and please have him see me ASAP."

Kelly finally realized that things were FUBAR, and the smile bled off his face. "Yes ma'am."

I rolled up my window and drove off, checking the rearview mirror. Behind me hydraulics whined, raising the spiked barricade to block the street.

I drove to the warehouse, and we came in through the business entrance. I walked into the conference room and used the intercom. "Family meeting in the conference room, please."

Runa took a seat. I sat down at the head of the table.

I'd been attacked by two corpses, saw my teenage crush stab a man in the heart, and then watched him jump out of a three-story window. I'd bullied an administrative assistant and stood up to the cops. Then I drove through heavy traffic, scanning it for enemies, and almost got into an accident in front of my damn house. My heart was still pounding. I wanted to jump up and run around the block to burn off the adrenaline.

Instead, I had to sit in a chair and appear professional. I could still feel the sharp desiccated fingers on my throat, squeezing to crush my windpipe. I would remember that awful smell as long as I lived. There was no time to deal with any of it.

The reanimated bodies were bad, but Alessandro was worse. I kept replaying that strike in my head. I wasn't sure I could've blocked it even with my magic. And his face. He'd looked relaxed. He'd stood there, with a human being sliding off his knife, and he'd looked relaxed.

My cell rang. An unlisted number.

I answered it on speaker. "Yes?"

"You're tracking me," Alessandro said.

Runa's eyes went big.

"I'm not tracking you," I told him. Technically, it wasn't even a lie.

"You're having me tracked. I understand that I'm irresistible. It's a cross I bear. But do try to have some self-control, Catalina. I'm embarrassed for you."

He . . . Argh. "As I recall, I never had a problem resisting you."

"I thought we agreed that you would drop this."

"I didn't agree to anything."

"Catalina, listen to me. This is serious, the people involved are dangerous, and your well-being is important to me."

Since when? "Why don't you tell me more about it? Maybe if I fully understand the danger, I'll stay out of it."

"No, you won't. You have no sense."

"I have all kinds of sense."

"This is your last warning, Catalina."

"Or what?"

"Trust me, you don't want to find out."

He hung up.

I glared at the phone. Insufferable ass. When I got my hands on him, I would pry his mind open like a tin can.

And then I would make him do a little dance, record it, and play it for him on a loop after I drained my magic off. *Irresistible. I'll show you irresistible. Just you wait.*

"'I have all kinds of sense'?" Runa quoted.

"I was too mad to think of a snappy comeback."

Mom and Bern walked into the conference room. I put my phone down.

"Where is everyone?" I asked.

"Closing Yarrow," Mom said. "There has been a development. Leon called for reinforcements. Your grandma and Arabella left about an hour ago."

"What kind of a development?"

"They wouldn't tell me, but they took Brick."

Brick was Grandma Frida's ultimate achievement. It started life as a military Humvee and was now the pinnacle of vehicular security. It couldn't go faster than sixty miles an hour, but my grandma claimed it could take a shot from a tank. She also refused to let any of us drive it.

The Yarrow case involved a woman who posed as a CPA and used her charm to worm her way into her friends' small businesses and then rob them blind. What in the world would they need Brick for?

I brought Mom up to speed on the events of this morning. "Also, I asked Mr. Abarca to join us after this meeting."

"Right," Mom said, loading a world of meaning into the single word. She and our head of security had been butting heads almost from the moment we hired him, and it was only getting worse.

I turned to Runa. "We need to figure out why your family was targeted. People kill for one of three reasons: emotion, power, or money. Not every House in Houston would have the audacity to pressure an AME.

The penalties are severe. Your mother made an enemy with a lot of power."

Runa spread her arms helplessly.

"How did your family make money?" I asked.

Runa frowned. "I don't exactly know. We just always had enough. We had some investments, I think. Once in a while, Mom would consult in criminal cases. She served as an expert witness."

"Any recent cases?" If someone's conviction hinged on her testimony, it could be a hell of a motive. That or revenge. Always a good one. I would have to pull up all the recent cases Sigourney Etterson had testified in.

"No." Runa shook her head. "She used to do it more frequently when I was younger. I remember her traveling a lot, especially right after my father bailed on us. But she told me a few years ago that she wanted to spend more time with us, and that the forensic work didn't pay well enough to justify her missing things in our lives."

I glanced at Bern. He met my gaze and frowned.

"What?" Runa asked.

Someone had to state the obvious and that someone was me, apparently. "You said your father cleaned out the family accounts and twelve years later you are worth eight million dollars."

"Less now. Some of it was the house," Runa said.

"Expert testimony can be profitable, but it doesn't pay *that* well," Bern said.

She bristled. "What are you saying?"

"We're not saying anything," I told her. "We're asking questions. Things are not making sense and we need to keep digging until they do."

Runa rubbed her face with both hands.

"Did your mother use any kind of remote backup?" Bern asked.

"I don't . . . Wait, yes," Runa said. "Yes, she did. She used Guardian, Ltd. All the important documents were backed up to a remote server. Her user name is Hemlock. The password is our three names, RunaHalleRagnar. She made me memorize it. I should have checked it. I'm so dumb. I didn't even think about it."

"You had a lot going on," Bern said. His fingers flew over his laptop's keyboard. "I'm in."

"Did she leave any letters for me? A message?"

"Not that I can see right away," he said. "I'll look."

The excitement drained from Runa's face. "Is that all the questions?" she asked quietly.

"For now," I told her.

"I'm going to go check on my brother. Please tell me if you find anything."

I waited until the door behind her closed and turned to Mom.

"Abarca?" she asked.

"The access road barrier wasn't up. We almost got hit by a truck coming from that street. The barricade by the security booth was down also and when I checked with Kelly, he thought the truck thing was funny. Kelly didn't have a battle buddy."

My mother rested her elbow on the table and leaned her chin on her fingers. This was her we-have-a-serious-problem pose.

When I agreed to become the Head of our House, I decided that I wouldn't repeat Nevada's mistake. I wouldn't try to do everything myself. I wasn't as strong as she was, and if I tried to carry it all, I would crumble; so I delegated. Bern oversaw all things digital that were more complex than our regular information searches. Grandma Frida handled our vehicles. Arabella collected payments. Mom took care of our security. That was her sphere, and I mostly stayed out of it. Delegating didn't mean anything if I questioned every decision she made.

The doorbell chimed. I got up, went to the front door, and checked the camera. Abarca stood on the other side. Lean and bronze-skinned, Abarca was forty-eight years old but looked ten years younger. He had a full head of hair, once black but now going to grey, and a pleasant face with dark eyes and an infectious grin.

As I opened the door, he gave me a bright smile. I smiled back, because it was polite, and shut the door behind him.

Three years ago, Nevada married Connor Rogan, also known by such fun nicknames as Mad Rogan, the Scourge of Mexico, and Huracan. Connor maintained his own private army, and for a while they provided our security.

We were all very naive back then. We actually looked into building a house next to Rogan and Nevada's, going as far as negotiating the price for the land. The deal fell through when I crunched the numbers and saw how much money we still owed Augustine and how much we would need to survive. Instead we had to concentrate on paying off our debt.

As time went on and we slowly crawled out of our financial hole, we decided to hire our own security team. We did it for two reasons. We didn't want to be a drain on House Rogan's resources, and we had to separate ourselves from Connor's long shadow. Always counting on Nevada and Connor to save us and provide for us wasn't fair to them. Once I understood that fact, I worked sixty-hour weeks.

When we started, I had no idea how much capital went into maintaining a private security force. We had to house them, feed them, and provide them with equipment. We had to carry insurance and employ an accountant to issue paychecks and file taxes. We had to retain a lawyer to file all the necessary permits. It was like piling money into a heap and setting it on fire twice a month.

Once we gathered enough capital to hire our own security, Mom brought Lieutenant Abarca in to oversee it. They'd served together, and he'd needed a job. Abarca supervised the hiring and the training of our guards, and he seemed competent. He was approachable and friendly, but as time went on, the cracks in our security became more and more apparent.

Abarca dropped into a chair. "Hi Pen."

Pen was not my mother's favorite nickname.

"The security barriers weren't up, George," she said. "I sent the alert myself. You acknowledged it. And then my daughter almost got hit by a truck that shouldn't have been on that road."

"It was Justin's truck. He delivers groceries to the DFAC, and he has done so for the last eight months. He was not a security risk and we were almost out of coffee. You know an army runs on coffee." He grinned.

His smile bounced off my mother like rubber bullets off a tank. "This isn't a joke. You put my children in danger. You put your own people in danger. Why was Kelly alone in the booth?"

"Merriweather's daughter had a recital," Abarca said. "These are people, Penelope. They have lives and families, just like you."

My mom gave him her thousand-yard stare. "Their families don't employ them, George. We do. And we have the right to demand a certain level of professionalism and discipline. Last night your people let an Illusion Prime roll right through the security checkpoint all the way to our front door."

"That was an extraordinary case. Nobody could have foreseen that."

"Really?" My mother leaned forward. "Our security personnel, who are supposed to maintain a log of departures and arrivals, didn't realize that Catalina was already home or think it odd that she came back in a strange car driven by a chauffeur none of them had ever seen before?"

Abarca's face took on a patient expression. "People are human. They make mistakes."

"They can make mistakes on someone else's dime." Mom's face held no mercy. "The two guards who let Montgomery through are fired."

Abarca stared at her in stunned silence. A moment passed.

"You can't mean that. Lopez is taking care of her sick mother and Walton has two kids."

"I have five kids and a mother in this house, and I want to keep them all alive. Mistakes like that get people killed."

Abarca shook his head. "I won't do it, Pen. If you want them gone, you're going to have to tell them yourself."

He and Mom locked gazes.

"Either you fire them, or you can pack your shit and go with them."

"We're not at war anymore," Abarca said.

"You're wrong," I said. "As of today, we are at war."

"You're dismissed," Mom said. "Let me know your decision by tomorrow."

Abarca looked at me, then at her, then at me again, stood up, and left.

I turned back to my mother.

"I know," she said. "If we don't fire him, he's going to get himself killed and our people too."

"Then let's fire him and hire someone else." We would give him a generous severance package. At this point, I would rather take a financial hit than keep at it. I knew everyone who worked for us. I didn't want any of them to die because we failed to properly train them. We needed better leadership.

Mom sighed. "It's not that simple. If we fire him, there is no telling how many of them will quit. They're loyal to him."

"Mom, they need to be loyal to us."

"I know," Mom said. "But at least they provide some protection. I don't want to fire him until we have a replacement ready."

"We could give Abarca a second chance," Bern said.

Mom's expression hardened. "We won't get a second chance, Bernard. We will be dead. Second chances are given when someone is good but makes an honest mistake or their nerves get the better of them. I gave Abarca the authority to hire his own unit. I questioned his choices at the time and he personally vouched for every soldier he brought to the table. It was his responsibility to train them and mold them into a cohesive unit. It's six months later, and they're failing at the basic security procedures. That's not nerves. That's incompetence. Hiring him was a mistake, my mistake. I wasted our time and money and I put us in danger . . ."

She looked like she was about to walk across hot coals barefoot. Oh, Mom.

"It wasn't a mistake," I said. "It just didn't work out. He looked really good on paper. He has all the qualifications. He's just . . ."

"He just cares about being liked more than he cares about doing his job," Mom finished. "I'll handle it."

Bern raised his head from his laptop. "Found something," he said.

I found Runa in the guest bedroom. She sat on the queen bed, next to Ragnar, who was curled up under a blanket. Sleep had softened his face. He looked so young right now.

"Hey," I said quietly.

"Hey. He's still asleep," Runa said. "Is that normal?"

"Yes. It's normal."

"Have you actually done this before?"

"Yes."

Last year one of Rogan's security people had developed an unhealthy obsession with Arabella and decided to break into our house in the middle of the night. I had fallen asleep in the media room, and he surprised me as he blundered past. He slept for two days, and once he woke up, he was an emotional zombie for a week. Rogan fired him and strongly encouraged him to move out of state. The last we heard, the man was in Alaska.

"What happens if he doesn't wake up tomorrow?"

"We'll put him on an IV and wait some more. His respiration is normal, his heartbeat is steady, and if we really tried, we could probably wake him up for a few seconds. He just needs rest, Runa."

She looked at her brother, reached over, and pulled a corner of the blanket up to expose his feet. "He always kicks the blanket off to stick his feet out. When he was little, it used to cause him anxiety. He wanted to sleep with his feet uncovered but he was scared that a monster from under the bed would grab his foot at night . . ." Her voice trailed off.

I wanted so much to make it better for her. "He will wake up."

Runa looked up at me and held her hand out. "Runa Etterson, Prime Venenata."

It was the way she had introduced herself at Nevada's wedding. Why were we doing the introductions again? "We've already met."

"No. I've met Catalina Baylor. She's shy and she tries to fade into the background. She gets embarrassed if anyone glances at her a second too long. I watched her at her sister's wedding and half of the time she looked like she was waiting for her chance to run away."

"I was."

"I saw you verbally eviscerate Conway a few hours ago. You had this look on your face like you were some ice princess and he'd trespassed in your kingdom. And then you cut my sister's reanimated corpse into four pieces."

"Conway was wrong to treat you the way he did, and reanimated bodies have to be disabled. The smaller the pieces, the lesser the threat."

She shook her head. "That's not my point and you know it. What the hell happened to you?"

I came over, sat on the other side of the bed, and put the small box I was carrying onto the covers.

"When we met at Nevada's wedding, I was panicking. That was the first time I was in charge of anything important. You were born a Prime, into a House of Primes. I was born a normal person, into a normal family, except that I had this terrible magic I had to hide so I wouldn't accidentally hurt people with it. I was only required to go to school, get good grades, and keep my magic hidden. Nobody expected me to take any responsibility for anything else. I had the luxury of covering my face and saying, 'This is too hard. I can't do this.' And I did."

"So what changed?"

I sighed. "We became a House. I was certified as a Prime. I had a nervous breakdown."

Runa blinked. "Why?"

"Because it was all too much. I needed rules. As long as I followed the rules, nobody got hurt and everybody left me alone. Suddenly, all my rules no longer applied and hiding in the background wasn't an option. I was freaking out. Then Rogan's mother found me and offered to mentor me. She made me see things from a different perspective."

"She taught you how to dismember a person with a knife?" Runa asked.

"She hired someone who did. Have you killed anyone before?"

"No."

"I'm sorry you had to do that today."

If I hadn't taken her with me, she wouldn't have killed Conway. But she would have to kill sooner or later. Maybe it was better this way. I had a feeling that whoever targeted her family wouldn't let go, not now, after their murder was confirmed.

"Have you killed anyone?" Runa asked.

"Physically, no. But what I do is much worse. Victoria Tremaine is my grandmother. When she requires the contents of your brain, she grasps your mind, wrenches it open, and takes whatever she wants. All your secrets, all of your hopes, your fantasies, your guilt over things you did years ago and tried your best to hide and forget, she sees it and rummages through it. Nevada has the same talent. I saw her interrogate a man once. He was a hardened mercenary and after she was done, he curled into a ball and cried like a child."

"Your magic is different."

I shrugged. "I don't use brute force. I entice, I seduce, but the end result is the same. I suppress your will. You'll tell me everything, and you will be happy to do it. It's the deepest violation of a person. I try not to do it unless I absolutely have to."

"But you've had to," Runa guessed.

"Yes. My mom is a veteran, and she once told me that nobody gets out of a war with their hands clean. We've been at war for the past three years."

"You do realize how fundamentally fucked up this is." Runa crossed her arms on her chest. "I feel like I lived my whole life with my eyes closed."

"Your mother took very good care of all of you. Runa, it doesn't have to be like this for you. I have no choice because of our circumstances, but there are plenty of Houses who don't often come into conflicts with each other."

"But why does it have to be you?"

"Because it's my turn. Nevada is married. She has her own threats and problems to deal with and I can't expect her to drop everything and run here to save us. My mother doesn't have the kind of magic that can protect us. Grandma Frida is past seventy. Here I am with all this power and I let everyone take care of me for most of my life, because it was too hard and scary and because I didn't want the guilt of hurting people. It wasn't fair. So, when Nevada decided to take a step back, I decided it was my turn to take care of everyone and do the ugly things nobody wants to do."

She shook her head.

"I'm the oldest ranking Prime in House Baylor," I told her. "It's my job to keep us fed, clothed, and safe. I still want to run away, Runa. But if someone tries to hurt my family, I'll kill them. It will cost me a great deal, but I'll do it."

Runa stared at me. "This is what being the Head of the House does to you."

It wasn't a question, but I answered it anyway. "Yes."

"I don't feel bad about killing Conway," she said. "I should. I took a life. But I don't."

"Guilt usually hits me late at night," I said.

"How do you deal with it?"

I pushed the box toward her. "I keep a stash of chocolate in my room."

"Does it help?"

"It does a little."

She opened the box. "Neuhaus truffles?"

"Mhm. Bern found some information on your mother's backup server. We have to go back to the conference room."

Runa's eyes widened. "Am I going to need these?"

"Yes."

 **Chapter 5**

"Most people tend to back up specific files or folders." Bern set his laptop in front of Runa. "Your mother went a step further. She backed up the entire hard drive. For all intents and purposes, this is an exact copy of her computer. The last session happened on the day she died."

I picked up my tablet. "We were able to view her activity log. She moved three files out of documents to the desktop. Here they are: Will, Financial Summary, and Bills and Utilities."

Runa clicked on the financial summary and scanned the contents. Bern and I had already looked at the file. It listed House Etterson's investments, the amounts current as of last Sunday. A short note at the bottom identified a financial adviser, Dennis Moody, with a notation, "Ask him if you have any questions." The other file documented the monthly bills, including utilities, insurance, and Ragnar's tuition.

Runa raised her head. "She knew she was going to die. That's why she moved the files where I would see them right away."

"It looks that way," Bern said.

"I don't understand." Runa leaned forward, her hands rolled into fists. "Why didn't she tell me? All she had to do was pick up the phone. Why didn't she hire somebody? Some sort of bodyguard?"

Those were all good questions. "There is more."

Bern reached over and tapped a couple of keys. A video filled the screen.

"Your mother recorded this on the day of her death just before midnight," Bern said.

"We haven't watched it," I said. "Would you like some privacy?"

"Yes. Thank you."

Bern and I stepped out into the hallway and I shut the door behind us.

"That financial summary bothers me," I said quietly. "Sigourney dumped a two-million-dollar investment with Diatheke, Ltd., on the day she died."

"I saw that," Bern said. "That's a large amount."

"It was also Sunday. What sort of investment firm or bank is open on Sunday?"

"A good question."

So far, we had this mysterious payment and Alessandro. Those were our only leads. If only I had gotten to Conway in time.

"Did you have time to look into Conway?" I asked.

Bern frowned. "I pulled his credit report. He has a line of credit from Texas State Employee Credit Union. Most likely, his accounts are there. All the first responders, cops, and firefighters bank there. They shell out the big bucks for online security. The guy who set up their system is a Significant cryptomage. It will take days to break, if I can do it at all. Not only is it illegal, but they'll come after me. Do you still want me to do it?"

Too risky. If they caught Bern, they would make an

example out of him. He would be the dirty hacker who compromised the hard-earned money of Texas heroes. Bern would serve real time and we would be done as a firm and a House.

"No," I told him. "Conway is a dead end. It's not worth it."

"Okay," he said.

The door swung open. Runa stood in the doorway. Tears wet her face. "You need to see this."

Bern and I followed her into the conference room. She reached toward the keyboard with trembling fingers and pressed enter. Sigourney Etterson filled the screen. She looked like an older copy of Runa: same wild red hair, same almost translucent skin, and same sharp green eyes.

"Hi sweetheart," Sigourney said. "I'm afraid this isn't a happy message, but I don't want you to be sad. Sometimes bad things happen. I don't regret my actions. I did what I felt was right. I love you so much. I'm so proud of you. You grew up to be a great person. You're kind, and responsible, and so smart. I couldn't wish for a better daughter."

Her words were like claws scratching on my heart.

"If I don't make it, you have to take care of your brother and sister. You have to be the Head of the House. It's a lot, but you can do it, darling."

A dark shadow moved behind Sigourney, approaching from the depths of the house, little more than a silhouette.

"I've named you as the executor of my estate. There will be a sharp learning curve. Dennis can answer some of your questions, but the primary burden will be on you. I don't trust anyone else enough to put them in charge of your inheritance."

The shadow glided forward.

"I'm sorry—" Sigourney fell silent in mid-sentence. Her gaze turned blank. Thick red drops slid from her eyes, ears, and mouth, painting crimson tracks down her pale face.

A gloved hand reached over Sigourney's shoulder to the keyboard. The video stopped.

He'd killed her. I couldn't explain how I knew it was a he, but I felt it deep in the pit of my stomach. He'd murdered Sigourney and he hadn't bothered to delete the video. The brutality of it was shocking. He just erased her like she was never there. Without laying a finger on her.

If he came for my family and I wasn't here, he would slaughter everyone.

Runa wiped her tears with her fingers. Her words came out sharp, as if they cut her mouth. "What kind of magic is that?"

"Probably a carnifex mage," I said. The instant internal injury fit their MO. Carnifexes normally went for the heart, not the brain. Anything protected by bone presented difficulty to them. If he was a carnifex, he was experienced and powerful.

"What's a carnifex?"

"A butcher," Bern said. "They cause lesions in internal organs."

She wiped her eyes again. The tears just kept running, and she kept flicking them away, her gaze locked on the screen.

A long, torturous minute slid by. I wished I could make it better. I wished so much that I could hug her, wave a magic wand, and undo all of this.

"What do we do now?" Runa asked.

"We go through your mother's accounts and her forensic testimony files."

"She kept meticulous records," Bern said.

"That's it?" Runa's voice vibrated with anger. "We look at files?"

"Yes," I told her.

"I just watched some prick murder my mother! We need to find him, so I can kill him. I'll poison him and fix him and poison him again until he can't take any more."

I understood. I wanted to find him too and make him regret ever being born. And when I found him, I would make sure he would never do that to another person. But right now, Runa needed cold water, not more gas on the fire.

"Okay," I said. "Where do we start looking?"

"I don't know. You're the investigator."

I stepped to the laptop, rewinded the video, and restarted it just as the shadow entered the room. "What we have here is a human dressed in dark grey. His face is covered with a mask, his hands are gloved. We can't even be certain it's a he, although judging by the height, this is probably an adult male. It could be a very tall woman. We don't know the exact nature of his magic, who he works for, or why he killed your mother."

The killer reached over Sigourney. That gloved hand looked odd, misshapen somehow . . .

"Then we need to find out! Don't you have someone? Like a snitch or an informant? Something!"

"This isn't a TV show," I said gently. Also, we were not hardened NY detectives who didn't play by the rules. "Confidential informants typically report on neighborhood and gang crime, because the people involved in those crimes don't know how to keep their mouths shut. This is a professional hit by a high-caliber magic user."

Runa squeezed her eyes shut and exhaled. Her fists relaxed. She opened her eyes. A little bit of the crazy had gone out, and I jumped on the chance.

"Your mother said she had no regrets. She was aware that her actions carried consequences. She did something, Runa, something that led to this murder. The sooner we figure out what that something is, the sooner we can find her killer. The answer is probably somewhere in her files."

"Okay," she said.

The forensic review didn't yield any results. After three hours, my eyes started to glaze over.

I turned down the sound and pulled up the video of Sigourney's murder in video editing software. Bump up the contrast, sharpen, levels, zoom . . . I ran the clip again. The glove's details came into focus.

It didn't look like a glove, more like a hand with greenish skin mottled with brown and orange, like a carapace of some beetle or the tail of a raw lobster. The tapered fingernails resembled claws, sharp and black.

This made zero sense.

A century and a half ago, several labs across Europe synthesized the Osiris serum. The Spanish were the first, followed by the English, Russians, and Chinese. They came to the discovery almost simultaneously, following up on the same research trail, with Germans and Americans being only slightly behind. Those who failed to discover the serum bought it or stole it.

An injection of the Osiris serum brought about one of three equally likely results: you died, you became a monster and then died, or your latent magical powers awakened. Despite the horrific odds of success, the serum spread across the planet like wildfire. The World War loomed on the horizon, and the major powers scrambled to crank out mages in hopes of gaining the upper hand. They gave it to everyone: the soldiers, the fading aristocracy, the captains of industry, people who had everything and those who had nothing.

Then the World War hit, bringing nightmares and atrocities beyond anyone's imagination, and it was quickly and unanimously decided that having people who could incinerate entire city blocks and spit poisonous gas into the trenches was a really bad idea. The Osiris serum was locked away, but by then it was too late. The magic proved to be hereditary.

The serum was inaccessible, but the experimentation into enhancing one's powers never stopped. Countless families and labs kept trying to find a way to make their magic stronger, and the only way to do it was to experiment on human beings, preferably those with some magic and very little money. Sometimes that experimentation caused a cataclysmic response, twisting the bodies of the research volunteers into inhuman monstrosities. The majority died on the spot. The few who survived were no longer human, physically or mentally. They became warped.

According to the numerous articles and scientific papers I'd read, the transformation permanently altered the subject's magic. Instead of their original powers, all their magic was now dedicated to keeping their warped bodies functioning. The constant magic drain killed them within two to three years.

No one magic-warped could have a magical talent by definition. Yet Sigourney's killer clearly did.

Not only that, but a warped human couldn't have pulled off this hit. It required critical thinking and performing a succession of tasks: break in, move quietly, kill the target, turn off the computer, stage the scene, set the house on fire. Nevada knew a warped woman, Cherry. Before Cherry died a couple of years ago, she'd spent her days swimming in the brackish water in a flooded part of Houston, eating fish and garbage. She couldn't carry on a conversation for longer than a minute. If you somehow convinced, bribed, or forced Cherry into assaulting a House, she would probably crash through a window or bang on the door until she forgot what she was doing there.

Maybe it wasn't a clawed hand. Maybe it was some sort of specialized glove. I peered at the screen.

My cell rang.

Across from me, Runa groaned. "Please answer it. My head hurts."

I took the call.

"Greetings, Ms. Baylor," Mr. Fullerton's precise voice said.

I put the call on speaker. "Hello, Mr. Fullerton. I hadn't expected to hear from you so soon." He had told me it would take at least twenty-four hours for the DNA results.

"The official results will be available tomorrow; however, under the circumstances, I felt urgency was in order. Is Ms. Etterson present?"

"Yes," Runa said.

"Very well. I can confirm that one of the bodies is that of Sigourney Etterson."

As expected.

"The other body doesn't match any of the profiles in House Etterson. It shares no similar genetic markers."

Runa jerked upright in her seat.

"Could you please repeat that?" I asked.

"The other body isn't Halle Etterson."

"Where is she then?" Runa demanded.

"I don't know. I know where she isn't. She isn't in the Forensic Institute's morgue. I hope this was helpful. Ms. Baylor, Ms. Etterson, good day."

Holy shit.

The three of us, Bern, Runa, and I, stared at each other.

Leon strode into the kitchen. He wore his blood-stained T-shirt on his head, like a turban, and his bare chest peeked through the gap of his open jacket. He was carrying a bucket of fried chicken in one hand and a bank deposit slip in the other.

"I closed Yarrow," he said. "The three of you look like you've just been slapped by a ghost."

"Neither of the bodies from the Etterson fire belongs to Halle Etterson," Bern said.

"Wow." Leon put the deposit slip in front of me, dropped into a chair, pulled the cardboard lid from the bucket, and fished out a drumstick.

"So, does this mean Halle's alive?" Runa asked.

I glanced at Bern, sitting at the table, but he apparently decided to impersonate a statue from Easter Island, because all I got back was an enigmatic look. I was on my own.

"No. It means that the other body in the morgue isn't your sister."

"So she could be alive?"

Runa jumped up and paced around the kitchen, circling the island. She was desperate and drowning in grief. The small chance that Halle might have survived was a lifeline and she clung to it. She was irrational before, and she would be completely unpredictable now. I had to make sure she stayed put. The last thing we needed was her running out to "investigate."

"She could be alive. If they killed her, why go through the trouble of planting a body? However, we aren't sure where she is or what condition she's in. Somebody went to great lengths to make sure she was officially dead.

They didn't want anyone to look for her. We have to tread carefully here. We may endanger her by our actions."

Runa stopped pacing and stared at me. "Catalina, if there is the slightest chance that my sister is alive, we have to find her. Nothing else matters; not revenge, not finding the murderer, nothing except Halle's life."

"I understand. Halle is the first priority." I turned to Bern. "Were you able to find that two million Sigourney liquidated on the day of her death?"

Bern frowned.

"I'll take that as a no."

"I've checked all of our accounts," Runa said. "It's not there. It wasn't wired in and then wired out or withdrawn. It didn't come in as a big chunk or in smaller deposits."

"Ramma munnuf," Leon said.

"Swallow your food," Bern told him.

Leon gulped his iced tea. "Ransom money."

Thank you, Captain Obvious. Just because we hadn't blurted it out in front of the client didn't mean we all weren't quietly thinking it.

Runa froze. "Do you think Halle was kidnapped and Mom withdrew the money to pay the ransom?"

"It's a possibility," I said, keeping my tone measured.

"Catalina, stop treating me like I'm made of glass! Everything is 'may' and 'possibility' and 'we're not sure'! I deserve an honest answer."

You know what, fine.

"Okay. Here is the truth: I don't know. I'm trying not to get your hopes up, because you're grieving, and it makes you prone to rash decisions." There, that was honest.

"Dun dun dun," Leon intoned dramatically.

"Rash decisions? Like what?" Runa demanded.

"Like poisoning the man who could've told us who hired him to cover up this murder."

Runa waved her arms. "My mother's body attacked us, I freaked out! And besides, it was your boyfriend who stabbed him."

"Please. Conway was a dead man walking before he left the room. You poisoned him so well that his body grew an inch of black fuzz after he was already dead. And for the last time, Alessandro isn't my boyfriend."

Runa's eyes narrowed. "When I saw you, you had your hand on his arm, as if you were walking into prom. You had that look on your face."

Leon and Bern looked like they were watching a great movie and had just come to the best part. Ugh.

"What look?" I asked.

"The I'm-touching-the-dreamiest-guy-in-the-universe look."

"I was flustered. I'd just watched him stab a man and then smile at me like nothing happened."

"Well, I was flustered too!"

Arabella walked into the kitchen. "I smell chicken. Give."

"You're gonna want to sit down for this," Leon told her. "Catalina and Runa are having a fight. We're about an inch from hair pulling."

"A fight?" Arabella's eyes widened. "A real fight?"

"Yes," Bern told her.

"Pass the popcorn," my sister said.

Why did I put up with all of this? Oh yeah, they were family and I loved them no matter what. But sometimes, like right now, I loved them significantly less.

I turned to Runa. "Your sister could have been kidnapped. The ransom would explain where the money went. But this scenario has problems."

"Okay," she said. "Like what?"

"First, if someone kidnapped Halle, and your mother

paid the ransom, why kill her and why plant a fake Halle? If your mother failed to pay the ransom, where is the money, and again, why the decoy? It would make much more sense to contact you and say that they killed your mother and they have your sister. You would pay whatever they asked. Also, your mother says in the video that she didn't regret her actions and that she did what she felt was right. That suggests that the fire was an act of punishment. She expected to be in danger, but she says nothing about your sister, and she made no effort to shield Halle by sending her away, for example, which implies your mother thought she was the only one in trouble. So no, none of this makes sense."

Runa pondered it. The silence stretched.

"Fair enough," she said finally. "What about this Diatheke thing?"

Bern cleared his throat. "On paper, they're an investment firm 'seeking partnership with high net worth individuals, families, and firms.' They mainly invest in enterprises in South America. Average Web site, pictures of corporate officers, which are old white guy, younger white guy, and some people in their thirties with good dentists and above average income."

So far, pretty average.

"There are no reviews or testimonials, which isn't unusual for a private investment firm," Bern continued. "Their Glassdoor listing is vague. Employees: one to eighty. Net worth: unknown. Revenue: unknown. Salaries: unknown. Again, not unusual. Bloomberg, which gets its info from S&P Global Market Intelligence, lists Randall Baker as a founder. He doesn't belong to any House and he isn't on Herald. He hasn't been indicted. He hasn't declared bankruptcy. The company never declared bankruptcy and has never been sued or sanctioned. They're a private equity firm like dozens of others in Houston. The only thing notable about them is that their founder is likely a figurehead."

"Why do you think that?" Runa asked.

"Because Randall Baker is ninety-two years old and his primary residence is in Naples, Florida," Bern said. "I broke into his home network and read his email. He hasn't been to Houston since before we became a House."

I rubbed my face. "Tomorrow I'll go to Diatheke and see what I can find out. They probably won't tell me where they wired the money, if they wired it, but at least we can confirm that the funds were transferred."

Runa looked at me. "I'll come with you."

"No," the four of us all said at the same time.

She threw her hands up. "I won't poison anybody."

"If you go there with Catalina," Bern said, "she'll have to concentrate on keeping you safe instead of finding your sister."

"What he said," Arabella said.

"Please stay here," I told Runa. "Besides, if Ragnar wakes up, he'll need to see you. He'll be in a strange place, with strange people, and waking up after my magic will be confusing enough."

"Okay," Runa said. "I'll stay here and sit on my hands. Doing nothing. While you go into danger on my behalf. Happy?"

"Ecstatic. Arabella, will you come talk to me upstairs?"

I marched into the hallway. As I climbed the ladder to my loft suite, I heard Bern behind me rumble, "She really wants to help you. Personal confrontations are very difficult for her."

Great. Look at all this respect I was getting as Head of House. So much respect.

Arabella knocked on the ladder and climbed up. "I'm so tired. What did you need?"

"Could you look into Halle Etterson for me?"

Arabella grimaced. "You think she killed her mother, planted a corpse, and made off with a cool two mil?"

"I don't know, but I want to find out."

My face felt too hot. I went to the window, unlatched it, and slid it open. The night exhaled cold air, cooling my skin. As much as I didn't want to admit it, Bern was right. I didn't like confrontations. Especially with people I cared about.

"Did Alessandro actually stab somebody?"

"Yes. He did it well too."

Arabella exhaled. "Well, I'm shook."

Shook was a good way to put it.

My window opened onto a street, behind which rose tall brick buildings. Between the buildings and the road an old oak tree spread its branches, its massive trunk encircled by a four-foot-high stone wall. A lone streetlamp fought a valiant battle against the night, illuminating some of the street and the tips of the branches.

I sighed. It was a long, long day, and I had so much work to do tomorrow . . .

Arabella said something.

"What?" I asked.

"I said you should have some chicken. Don't be pulling a Nevada on me."

"I will. I just didn't want to ask you in front of Runa."

Movement troubled the oak. I focused on it.

Alessandro sat on the thick branch directly across from my window. He wore charcoal grey, and his hair was brushed back from his face.

He raised his hand and waved at me.

I caught my hand rising to wave back and spun to my sister. "He's here!"

"Who?"

"Alessandro! He's sitting in the oak."

Arabella dashed to the window. "Where?"

The tree was empty.

I pointed to where he had been a moment before. "Right there. He waved at me."

I grabbed my phone and dialed the emergency contact for Abarca.

"Chicken," my sister said. "Lots and lots of chicken. Helps with hunger-induced hallucinations."

"I saw him." The phone rang and rang.

"I believe that you think you saw him. The heart wants what the heart wants, Catalina."

"My heart doesn't want anything. I saw him stab a man in the chest and now he's in the oak, bypassing our security like it's not even there."

"Chicken and then a nap. How about a nice long nap?"

"I'll put you into a nice long nap."

She snorted. "You and what army?"

"Abarca!" the phone said.

"There is an intruder on the premises."

"Are you sure?" Abarca asked.

"Yes, I'm sure. He was in the tree by my window. If he was a sniper, I would be dead, or Arabella would be dead."

"I find it highly unlikely," Abarca said. "We've got the place locked down tight. Are you sure . . ."

"My sister said she saw an intruder," Arabella yelled. "Do something!"

"We're on it." Abarca hung up.

I dialed Bug.

"If you're calling about that ass clown, I don't have him yet. He got away from me this afternoon, but I'll find him . . ."

Ass clown. What did that even mean . . . "He was in the oak by my window twenty seconds ago."

"Dickfucker!"

Bug hung up.

"Food. Now," Arabella ordered.

"Okay, okay." I headed for the door. "I did see him."

"Maybe you'll see him in your dreams. By the way, I called our insurance company to give them a heads-up about the Yarrow case."

"Why?"

"We rammed a house with Brick."

I made a one-eighty. "You what?"

"It was a hostage situation," she said. "The damages aren't that bad."

"How bad?"

"We took out a wall and a panic room door."

I opened my mouth. Too many words tried to come out at once, and I just stood there, trying to sort them out.

"Anyway, our insurance is canceled as of last month."

"What? Are they claiming we didn't pay the bill? Because I had them on direct deposit!"

My sister sighed. "No, they canceled because our grace period expires tomorrow, and we're 'high risk.'"

"Nice. Do they expect us to immediately die in horrible ways?"

Arabella nodded. "Pretty much. Let's go get some dinner."

 **Chapter 6**

I woke up because my alarm went off and it was my turn to cook breakfast.

Cooking was basically my and Mom's job. When Nevada lived with us, she was too busy keeping us afloat financially. Bern and Leon had kitchen duty once a week and usually made meat, preferably steak, and they served it charred on top and raw in the middle. Grandma Frida came from the generation when things weren't cooked unless they were mushy or slightly burned, and my younger sister, who was actually a decent cook when she had to be, couldn't be trusted to stay in the kitchen for the duration of the cooking process. She'd start frying and then end up outside texting to her friends or in the media room laughing at some show, until the smoke detectors went off and we had to race to save the food and put out the fire.

I set about making things. Since it was a weekday, I decided on a simple menu. I put two packs of bacon into two baking pans and popped them in the oven. Then I mixed the batter for the blueberry pancakes.

The best part about cooking, besides making delicious

things, was that it gave you time to think while your hands were busy.

I had spent a few more hours last night going through Sigourney's case files. Most of the people she testified against were still incarcerated. Two had died and one was released and had moved out of the country. The revenge angle was looking unlikely.

Every minute we wasted chasing down dead ends made recovering Halle that much less probable. The first seventy-two hours in a missing person case were crucial. The fire happened early Monday morning. Today was Thursday. The seventy-two hours had come and gone, and we hadn't even realized she was missing for most of it.

I imagined Runa finding her sister's body after thinking Halle was alive, and shuddered. How much loss could Runa and her brother take? To have that hope and then have it crushed was almost worse than not having it at all. And where was Halle? If I was right, someone dragged her out of her house in the middle of the night while her mother burned to death. It made me angry. Violently angry.

We had to make some progress today. Bug hadn't reported in, so right now Diatheke was the most obvious choice. They opened their doors at nine and I would be there exactly one minute after that. I had the legal backing and my magic. They would tell me what I wanted to know whether they liked it or not.

I called Nevada while chopping mushrooms for the egg, mushroom, and cheese scramble.

My sister answered on the second ring. "Yes?"

"How's Spain?"

"Sunny and beautiful. How's Houston?"

"Cold. My toes are cold. Anyway, do you remember Runa Etterson?"

"Yes."

"Her family was murdered." I summarized things for her.

"In the heart, huh?"

"Yes. It was smooth, Nevada. Practiced."

"Well, that's a hell of a thing. Do you need me?"

"No. If we do, I'll call you, I promise. I don't want you to worry."

Nevada snorted. "You sound like Mom. Speaking of Mom, how are things with Abarca?"

Yep, she'd heard about Augustine waltzing into our house at two o'clock in the morning. I knew Rogan left someone to watch us. The man couldn't help himself. Served us right for not spotting the observer. If our security was better, they wouldn't have gotten so close. If I told Abarca about it, he wouldn't believe me. According to our valiant security chief, there was "no way" for anyone to penetrate our perimeter, climb an oak, and then wave at me. His exact words were "not even a squirrel." In fact, he heavily implied that I hallucinated the entire thing.

"We may have to let him go," I said. "Mom is beating herself up over the whole thing."

"They were friends and Abarca looked good on paper."

"That's what I told her."

"Catalina, if you really get in trouble, call Heart. I'll text you the number. He's in the States and between wars right now."

He headed Rogan's elite unit, fighting in conflicts all over the world for astronomical prices. We couldn't afford Heart, even with Rogan's discount.

"I will," I told her. "Does he take installment payments?"

"Seriously," Nevada said. "Call him. I don't want to come back home to burned bodies."

"You worry too much," I told her.

"I worry just enough. I would worry less if you promise to call Heart."

"If things get bad, I promise I'll call Heart. Love you."

"Love you too." There was a pause as my sister hesitated. "Catalina, kidnapping cases rip your soul right out. Especially if you know the client. Take care of yourself."

"I will."

I hung up. My stack of pancakes was almost finished, and the mushrooms had browned nicely.

Someone cried out. It was a very short, startled sound, cut off in mid-note. Now what?

I turned off the gas burners, wiped my hands on a kitchen towel, hung it over my shoulder, and went to investigate.

The door to the spare bedroom stood ajar. A deep rumbling sound came from within, a soft kind of snarl born deep in a huge throat. It sounded demonic. I pushed the door open with my fingertips.

Ragnar sat on the bed, his back pressed against the headboard, his face pale, his eyes opened as wide as they could go. An indigo-blue beast sprawled on the floor by the bed. Six feet long, not counting the tail, with a tiger's thickness and a muzzle with four nostrils, the creature watched Ragnar with electric-blue eyes. His paws were as big as my head.

Ah. Cornelius and Matilda were back. I would have to put more eggs into the scramble.

The otherworldly feline saw me. A fringe of tendrils rose around his neck. Sickle claws shot out of his velvet paws and vanished.

"Zeus, what did I tell you about scratching the rug?"

Zeus made a short noise somewhere between a bull and a sea lion.

"Don't sass me."

The beast resumed his throaty snarling.

"Hi," I said to Ragnar. "Remember me?"

Ragnar shook his head, his gaze fixed on Zeus. "No."

"That's good," I told him.

"What is he?" Ragnar asked.

"He's a summoning. A few years ago, a summoner pulled him out of the arcane realm. He made friends with an animal mage here. Nobody has ever seen anything quite like him before, but he stays with us now. Come on, Zeus. Out."

Zeus refused to move. That meant one thing: someone higher than me in his pack told him to stay here.

I raised my voice. "Matilda!"

A moment later Matilda walked into the room. Prince Henry, a ball of white fluff made of cuteness with blue eyes and an absurdly fluffy tail, trailed her. Matilda and Cornelius claimed he was a Himalayan cat, but I had my doubts.

Slight for her age, with long dark hair and big chocolate-brown eyes, Matilda looked a lot like Nari, her Korean mother. Nari was murdered three and a half years ago, which was how Cornelius came to work for us. Matilda split her time between school, her aunt's house, and our warehouse, and when Cornelius was in the office, she was usually here.

"Is your dad here?"

"He dropped me off."

"Could you tell me why you asked Zeus to stay here?" I asked.

Matilda looked at Ragnar. "He slept too long, and it was time for him to wake up."

I had sent Cornelius an email last night catching him up on the case. Clearly, Matilda read it. "Yes, but why Zeus?"

"Medical studies indicate that hearing a cat purring lowers human blood pressure and promotes calm," Matilda recited.

"Matilda," I said gently, "most people find Zeus scary. The article probably meant house cats, not enormous blue tigers from the arcane realm."

She shook her head. "There is no difference in purr quality between Zeus and Prince Henry. If he doesn't understand that, it's up to him to educate himself."

Sometimes dealing with her was like talking to a fussy forty-year-old. "Please ask Zeus to exit."

Matilda rolled her eyes. "Fine. Come, Zeus, you are wasted on this stupidhead."

I had no idea if she meant me or Ragnar.

She left the room, and Zeus trotted out, following Matilda deeper into the house.

I turned to Ragnar. "My name is Catalina. You and Runa are staying with us for now. Runa helped our family a few years ago and now we're investigating what happened to your mother and your sister."

Some color came back into his face. "They died in a fire."

I really needed Runa for this conversation. "We confirmed that your mother is dead. However, the other body the firefighters recovered doesn't match Halle. There is a small chance that Halle might be alive."

He nodded at me, his expression serious and calm. "Okay."

Magic drain was a hell of a thing.

"When you're ready, there will be breakfast in the kitchen. Follow the smell of pancakes and bacon."

"Okay," he said again, "Thank you."

I turned to leave.

"Excuse me," Ragnar said. "Where is my sister?"

Shit.

Five minutes later, I watched the security footage of Runa exiting the warehouse. She got into her Nissan Rogue and drove off.

Damn it. There was no telling where she went.

She wasn't a prisoner. She was a guest and a client. She could leave as she wished. Even if it was dangerous and stupid.

On the recording, Bern slipped out the door. I whipped out my phone and texted him.

Where are you?

Watching Runa.

What is she doing?

She's sitting in the remains of her house and crying. I'm going to let her cry it out and then follow her to make sure she gets home.

Ragnar is awake.

I'll tell her.

I exhaled. Today would be a long day.

When people thought of Houston downtown, they imagined modern towers made of steel and glass. Which was true. But Houston had another downtown, older, more ornate, born during the 1920s and 1930s, when

Art Deco skyscrapers set new height records and the recent invention of air-conditioning made the oppressive heat and humidity of the Houston swamps bearable.

The Great Southwest Building, which now housed Diatheke, was built in a single year during that boom. The blocky limestone and brick tower rose above Texas Avenue, rectangular for most of its twenty-two floors, except near the top, where the upper floors were stepped back to mirror the Mayan pyramids that inspired its design. Carved reliefs adorned the walls. Mesoamerican dragons and warriors stared down at passersby from above the ornate arches.

I walked through its doors wearing my work clothes. Dark pants, white turtleneck, and my favorite Burberry coat with my knife in it. I carried a folder containing the legal equivalent of a loaded Howitzer, everything from our license to the limited power of attorney and urgent request for information, which I had Runa sign last night.

The lobby was just as grand as the outside. The polished parquet floor gleamed like a mirror, reflecting red marble walls. To the left, a small marble counter, decorated with an elegant white orchid, sheltered a lone receptionist. Past her, two elevators interrupted the marble wall. Directly across from the receptionist, to the right, a small sitting area offered two plush loveseats and a low coffee table with a glass vase filled with bright Christmas ornaments.

Typically, a lobby would have more than one exit, but the only other door, in the far wall, wasn't marked as such. It probably led to the stairs. The door looked remarkably solid, steel and modern, with a keycard lock.

I approached the counter. A middle-aged black woman wearing a charcoal suit and a pair of black framed glasses looked up from her computer screen and smiled at me.

She had short hair, minimal makeup, and a string of pearls around her neck.

"How may I help you?"

"Catalina Baylor, of House Baylor. I'm here to speak with someone regarding the House Etterson account."

"Do you have an appointment?"

"No. However, the principal account holder is dead, and the matter is urgent."

"Oh my goodness. That's not good. Please have a seat and someone will be right with you."

I walked over to the loveseats and sat in the corner, so I could watch both doors. The elevators had a keycard access box, meaning nobody without a card could even call the elevator to the floor. There had to be surveillance cameras, although I couldn't see any. For an older building, they sure had a lot of high-tech security.

Bug still hadn't reported in, which meant Alessandro had given him the slip twice. Bug had to be livid. On the other hand, Alessandro was now a challenge and would get his complete attention. No texts from Leon or Bern, which hopefully meant that Runa was still alive and hadn't murdered anyone. The last I'd seen of Arabella, she'd armed herself with a doughnut and a ridiculously large Starbucks latte and was shoulder-deep in Halle's online social life.

I looked up from my phone. The receptionist sipped something from a white mug with golden letters spelling out "Baby, it's cold outside." If she locked the front door, I would be trapped. The elevators were inoperable without a keycard. Same for the door leading to the stairs. There were no windows at this level except for the front door glass panels, and I had caught a glimpse of a metal grate that could be lowered, blocking the exit.

It was all rather dungeonlike.

The left elevator doors opened with a whisper. None of the numbers above it had lit up. Nothing indicated from which floor it had descended or that it was even on the way. Curiouser and curiouser. Unlike Alice, I couldn't grow to giant size in case of trouble. That was okay, I had other tricks up my sleeve.

A white woman in her late forties or early fifties stepped out of the elevator. Short and petite, she wore a pale pink Chanel suit with black piping, beige stockings, and black kitten heels. She'd chosen a chunky rose-gold necklace and a matching bracelet as her accessories. Her glasses matched her jewelry. Her dark hair, pulled back into a conservative bun, completed the look. She hurried toward me, her heels clicking on the polished wood floor.

I got up.

"Celia Scott." She offered me her small hand with rose-gold acrylic nails.

"Catalina Baylor."

She squeezed my hand, trying to reassure. "I'm so sorry about Sigourney. What a horrible tragedy. Let's talk in my office."

I followed her to the elevator. She pulled a slim plastic card out of her jacket pocket, waved it in front of the dark window above the call button, and the elevator doors opened. We stepped inside, and she waved the card again, this time above the floor numbers, and pushed the button for the fifteenth floor.

"How is Runa?"

"Shaken up."

"Perfectly understandable given the circumstances."

The doors opened, revealing a surprisingly modern hallway with a tasteful modern rug with splashes of red and turquoise, and eggshell white walls. Wow, fast elevator.

Celia took off down the hallway to the left, and I had to speed up to keep pace.

"What a beautiful building," I said.

"Isn't it? So much history here. If only these walls could talk."

Celia waved her keycard in front of a door on our right. The electronic lock clicked, and she swung the door open. I walked inside into a comfortable but decidedly modern office with an ergonomic desk and black leather designer chairs.

"Sit, sit." Celia waved at the chairs.

I sat. Three pictures in rose-gold frames sat on a corner of her desk; one showing Celia holding a baby, one with her and a middle-aged man in ski outfits, standing on a snowy slope, and one of a ridiculously groomed white poodle about the size of a cat. I was kind of surprised the poodle didn't sport a rose-gold collar.

Celia sat in her chair and smiled at me. Her mouth stretched, but no emotion reached her eyes. "So what can I do for you?"

I opened my folder and unleashed my bona fides. It took her about three minutes to get through it.

"A private investigator. How exciting. How did you get into that? You don't look the type."

"What is the type?"

She rolled her eyes. "Uh, burly, older, male?"

"We're not those kinds of detectives." I smiled back at her. "Strictly white-collar investigations here. We deal with insurance companies rather than distraught dames."

Celia laughed. "A pity."

"I'm here in a friend-of-the-family capacity. Runa is too upset to sort through her mother's affairs and we're trying to prep everything for her takeover."

"Of course, of course."

"Ms. Etterson kept meticulous records and they show a withdrawal of two-point-two million dollars from her Diatheke account. Can you confirm that a withdrawal took place, the status of the account, and the account to which the funds were deposited?"

Celia frowned. "I'm so sorry, but it is our policy to process such requests in writing. If you submit a written request, I should be able to get back to you in a couple of weeks. By Friday after next, at the latest."

Two weeks.

We didn't have two weeks. More importantly, she was lying.

Online resources and crime dramas stressed the importance of microexpressions or signs of nervousness when trying to judge when someone was telling the truth. Shifting eyes, looking up in the direction opposite of your dominant hand, sweating, pursed mouth, and so on. Accomplished liars exhibited none of those. However, I had grown up with a human lie detector of a sister, and Nevada had clued me in on an indicator that proved right most of the time.

Frequent liars maintained eye contact.

When I was little, my mother would sit me and Arabella down and ask who started the fight. "Look me in the eye and tell me you didn't do it." We both quickly figured out that as long as we looked her in the eye while we lied, she was much more likely to trust us. I had no idea why parents believed in the supernatural truth-serum power of their gaze, but most of them did. And they taught their children that shifty-eyed liars didn't meet one's stare under tough questioning.

Celia had maintained eye contact like a champ. So much so, it was slightly unsettling. Most people looked away when they were embarrassed, or uncomfortable, or when they tried to process things. Denying help to someone whose family had just died in a fire was about as uncomfortable as it could get, but Celia had stared straight at me, emitting trustworthiness.

I concentrated.

Nearly all mages had an active and a passive field. Active magical abilities required effort on the mage's part, while passive powers were always present: automatic, involuntary, and continuous, like breathing. Cornelius always scanned his surroundings for animals. His subconscious did it on autopilot. However, if he wanted to make friends with a particular animal, he had to apply his magic. In my case, I spent most of my time actively suppressing my passive field around strangers. Relaxing control now felt like letting out a breath I had been holding.

"Such a long time," I said, sinking some of my magic into my words. It stretched to Celia, winding around her. Her smile grew slightly, suffused with genuine warmth. I let her see a hint of my feathers, just a shimmer for half a second. "Runa has already been through so much. She lost her mother."

Another strand of magic.

"She lost her sister."

Another strand.

"She lost her house. And now she's missing two million dollars. Are you sure nothing can be done?"

Celia sat very still for a moment, then waved her arms. "Okay, okay. Just this once. And you have to keep it between us. Sigourney came in and closed out her account. Cash, of course."

Two million in cash?

"If you can't find it, it's probably in her pro account." Celia leaned forward. "Between you and me, I was surprised by the whole thing. Sigourney was a professional, with a long tenure. She knew how the game was played . . ."

The office door opened and a tall Asian man in a slick silver suit stepped inside.

Celia clamped her mouth shut.

"Ms. Baylor," the man said. "Mr. De Lacy requests the pleasure of your company. He asked me to invite you to his office."

"You better go, dear," Celia said. "Mr. De Lacy is our VP of operations. Very big deal."

The man fixed Celia with a cold stare. "Thank you, Ms. Scott, that will be all."

We walked to the elevator in silence, got in, and my escort swiped his card and pushed the button for the top floor. The elevator sped upward, coming to a smooth stop. The doors opened, and the man gestured me forward. "Please."

I stepped out. The doors shut behind me, and a faint whisper announced the elevator carrying my guide down.

No good-bye hug. How disappointing.

I was standing in a small hallway, framed by mahogany walls on both ends, each offering a door. The door on the right bore a heavy metal sign reading "Randall Baker." The door on my left said "Benedict De Lacy."

Benedict had Celia watched and pulled the plug on my interview the second she went off script. Sigourney was important to him and I couldn't wait to find out why.

I turned to the left. The door swung open under the pressure of my hand, opening with a soft chime. A huge office spread in front of me. You could fit a four-bedroom apartment in here and then some.

Persian rugs lined a floor of white Italian marble. A

life-size bronze statue of a running horse guarded the entrance. To the left, a sitting area offered antique French furniture that would have wiped out our entire annual budget. I had seen some luxurious accommodations, but this space was opulent, even by House standards.

Nobody came out to greet me.

I walked deeper into the "office." The next room offered an antique hand-knotted Turkish rug, delicate inlaid wooden tables, and a magnificent Syrian-style sofa, adorned with mother of pearl. Weapons decorated the walls between ornate shields: a Turkish yatagan, a shamshir, blades of Damascus steel, and French hand-and-a-half knight swords. Marble statuettes rested in wall niches vying for attention along with framed art. This wasn't the collection of a poser trying to impress. Too eclectic. No, Mr. De Lacy was a connoisseur.

And he was nowhere to be found. This was simply annoying.

The room ended in a long hallway. To the left was a wall with a door. To the right, another interior wall sectioned off a generous portion of the floor space. I turned right and walked into a study. Shelves filled with books and small busts lined the walls, interrupted by tall windows. A heavy oak desk dominated the space. Carved knights in full armor jousted across its front and sides. Behind it, in a thoroughly modern ergonomic chair, a blond man sat in front of a computer, holding a phone to his ear.

He looked up and raised his index finger at me.

Fine. I would wait. I sat in a plush chair upholstered with a kilim rug.

De Lacy listened to his phone. He was in his early thirties, tall, lean, with a powerful frame shown off by a tailored vest he wore over a pale-blue shirt. A suit jacket hung over his chair. He looked like he'd been up for a while. His hair was tousled, and stubble sheathed his jaw.

His face was handsome in that traditional way of good breeding and money: square jaw, patrician nose; good cheekbones; all the features a child could inherit from generations of very rich men marrying very beautiful women. Sometimes the offspring of those families looked softened by the luxury they were born into. There was nothing soft about Benedict. His eyes were sharp and cold, two chunks of ice radiating intelligence and menace.

A trace of magic brushed against me, the hint of a glacial mind. My instincts screamed in alarm. I let it wash over me. I had become so good at suppressing my magic, I looked inert to others. The magic drenched me and withdrew. A Prime. Some sort of mental branch. Very strong.

If this was a private equity firm, I would eat my coat.

"Authorization granted," he said, and hung up. His voice matched him, smooth and resonant, with a practiced quality to it, as if he'd spent some time with a vocal coach. "I see you found me, Ms. Baylor."

I had no idea what he was, but he had no idea what I was either. If I let him think he rattled me, I might not get out of this alive.

"It was touch and go for a while," I said. "I almost made camp in the Ottoman room but decided to press on."

Benedict smiled. The small hairs on the back of my neck rose.

"Why are you here, Ms. Baylor?"

"I've been retained by House Etterson. It's my understanding Sigourney Etterson had an investment account with your firm. Her records indicate she liquidated it. I'm attempting to locate those funds."

"An admirable pursuit."

"My client is in severe emotional distress after the death of her mother and sister. Her family home is gone, and she's trying to pick up the pieces. She needs every dime of her inheritance to rebuild her House. We're unable to account for the two million dollars. We would appreciate any assistance you could provide us."

Benedict pondered me.

The next step would be to threaten him with a lawsuit if his firm failed to cough up the information. I didn't want to push that far, not yet. I was alone in the office of an unknown Prime, asking uncomfortable questions and skating on thin ice.

Silence stretched.

Benedict turned his monitor sideways, so I could see it. On the screen Celia leaned forward and smiled at me.

"You come into my house, Ms. Baylor, and use magic on my staff. You can see how it presents me with a dilemma."

I waited. Silence stretched.

"I find it interesting that you feel absolutely no pressure to fill the lull in the conversation," he said.

"What makes you think I used magic? Perhaps Celia simply felt some compassion for the two young people who are now orphaned."

Benedict smiled at me, a quick, precise baring of perfect teeth. "You're right. I could blame Celia for her sudden attack of kindness. Unfortunately, Celia doesn't understand the meaning of the word. She approximates human emotions the same way a chameleon mimics his environment to survive. I'll be blunt: you intrigue me. You don't taste like a psionic; they give off a mental stench they can't mask. I don't detect the sharpness of a telepath or the particular flavor of a dominator. You're definitely not an empath. I tend to disturb them beyond their level of comfort. You almost taste like nothing, yet there is this slight hint of spice. A beguiling after-taste."

And he went right into creepy. "I think you give yourself too little credit, Mr. De Lacy. Empaths aren't the only people you disturb beyond their comfort level."

Benedict chuckled, got up, and strolled over to the window, where a blue crystal elephant stood on a small table next to a collection of matching heavy tumblers. The beast wore a delicate harness of gold that looked spun rather than forged and carried a decanter on its back, half full of what looked like whiskey. Baccarat crystal, antique, midnight shade of blue . . . a hundred thousand, maybe more.

He poured two fingers of amber liquor into a tumbler. "Whiskey?"

"Nine-thirty in the morning is a bit early for me."

Benedict raised his glass to his lips. "I've been up for twenty-two hours. You and this whiskey are a pleasant diversion at the end of a very long day."

The way he said it set my teeth on edge. Every woman had an instinct that warned her when things were about to spin out of control, and that instinct took in the way he looked at me and started screaming. I had to get out of this office.

I reached deep down and pulled Victoria Tremaine's granddaughter out. Surprisingly, it was easier than I re-membered.

"Since we agreed on being blunt, I hope you don't mind if I indulge."

"Please." He invited me with a sweep of his hand.

"I came here with a simple request for information, and instead I've been kept waiting, given the runaround, and now we're here in your multimillion-dollar man cave, while you are going out of your way to be gauche and vaguely threatening. Why, I can't imagine."

He laughed.

Right. I rose. "Mr. De Lacy, thank you for this incredibly frustrating and fruitless visit. Your time is valuable but so is mine. I'm done. I'll see you in court."

"I'm afraid I can't let you leave, Ms. Baylor." He stared at me. A shockwave of alarm punched through my spine. "I simply must know what you are. Fortunately for me, there is an easy way to find out."

Power splayed out of him, piercing my senses. I saw it through the prism of my magic, a dark, churning cloud, erupting from him like a nest of dark serpents. It hung around him, streaked with flashes of purple and red. Phantom mouths snapped the air with ghostly fangs, melting and re-forming, each cluster of darkness a living, malevolent thing wanting to bite and tear with those awful teeth.

Fear slammed into me. Every fiber of my being wanted to flee.

Benedict smiled at me from within that seething cloud. The mouths snapped, reaching for me.

The elephant decanter next to Benedict exploded. Glittering shards of blue crystal rained down on the rug and the table. Behind it, a hole gaped in the window panel. A sniper shot, most likely from the top of the high-rise apartment under construction across the street.

The serpent nest folded in on itself, sucked back into Benedict. He chuckled. "You have interesting friends, Ms. Baylor."

I had no idea who'd shot the decanter. Right now it didn't matter. I had to get the hell out of here, before De Lacy decided it wasn't funny anymore. The sniper had saved my life.

"Perhaps you simply have incompetent enemies. My friends wouldn't have missed. Good day, Mr. De Lacy. I'll show myself out. Please have one of your minions meet me at the elevator."

He raised his glass in a kind of salute. "Say hello to Montgomery for me."

He thought I worked for Augustine. I had no idea why, but I'd sort it out later.

I turned and made the long trek to the door. My knees shook. If nobody met me at that elevator, I would have to go back in there. I reached into my pocket. My fingers closed about a reassuring length of chalk.

If I did get trapped, I would make my stand by the elevator. No matter what kind of hell he fermented inside him, I could draw an arcane circle faster than he could, and once I had that boost, my chances shot up. He liked surprises? Well, I would give him one he would never forget.

I opened the door and stepped into the hallway. The elevator stood open, the same Asian man waiting inside with the same serious expression.

A few moments later, the elevator released me into the lobby. No sign of the receptionist.

I crossed the floor. My heart was beating too fast. I reached the doors.

Please be open.

The door swung open under the pressure of my hand and I walked back into the sunshine.

 **Chapter 7**

I was on Katy Freeway, driving home, when I noticed a tail. It would have been harder to spot it if they weren't driving two IAG Guardian light-armored personnel carriers. The Guardian was a favorite among the Houses that had to transport their private armies, and Grandma Frida had worked on about a million of them.

The Guardian resembled an SUV that had been kidnapped by a paramilitary organization and force-fed steroids. Armored enough to withstand multiple hits from high-power rifles and light machine guns, the Guardian came equipped with off-road capabilities and could be customized to mount light and heavy machine guns. The goons chasing me had opted for a toned-down "city profile" without all of the scary protruding barrels. They religiously changed lanes when I did, and when I slowed to fifty-five miles an hour, which would cause any sensible Texan to blow by me, they hung back and waited.

Benedict De Lacy didn't like losing his decanter.

Nobody except family knew where I would be today. The two vehicles weren't behind me when I'd left

Diatheke, so they must've bugged the Element while I was inside.

When the sniper shot the elephant, he or she had given Benedict a sign that I had backup. Diatheke wasn't what it seemed, and Benedict probably hated any kind of spotlight. If the sniper and I were on the same team and I failed to exit the building, there would be consequences. Benedict had decided on a wiser course of action—let me leave and hit me en route with a team that couldn't be traced to his firm.

Two Guardians, maximum carrying capacity of ten people each. I didn't know who rode inside, but they would likely be good at killing.

We had ten soldiers, of which only six were currently on duty. Considering the recent examples of their battle readiness, twenty professional killers would tear through them like they were tissue paper and move on to the warehouse. Bern hadn't checked in, so he and Runa were still out. Arabella had planned on leaving to talk with Halle's friends in person, so right now the warehouse sheltered Ragnar and Matilda with only Grandma, Mom, and Leon.

If I called Abarca right now and told him that I was being followed by two armored personnel carriers, would he even believe me?

I couldn't go home.

I had to defend my family. I had to kill the strike team. That's what Heads of Houses did.

Suddenly everything was clear. I felt cold and calm, oddly flat, as if all the emotion drained out of me and only my mind remained.

I couldn't fight twenty people at once. They would simply shoot me before I had a chance to open my mouth. My power worked best when my targets could both see and hear me. Benedict wasn't an idiot and he'd watched me work on Celia, so it was highly possible the people riding in the Guardians wore ear protection.

Given a couple of days to prepare, I could open this car window and sing the crews of the Guardians and everyone else within hearing range into blindly doing my bidding. At this distance and with my song amplified by magic, no earplugs would save them from my voice. However, once I did that, I'd have an adoring mob on my hands and no way to escape it. The longer they remained beguiled, the stronger my magic affected them. Eventually they would rip me to pieces. The two times I had used my magic to its full extent, my sisters had evacuated me right after I was done.

No, this called for a subtle approach. I needed a place to hide, somewhere secluded and out of the way, where they would be forced to fan out and search for me and I could stagger them.

Where could I find that in the middle of the city?

In the rearview mirror, the two Guardians stayed about three car lengths back. The heavy traffic didn't permit much maneuvering, but an opportunistic sporty-looking Subaru wove in and out between cars, trying to squeeze a few extra feet here and there. It slid behind me and promptly rode my ass.

Keystone Mall.

Fifty years old and looking every bit of it, Keystone Mall sat near the new 290/610 interchange. It had been dying since I was a kid. Hurricane Ike had killed its Macy's a decade ago, leaving the mall with just one an-chor store—JC Penney, which bit the dust last January. The mall closed shortly after. Bayou City Fright Fest had rented it this last Halloween for their annual Haunted House and Arabella dragged me to it. We spent seventy dollars apiece to wander through the dilapidated husk of a building, while zombie clowns jumped out at us from every dark corner. It had been horrible, and I didn't talk to her for two hours after that. Predictably, she'd loved it.

If I got out of this alive, I would thank her.

I dropped my speed by about five miles an hour. The Subaru looked for a way to pass, but the lane to the left of us was clogged with big rigs. He settled for getting within a hair of my bumper. *Perfect, stay right there.*

The exit sign for 762B flashed by. One mile.

The Subaru honked at me. *You stupid jerk. All the lanes are full. Even if you get in front of me, where do you think you're going to go?*

The exit lane peeled off the freeway to the right. One, two, three . . .

I wrenched my wheel to the right, cutting into the exit lane mere feet from the black impact barrels cushioning against a head-on collision with the concrete barrier. The Subaru slammed on its brakes out of sheer surprise. Behind it, the Guardians screeched, trying to avoid plowing into the smaller vehicle.

I tore down the exit lane at top speed, caught a green light on Old Katy Road, made a left, then a right onto Post Oak Road, and sped north. It wouldn't buy me much time, but hopefully it bought enough.

I crossed the railroad tracks and drove straight into Keystone's parking lot. At night, it had looked scary. The daylight stripped the horror mystique from it and now it just seemed grim and sad, gazing at the world with dark, empty windows. I parked near the entrance, jumped out, and popped the back hatch.

A large metal safe box waited for me. Grandma Frida had bolted it to the floor in the back, so there was no chance of it being stolen. I keyed the code into the lock. It popped open and I flipped the lid. A row of blades lay on black fabric, secured by leather straps. Two pistols rested in the top corners, a Glock 43 for the times I needed a subcompact for concealed carry and a Beretta APX.

Unlike Leon, my mom, and Nevada, I couldn't rely on my magic for flawless targeting when it came to guns, but Mom made sure that all of us knew how to handle a firearm. My accuracy was decent. I was a simple, no-nonsense shooter and the Beretta was a simple, no-nonsense gun, designed for daily use by the military and law enforcement. Roughly seven and a half inches long and five and a half inches tall, the gun weighed twenty-eight ounces empty and had a six-pound trigger. Firing it felt very deliberate; it was solid, and the heavy but crisp trigger guaranteed I wouldn't accidentally discharge it.

I grabbed a tactical belt, put it on, and clipped the black nylon holster to it. The Beretta went into the holster. I had opted for the .40, which gave me fifteen rounds, and the spare magazine in the built-in holster pocket brought my ammo count to thirty.

The sword was next. I had a choice between a tactical saber, a machete, or a gladius. I went with the gladius. Solid black, with a sixteen-inch double-edged blade of 80CRV2 steel, it weighed a pound and a half and let me cut or thrust with equal efficiency.

A canister of mace was last, just in case.

I locked the box, locked the car, and ran to the front doors. Logic said that whatever security this place had, if it had any, would clear out the moment the two Guardians pulled into the parking lot. They would take pictures of the license plates, submit a report, and let the cops and insurance company sort it out.

The door was locked. I smashed the butt of the gladius' hilt into the lower glass pane of the entrance door.

The glass panel fractured. I cleared it with my blade and ducked through. The interior door took another couple of seconds and I ran into the gloomy old mall.

The inside of the Keystone Mall smelled of dust and decay. On my right, an entrance to an old movie multiplex gaped open, a black hole in the pale marble wall bordered by ornate plaster columns. The theater was a deathtrap. It was sectioned off from the rest of the mall, and the only way in or out lay through that entrance in front of me. The individual theaters had emergency exits to the outside, but I didn't want to go outside. I wanted to stay in the mall and force them to fan out, searching for me.

I moved on.

A little farther, on my left, lay the food court, a large space with fast-food shops on one side. In the corner between the restaurants, a narrow tunnel led to the restrooms. The cheap plastic dining tables were still there, bolted to the floor, but all the chairs were gone. The air smelled of old corndogs.

Another dead end.

I passed the food court and paused at the top of the frozen escalator. The mall lay in front of me, a long narrow rectangle, two stories high and anchored by Macy's on the left end and JC Penney on the right. Weak daylight sifted through the dirty panes of a slender skylight, illuminating the little shops lining the sides; the has-been shoe stores and fashion boutiques. Without merchandise, they were little more than bare rectangles with a single back room sectioned off from the main space. No place to hide there.

The two anchor stores were my best bet; they were

large and confusing. Of the two, Macy's would be more open, a vast expanse of waist-high counters with barely any interior walls. JC Penney offered more partitions and better places to hide. Plus it had Sephora. The name-brand cosmetics store had its own shop in the middle of JC Penney's ground floor, a separate retail space defined by distinct black and white walls. Some Sephoras had three entrances, others had two, but in any case, it was a good place to set up an ambush.

I ran down the dead escalator and sprinted to the right.

The empty stores flew by. My steps sounded too loud in the cavernous mall, scattering echoes through the abandoned hallway. Traces of Fright Fest still lingered—a plastic curtain stained with fake blood hanging from Payless shoe store, a synthetic spiderweb in the broken window of a prom dress shop, a plastic prop knife on the floor . . . As if the place wasn't creepy enough already.

Twenty people. At least two to watch from outside in case I came out, two each for the two escalators inside the mall to make sure I didn't keep switching floors on them. Fourteen people to hunt me down. Way too many. I never tried to beguile more than three without going all out with my power.

The entrance to JC Penney loomed ahead, shrouded in shadow, like the mouth of a cave. The weak sunshine from the skylight barely reached it. Empty metal clothes racks crowded the floor, pushed all around at odd angles. Abandoned jewelry counters and wheeled displays added to the chaos, turning the inside of the store into an ominous labyrinth. The place was a mess and it was perfect.

I padded inside, running on my toes. Glass crunched under my feet. Someone must have taken a bat to the glass display cases. A cloying mélange of fruity scents hung in the air, the ghost of broken perfume bottles. To the right the boxy walls of Sephora waited, still painted black and white.

A thud echoed through the empty hallway. Glass shattered. The hunters were here.

I turned toward the Sephora. An empty counter blocked my way. I sidestepped it and saw the outline of a person in the gloom behind it.

I dropped to the floor, the gladius still in my hand. My heart hammered against my ribs. Crap.

That was too fast. They couldn't have gotten here ahead of me. Was it some junkie or a squatter? Shooting him would sign my death warrant. The sound of the shot would carry. I might as well ring a bell and scream, "Here I am, come and get me."

I strained, listening for any hint of a noise.

Nothing.

Maybe he hadn't seen me. I inched to the right, trying to get around the counter in front of me. If I could get a better look . . .

The deep ink-black shadows under the counter shifted.

I froze.

An eerie rustling sound came from the darkness, the whispery noise of some sort of creature moving around. The stench hit me, a foul, sour reek of excrement and animal fur.

The hair on the back of my neck stood straight up.

Don't see me. I'm not here. Just stay where you are.

The thing in the darkness crept forward.

It had to be a rat. Just a rat. Nothing special.

The thing shimmied closer.

Not a rat. Too big. An opossum? A raccoon? A small monster? I could stab it with my sword, but I didn't want to kill it before figuring out what it was.

The dry staccato of claws on a concrete floor echoed softly. Click. Click. Click.

I lay perfectly still.

Click. Click.

Click.

A long black muzzle framed by matted hair emerged from under the counter. Two big round eyes stared into mine. The muzzle split open, showing sharp white teeth. A little pink tongue slid out and licked my nose.

A dog. A small, filthy, matted dog.

The dog licked my face again and whimpered.

Whoever was hiding behind the counter had to have heard it. I had to strike first.

I took a deep steadying breath, rolled to the right, came up on one knee, and lunged, thrusting my sword. The gladius sliced into fabric and fiberglass.

A zombie face, half rotten and stained with dry green pus, leered back at me with plastic eyes, its mouth twisted in a grin, showing off rotten yellow fangs.

Fuck!

I landed on my butt and let out a breath. The zombie mannequin laughed at me, a hideous sequined dress the color of blood hanging off its bony shoulders. Prom Queen Zombie. Fucking Fright Fest.

The little dog trotted over to me, curled up against my thigh, and licked my pant leg. Its black tail wagged, sweeping broken glass in all directions. You could barely make out its shape under the mass of matted fur.

I reached over and gently stroked its back. The tail wagged harder.

"What are you doing here?" I whispered. How had it survived here? What did it eat? On second thought, I didn't want to know.

The dog stared up at me with big brown eyes full of endless canine devotion. It seemed to be saying, *Please don't leave me alone in the dark. I'm hungry and dirty and lonely with no one to take care of me.*

The beam of a flashlight sliced through the gloom in the hallway behind me.

"Bad people are coming," I whispered. "What am I going to do with you?"

The little dog scooted closer to me.

I scooped the dog off the floor. It was so light, it had to have been starving.

Another thud. They were getting closer.

If I left the doggie in the open, it would make noise and they would shoot it and me. No, that would not be happening.

I squinted at the store, taking in the width of the entrance, the distance to Sephora, and the piles of debris. I'd have to take off my shoes for this plan to work.

"Time to go." I ran into Sephora. Here's hoping I had time to prepare a nice surprise.

Ten minutes later, the hunter team entered JC Penney in a standard formation for clearing large rooms. There were three rules all SWAT and military teams lived by when searching a building: never enter alone, don't move faster than you can think, and stay out of your partner's line of fire. I had hoped for some wannabes who would wander around in groups of one or two doing the dynamic entry with dramatic jumping and running, but no. These people knew their business.

The first two hunters, dressed in black tactical gear and wearing ballistic vests, walked in at opposite sides of the wide entrance and halted, each of them covering their sector of the room, slow and methodical. They knew I was alone, and they had cleared the rest of the mall, so they had me cornered.

The two sentries stopped, just as I thought they would. The one on the right halted less than five feet from where I lay under dirty plastic stained with fake blood. I had arranged the debris into a pile of generic garbage identical to other such piles scattered around the mall and buried myself in it.

A five-man team moved forward between the sentries, passed them, and cautiously walked deeper into the store, heading for Sephora. There should have been more of them. They must have split up and left the second team upstairs to clear the upper floor.

The clearing team kept walking. Nobody spoke. No static came from their radios. Nobody wore low-light gear. The inside of the store wasn't dark enough.

Five minds. I had hoped for smaller teams of two or three. I would have to beguile them with voice alone and do it fast. My magic took a little while to gain a hold. The moment the first word came out of my mouth, they would shoot at me. I needed to be heard but not seen. There was no margin for error.

They should've been close enough by now. I held my breath.

Behind me, my cell phone alarm went off.

If they had been amateurs, they would have dropped everything, and all run over to look for the phone. Instead, the clearing team ignored it. Looking for it meant they would have to turn their backs to Sephora, and since the ringing cell was obviously a distraction, they surmised that I wanted them to keep away from Sephora, so they stayed on their present course.

The sentry closest to me turned right and walked toward the sound. His buddy didn't move, covering the left side of the room.

A step.

Another step.

A black combat boot landed mere inches from my face. Glass crunched under the heavy rubber sole. I could reach out and touch it.

Another step.

I tried not to breathe.

Another.

He moved past me. The phone kept playing, eerily loud in the silence. I had hidden it under more plastic. It would take him a bit to find it.

Now. I had to do it now.

I slipped from under the plastic and dashed to the remaining sentry. He never saw me coming. My magic pulled me. I lunged, following its lead, and sliced his throat, severing the jugular and the carotid in one smooth thrust. Blood wet the blade. The sentry spun, choking on his own blood, unable to cry out. I thrust, putting three years of practice behind my sword. Funny thing about ballistic vests, they were designed to disperse the kinetic impact of a bullet, not stop a blade. My gladius cut through the Kevlar like it was a quilt, severing the man's aorta. I sprinted to the other hunter, my socks muffling my steps.

He'd reached the counter where I'd hidden the phone and was pulling the plastic off it. I clamped my left hand over his mouth and drove the gladius into his lower back, just under the body armor and into his kidney. The sharp blade sliced through the bundle of nerves and pain receptors, drowning the hunter in agony. I jerked his head back and slit his throat, cutting through the carotid and the trachea. The man sagged, and I gently lowered him to the floor.

A harsh metallic taste washed over my tongue. My hands shook. Blood dripped from my gladius onto the floor.

I'd just killed two people.

This was it; they were dead, and I could never take it back.

A two-shot burst crackled inside Sephora. Someone found the Prom Queen wearing my favorite coat.

In a moment, they would come out and realize they were missing two of their own people. I had to move or die.

I sprinted to the right, behind the clothes racks, which I had pushed together into a crescent shape around Sephora. The still ringing phone would buy me a few precious seconds but not many.

A dark, human-shaped shadow moved away from the group and came straight for me. That was not the plan. I crouched to the right of the gap in my makeshift barricade.

The sound of his footsteps drew closer. The dark outline of a gun emerged, followed by his arms, then his leg.

I held my breath.

The hunter turned to my left toward the phone, exposing his back. I lunged from a crouch and slashed across his spine, just under the bulletproof vest. He cried out and swung around. I stabbed him in the throat and withdrew. He collapsed. They had to have heard his gasp. Now or never.

I took a deep breath and sang out, pouring carefully measured magic into my words, "Baa, baa, black sheep . . ."

Gunfire tore through the store, but I was already moving, sprinting behind the metal clothes racks. To my magic-enhanced vision, the four remaining hunter minds fluoresced in response to my song, pale smudges of grey light in the darkness of the store.

The shots died.

"Have you any wool?"

Bullets ricocheted from the clothes racks, tracking my voice. I dropped to the floor and crawled behind some wooden displays. They stopped shooting.

"Yes sir, yes sir, three bags full."

A bullet tore a chunk from the plywood counter just in front of me. I scrambled to my feet and dashed the other way. The rest of the hunters moved toward me, closing in on my position like sharks.

"One for my master, one for my dame . . ."

The gunfire died. Silence claimed the store. I inhaled.

Four voices chorused in perfect unison. "And one for the little boy who lives down the lane."

I had them. They were mine.

Oh my God.

I straightened. The four hunters emerged from behind Sephora's walls. The leading hunter pulled his ski mask off his head, revealing the scarred face of a white man in his thirties, and gave me a shy little smile.

"Hello," I said.

"Hi," they chorused. A woman on my right gave me a little wave with her HK MP5. If she had shot me with it, the spray of bullets would've cut me in half.

"Tell the team upstairs that everything is clear. So they don't have to worry."

The scarred man got on his radio. "False alarm. Continue the sweep. Clear. Over."

A static-softened answer came back. *"Copy."*

I slid the sword into its sheath on my belt. "Can one of you bring me my cell phone and my coat? It's the one that was on the zombie mannequin."

The scarred man jerked his head at one of the other hunters. The hunter took off at a run and returned with my cell phone and my expensive coat, which now sported a couple of fresh bullet holes. Damn it. I turned the phone's alarm off.

"Follow me, please. I have to get my shoes." I walked to the corner of the store, where a lone cash register had somehow survived the looting. The hunters trailed me.

"Who sent you here?"

"Mr. De Lacy," the scarred man told me.

"What were your orders?"

"We're supposed to apprehend you and bring you back to his residence."

Benedict was a sick asshole.

"We're supposed to kill you if we couldn't capture you," a female hunter added.

"Sorry," the scarred leader said.

Sorry didn't quite cover it.

I took my boots from where I'd hidden them under the counter and put them and my ruined coat back on. My new bodyguards watched. I pushed aside the debris I had piled against a cabinet to keep it closed, opened the door, and took the little dog out. It licked my face.

I cradled the dog in my arms. "The people upstairs don't realize I'm nice. They'll try to kill me. You'll keep me safe, won't you?"

"Of course," the leader said. "Don't worry, Ms. Baylor. We've got this."

"We'll keep you intact," another man said.

"We need to take them out," the leader said. "It's the safest way."

The woman with the HK smiled. "The escalator is nice and narrow."

The scarred hunter touched his radio. "We have her pinned down. Take the escalator down and cover us."

"Copy."

The leader pointed to a spot on the floor. "Stand there please."

I stood. The four hunters flanked the escalator. Two hunters came down the steps, sticking close together, a third slightly behind. My four bodyguards let them get halfway down. Gunfire burst, deafening in the silence of the mall. Three bloody bodies fell.

Three more people I killed. I would deal with the guilt later. Right now, I had to survive.

The leader turned to me. "We should take care of the rest of the crew as well, while we're at it. Safer that way."

I forced my mouth to move. "Good idea."

The hunters fell into a defensive formation around me, the scarred leader in front, two people on the sides, and the female hunter covering the rear. We walked back to the Keystone Mall entrance.

"Do you often capture people for Mr. De Lacy?"

"We've done it a few times," the leader said. "Mostly we're given termination jobs."

"Was Sigourney Etterson one of your contracts? It would've been last Sunday."

"No," the scarred man said without a pause. "We did a wet job last Saturday. Sunday we were dark. I got some killer fishing done."

Killer fishing. He didn't even realize what he'd said.

"Did you go out on your boat?" the hunter on the right asked.

"Naah. Went kayak fishing on Lake Anahuac. Got a six-pound largemouth bass."

"Nice!" the hunter on the right said.

"Who did you kill on Saturday?" I asked.

"Some lawyer," the leader said. "A clean, easy job. He came home, we put a gun into his mouth, pulled the trigger. Left him for the wife to find."

"I wish they were all that easy," the female hunter said.

"Ain't that the truth?" the hunter on the left added.

The first set of escalators came into view, a pair of guards by it. My escorts snapped their weapons up. The guns spat noise and bullets, and two corpses hit the floor. As we moved past them, the female hunter kicked one of the bodies. "I never liked that guy."

"What kind of work does Mr. De Lacy do? How did you end up working for him?"

"Technically, we work for Diatheke," the female hunter said.

"I don't know what he does," the leader said. "All I know is we get a name, we show up, do our thing, and we get paid."

"Yes," the guard on the right said. "Do you have any idea how much a year of college costs? I've got two kids in elementary, and the wife and I already have to start saving."

"Did the lawyer you killed have any kids?" I asked.

The guard on the right nodded. "Oh yeah. Two girls, both in Texas A&M. That's some money, right there."

The female guard snorted. "Hope he had insurance."

"His kind always do," the leader said.

It didn't even bother them. Maybe it had at some point, but not enough to stop.

We reached an abandoned booth in the middle of the floor.

"Wait here," the scarred man said.

My escort halted. The leader moved ahead along the wall and out of sight. His mind receded, tendrils of my magic stretching after him. Two twin bursts of gunfire popped. The scarred hunter came running back, a big grin on his face. "Never saw me coming."

The woman chuckled. "Fucking amateurs."

The leader smiled at me. "It was hard being gone. I was worried bad things might happen to you. I'm not letting you out of my sight, young lady."

"Let's go to the door," I told him.

"You heard her." He indicated the way with his index and middle finger. "Move out."

We approached the escalator. A dead hunter sprawled on the floor, blood pooling around his body, a shocking vivid red on the once white floor. A pair of boots stuck out from behind the escalator rail. We skirted the first corpse, and the scarred hunter moved up the steps. The two hunters flanking me followed. I was next, with the female hunter guarding my back.

At the top we turned left. The food court came into view.

"Act natural," the leader advised me. "Pretend you're in our custody."

We turned the corner. Four hunters guarded the entrance. They focused on us, guns raised.

The leader opened his mouth.

Alessandro shot out of the movie theater entrance, blindingly fast. A long piece of broken metal pipe appeared in his hand. He stabbed it into the closest hunter's throat, turned, graceful, like he could hear music in his head, and drove his makeshift spear into the second man's mouth.

Oh my God. "Hold your fire!" I snapped.

Alessandro yanked the pipe out, dropped it, and hurled the dying man into the third hunter. The woman stumbled, Alessandro darted around her, and she clutched her throat. Blood gushed out between her fingers. Alessandro lunged at the fourth gunman. A wicked-looking knife flashed in his hand. He caught the man's HK with his left hand, pushed it aside, and stabbed the hunter once, twice, three times, his hand a blur.

The hair on the back of my neck rose.

"Damn . . ." the scarred hunter said, his voice too loud.

Alessandro whipped around, pulled a gun from a holster on his thigh, and fired four times. The hunters protecting me collapsed like puppets cut from their strings.

He did it again. He killed my source of information.

Alessandro marched up to me. His magic coiled and flexed around him, so potent I could actually see it. It shimmered like hot air rising from scalding pavement, flashing with orange fire that burst into life for the briefest of moments and melted back into transparent heat. He walked like he was a fallen angel, looking for someone to punish.

Breath caught in my throat. So much power . . .

He reached to grab my forearm. "We have to go!"

I stepped out of the way. The little dog let out a surprisingly vicious snarl.

Alessandro halted. "What the hell is that?"

"It's my dog."

"Fine, bring it, but we have to leave. Now."

"I'm not going anywhere with you."

"Catalina, we can't stay here. They called for backup when they got here. More of them are on the way."

"That's fine." I couldn't go anywhere with him. I had no idea how he was involved in any of this. "You go your way and I'll go mine."

"How? They shredded your tires. Your car isn't going anywhere, you're not going anywhere, your little dog isn't going anywhere. Come with me."

"No." I jerked back from him.

"I'm trying to keep you alive!"

"I don't need your help. I'm doing fine on my own."

"Don't make me carry you out of here," he snarled.

"Try it."

"Don't tempt me."

The little dog barked at him.

"We don't have time for this." He spaced his words out, speaking slowly and clearly as if to a child. "Why are you being . . . difficult?"

"You just killed eight people! I don't even know why you're here, how you're involved in this or why, and you want me to just get into the car with you."

He growled and thrust his gun into my hands. "Here, you can have my gun. You can point it at me the entire way."

"No thanks. I have my own."

"*Cazzo*." He raised his arms. "Is there another elephant I can shoot to make you come with me?"

I shut up and ran for the door.

 **Chapter 8**

I jumped into the passenger seat of a silver Alfa Romeo 4C and buckled my seat belt, the little dog on my lap. Alessandro slid behind the wheel and pushed the start button. The tiny car purred. He fastened his seat belt, put the Alfa into gear, and we sped off.

"You shot the elephant?"

The remains of my Element with bald wheels and bullet hole scars in the doors flashed by us.

"Of course I shot the damn elephant."

At the other end of the parking lot another Guardian roared, coming up the street. Alessandro took a turn at an insane speed. The Alfa all but floated above the pavement. We circled the mall and shot out onto Old Post Road like a bullet.

"Who's in that Guardian?"

"Celia."

"What? Rose-gold Celia?"

"Yes. I told you to let it go. I told you to go home. And what did you do?" His magic pulsed with a flash of orange. "You flounced straight into that snake pit."

"Flounced?"

"Like a lamb, Catalina. Like a stupid, pretty little lamb bouncing over green grass straight into the wolf's den. Do you have any idea what Benedict does to women?"

"No, why don't you enlighten me?"

"The man is a degenerate. *Ma porca puttana!* What were you thinking?"

Well, look who lost his temper. I would have agreed with his assessment of Benedict, except in Italy "that whore of a pig" only applied to situations, and never to a person.

"I was thinking I have a client whose mother was murdered and whose seventeen-year-old sister is missing. Instead of posturing and cursing, you could help me. Where is Halle, Alessandro?"

"I wish I knew so I could kidnap her back and leave her on your doorstep with a bow to keep you from sticking your pretty nose into things you don't understand."

He said I had a pretty nose. "Stop treating me like I'm an idiot."

My phone rang. I answered it. "Hello?"

"Good news," Bug said.

I put him on speaker.

"I found your vomit muffin. He's driving a crappy silver Italian import. He's about to merge onto the I-10. Where are you?"

"In the passenger seat of the crappy import."

"This is a great car." Alessandro executed a hair-raising merge and cut across three lanes of traffic with three inches of room to spare. "Italians make the best cars."

Bug sputtered. "Ask Captain Vapid if he knows what Fiat stands for. Fix It Again, Tony!"

Alessandro shifted lanes again. "You better ask Tony how good he is at fixing surveillance drones."

"You son of a bitch! When I get my hands on you—"

"You'll wish you hadn't."

"Will the two of you shut up?" I snapped. "Bug, there is a Guardian following us. We need to lose it."

Alessandro cut across two lanes to the right, weaving in and out of traffic. The Alfa slid between two trucks about an inch from the front vehicle's bumper. Someone laid on their horn.

"I don't understand why we couldn't just fight her at the mall," I squeezed out through clenched teeth.

"Because your magic won't work on her in her active state and I don't have a gun large enough to take her down. I looked."

"I have the Guardian," Bug reported. "Bad news. They've got a Cockerill MK III 90mm cannon mounted on that thing. People are getting out of their way like the Red Sea before Moses."

Alessandro stepped on the gas. The Alfa jumped forward into the lane on our left, sped around a semi, and slid in front of it, nearly skidding.

"Find us an exit strategy," I barked. "Before we wreck."

"We won't wreck." Alessandro's voice was completely calm.

"If you keep driving this way, we won't have to. This is Texas, someone will shoot us."

"It's not my fault you have barbaric gun laws." He switched lanes again.

"Stop driving like a maniac!" Bug yelled. "Slow down."

Behind us a horn blared. I turned. The huge semi we'd passed was moving into the left lane, which was illegal.

"Oh shit," Bug said.

The semi finally merged over. Behind it the Guardian sped up, a huge barrel pointing at us. Holy crap, that thing could put a hole in a tank.

"There's no way they can fire that cannon at us," I

said. "The shell would go through our car and wipe out three lanes around us. Diatheke would be finished."

"That's not for us," Alessandro said. His eyes scanned the lanes ahead of us, but there was no opening. We were stuck.

The top of the Guardian came open and Celia climbed out in her pink Chanel suit. She stood, her arms out, trying to balance on top of the Guardian in her pumps.

What the hell was she doing?

Long dark quills thrust out of her, piercing her suit. Her skin stretched and tore, and a creature twice her size burst out of her, muscles bulging under dense red fur. It sat on its haunches, the sickle-shaped tiger claws of its hind feet digging into the metal of the Guardian. Its forelimbs, thick and powerful, like a gorilla's, clutched at the barrel of the Guardian, anchoring the beast. A dense red mane that was more hair than fur thrust from its head and shoulders. Two-foot-long quills protruded from the mane and the backs of its forelimbs. Its face was horrible; a meld of cat and ape, with beady eyes sunken deep into its skull, a simian nose with huge nostrils, and feline mouth filled with long dagger teeth. A long, whiplike tail snapped behind it.

A metamorphosis mage. Shit.

The gun wasn't for us. That cannon was for her, in case she went off the rails. When a metamorphosis mage transformed, they lost most of their ability to reason, reverting to a primal state somewhere between an attack dog and an enraged ape. There would be no reasoning with her. Anything short of a lethal injury would just piss her off.

"Can you nullify her with your magic?" I asked.

"Not once she's in that shape. She's fucking immune to everything."

Celia's enraged eyes fixed on us. She opened her mouth and howled, flinging spit into the wind. Oh God.

"Drive faster, Alessandro!"

"Go," Bug screamed from the phone. "Go, go, go!"

There was nowhere to go. We were in the second lane from the right. Traffic clogged the interstate ahead of us. Even if we managed to force our way into the far-right lane, this section of the I-10 ran above the ground and a concrete wall guarded the edge. We couldn't jump it. The Alfa was too small and low.

We had to exit.

"We can't maneuver here. There's an exit ahead," I said. "Take Bunker Hill. We'll lose them on the surface roads."

"No!" Bug yelled. "Don't take Bunker Hill, it's closed. The tanker truck, remember?"

Two weeks ago, a tanker truck carrying thousands of gallons of gasoline overturned on the Bunker Hill exit and burst into flames. It burned for hours, and the fire ate through the concrete. A section of the exit had collapsed, plunging the burning wreck down to the street below. It was the biggest story on the news for a week.

"Bug's right, don't take the exit, there is a hole in it."

"How big a hole?" Alessandro asked.

"Too big," Bug said. "Twenty feet."

"How many meters is that?"

"Six."

"Ascending or descending?"

"Descending, right at the top of the curve."

Alessandro darted into a tiny gap between a white truck and a black SUV on our right.

"Don't do it, dickass!" Bug barked.

The green exit sign flashed over our heads, an orange warning strip across it screaming, "EXIT CLOSED."

If h is the difference in height between the two sides of the gap, then θ is the angle of the exit's slope, V is the velocity, and g is the standard acceleration of free fall at 9.8 m/s²; the required velocity would equal the square root of g *36m² divided by 2(h+6tan θ)*cos² θ . . .

I kept my voice calm. "Alessandro, you're going to kill us. This only works in the movies and it requires a ramp. The moment our wheels leave the ground, the car will start dropping. Even if we make it, the vehicle will be crushed from the impact."

"It will be fine." The Alfa roared up the slope, accelerating.

"How? How will it be fine?"

He looked over at me. "This car is very light and we're going to drive very fast."

Striped white and orange barriers blocked the way. The small sports car smashed through them. Chunks of wood flew. Behind us the Guardian lumbered onto the exit, speeding up.

"No!" Bug screamed.

Construction vehicles flashed by on our sides. In the sideview mirror the Guardian tore up the slope, squeezing everything it could out of its engine to catch us.

"Please don't do it," I said.

Alessandro glanced at me for half a second and hit me with a dazzling smile. "Trust me."

Black scorch marks stained the pavement ahead. Alessandro stood on the gas. The digital speedometer flashed 145. We were almost to the top of the slope.

I hugged the little dog to me.

The Guardian skidded to a stop. Celia leaped from the top of it, flying through the air like she had wings.

The Alfa went airborne.

I expected my life to flash before my eyes. Instead I went weightless, floating . . .

The Alfa crashed to the pavement and bounced hard. I pitched forward. My seat belt yanked me back. The Alfa skidded to a stop.

We made it. Oh my God.

"For fuck's sake!" Bug cried out.

"See?" Alessandro grinned.

A heavy thud rocked the car. Celia landed on the roof. Two huge clawed fists smashed into the windshield like sledgehammers. The laminated glass cracked in a spiderweb pattern but didn't shatter. Celia's hand-paw broke through the glass and plastic. She clutched the edge of the hole and ripped the windshield out.

The little dog erupted into barks.

I pulled my Beretta out, pinned the dog with my left hand to keep it out of the way, and fired four shots through the roof. An angry shriek answered.

Eleven bullets left.

Alessandro stepped on the gas. The Alfa screeched in protest but rolled forward, weaving between the heavy construction equipment. Something must have broken on landing. We picked up speed . . .

Alessandro threw his arm in front of me and slammed on the brakes, spinning the car to the left. Celia slid off the roof, landed on the pavement on all fours, and rolled to her feet. Her maw gaped and she roared.

We had to get past Celia before the Guardian decided to start blasting the cement mixers and dump trucks blocking its view of us on the off chance the shrapnel and debris would hit the Alfa. Ramming her wouldn't work. We didn't have the mass and if she destroyed the car, we would be stranded on this exit.

Alessandro jumped out. Two guns appeared in his hands out of thin air. He fired at Celia.

I unbuckled my seat belt and scrambled out of the vehicle. The little dog tried to follow, but I slammed the door in its face.

The stream of bullets from Alessandro's firearms pounded Celia. She jerked, snarled, and charged, loping forward in great leaps. I sighted her and fired. The Beretta pumped out bullets.

Eleven, ten, nine, eight, seven.

The shots tore into Celia without any visible damage. No blood.

Alessandro darted out of the way. A shotgun materialized in his hands. He pumped it and sank a burst into Celia's stomach. She recoiled.

Six, five, four.

He pumped it again and fired at her face. She leaped aside, nimble like a cat, and flexed her tail. It whipped Alessandro, nearly taking him off his feet. He grunted and shot her again.

Three, two, one. Out.

Celia reared, swinging her arms in a frenzy. Her clawed hand closed on Alessandro's shotgun and she tore it from his grasp, knocking him back. He stumbled and she chased him, claws rending the air.

"Celia!" I snapped. "Look at me!"

She spun toward me. I opened my wings and let my magic rip. The focused torrent of power drowned her.

"Come here," I called, sinking enough magic to seduce a room full of people into it.

Celia rushed me. Her huge arm swung, and she backhanded me. I flew and hit a hard surface with my right side. Pain tore through my hip. Something crunched. Ow. A dump truck had thoughtfully broken my fall.

I looked up and saw Celia leaping toward me, claws ready to rend, mouth gaping. I dropped to my knees and scrambled under the truck.

Celia slammed into the vehicle with a thud and hugged the ground. Her terrible face thrust into the gap between the wheels. Tiny hate-filled eyes bore into me. She tried to squeeze in after me. I held my breath. She wiggled, pushing in another inch, and stopped. The truck sat too low.

Celia bared a mouthful of monster teeth and thrust her arm under the truck, trying to hook me with her claws. I shimmied back. She shrieked, frustrated, jumped to her feet, and gripped the truck, trying to lift it. The huge vehicle rocked.

How strong was she?

Celia shrieked again and dropped down to the ground, her face only feet away from mine. I pulled the mace out of my pocket and sprayed her in the eyes.

Celia screamed and clawed at her face. The telltale roar of a chain saw answered. Blood spray wet the asphalt. Celia squirmed from under the truck and disappeared.

I crawled to the right, out from under the vehicle, and dashed around it.

Alessandro chased Celia with a chain saw. She dashed back and forth. Her left arm hung off her shoulder on a string of flesh, gushing blood. Bone glared from the stump. A gash sliced across her left hind leg.

I pulled my sword out and sprinted after them.

Alessandro backed Celia against the pavement roller and sliced the chain saw across her stomach. A horrible scream tore out of Celia. She threw herself at him, and the sheer weight of her took Alessandro off his feet. He fell, buried under her bleeding body.

No! I ran like I'd never run before in my whole life.

She opened her mouth and aimed for his face.

I drove my gladius into her neck. The sword slid into flesh and found bone.

Boom!

Bullets tore out of the back of her skull. Bone and brain exploded, spraying me.

I yanked the gladius out and brought it back down with everything I had. The blade carved through reinforced vertebrae. Celia jerked and collapsed. Who is your pretty little lamb now?

I dropped to my knees. "Alessandro?"

Please be alive, please be alive . . .

Celia's body shuddered, rose, and Alessandro heaved it aside, pulling a Smith & Wesson 460XVR revolver out of her mouth. He stared at the massive gun's fourteen-inch barrel and then looked at me, his eyes incredulous.

"It's a hunting revolver." I slumped back. "It's for big game hunting."

"Texas," Alessandro said, loading a state's worth of meaning into a single word.

The Alfa still worked. It wasn't as fast or as smooth, and riding without a windshield in a tiny seat with every bump jabbing a spike of pain through my hip was a new kind of torture, but we made it off the exit onto Frontage Road.

I hugged the dog to me with one hand and dialed our lawyer with the other. Sabrian listened to my recap without a word.

"Any injured civilians?"

"Not that we know of."

"Fine," she said. "I'm on it. I'll be emailing you documents. Read, print, sign, scan, email back, get the originals to me by courier, today."

"Thank you."

"Don't thank me, just be on time with papers and payment."

I hung up.

Next to me, Alessandro drove as if we were enjoying a pleasant excursion on the Pacific Coast Highway, winding our way through picturesque hills with a blue ocean on our side. A relaxed smile played on his lips.

"What are you so happy about?"

"We're alive. I told you it would work."

"Your car is ruined."

"It's just a car. It's replaceable. You're not."

What did it mean? Why did he even care? He saw me for fifteen minutes during the trials, then for another fifteen minutes when he showed up asking me to go for a drive, and then we hadn't spoken for three years.

"How are you involved in this?"

The smile died. It was like the sun being turned off. I felt like a moment of silence was in order.

"Not that again," he said.

"Yes, again. I have to find Halle."

"What part of 'drop it' don't you understand?"

"The part where you keep interfering with my investigation and shooting people I need to interrogate."

"Interrogate? I must not understand the meaning of that word, because from where I'm sitting, you blunder around asking people questions until they try to kill you."

Oh, you ass.

"You haven't even thanked me for the elephant. When someone saves your life, you're supposed to be grateful. Do they have laws against expressing gratitude here?"

Argh. "Thank you so much, Alessandro, for providing help I didn't need. I so appreciate you taking the time out of your busy schedule of Instagram posing and luxury car wrecking to murder every person who could conceivably shed some light on this investigation. Thank you ever, ever so much."

We glared at each other.

He raised his eyebrows. "Wait, I know. Since you insist on doing the opposite of what I tell you, let's try this. Don't stay home, Catalina. Don't drop this case. Don't stay safe. Is it working? Please tell me it's working."

"God, you are an asshole." It just kind of came out.

Alessandro drew back. "Such a dirty mouth. Oh, the possibilities."

"You have no possibilities with my mouth! Nobody has any possibilities with my mouth!" I did not just say that.

He laughed. He *laughed* at me.

"Halle's seventeen, Alessandro. She's innocent. Whatever her mother did or didn't do, she shouldn't be paying the price for it. Tell me what's going on so I can find her. Don't you have any compassion at all?"

"The sooner you realize that I'll tell you nothing, the easier it will be. Give up, Catalina. It's being handled."

He turned onto our street.

"Stop the car."

The Alfa slid to a stop with a metallic groan. I unbuckled my seat belt.

"Catalina, let me take you to the door. I know your leg hurts."

I climbed out of the car clutching my dog and my sword.

"Don't be a hero," he called.

I wished I had a free hand so I could flip him off. I marched toward the security booth, grimly determined to not limp.

"Hey," he shouted. "At least we finally had our drive."

"Drop dead."

I marched to the booth, the grinding noise of the Alfa driving away receding behind me.

The two guards in the booth stared at me. I saw my reflection in the glass as I passed them. Most of me was covered with a uniform layer of dirt and dust from lying on the floor of the mall. Blood splattered my face, my neck, and my white turtleneck. Bits of Celia's skull and brains hung in my hair. Two bullet holes punctured my coat, right in the middle of the chest and a little to the left.

Terrific. Just terrific.

The dirty, matted dog whined softly in my arms.

"I know, right?" Some pair we made.

If I walked like this through the front door, my family would suffer a collective apoplexy. I needed to clean myself up. My best bet would be to go through the motor pool, at least wash my face and hands, and then try to sneak upstairs to my room. That meant circling the warehouse.

I turned into the narrow space between the warehouse and a concrete wall separating it from the next parking lot and limped on.

Ow. Ow.

I never quite realized how large our place was.

Ow.

Did we really need a warehouse this big?

The little dog whined again, overcome with some sort of canine sadness.

"Shh. You'll blow our cover."

I finally turned the corner. The huge industrial bay doors stood open and the motor pool inside seemed deserted. Everything was in its regular place: Brick and Romeo, Grandma's pet tank, covered with tarps, the armored Humvee we used for dangerous jobs, and Grandma's latest commission, a medium-size track vehicle waiting in the middle of the floor.

A lopsided tangle of blue yarn on circular needles lay

on the worktable. Nevada once told Grandma Frida that other grandmas knitted things for their grandchildren. Ever since then she made valiant efforts to knit presents for each of us, and the current Gordian knot was supposed to be my sweater. Usually she took it with her when she was done for the day.

I stopped and listened. The motor pool lay silent. Nothing moved. The coast was clear.

Maybe Grandma Frida had run inside to use the bathroom.

I limped through the doors and headed toward the sink. Grandma Frida chose that moment to jump out of a track vehicle's cab. She stared at me, her blue eyes widening.

I had to distract her, quick. "The Honda might be totaled, but I left two Guardians without drivers at Keystone Mall. They're all yours, just don't forget to disable their GPS . . ."

Grandma Frida walked past me and pressed the intercom.

"Please, please don't," I begged.

My grandmother mashed the intercom button. "Penelope, the baby is hurt."

I wasn't a baby. I was twenty-one years old, but it didn't matter. To Grandma Frida all three of us would always remain babies. "I said please."

Grandma's eyes held no mercy. "She's got two bullet holes in her coat and someone's brains in her hair. Come quick."

Damn it.

The world was full of interesting words used to describe complicated things. There was *tartle*, a Scottish word for the panicked pause you experience when you have to introduce someone, but you don't remember their name. There was *backpafeifengesicht*, a German term for a face you'd love to punch. There was *gigil*, a Filipino word for the urge to squeeze an item because it is unbearably cute.

I didn't know if there was a word for the whirlwind my very upset family created while they tried to treat my wounds, clean me up, and interrogate me all at the same time while talking over each other, but if there was one, I would definitely have to learn it. I refused to answer any questions until after they let me shower. My demand was met with howls of protest, but I held firm in the face of adversity, and when Bug conveniently sent the drone video of our fight with Celia, the family surrendered and released me so they could watch it.

The little dog was a girl. It took fifteen minutes of strategic mat cutting to reveal that fact. After I trimmed the worst of her fur, I had taken her into the shower with me. At first, she cowered in the corner, but by the end of it, she decided bath time wasn't so bad. The water that ran off her on the first rinse was black and smelled like a sewer. I had to shampoo her with Dawn dish soap twice.

After the shower, she dashed into my loft, running in circles while I dried myself off. One of her parents had to have been a dachshund and the other a Scottish terrier or some similar breed. Her little body was long with short legs that looked delicate. Her black and now glossy fur grew longer and coarser on her back and butt, where it curled backward in clumps. Her ears were floppy, her jaws long and framed with sideburns reminiscent of a Scotty, and when she opened her mouth, her teeth were huge in proportion to her head. It looked like a bear trap from old cartoons.

She was also painfully thin. Getting rid of the mats

must've cut her weight by a third. Her ribs stuck out and vertebrae protruded from her spine.

I ended up chasing her with a towel for three whole minutes, until inspiration struck, and I threw it on the floor. She burrowed under it and I caught her and dried her off.

Someone knocked on my door. Well, that didn't take long.

"Who is it?"

"It's me," Mom said.

I knew this was coming. The last thing I wanted was to talk to Mom.

After Dad died, everything had been in shambles. The business was failing; our house was gone; we had to change schools, which to most people would be no big deal and to me was catastrophic; and most importantly, Dad wasn't there. When my mother deployed, Dad took care of us. When I had a problem, I went to Dad before I went to Mom. Up to that point, Dad knew more about me and he always managed to talk me off whatever ledge I had climbed on.

I'd been twelve years old and the idea that he would never be there again was apocalyptic. It felt like my world had ended.

And then Mom somehow picked us all up and made it okay. It took me nearly half a decade to realize Mom herself was not okay.

My mother had spent months as a POW in the Bosnian Conflict. It left her with a permanent limp and enough invisible scars to last a lifetime. She never dealt with it because her husband became sick, so she'd had to go from being deployed six months out of a year to being a full-time parent, and the sky was falling. It came back to haunt her at the worst possible moment. She lost her PI license and the only way she could provide for us. Nevada had to become the breadwinner before she even finished high school. My mother was no longer a soldier or a PI. It made her feel helpless.

The conversation we were about to have would make her feel helpless again, and there was nothing I could do to avoid it. She'd climbed my ladder with her limp and she wouldn't go away until I leveled with her.

"Catalina?"

I got up off the floor and opened the door.

"Let me see that hip," Mom asked.

I turned and pulled down my sweatpants. "It's just bruised. Look, I can put weight on it and everything." I heroically stood on one foot.

"Are you sure?"

"Yes. Nothing broken."

"Your grandma took your sister and two guards and left. She said something about two Guardians at the Keystone Mall."

That was exactly the line of questioning I was hoping to avoid. "Uh-huh."

Mom pinned me with her stare. "Why are there Guardians at an abandoned mall?"

To lie or not to lie? I hated to lie to Mom.

"You went to Diatheke and then what happened?"

"I left."

"Did someone follow you? Is that why you went to Keystone?"

Crap. My short answers clearly didn't work. "Yes."

"Why didn't you come home?"

Because I was followed by twenty highly trained killers who would've carved through our security and stormed the warehouse with children inside. "I wasn't thinking clearly."

My mother's face fell. She knew.

"I'll ask you one more question, but I want an honest answer. If Rogan's people were here, would you have come home?"

I shut my eyes. "Yes."

She stepped close to me and hugged me. If I had any tears left, I would've cried.

"Was it bad?" she asked quietly.

"Yes."

Mom let go of me. "I'll fix this. I promise you. It will be fixed tonight."

She turned around and went down the ladder.

I looked at the little dog. "I suck."

The little dog squatted and peed on the floor. Right.

"It's okay," I told her. "You'll figure it out."

I cleaned up the mess and took her downstairs. At the kitchen table Bern, Leon, Runa, and Ragnar crowded around Bern's laptop. On it, Celia was paused in mid-leap.

I got some rotisserie chicken out of the fridge, pulled a generous chunk of the breast meat off the bone, and shredded it into a small bowl. The dog spun in circles at my feet.

The sounds of a chain saw came from the screen.

I put the dish on the floor. The dog attacked it like her life depended on her victory over the cold chicken. I got myself a plate and set about assembling two tacos.

"Pause it. Right there," Leon said.

"It just . . . appears in his hand," Ragnar said, his voice full of wonder. "How is he doing that?"

"It seems completely subconscious," Runa said. "He needs a weapon and poof!"

"Poof?" Bern said.

Runa turned to him. "Yes. Start it for a second. Notice how he's looking at the chain saw. He's clearly never seen it before."

"So, you think it's a passive field effect?" Bern thought out loud.

"It would make sense," Runa said.

"What would an active effect of this look like?" Bern wondered.

"It doesn't matter if it's passive or active." Leon leaned closer to the screen. "I want to know if he's teleporting items he has seen before, or does he snatch them up within a certain area of effect."

"Why?" Ragnar asked.

"Because I need to know if I have to worry about this asshole teleporting my guns into his hands when I fight him."

Everyone pondered that.

"Maybe he doesn't teleport them," Ragnar said. "Maybe his magic duplicates them."

"That would be a hell of a thing," Leon said.

"What kind of magic is it anyway?" Runa said. "I thought he was an Antistasi."

"He is," I said.

They turned to me.

I put my plate down. I wasn't hungry anyway. "The Antistasi magic occurs roughly five times as often as truthseeking. It's not the rarest, but Antistasi Primes are exceptionally rare. There are three truthseeker Houses in the entire continental US, and only two Antistasi Houses. There are five Houses in the whole of the European Union, two in Africa, we don't know how many in China, and another three in the Russian Imperium. Of all of these, House Sagredo is the oldest."

"Your stalking of Alessandro is truly impressive," Runa said.

She had no idea. "The point is, we know what the Antistasi can do because of what they choose to reveal to us. Perhaps whatever Alessandro is doing is the ultimate expression of that talent and the handful of Antistasi Primes are keeping it secret. Perhaps he's in a league of his own like Rogan. What matters is, he's dangerous."

Leon smirked. Oh no, you don't.

"Forget Instagram," I said. "Forget all the yachts, and cars, and women. It's a smoke screen. This man is lethal. Diatheke sent an experienced, well-armed strike team after me. I watched Alessandro kill eight of them. He impaled two of them with a piece of broken pipe, murdered the remaining pair with a knife, and then he shot the four people I beguiled. One shot, one kill, every bullet in the T-zone."

If you drew a rectangle around both eyes and another around the nose, you would get a target area in the rough shape of a T. Shots to the T-zone were almost always fatal.

"From how far?" Leon asked.

"About twenty yards. He's precise, calm, and he can use a wide variety of weapons. And he can negate our magic whenever he feels like it. The Antistasi are only supposed to negate mental magic, but when I asked him if he could nullify the metamorphosis mage, he said, 'Not in her current form.' Which means he could have nullified her prior to transformation. Metamorphosis is arcane, not mental. If you see him, do not engage him alone. He'll kill you. I mean it, Leon. Don't get into a pissing match with him alone. Take it as an order."

He smiled at me.

"Leon!"

He raised his hands. "Okay, okay. So did you figure out what happened to the two million?"

He changed the subject way too fast. He would try to take on Alessandro the moment he saw him and then die trying to outshoot him. Leon was lethal, but Alessandro was versatile, more experienced, and stone cold.

They were waiting for an answer.

"They're claiming Ms. Etterson withdrew the two million dollars in cash."

"In cash?" Bern asked.

I sighed. "Yes. We need to look further into Diatheke. It's not what it seems."

I slipped out of the kitchen and headed to my office. The little dog trailed me. I really had to give her a name. I was just about to duck into my office when I heard my mother's voice coming from the conference room through the half-open door.

". . . a strike team," my mother was saying. "She had to kill some of them, I'm almost sure of it. Then she fought a metamorphosis mage."

I snuck forward on my toes and leaned to look through the glass wall. Mom sat at the conference table, an open laptop in front of her.

"Is she okay?" a familiar male voice asked.

She was Skyping with Sergeant Heart.

"She's alive. She won't tell me anything. I watched my daughter chop off a monster's head with a sword."

Mom paused. Her tone had an odd note in it. If I didn't know better, I would say it stopped just short of being fear, except my mother would never show fear to anyone outside the family.

"We need protection," she said. "I can't tell you for how long, but I promise you that however long it is, we will pay you . . ."

"Penelope."

He said it with warmth in his voice, and I almost did a double take. Sergeant Heart didn't do warm. He did efficient and scary.

It must have startled my mother too, because she stopped talking mid-word.

"All you ever have to say is that you need my help," Sergeant Heart said. "Do you need me, Penelope?"

There was a long pause.

"Yes, Benjiro, I need you."

"Ah, you know my name. I'll be there tomorrow at 20:00 hours. Can you hold until then?"

"Yes," Mom said.

I quietly backed away and into my office. The little black dog scampered in and went straight to the loveseat in the corner.

There was no way she could jump that high on her short little legs.

The dog leaped onto the loveseat and started making circles on the folded blanket Arabella used when she hid in my office to nap.

Well. I stood corrected.

I gently shut the door, sat at my desk, and put my headphones on in case Mom noticed me when she left the conference room. *What, you had a tender, almost intimate conversation with deadly and almost superhuman Sergeant Heart? No, I didn't hear a thing. I had my headphones on the whole time.*

Sergeant Heart liked my mother. I wasn't sure how she felt about that. I wasn't sure how I felt about that either.

I opened the Etterson file on my computer and stared at it. Making a list of everything I knew usually helped me, so I started a new file and wrote out my list.

- Sigourney Etterson was a poison Prime who amassed a fortune of almost ten million dollars in twelve years by unknown means.
- She knew her life was in danger.
- Someone killed her and possibly kidnapped her second daughter.
- Before she died, Sigourney visited Diatheke, Ltd., to withdraw two million dollars, in cash.
- Diatheke had no problem filling a bag with two million dollars in cash on the spot. Celia, who worked at Diatheke, didn't find this odd.
- Celia described Sigourney as a "pro." She also implied Sigourney had a secret account, and acted like getting killed was a known occupational hazard for pros.
- Benedict De Lacy, who is a screwed-up mental Prime, didn't ask any of the usual questions most people ask when learning about the death of an acquaintance or a client. He didn't show surprise or express condolences.
- Diatheke routinely employs a trained strike team of killers.
- Celia was a metamorphosis mage, probably at least a Significant, and she tried to murder me. I was her primary target.

There was only one reasonable conclusion to all of this. Sigourney Etterson worked for Diatheke as an assassin. They either knew she was about to die, or they killed her. Other convoluted ways to interpret that list existed, but this was the simplest and most straightforward.

Did Benedict have her murdered over the two million dollars? I had no doubt that Diatheke gave Sigourney her money. If they hadn't, Celia would have told me. By the time Sigourney cashed out the account, she had already moved her will to her desktop, which meant the threat existed before she went to Diatheke. If they intended to kill her, why cash her out?

I still had no idea what Diatheke actually did. Private security teams, like the one that almost killed me today, usually served prominent, wealthy Houses. On paper, Diatheke wasn't associated with any House, but it sure was run like one, with a Prime at the top.

A metamorphosis mage of Celia's caliber required careful management. Arabella was a metamorphosis mage. There was no comparison between the two, because my sister was one of a kind, but similarities existed. For one, deploying Celia would've been a gamble every time. Very few metamorphosis mages retained the ability to reason while transformed. They were the magic equivalent of a directional antipersonnel mine. Point the right side toward the enemy and hope for the best. Diatheke would have to maintain a suppression team to neutralize her if she went off the rails.

What kind of nasty shit was Diatheke involved in that they needed Celia on their team? There was a simple answer to that, and I didn't like it.

Bern had already done a search on Diatheke and came up with nothing out of the ordinary. That left Benedict De Lacy. Mental Primes with that sort of power didn't just pop out of nowhere.

Most of his furniture and artifacts dated between the fourteenth and sixteenth centuries, during the rise and peak of the Ottoman Empire, and came from that specific region, with the exception of some medieval European swords and French furniture. To acquire that collection took not only ridiculous wealth, but education. He had to have gone to college, probably an Ivy League university somewhere. I pictured his office in my mind. No, he didn't have any diplomas framed on his wall.

I logged into Herald and searched for Benedict De Lacy. Nothing.

House De Lacy?

Herald spat out two search results, one for some aquakinetics in Canada and the other for some harmonizers in New York. The aquakinetics imported bottled spring water, and the harmonizers, whose specialty was creating living spaces that evoked a particular feeling, owned an interior design firm. I checked both out of due diligence. Neither listed any Benedicts and none of the family members looked anything like Benedict.

He was something though. I had spent enough time with Arrosa to recognize old wealth and breeding. Perhaps he was using an assumed name. If he was a bastard child of some high-ranking Prime, he would be nearly impossible to identify. Family resemblance would be my best bet.

I accessed the Herald's Prime visual database and went to advanced search. I typed in male, white, fifty to eighty, Prime, mental branch of magic. It resulted in two thousand hits.

Great. Here's hoping Benedict had a living father who looked like him.

I was on page seven when I smelled blood. The salty metallic stench cut across my senses like a razor. It came from my sword.

It made no sense. I'd wiped the gladius with an oiled rag before putting it back in its bracket on the wall. It hung there, five feet away from me, the blade shining slightly, reflecting the light of my lamp. I knew it was clean.

I had killed three people with it. I'd cut their throats. They'd died while my hands were on them. I could still feel the warmth of the second man's face as I clamped my fingers over his mouth. I remembered the heat of his breath when he exhaled as I drove my sword into his flesh.

My hands shook. The scent of blood was everywhere now, saturating the air and settling on my skin in a sticky patina. I inhaled it with every breath.

I gagged and tasted acid in my mouth. Tears wet my eyes, blurring my vision. I wished I could open a window, but the office had none.

I swiped at my eyes and heard myself sob. The office blurred. I got up, locked the door, and lowered the shades on the glass wall facing the hallway. Then I collapsed in the chair, put my hands over my face, and cried.

I wished I could take it back. I wished I could rewind today or wake up and realize I'd had a nightmare. It felt like a sharp shard was inside me trying to cut its way out. It hurt so much.

The little black dog stood on her hind legs, put her front paws on my knee, and wagged her tail. I petted her shaggy head. The tears kept coming. I just couldn't stop.

My phone rang. Bug. I answered and hit the speaker icon.

"Hey," he said. "Your grandma and your sister made it to Keystone okay, got the Guardians, and are heading back. Arabella made a slight detour, so I thought I'd tell you so you don't freak out."

"That's great," I choked out. My voice sounded strained and sharp.

"I detect some hostility," Bug said. "Is everything okay?"

"It's great."

"Catalina, where are you? What's wrong?"

"I killed three people." I was trying to keep it together, but saying it out loud proved too much. The sobs broke through.

"What people? Where?"

"At Keystone Mall. Actually, I killed ten people, three myself and seven through people I beguiled. Ten people, Bug. They can never go home. They had families . . ."

"It's okay." Bug's voice turned soothing. "It's okay. Why were you at the mall?"

"Things didn't go well after Diatheke. I picked up a tail, took them to the mall, and killed them."

"The crew from the Guardians?" Bug guessed.

"Yes."

"Catalina, they followed you to the mall. You didn't chase them down. They could've walked away at any point. Those fuckers made a deliberate choice to hunt you down instead. It was you or them. Listen to me. You didn't do anything wrong. You killed ten bad people."

The rational part of me knew he was right, but it didn't make me feel any better. I took ten lives.

"If you hadn't killed them, they would have killed you and then tomorrow or next week, they would have killed someone else. Talk to me. Are you there?"

"Yes. I just can't stop crying."

"It's adrenaline overload. Listen to me, listen to my voice: they were wrong, you were right. People who ride around in Guardians so they can hunt down a lone woman in an abandoned mall don't deserve mercy. They're the worst kind of assholes. The world can use less assholes."

I took a deep breath, trying to steady myself. "I'm better," I told him. "I've got it."

"Good, because your sister just passed the security checkpoint."

I grabbed a handful of tissues and wiped my face.

"Bug?"

"Yes?"

"Please don't tell anybody."

"I won't," he promised. "She's at the front door."

I jumped up, opened the shades, unlocked the door, and sat back at my desk. The front door swung open. There was a grunt. The door swung shut. Arabella staggered down the hallway and into my office carrying an armload of stuff and dumped it on the floor.

"What's this?" I asked. My face was red, my eyes bloodshot, and we both pretended they weren't.

She sat on the floor and dug through the bags, raising each item like she was auctioning it off. "Dog food bowl, water bowl, collar, leash, dog food; goes in the bowl, puppy pads; go on the floor, special cleaner with enzymes to clean up messes, chewy toys, an almost life-like squirrel, a rubber hamburger, little tennis balls, a blankie, a dog pillow, special dog shampoo, and a grooming brush."

Wow.

"Thank you."

"You're welcome."

"How did you know what to get?"

"I asked Matilda."

The little dog trotted over to the pile of loot and bit the rubber hamburger. It squeaked. The dog dropped the hamburger and dashed under my desk.

"A paragon of bravery," Arabella observed.

"She's been through a lot. Why the sudden attack of kindness?" I asked.

She got up off the floor and hugged me. We almost never hugged anymore.

Arabella headed to the door.

"Hey," I called.

She turned back to me.

I lowered my voice. "Sergeant Heart has a thing for Mom."

She blinked, then her eyes went wide. "How do you know?"

"She Skyped with him and he told her that all she had to do was let him know that she needed him. And she said, 'Benjiro, I need you,' and then he got terribly excited that she knew his first name."

"He has a first name?"

"Don't say anything," I warned.

"I won't."

"I mean it. He's coming here tomorrow night."

"What, like a date?"

"No." I waved my hand. "He and his team are coming to replace Abarca."

Arabella sagged against the door frame. "Don't scare me like that."

I made a face at her and she left.

I stared at the pile of doggie goods on the floor. I loved my sister so much. I loved my whole family more than anything. I had to make sure they kept breathing.

I looked back to the screen, switched to the browser, and clicked to go to the next page of headshots.

 **Chapter 9**

I woke up because the little black dog licked my nose. I hugged her to me, turned on my side, and tried to steal more sleep, but my alarm went off and dragged me out of bed.

The little dog spun in circles at my feet, ridiculously excited that I was conscious. I took a step toward the bathroom and my foot landed in a puddle of cold pee. Awesome.

I hopped to the bathroom on one foot.

Looking at all the male Primes yesterday had gotten me nothing except a pounding headache. I would've accomplished more cold-calling random Houses and demanding to know if their Primes had sired any bastards with freaky powers.

After I finished my fruitless search, I spent an hour researching Alessandro. I learned the same things I already knew. Italian count, Antistasi Prime, old family, wealthy, handsome, three broken engagements, no long-term relationships. The shield he presented to the public was bulletproof.

I would've searched more, but the documents from

Sabrian landed in my inbox. The good news was that Sabrian was confident that Celia's attack would be classified by the authorities as House warfare or a metamorphosis mage going berserk. The bad news was that the House unit of Houston PD wasn't staffed with idiots. The moment our packet of documents hit, the cops would realize that Celia attacked me while I was in a car with a man matching the description of the guy who had knifed Conway.

I spent the next few hours carefully reading the documents and then writing two versions of a detailed statement, one with Alessandro in it and the other without. In version number two, I was driving "a vehicle" all by my lonesome. I emailed everything back to Sabrian and instructed her to use her discretion. She told me she would sit on it until she had no choice.

All of that had taken me the entire afternoon and most of the evening. By the time I finished, the sun had set and the little dog had declared victory over the rubber hamburger. Just before dinner I went up to my room "for a minute" because I needed to clear my head, collapsed on my bed, and passed out. And my family apparently let me sleep the whole time because I was still wearing my T-shirt and sweatpants from yesterday. My career as a respected and admired, all-important Head of the House was clearly on the upswing. Not.

I looked like death. My hip hurt. And the worst part of all of this, I had slept for thirteen hours and I was still tired.

I washed my foot in the sink and lifted my shirt and pulled down my sweatpants to look at my hip.

Oh God.

My whole side from the waist down all the way to mid-thigh was black and blue. I poked my thigh and jerked my finger away. Ouch. The bruising was real, and not just a funny prank perpetrated while I was asleep.

The great detective Catalina Baylor. When confronted with undeniable empirical evidence, perform a field test anyway.

I took the little dog outside, where she sat on her butt and stared at me adoringly for ten minutes. Clearly, she had no pee left because she'd emptied her bladder on my floor. I let her back inside, zombie-staggered into the kitchen, mumbled good morning at Mom, made myself a cup of tea, and escaped into my office.

My inbox presented me with an email from Sabrian acknowledging the receipt of the documents I had couriered over yesterday. The rest was bills. I drank my tea and stared at them in the hopes they would disappear.

Day three of the investigation, and still no Halle.

I dialed Bug's number.

Bug answered on the first ring. "I lost him yesterday and I don't have him yet."

"Never mind Alessandro. I need another favor, but it's complicated, so it might be better if I explain in person. Can I visit you?"

There was a slight pause. I had planned to call him about this yesterday, but too many things had happened. Face-planting on my bed was so not the plan. I hadn't even taken any of the doggie things to my room.

I should feed the dog. She was probably starving. I got up and filled a dish with dog food. How much food would a dog of this size need . . .

"Bug?"

"Yeah."

Yeah what? Yeah, you can visit, or yeah, I'm still here and thinking about it?

I set the dish down and the dog dove into it. Apparently, she needed all the food.

Bug still hadn't said anything. "When would be a good time?"

"Now would be okay."

"Are you at Rogan's?"

"Kind of."

"What do you mean 'kind of'?"

There was another pause.

Bug sighed. "I'm at the old HQ across the street."

Wait, what? "Across the street from me?"

"Yes."

"I'll be right there."

I grabbed my phone and went to the door. The black dog licked her empty bowl, picked up her rubber hamburger, and followed me.

"I'm going to call you Shadow."

Shadow wagged her tail.

I walked into bright sunshine, and Shadow and I crossed the street to the old industrial building. Three years ago, when Nevada and Rogan were in the middle of trying to save Houston, my paranoid brother-in-law bought all the buildings around the warehouse in an effort to make us safe. We had since bought some of them back from him, but this one was still his. It housed a secondary HQ, and when Nevada and Rogan came to visit us, they stayed in the apartment on the top floor.

The metal door was unlocked. I crossed the empty bottom floor, which once served as the motor pool for Rogan's private army, climbed the metal staircase, heroically trying not to wince and failing, and emerged on the second floor. A massive computer station dominated the space, a gathering of servers and workstations, connected to nine large monitors arranged in a three-by-three grid on a wire cage. Behind the screens lay a small living space, with two couches on the right and a kitchen on the left. A tower of pizza boxes flanked by a brigade of empty Mello Yello bottles filled the kitchen island.

In front of the screens, perched in a rolling chair, sat Bug. Thin and wiry, Bug was never still, so much so that he seemed to almost vibrate, as if his body was struggling to contain the nervous energy within. Bug had enlisted in the Air Force as soon as he turned eighteen, and while he was in, the military offered him a deal: they would pay him an outrageous bonus and in return he would allow them to augment him. A specialist mage had reached into the arcane realm, pulled out a swarm of magical insects, and implanted them into Bug.

Nobody understood how swarms worked or the exact nature of their implantation. Most people didn't survive the procedure. Those who did gained an ability to process visual information and sometimes computer code at superhuman speeds. They burned bright and died fast. The normal life expectancy for a swarmer was about two years. That's why the military offered them a truckload of money. It was essentially a delayed suicide.

Somehow Bug survived. When Nevada first met him, he was an obsessed, manic wreck. Rogan was able to steady him through a cocktail of carefully curated medication and a stable environment, and usually he could almost pass for a normal person.

Right now, there was nothing normal about him. His brown hair stuck out at odd angles. His rumpled T-shirt, decorated with pizza stains of various shapes and ages, hung on his slight frame. His movements were quick and jittery, the agitation rolling off him in spasmodic waves.

"How long have you been here?"

Bug glanced at the kitchen island. "Four days."

"Did you have to count the pizza boxes?"

"Yes."

He had been here since Rogan and Nevada left for New York before traveling on to Spain for the funeral.

"Why didn't you stay on base?"

Rogan's estate contained a fully functional compound, complete with a barracks, commissary, gym, and everything else a small army would need to stay sharp. He used to just run everything from his enormous house, but after getting married, he and Nevada wanted privacy.

"There's nobody on base," Bug said. "It's the holidays. With the Major gone, there's only a skeleton crew protecting the house. I got lonely. And your security sucks. I've been here for half a week and they didn't notice. People deliver pizza to the door downstairs and nobody asked why."

For a second, I didn't know what I wanted more, to hug Bug or to scream in Abarca's face.

"No more pizza," I told him.

"What are you, the pizza police?"

"You're going to come home with me and you're going to have a normal dinner. With vegetables."

"I have mushrooms and tomato sauce on pizza. Add the meat, bread, and cheese and you've got all the food groups."

"Tomato is a berry, mushrooms are a fungus, and that isn't cheese, it's a cheese product. I don't even know if it can be classified as dairy. You're going to have a nice dinner, and you're going to bring your laundry, and you're going to take a long shower."

Bug tried to sniff his armpit and jerked his head away. He looked at me. "There will be people there."

"You know everybody, and everybody likes you. You and Bern are friends. The only new people are Runa and Ragnar, and they're nice."

Bug pondered it.

"You can play with my new dog."

Bug looked at Shadow. Shadow wagged her tail.

"Is it too soon?" Bug asked.

It was clearly a rhetorical question, so I didn't answer. Bug's old French bulldog mix, Napoleon, had died a year ago. Bug had rescued him off the street, and Napoleon enjoyed a spoiled, carefree life until time took its inevitable toll.

Bug dug in the desk drawer and fished out an ancient dog biscuit.

"How old is that thing?"

"It's a Milk Bone. They're like Twinkies, they don't go bad."

Shadow took the bone from his fingers and hid under the couch.

"I'll come to dinner," he said.

"Thank you."

"What do you need?"

I brought him up to speed on Diatheke, Benedict, and the missing two million dollars.

"I need you to go back to Sunday on CCTV and see if you can spot Sigourney leaving Diatheke. Assuming Diatheke didn't send a hit squad after her to steal the money back, I want to know what she did with it."

Bug's fingers flew over the keyboard. "What kind of name is Diatheke anyway?"

"It's ancient Greek. According to biblical scholars it means a contract, specifically the last disposition of all earthly possessions after death, or a covenant."

"So like a will?"

"Kind of. It can also mean a business agreement between two parties."

"Umm. Their name means make your final arrangements, and Sigourney was a poison Prime, and she worked for them . . ."

I raised my hand. "I know what you're thinking. I'm thinking it too, but I have no proof and I don't want to jump to any conclusions."

Bug shrugged and turned to his screens. I went to the kitchen, pulled up the sleeves of my sweatshirt, and attacked the mess on the island.

It took me twenty minutes to bring the kitchen to a state of cleanliness that didn't send shivers of horror down my spine. I took out three bags of trash and filled the recycling bin halfway. How someone could exist on pizza and Mello Yello alone, I would never know. Once I cleaned up, I settled on the couch with my phone and Shadow.

"Got her," Bug said finally.

I walked over to stand by him. On the central screen, Sigourney Etterson stood frozen in the process of walking into Diatheke, Ltd. The image was slightly out of focus, but I'd know that red hair anywhere. Judging by the angle, the footage was recorded from across the street.

"Apartment building?"

"Yeah. It's under construction and the construction crews always have good surveillance. Helps to cut down on material theft. 10:00 a.m. on the dot." Bug pressed a key and the grainy picture sped up. "She walks in and seventeen minutes later, she's out."

On the screen Sigourney emerged into the street, pulling a wheeled suitcase behind her.

"What's in the bag?!" Bug screamed dramatically.

"Probably the money."

"I was quoting a movie."

"You were misquoting a movie." The movie referenced a box.

"Whatever."

Sigourney walked to the parking lot and loaded the suitcase into a blue BMW SUV. She climbed into the driver's seat and drove offscreen.

The eight monitors around the central screen ignited, showing the images of Sigourney's SUV from various angles and cameras.

"X6 M," Bug said. "A hundred K, before modifications. Clearly, whatever she did for them paid well."

"Where is she going?"

"You'll see."

The video sped up, changing on the screens as different cameras tracked the SUV through the streets. Finally, it came to a stop before a metal gate. Beyond the gate stretched a long rectangular building with bright yellow doors.

"CubeSmart Self Storage," Bug said. "They're all over Houston."

The view switched, showing a shot of Sigourney's vehicle from the driver's side. She rolled down the window, punched a code into the box by the gate, the gate swung open, and she drove in.

"She rented the unit in advance," I thought out loud.

"Yep. She leaves six minutes later. I can't see it, but I assume the bag is no longer in the car."

"Thank you. You're a wizard."

Bug turned to me, his eyes shining. "But wait. There's more."

The video feed turned blurry as the images flew by.

"Wait for it . . ."

"How can you possibly keep track of anything at that speed?"

"Magic. There it is."

He pressed a key and the recording slowed to normal speed. A white Jeep Renegade pulled up to the gate. The driver's-side window slid down and Alessandro's shockingly handsome face came into view.

"Son of a bitch!" I leaned closer to the screen.

"I know, right? This must be his blend-in-with-the-locals car. I guess his Italian wheels were too flashy. How can that ass clown look so good on a damn surveillance camera? The guy flew in from Sydney, eighteen hours in the air, drove straight from the airport here, and he looks like a million bucks. Two million to be precise."

"When did he get in?"

"Monday at 8:42 a.m."

Sigourney was already dead then. A weight dropped off me. It wasn't that I suspected Alessandro murdered her, but I hadn't been able to discount that possibility until now.

Bug turned to me. "I have been chasing that shit monkey all over the fucking city. He destroyed three of my drones. He mocked me."

The top right screen showed a view from above, clearly from a drone. The screen shuddered, the view plunged to the ground, and rose again as someone picked up the fallen drone. Alessandro appeared in the camera, grinned, gave us a thumbs-up, and the screen went black.

"Do you see what I've had to put up with? But now, I have redeemed myself. And there is still more."

Bug dramatically paused.

"Tell me before I explode from anticipation."

Bug reached over and held his finger above the keyboard. The finger descended in slow motion.

I would strangle him. I swear, the court would understand.

"Bug!"

The finger kept dropping. Bug finally touched the keyboard. The image of the white Jeep Renegade filled the monitor, the nine screens presenting a single picture, like a mosaic.

The street by the Jeep looked eerily familiar.

Oh my God. "Is that our oak?"

"Yes, it is. He's parked it here, under the carport across from this building, every night since Monday. I checked the feed from your cameras while you waited. He swapped the plates with the cleaning crew truck, and your idiot toy soldiers have been letting him in because the license number is on their approved list. Yesterday he brought them coffee." Bug opened his eyes as wide as he could. "The calls are coming from inside the house, Catalina!"

I took off running.

The Jeep sat in the carport, its windows so tinted, they bordered on illegal. I peered through the windshield.

Empty.

I tried the doors. Locked.

I crossed the street and headed around the warehouse to Grandma Frida's motor pool. Shadow trotted after me.

Grandma poked her head out of a familiar-looking Guardian. Its twin sat on the left, with its doors open. I walked to the tool bench, grabbed the largest flathead screwdriver on it, took the reciprocating saw from the wall, and walked out.

"Safety glasses, Catalina!"

I did a one-eighty, snagged the safety goggles off a peg on the tool wall, and kept going.

"Catalina," Grandma Frida called out behind me. "When you're done cutting up the body, call me. I'll help you hide it."

I turned and looked at her.

Grandma flexed her arm. "Ride or die."

I squinted at her. "I'm still mad at you for ratting me out."

"You looked like death warmed over," Grandma said. "You may be the Head of House Baylor, but you're still my granddaughter and I won't be taking any of your bullshit."

"How is my sweater coming along, Grandma? Have you knitted more than two inches yet?"

Grandma Frida gave me the Look of Death.

I walked back to the Jeep and stabbed the two tires on the driver's side. The sound of the air hissing out was very satisfying. Shadow jumped back and hid behind the low stone wall bordering the oak. I put the safety glasses on and jammed the screwdriver into the driver's-side window. It cracked with a loud crunch but held. That's what I thought. Laminated glass.

Car windows came in two types, tempered and laminated. Tempered glass shattered into dull pieces. Laminated glass was made by sandwiching a layer of plastic between two panes of glass. Traditional escape tools did nothing to it. The Jeep was new enough to have all its windows laminated.

I pictured Alessandro's smirking face and stabbed the crack in the window. Stab, stab, stab. The glass finally gave, and I slid the blade of the saw into the small hole I had made.

Abarca came out of the mess hall down the street and zeroed in on me.

Keep going. Don't see me, don't talk to me. I have a screwdriver, and I'm not afraid to use it.

I turned the saw on. The blade chewed through glass and plastic. Abarca wandered over and stood next to me.

"Would you like some help?"

Yes, I'd like some help. I'd like you to help me understand how an Antistasi Prime has been driving in and out of our territory, parking his car fifty feet from our front door, and your elite security force, which had this place locked down so tight "not even a squirrel" could get through, has been letting him in and out and accepting his coffee. Help me understand that. "No."

Shadow poked her head from behind the wall and barked. For a small dog, she sounded surprisingly fierce.

Abarca ignored her. "I realize this might not be the best time to discuss this, but it can't wait."

"I'm listening." *Ask me why I'm cutting the window out of this car. Ask me whose car this is. Go ahead, I dare you.*

He raised his voice, trying to be heard over the dry grinding of the saw. "As you know, we had to let Lopez and Walton go. It was a difficult decision, but ultimately it was for the best."

He seemed to have forgotten that I was in the room when Mom told him to fire those two or pack his bags. He didn't have to make any decisions, just follow orders.

"We need to fill those two open slots as soon as possible. I submitted a list of candidates to Pen, but we don't seem to be on the same page."

Same page? He and Mom weren't even on the same bookshelf.

"The two individuals I've chosen have spotless track

records, and I have no doubt they would make fine additions to the team."

The team which would be replaced tomorrow night.

Abarca fell silent, clearly anticipating some sort of response. He was trying to go over Mom's head to get his guys hired.

"I'm confused. What exactly would you like me to do?"

Abarca smiled at me. "I value your opinion."

Since when?

"I'd like you to review the candidates."

"All security matters must go through my mother."

"But you're the Head of the House."

I turned the saw off and faced him. "I *am* the Head of the House and I'm telling you that all security matters must go through and be approved by my mother. If she wants my opinion, she'll consult me. Was there anything else?"

Abarca opened his mouth, hesitated, then said, "No. That's it."

"I'm glad we cleared that up." I turned the saw back on and continued my slow cutting.

Abarca walked away. If I wasn't hacking at Alessandro's car, I would almost feel sorry for him. It wasn't altogether his fault. He was trying to do a job that he wasn't qualified for, but we were the ones who hired him for that job in the first place. I didn't blame him for taking the position. He'd needed the work in the worst way, from what Mom had said. And I didn't blame Mom for hiring him. She was trying to help a friend and keep us safe. But I was really glad Heart was on his way.

If only I knew where we could find the money to pay him.

The saw tasted air. I had cut a ragged rectangle in

the window. I turned it off and hit the window with the handle of the screwdriver. It fell in onto the driver's seat.

I popped the lock and opened the hatchback. The back was empty, except for a folded blanket, a rain poncho, and a garment bag. I unzipped the bag. A tuxedo, good quality. Typical.

I opened the back doors and went about searching the car.

I climbed the ladder to my loft, carrying the dog pillow, my arms filled with dog shampoo and puppy pads. Shadow bounded up the steps ahead of me and sprinted into my room.

The Jeep yielded no clues. I found no hidden stashes of weapons or gold coins, no fake IDs or passports, no rental agreement, no paperwork of any kind, not even a fast-food receipt. For some reason Sigourney Etterson had paid Alessandro two million dollars and I had no idea why.

I'd returned the tools to Grandma. Bug was watching the Jeep, so we would know the moment Alessandro reappeared. At least he would be in for a hell of a surprise when he came back to the car. I would actually raid our overstretched budget and pay good money to see the look on his face.

My hip hurt. I would put the dog pillow down for Shadow, then I would wash my hands and go down to eat some lunch, during which I would sit across from Runa and Ragnar and have to think of some way to explain why I hadn't found their sister yet. Ugh.

I walked into my loft.

Alessandro Sagredo lounged on my bed. He lay propped on one elbow, his large, muscular frame taking up the entire space. He couldn't be real; he had to be a painting made to tempt women; masculine, handsome, erotic, from the broad spread of his shoulders and his flat stomach to his long legs.

Shadow lay next to him, chewing on some yellow rectangular thing.

Alessandro raised his head. His amber eyes lit up and he smiled a slow, lazy smile, like a wolf cornering a doe.

He was holding the pink frame with his picture in it, which I had left on my nightstand.

The enormity of it hit me all at once. I wanted to fall through the floor, strangle him, grab my dog, and scream at the same time. My brain took those conflicting urges and compromised. I dropped the dog pillow and hurled the pack of puppy pads at his head.

Alessandro caught the pack one-handed and tossed it to the floor. He didn't even move, the son of a bitch. Just raised his hand, caught the pack, and went back to looking at the picture.

He turned the frame, so I could see his picture in it. "Smoochie poo?"

"It's Italian for ass clown. What are you doing in my room?"

"Admiring your taste in arts and crafts?" He tilted the frame. "The application of glitter could use some work."

"Shadow, come here."

Shadow wagged her tail and stayed exactly where she was.

"What is she eating?"

"A Himalayan yak treat. Unlike you, your dog can be reasoned with."

"Yak what? What part of the yak?"

"Relax. It's made of cheese." He tilted the photograph

toward me, so the light caught the pink glitter. "Can we postpone the topic of dog treats and go back to the fact that you have my picture in a pink frame on your nightstand?"

"It came with the frame."

He grinned.

If I had a gun, I would've shot him. I did have a gun. It was locked in the nightstand. Getting it would mean risking being within his reach, and he was very fast.

"I took some pics in Sydney last week, on the beach. With my shirt off. I can send a few to your phone, if you'd like."

How dare . . . "No, I wouldn't like."

Alessandro raised his eyebrows. "Are you sure? Judging by the condition of my car, you have a lot of pent-up anger."

He'd watched me take apart his Jeep. Probably while searching my room. It was good that humans couldn't spontaneously explode, because otherwise I would have disintegrated.

"What does my anger have to do with your selfies?"

"You might find having a hot pic of me by your bed relaxing."

He did not just imply what I thought he implied.

Yes, yes, he did.

"If I wanted a hot pic by my bed for relaxation, it wouldn't be yours." There.

"You're right. Why settle for a picture when you can have the real thing?" He spread his arms. "I'm right here."

Oh my God.

"In your bed. Waiting."

Yes . . . No. No!

He was looking at me as if I was naked.

It was my most secret fantasy. He was in my room. On

my bed. Looking at me. Smiling at me like he wanted me. Everything I'd ever dreamed of was right there.

My heart pounded in my chest at a million beats per minute. My cheeks grew warm. I gathered all my will into a steel fist. *Do not blush. Do NOT blush.* Why was this happening to me? He wasn't even doing anything. He was just looking at me and talking.

Alessandro studied me, and when he spoke, his tone sent tiny shivers down my neck. It was intimate and seductive, and it promised me all the things I wanted and couldn't have. "Is it because your family is downstairs? Don't worry, we can be very quiet."

The temptation to cross the room and touch him was almost too much. I could . . . No, I couldn't. He was mocking me. He saw the picture, put two and two together, and now he was taunting me with it.

The entire floor of my bedroom was a single arcane circle. I had drawn it with soap on the floorboards to trap a possible intruder. If I activated it, all his jokes would dry up real fast.

If I activated the circle, I would lose all my work, and it would turn our conversation into combat. Using my wings would get us there even faster. There would be no coming back from that, and I needed Alessandro. I needed the information locked in his head.

Oh, how I would love to wipe that smug grin off his face.

I forced myself to relax. It was like trying to stretch a really wide rubber band. My body resisted. Every cell I had wanted to keep focusing on him. On his hands. On his face. On his amber eyes . . .

"What do you want? Make it quick, Alessandro, I'm busy."

He sat up. "That's not typically a request I get."

So funny, so clever. Jackass.

I folded my arms across my chest. "Today."

He reached over and patted Shadow on her fuzzy head. "After our fun trip to the mall, I asked myself if you would ever see reason and walk away from this mess. Would you like to know my conclusion?"

"No."

"I believe you won't, and I'll tell you why. You are the kind of woman who stops in the middle of fighting hired killers to rescue a small, foul-smelling, doglike creature."

"What does that have to do with anything?"

He swung himself into a sitting position. "Please hold all questions until the end of the speech. Runa Etterson did your family a favor during your sister's wedding by removing poison from the wedding cake. She's your friend, probably your only friend."

"I have tons of friends."

"And I have access to a computer and your social media profiles. Your younger sister has tons of friends. Your Instagram has five followers, all of whom are related to you, and your most popular post is a book review of *The Geometry of Arcane Circles*, where you called the author an 'epic idiot.'"

I gave him my Tremaine sneer. If I had been an ice mage, the air between us would've frozen. "Prime Sagredo, my House is none of your business. My sisters, my cousins, my grandmother, and their social media are none of your business. You have now repeatedly violated the sovereign domain of my family. Get to the point and get out."

"That's new," Alessandro observed. "I like."

What wouldn't I give to brain him with something heavy . . . "I'm so pleased."

"May I finish, Dread Mistress?"

"I wish you would."

"The point is, you can't abandon Runa. You're going to turn yourself inside out to help her. It is literally who you are."

Alessandro set the pink frame back on the nightstand. All humor drained from his face. Only cold menace remained, sharpened by intelligence and resolve.

"Unfortunately, you are in over your head. That leaves me with two choices. I can watch you die in a nasty way or I can throw you a rope."

Was he trying to con me? Did he need information from me? Trusting him was a mistake, I was sure of it. I'd cyberstalked him, I had researched his family, and I could name his favorite car, wine, and band, but I knew exactly zip about who he actually was. If he told me the sun was shining, I'd run outside to double-check.

But Halle was still missing. If he knew anything about it, I had to get it out of him. He kept thinking of me as a dilettante. He wouldn't tell me anything until he saw me as an equal.

"Keep your rope. I want to know what you did with the two million dollars Sigourney paid you."

He came off the bed in a single spring-loaded movement, covering the distance between us in a fraction of a second. Suddenly he was too close.

My heart sped up, and I didn't know if it was from fear or excitement.

Alessandro's eyes measured me. He moved to the side, light on his feet, a deadly human predator, like a gladiator looking for an opportunity to close in for a kill. I was being hunted.

"Be careful," I warned him, turning to keep him in my view.

He tilted his head, his tawny eyes sharp. "Planning to fight me?"

"If you force me to." Big talker, that's me.

The air between us vibrated with tension. Magic nipped at my fingertips, ready to punch the arcane circle under my feet.

"You want to find Halle," he said. "I need to identify Sigourney's killer. Two roads going to the same place."

He was right. Whoever killed Sigourney likely had her daughter. "Why do you need to find Sigourney's murderer?"

"Because she paid me to kill them."

"How did she know to hire you? She didn't pick your name out of a hat. Why did you think that you could kill an assassin?"

"Some people know I'm good at killing."

The planet stopped. My mind struggled to process it. He was a professional killer. No different than the people who'd come after me in the mall. No different than the person who killed Runa's mother.

The little hopeless dream I carried inside me died.

Why? He had everything going for him. Why?

"Work with me and we'll get this done together," he said.

Working with him would be a nightmare.

This wasn't an emotional problem. My feelings didn't matter. I had to look at this rationally. All I had was the money and that trail ended with him. If I refused to work with him, he would continue his search on his own and we would keep tripping over each other. I would rather have him on our side than competing with me. Two was better than one.

"If I work with you, will you share what you know about Sigourney's death?"

"Yes."

"Prove it. Tell me what you know about Diatheke and Benedict De Lacy."

He leaned forward half an inch. It was a small movement, but it felt like he had pounced on me.

I held still and stared back at him. *No, you're not getting an inch. I'm going to stay right where I am.*

Alessandro studied me. "When I first met you, I thought you were a shy, innocent, honest girl who was overwhelmed by her sudden rise. But you're not, are you?"

Not anymore.

"You're smart, ruthless, and calculating. Conniving even."

Conniving was going too far.

He flashed a grin, a quick baring of teeth. "I love it."

"I changed my mind. I don't need your help."

"How fortunate for me that it's not up to you." He looked over my shoulder. "Why don't we ask your friend if she wants me to help you find her sister?"

I wasn't about to turn my back to him. "Runa, are you behind me?"

"Yes."

Crap.

"My condolences on your loss, Prime Etterson," Alessandro said.

"Did you kill my mother?"

I'd heard that brittle edge in her voice just before Conway started sprouting black fuzz. Alarm pulsed through me. I spun to face her, putting myself between her and Alessandro. Runa's face had gone so white, it looked bloodless.

"No," Alessandro and I said at the same time.

"He was in Australia at the time of her murder," I added. "I've verified this."

"I have useful information," he said. "I'm willing to help Catalina find Halle, but this is a one-time offer. Once I leave here, that's it. Make a decision."

I knew exactly what she would say before she even opened her mouth.

"I accept," Runa said.

Whatever little negotiating power I'd had just evaporated. I had to salvage what I could. "Give us some information as a show of good faith and we have a deal."

Alessandro flicked his fingers and tossed a black flash drive to Runa. "Your mother was a professional assassin. This is a record of her sins."

Runa looked at the flash drive in her hand like it was a snake. "Find my sister. That's all that matters now."

She turned and walked down the stairs.

The skin on the back of my neck prickled. Alessandro was right behind me, so close, I felt the heat of his body.

"You tried to save me," the wolf's voice said inches from my ear. "I'm so touched."

The small hairs on the back of my neck stood up. In my head, he leaned in and kissed me, his lips scorching hot on my skin. Having him near me was excruciating, and I'd just tied myself to him for however long the investigation would take. This was so messed up. So, so messed up.

Slowly, deliberately, I turned around. "Don't read too much into it. Do you think Benedict killed Sigourney?"

"I don't know," he said. "The body was too burned. I do know that he either did it himself or had it done. When I spoke to Sigourney, she told me Diatheke would be targeting her."

"Then Diatheke has Halle."

"It appears so." Alessandro grimaced. "The more pressing issue is that Benedict will retaliate, and soon.

He lost one crystal elephant, two Guardians, eighteen killers, and a metamorphosis mage. Reputation is everything in his business."

"What exactly is his business?"

Alessandro tilted his head. "Does this often work for you?"

"What?"

"Pretending you don't know things you have already figured out."

I raised my eyebrows at him. "Why don't you answer my question and I'll tell you."

"Let me put it to you this way: everyone you met inside that building is a trained killer. Any account managers you met, they are killers. Their managers are killers. If you met a custodian, he's a killer. The nice receptionist who greeted you, killer."

That's what I'd suspected. "They're an assassin firm."

He nodded.

Assassin firms were the magical elite's dirty secret. Not every House had combat Primes, but most prominent magical dynasties had money and a willingness to settle their private feuds through murder. The assassin firms operated in the shadows, selling their services to the highest bidder. Somehow, I never thought I would run across one in Houston.

"This is a specific type of industry, where reputation is very important," Alessandro said. "Diatheke is in the middle of a rapid expansion. A year ago, they were still a small firm. Now they're in the top eight worldwide. Benedict can afford anything he wants, except looking weak. He'll hit back to save face and to silence."

"Silence me?"

"You, Runa, your family, anyone who works for you. Anyone who can expose them for what they are."

The Herald was full of Prime fanfic involving sexy assassins who were secretly bastard sons and daughters of the rich and powerful and went on to have edgy adventures. The reality was uglier and much more brutal. Nobody wanted the assassin firms to exist. People who had engaged their services wanted to silence them to tie up loose ends. Combat Primes wanted to eliminate them to maintain their power. Law enforcement wanted them gone because murder for hire was illegal and difficult to solve. The few times assassin firms had been discovered, the authorities broke them up with the assistance of the local Assemblies. I knew of four cases in the last fifty years and every one of them had ended in a slaughter. The loss of human life on both sides was catastrophic.

"Do you understand now?" Alessandro asked softly.

The enormity of the can of worms I had opened finally hit home. Benedict would do everything he could to keep from being discovered. He had a building full of killers at his disposal and he would just keep sending them after us until we were all dead. And if we went to the authorities with what we knew, we would sign Halle's death warrant. They would slit her throat in retaliation.

This would end in blood.

What do I do? How do we prepare to fight this? How did I blunder so badly? Thoughts raced and collided in my head, too fast to make sense.

Alessandro dipped his head to look me in the eyes. "We're going to be best friends from now on, you and me. We're going to do everything together."

I managed to pin a thought down and made my mouth move. "Where are you staying?"

"In the building across the street on the left of the big tree. I like to keep an eye on you. Your security is shit."

I was getting really tired of people telling me that.

Arrosa always said, "When backed into a corner, handle it with grace." I scrounged up some grace. I had to look very hard for it.

"How much do you know about the assassins Diatheke employs?"

"Enough."

"I have a recording of Sigourney's death."

He came to life like a shark smelling blood in the water. "Show me."

"I'll bring it over. First, rules. One, do not attack or endanger my family. Two, share. If I find out that you discovered something and took off without telling me, the deal is off. And three, don't give snacks to my dog without asking me first."

"Agreed." He winked at me.

"House Baylor is delighted to offer our hospitality to you, Mr. Sagredo. Dinner will be tonight at six. I'll bring the recording by shortly."

He bowed with an exaggerated flourish, went to my window, opened it, and jumped out.

I ran downstairs and burst into the media room. It was empty. I turned and sprinted into the kitchen. Empty. Where the hell was everybody?

I tore through the warehouse to the office and all but flew through the door.

Bern, Runa, and Ragnar sat at the table in the conference room with two laptops, a tablet, and notebooks with scribbled notes. In the corner Mom rested in her favorite chair, scrolling through her tablet. The four of them raised their heads and looked at me.

"Where is everybody?"

"Leon is passed out in his room, because he hasn't

slept for two days," Bern said. "Grandma Frida is in the motor pool still working on the Guardians."

"Where is Arabella?"

"She said she had an errand," Mom said.

I pulled out my phone and texted Arabella. **Where are you?**

No answer.

I dialed her number. It went to voice mail. Would it kill her to charge her phone? Half of the time her phone was dead and the rest it was dying, because she was always on it. Argh.

"Something bad happened," Runa guessed.

"Diatheke is an assassin firm. They ordered the hit on your mother."

Mom sat up straight. "How sure are you?"

"Pretty damn sure. We're putting them at risk of exposure."

Ragnar tilted his head as if he was considering a thorny logical problem. When he finally recovered from the magic drain and his emotions returned, there would be hell to pay. "We should notify the authorities."

Runa's face went white again. "We can't."

"Why?" he asked.

"Because they have your sister," Bern said. "They'll kill her."

Runa clenched her hands together. "Not if I get them first."

"You would never get to her in time," Mom said.

"We don't know where they're holding her," I told her. "Diatheke's building downtown is a fortress. Everything requires a keycard. Once you're in the lobby, they can drop the grate over the front door and shoot you remotely. You won't get the chance to kill anyone or to ask any questions."

"So we just sit here. Again."

"No," Mom said. "We prepare."

"They'll hit us, sooner rather than later," Bern told her. "If we can, we need to take some of them alive, so we can bargain. If we get ahold of someone valuable enough, we can trade them to Diatheke for your sister."

Runa stood up. "I need some air." She walked out of the room.

"Stay close to the warehouse," Mom called.

"I'll keep an eye on her." Bern got up and followed her out.

I looked at Mom. Bern had voluntarily left the warehouse. Again. Since graduating from college, Bern did his best to impersonate a mushroom: he parked himself in the Hut of Evil with his servers and basked in the glow of the monitors, escaping only to use the bathroom and consume food. Going outside wasn't in his repertoire.

Mom shrugged.

Ragnar got up. "I'm going to the kitchen to get snacks. Please don't worry. I won't go outside, and I'll try very hard to not kill anyone."

He left. It was just me and Mom.

"It won't work," I told her. "They'll never trade Halle. She's a potential witness."

"I know," she said. "We have to bleed them. We have to make it so expensive that they'll drop it. They're a business."

"We're gambling with her life." Anxiety churned inside me.

"It's not about Halle now," Mom said. "It's about keeping that wild wrecking ball and her brother alive."

My stomach dropped. "I'm going to try, Mom. Halle's still alive. There is still a chance."

"Then you go and try. Heart and his people will be

here tonight. That should give you some freedom of movement." Mom sighed. "I miss doing small, quiet jobs. Insurance fraud. Cheating spouses."

"I miss them too," I told her. "But we are who we are. There's no going back."

Alessandro had taken the top floor in the three-story brick building that used to be a fire station years ago. Rogan purchased it but never did anything with it, and eventually we bought it from him.

I had walked through this building before when we purchased it. The first floor, with an unusually high ceiling, served as the garage for the fire trucks. The second, accessible by an iron staircase, housed the offices, and the third contained the rec room, sleeping quarters, and a big kitchen once capable of serving food to an entire fire team.

I climbed the iron stairs, with my hip screaming at me the entire way. I had left Shadow in the warehouse. She seemed susceptible to his bribes, and I had no idea what sort of bizarre thing he would try to feed her this time.

The original plan was to turn the fire station into barracks, but the building proved to be too old. Fixing it up would be more expensive than building a brand-new structure. Rogan let it go for next to nothing. At some point, Leon, obsessed with the fire pole, had tried to convince Bern to move there with him and turn it into a "hip bro cave." That plan died when they realized rewiring the place was out of their budget.

The stairs brought me to a wide-open door. I stepped through and ended up in the rec room, flooded with daylight from huge windows. Someone had swept the concrete floor. On the right a large pack of bottled water waited on the counter of a kitchen right out of the seventies, complete with wooden paneling. Straight ahead, in the corner, an inflatable mattress rested on the floor. Between me and the mattress stood two plastic fold-out tables filled with weapons and equipment. A high-tech-looking laptop, parts of a drone, six, no, nine guns, including a BFR, four knives, two daggers, a machete, a garrote, and a compound bow. The assassin's tool kit.

The assassin himself was nowhere to be seen. I walked to the tables. Whatever his faults were, Alessandro had excellent taste in blades. Everything was functional, sharp, and sturdy. And generic. No custom-made pieces, no family heirlooms. Nothing irreplaceable or that could be traced.

I reached for the Ka-Bar and tested the balance. Seven-inch straight blade angled at the tip. Heavy.

I turned to get better light. Alessandro sat on the kitchen counter, one leg bent, the other hanging free. I almost threw the Ka-Bar.

"Adorable," Alessandro said. "Do that little jump again."

I put the Ka-Bar down before the temptation got the better of me. "I brought you the recording." I held up the thumb drive.

He jumped off the counter and stalked toward me.

I circled the tables, looking at his collection and keeping the furniture between us. "You seem to know a lot about Benedict."

"Mhm."

"What is he?"

"You were with him. What do you think he is? What did you feel?"

"Revulsion and fear. His magic manifested as dark

phantom serpents. He opened himself, and a nest of ghost snakes slithered out wanting to bite me."

"That's why he calls himself the Adder," he said.

"The Adder? Really?"

"It goes with the territory. Nobody wants to hire a Mr. De Lacy or Madame Laurent. They want to hire the Adder or Mort Noire."

"Please tell me there isn't an assassin calling herself the Black Death?"

"More than one."

It seemed so childish except people were dying. "So, what's your nickname? Instagram Famous? Playboy Killer?"

"Are you teasing me, you sexy beast?"

The careful train of my thoughts derailed, flipped over in the air, and burst on fire. *Think of a witty comeback, come on* . . . How did he keep short-circuiting my brain?

He laughed. "If looks could kill."

I resumed our dance around the tables. "Benedict is a psionic, isn't he? Probably a phobic subtype."

Psionic mages affected survival emotions. Fear, disgust, rage, anxiety, shame. The primal, powerful urges that kept humans breathing thousands of years before tools and weapons came along. Psionics induced these emotions in their targets. Phobics specialized in fear. They had an innate ability to find your worst phobia and project it into your mind, dragging you into paralyzing madness. I'd dealt with a phobic before, although she wasn't a Prime. Benedict's magic elicited that same instinctual punch of revulsion and terror.

"Close," Alessandro said. "His mother is a phobic. His father is a mind cutter."

A menincissor mage. A particularly nasty branch of

mental magic that attacked consciousness. Mind cutters punctured mental shields and induced pain and the inability to think. They weren't lethal on their own, but they excelled at disabling their target.

"Are you running away from me?" Alessandro asked.

"No." We had come full circle around the tables.

"Yes, you are. Are you afraid of what I'll do if I catch you?" He raised his eyebrows at me. "Or are you scared of what you might do?"

I stopped. "I'm not afraid of anything."

He vaulted over a table and landed next to me. I tilted my head and looked at him. Magic roiled just under his skin. His amber eyes all but glowed.

Kiss me.

"When a phobic and a mind cutter have a child . . ." He spoke softly, his voice warm and low, meant just for me. When he told someone he loved them, he might sound just like that. ". . . they have a one in a quarter chance of producing a crime against nature called a mind ripper. Benedict can penetrate mental defenses like his father and then scramble the mind, inducing panic like his mother. Benedict didn't just happen; he was a planned project by a mind cutter House. They wanted a dark horse to handle their dirty deeds."

He was standing way too close. Looking at him made it difficult to concentrate. "What happened?"

"They had a difference of opinion. Now House Weber is no more."

I held out the USB drive. He took it from my hand. His long fingers brushed mine.

Alessandro opened the laptop and plugged the drive in. Sigourney appeared on the screen.

I crossed my arms on my chest and leaned against the wall by the window. If Alessandro ever kissed me, I wouldn't want him to stop. When he came to see me that time after the trials, asking me to go for a ride, I wanted him so much, it took all of my will to not open my wings and make him love me. In that moment, it didn't matter that it wouldn't be real. Being loved by him was all I had cared about.

I got so scared that I would lose control, I called the police and asked them to make him leave. I did it because my magic would take away his free will and chain him to me. I didn't want that for him. I wanted him to have a long, happy life with whoever he chose. I had to let him go.

The more I looked at his Instagram over the years, the less happy he seemed. Now I knew—the Instagram Alessandro was bullshit. He had created a fantasy and held it up to the world like a shield. This Alessandro, the one in front of me staring at the laptop with the single-minded focus of a predator; this was the real man. Knowing this should have freed me, but I only wanted him more.

My phone chimed. An Instagram alert for Alessandro's account. On my phone Alessandro surfed, a crystal blue wave curling around him. His wet hair flared around his face. Muscle corded his body under bronze skin. I looked at the tag and held the phone out to him. "Maui, really?"

"Mhm. I'm currently in Hawaii. Did you see his hand when he reached over her?" He paused the recording just before Sigourney's killer turned off the PC.

"I did. I digitally enhanced it." I hadn't mentioned it, because I wanted to know if he would notice it too.

He glanced at me. All the flirting had evaporated. His eyes were clear and cold. He had seen his target.

Alessandro the killer. And if I let my mind wander, it

would drift off into imagining the glide of his fingertips against my skin, the warm heat of his lips on mine, the power of his arms around me . . . It would construct impossible scenarios where somehow he fell in love with me and stopped being an assassin and we lived happily ever after.

I was morally bankrupt.

He must've seen it in my face because humor sparked in his eyes.

"Can I see the enhanced image? Or will you make me beg?"

"It's the second file on the drive. You know, you don't have to pretend to flirt with me. I said I would work with you and I meant it."

He smiled at me. It wasn't his dazzling bachelor-of-the-year grin, it was a simple quick smile. "I never pretend with you. Tease you, maybe. Flirt, yes. But never that."

I wished he hadn't said that to me. Not helping, Alessandro. Not even a little bit.

"These fingers have claws," he told me.

"And the knuckles of the hand are abnormally large and oddly shaped. If this was a normal person, he or she would have advanced arthritis. Doesn't seem like a desirable trait in an assassin."

He frowned. "If this is arthritis, he wouldn't be able to open a door. No, I think this is reinforcement to account for the additional finger weight and length of the claws."

"Yes. The distal phalanges are wider and longer as well. The whole hand appears stronger."

He leaned back from the laptop. "The warped can't do magic by definition."

"Yet here we are. It looks like she had a massive stroke with catastrophic bleeding. Is this a carnifex mage?"

"A butcher? It's possible, but they typically target the heart. It's a guaranteed kill. Going for the brain is a lot harder. You would really have to know what you were doing."

I shook my head. "He couldn't go for the heart. He needed her breathing so she could die of smoke inhalation."

His fingers tapped the keyboard. A carousel of portraits appeared, each on its own card, listing name and power. Benedict's handsome face looked at me with glacier eyes. The card said "Kurt Weber, Ratiocissor, Prime."

Alessandro swiped across the track pad, and the ring of portraits turned, presenting us with the next face, a Hispanic woman in her late fifties. "Alba Gonzales, Telekinetic, Prime." The following card showed a black man in his mid-twenties. "Kendrell Cooper, Aerokinetic, Prime."

How many Primes did Diatheke have? If they were a House, they would be unstoppable.

Alessandro kept swiping, the faces moving too fast for me to register them. He hardly looked at the screen. He must've memorized them and was now going through them just to reassure himself.

I counted eighteen cards. The last one said "Average" so they weren't all Primes. Still. That many killers under one roof would give anyone pause.

Finally, Alessandro straightened. "There are no butchers in their roster."

"How complete are your records?"

"Complete enough." He locked his jaw.

"Maybe he's a recent hire?"

Alessandro shook his head. "Etterson was an experienced assassin. They wouldn't send a rookie after her."

He stared at the laptop, his expression dark. How did he get those files? More importantly, why? This went beyond any due diligence one would do to research his competitors. It would have taken months, possibly years to compile this database. Alessandro was hunting Diatheke.

"My turn to ask questions," I said.

He smiled. "Go."

"Are you trying to take out a competitor? Is there another assassin firm pulling your strings?"

"I don't work for a firm. I'm here to kill Sigourney's murderer."

I raised my eyebrows and nodded at his laptop. "And so you threw this together on the fly?"

"Fair enough." Alessandro leaned back against the table and crossed his arms. "Benedict has been on my radar for a while. I need to ask him some questions on an unrelated matter. It has nothing to do with House Etterson."

"How important are those questions to you?"

"If it's a choice between the Etterson contract and his life, I'll kill him. I can find my answers in another way."

"How did Sigourney hire you, what are the terms of your contract, what do you know about Halle?"

"She hired me through an intermediary. She was in the business, and she was aware of my particular job requirements."

"Which are?"

"Privileged."

"Alessandro, she'd been out of the game for almost ten years. How did she even know about you? You would've been in your teens when she quit. Have you been doing this since you were fifteen?"

His face shut down. "I have a certain reputation."

"What kind of reputation?"

"The kind people like Sigourney make a point to note."

What the hell did that mean?

"The intermediary arranged a call," he continued, "during which Sigourney told me that her old firm was coming after her. She indicated they had pressured her to come out of retirement for a high-profile job, which she declined. She didn't tell me who the target was, said we would discuss it in person. She didn't think Diatheke would move on her immediately. She expected them to come back with a higher offer, which she also intended to reject."

"Clearly she was wrong."

"Yes."

I thought out loud. "For them to insist that she come out of retirement after so many years means the target was someone she had access to and they didn't."

"Or they didn't want it traced to them."

"Did she say why she wouldn't do it?"

Alessandro grimaced. "She said that if she didn't kill him, she would be in danger. If she did kill him, her entire family would be done. I got the feeling that she wasn't sure she could complete the job. It was a no-win situation. One way or the other, someone would die."

"So a dangerous, high-profile target. Male. Someone she knew." We would have to go through Sigourney's files again.

"Someone who scared her," Alessandro added.

"I don't understand why Diatheke let her walk into their building and take out the money. They knew they were going to kill her." That had to be some conversation.

"Two separate things. She earned the money, and if they didn't pay her, nobody else would work with them.

The greatest sin in this business is to withhold money earned." His voice dripped with disgust. "They have no problem killing a parent in front of their kids or blowing up a car full of charity workers; but if they don't get paid, they lose their shit."

For a hired killer, he had a lot of disdain for the profession. And he didn't say *we*. He said *they*.

He made sense though. It probably wasn't the best idea to cheat an assassin out of their paycheck.

"She didn't think her children would be in danger."

"Normally, they wouldn't be." Alessandro shrugged.

"Professional courtesy?" I couldn't quite keep the skepticism out of my voice.

"There's no such thing. If you must eliminate an assassin and things go sour, leaking the fact that they were a hired killer douses the heat. Nobody extends sympathy to murderers. But if a minor is killed, there is an elevated risk of public outcry and pressure to solve it. Halle should've been safe."

"It has to be her magic," I said. What else was there? Halle was too dangerous to sell or contain.

Alessandro met my gaze. "They bothered with this elaborate ruse because they need her alive. Catalina, we'll find her. I promise you. We'll get her back."

He said it like he meant every word.

"Thank you for leveling with me." I moved to the door.

He got there ahead of me and leaned on the door frame. "Leaving so soon?"

"Things to do."

"What if I asked you to stay? What if I said, 'Don't go, Catalina. I'll be lonely without you.'"

If he actually said that and was serious, I might move into this room with him. "I have to go."

"Stay," he said. "We can compare notes on murderers. It will be fun."

His voice pulled me in, and for a second, I didn't know which one of us was the siren.

"No. I have to go." If I kept repeating it, I might actually believe it. "I have to look through Sigourney's files and make dinner."

"Or you could bring your laptop over here. We could order Chinese takeout and wash it down with some bad American wine."

His eyes were so warm and inviting. It would be so easy just to stay here with him.

"I'll tell you funny stories," he offered.

I would give anything to spend an evening here, figuring out what made him laugh. "I have to go."

He gave me a resigned smile and invited me to exit with an elegant sweep of his hand.

I had to leave. I said I would. I insisted on it. I walked through the doorway.

"If you think of anything else," I said.

"I know where you live."

I was going to say text me. A sudden thought hit me like a bolt of lightning. "Alessandro, one last thing. Stay out of my room."

"Not a chance," he told me.

Thirty seconds after I finished putting dinner into the oven and invited Runa into my office to brief her, Shadow started sniffing my office floor and running around in circles. Runa and I had to grab her and sprint outside.

Grass was in short supply and the only tree, the massive oak across the road, was protected by a stone wall four feet high. I would have to drop her over it and then somehow scoop her out. I imagined loading Shadow into a bucket and lowering her to the roots of the oak with a rope. In my little fantasy Shadow wore a yellow mining helmet with a round light.

Clearly, I'd been staring at the computer for too long.

We took Shadow to the area behind the motor pool instead. Grandma Frida had set up a picnic table to the right, and we landed there, deposited the little dog on the pavement, and chorused, "Go potty!" in encouraging voices.

Shadow looked at us and wagged her little black tail.

"Whatever is cooking in the kitchen smells amazing. What are we having?" Runa asked.

"Lemon roasted chicken with rosemary baked potatoes, chive butter, kale and Brussels sprout salad with tahini maple dressing, and an apple pithivier."

Runa gave me a long look.

"I cook when I'm stressed out. It sounds more complicated than it is. In reality, it's mostly season things, dump them in a baking pan, and stick them in the oven."

The little dog wandered off.

"What's a PTVA?"

"It's a French pie-cake made with puff pastry. The traditional version uses rum and almonds, but nobody likes rum, so I make mine with apples."

Shadow trotted around, periodically paused to sniff at some random spot of asphalt, carefully considered it, then moved on. Apparently, selecting the perfect place to pee was vitally important.

"I need to catch you up on what we have so far." I summarized the last few days for her; Diatheke, Celia, Benedict, Keystone, the chase, and Alessandro's involvement. I kept the information about his database private. I didn't know what it meant yet in the big picture.

She rubbed her face with both hands. "I'm sorry you had to go through all that."

"It's my job." But yeah, it sucked. "I'm sorry we haven't found Halle. But so far the evidence seems to point to kidnapping, not murder."

Professionally I knew that we were doing everything we could. Personally, the guilt drowned me. No matter how many times I warned myself, I thought of Runa as my friend. I desperately needed to fix this for her, and this case was a quicksand trap. Just when I thought I was on my way up, I sank deeper in. It was driving me up the wall.

"So where do we go from here?" Runa asked.

"Well, first things first. We're now in the crosshairs of an assassin firm, so we'll get attacked. It's not an 'if,' it's a 'when.' I called Matilda's aunt. Unfortunately, she's out of town, but she said a friend will be coming by to pick her up. Would you like to send Ragnar with them?"

"No." She didn't even pause. "Right now, the last thing he remembers is getting off the plane and he's so calm, it's borderline freaky. I don't know how long this will last, but if his memory and emotions come back, I don't want him climbing onto another roof. I need to be there to steady him."

"Okay." It was her decision. "The next step is to identify your mother's target. We know he's male, powerful, and his death would cause an uproar. Diatheke wants him dead, but they don't want the heat that will come with it."

Runa shook her head. "No clue. Mom didn't socialize. Sometimes she didn't leave the house for weeks."

"I looked at your mother's social calendar. The last ten years are backed up. How much do you know about the Texas Assembly?"

Runa sighed. "Just what everyone knows. It's a legislative body that governs the Houses in Texas. Each House has one voting seat. If you are a Prime or a Significant, you are entitled to view the sessions but only the designated House representative can vote. Most people don't go to the sessions unless something important happens. Mom usually went. She liked to know what was happening in the political world."

I nodded. "The Texas Assembly has two main political factions: the Civil Majority and the Stewards. The Civil Majority thinks Houses have enough power and want to keep to themselves. The Stewards want to rule everyone and everything. Every three years the Assembly elects a Speaker. The winning party receives the Gold Staff and the loser is given the Silver Staff. Nine years ago, when the Civil Majority was in power, your mother served as the Gold Staff."

Runa frowned. "I think I remember that. Isn't it mostly ceremonial? She would bring the staff out and bang it onto the floor at the start and end of each Assembly session."

"It is. But it also means that she met most of the Assembly's members and knew all of the major players."

Runa groaned. "It could literally be any member of any House in the state."

"Yep."

The political undercurrents within the Assembly were so complex it would take a supercomputer to sort them out. I made a note of everyone Sigourney was in office with, starting with the former Speaker Linus Duncan. Linus would take my call. He'd served as a witness to the formation of our House. Whether he'd tell me anything was a different question entirely.

We watched Shadow wander about. Arabella was still MIA and worry gnawed at me. My sister could handle herself, but Diatheke's roster of killers was nothing to sneeze at.

"My brother is an emotional zombie, my sister is missing, and I found out that my mom was a hit woman." Runa sighed.

"I'm sorry."

"I suspected. The math just wasn't adding up. She didn't make enough from her forensic work to cover our bills. I mean, it wouldn't even pay my tuition. When you asked me to go through her bank statements, I went back to the beginning of her records twelve years ago. You know what I found? Large deposits for consulting work. A hundred grand, two hundred grand. One was for half a million. Half a million, Catalina."

"Must have been a high-risk target."

"At least she was good at her job, right?" Runa gave a short laugh. "It's one consulting fee after another, and then eight years ago everything just stopped. This was right about the time she told me that she wanted to spend more time with us. She must have stopped 'consulting.'"

"I'm sorry," I told her again.

"I can't ask her any questions. I can't say, 'How could you do this?' or 'What were you thinking?' So I went to my house yesterday. I talked to the ash and then I cried. I might be losing it."

"No," I said. "You're keeping it together just fine. Better than I would."

Runa shook her head. "I looked at the files on the flash drive. I thought maybe she was a kind of Robin Hood, who only killed bad people. She wasn't. She killed whoever they paid her to kill."

In the real world, there was no honor among thieves and no Robin Hood assassins.

She turned to me. "Ragnar can never find out. He wouldn't understand. I can rationalize it somewhat. We were in debt, we were about to lose the house, we would go hungry. I don't condone it, but all my mom knew was how to be a mother, a wife, and a superb poisoner. She was an amazing assassin. I don't even know how she did half of the stuff on that flash drive. So, I'll deal with it. I have no choice. But my brother can never be told. Promise me."

"I promise," I said.

Shadow squatted and peed at a random spot.

I clapped my hands and crooned in a high-pitched voice, "Good girl, good girl."

Runa whistled and made "woo" noises.

Shadow kicked her back legs, trying to scour the pavement, and strutted off.

"About Alessandro," Runa said. "I shouldn't have made the decision to work with him without talking to you. He was there, and he asked me, and I answered honestly. Brain wasn't engaged."

"Don't worry about it. I was just trying to squeeze more information out of him. Your mother hired him to kill her assassin. He isn't going away until he nukes them, so we can either work together or we can keep bumping into each other with unpredictable consequences."

Runa raised her eyebrows. "Are you sure you don't want to keep bumping into him, just a little bit?"

I gave her the Look of Death. "No. I found out that Alessandro has been staying across the street, so I disassembled his car window and then walked into my bedroom and found him posing on my bed like some sort of erotic poster."

"He was posing on your bed? Was he naked?"

"No." *I wish.* "But he was holding the picture I had left on the nightstand."

Runa frowned. "Wait, the picture? The pink, glitter heart picture?"

I nodded. "Yep. That's the one. I took it to my room. And now he knows about my kid crush and he's mocking me."

"Well fuck," Runa said.

"Fuck" was a good way to put it.

"Look on the bright side," Runa said. "If he steps out of line, I can poison him, so blood will come out of both ends simultaneously and continuously."

"Thank you, I think."

"You must think I'm crazy." The smile slid off Runa's face. "Joking while my mother is dead, and my sister is missing. Maybe I am, a little, and if I was by myself, things might be different. But I have my brother. I'm trying my best to not freak the fuck out. I'm trying to be positive and hopeful, and pretending that everything will be okay. But I know nothing is okay and sometimes I just want to scream myself hoarse."

I hugged her. "Runa, you don't owe me or anyone an explanation or an apology. Terrible things have happened to both of you, and you do whatever you need to do to get through it. If you want to strip naked and dance in the street throwing glitter in the air, nobody would blink an eye. It's your grief. You own it."

She wiped her eyes.

The door of Rogan's HQ opened, and Bug emerged into the light of the streetlamp. He wore a clean khaki T-shirt and a pair of dark pants. His face was clean, and his hair was damp and brushed.

"That's my cue to go inside," I told Runa. "This is Bug,

Rogan's surveillance guy I told you about. He doesn't do well with strangers."

"No sudden moves?"

"No, he's okay with sudden moves. Just don't expect him to do small talk."

Runa was right. The lemon roasted chicken did smell amazing.

The entire family had gathered for dinner, all except Arabella. She'd finally charged her phone and replied to my seven texts with "I'm okay, keep your panties on." I composed an eloquent reply rich with four-letter words, sent it to her, and hadn't heard anything back.

The table was full. Mom and Grandma talked quietly; Runa was making eyes at the chicken; Bern and Bug carried on a conversation in low voices. Matilda took the bread rolls off the baking pan and arranged them in a basket. Ragnar volunteered to distribute forks, knives, and napkins. Just a normal Baylor dinner.

Leon, wearing oven mitts, pulled the enormous roasting pan filled with potatoes out of the oven and held it while I scooped them into a pretty white dish.

"Grandma, Aunt Penelope, me and Bern, Bug, Runa and Ragnar, Matilda, and you," Leon said. "Nine people, but ten plates. Who is the extra plate for?"

"We might have a guest for dinner." I put the salad dressing on the table.

"Like who?" He put the pan onto the stove and pulled the oven mitts off.

I opened my mouth to answer. The doorbell rang, echoing through all of our cell phones. Leon tapped his phone. His eyes sparked with indignation. "You've got to be kidding me."

I went to answer the door.

The icy assassin who killed the strike team and then stalked me in my own room was gone. Instead, Instagram Alessandro stood in the doorway, carrying a bottle of wine. He wore impeccably tailored brown pants and an indigo blue dress shirt with the sleeves casually rolled up to his elbows and the top two buttons open, just enough to give a great view of his muscular neck. His boots, leather, ankle-high, and expensive, matched the outfit. His brushed then artfully tousled hair framed his face. He'd shaved, and the masculine perfection of his features was on full display; the sharp angles of his cheekbones, the strong, clean line of his jaw, his sensual mouth . . .

My brain did that thing again, the one where I lost all ability to reason and form complete sentences.

Say something. Something smart.

Our stares connected. His eyes were still the same; calculating, lupine, and heated by amber magic from within.

"You're late," I told him. Yes! Brilliant. I said a thing and it made sense. It had a subject and a verb and they went together. Catalina Baylor one, Instagram Alessandro a big fat zero.

"Beauty takes time."

"Oh, get over yourself." I stepped aside.

He stepped through. *"Permesso."*

I almost answered, *Avanti,* but caught myself. He didn't need to know how much Italian I understood. Instead, I locked the door behind him, and we walked deeper into the house, through the office, through the hallway, and into the kitchen.

Nobody had started eating yet, but people were passing dishes and fixing their plates. They saw Alessandro.

Everything stopped.

He smiled at them, a dazzling, charming smile, warm and happy and a touch shy. When they said a smile could launch a thousand ships, this was the smile they had imagined.

Grandma Frida put down the salad bowl, raised her phone, and snapped a pic.

"No phones at the table," Mom said on autopilot, her gaze fixed on Alessandro.

"I'm not missing this shot, Penelope."

"*Buonasera*," Alessandro crooned. "Thank you so much for inviting me to dinner. I haven't had a home-made meal in weeks."

When I'd spoken to him an hour ago, he'd had a mere trace of an accent. Now he sounded like he'd jumped out of a Fellini film onto the red carpet.

Bern crossed his arms. Leon scowled. Bug looked like a surprised hedgehog with all his needles up in the air.

Alessandro pretended not to notice and handed the wine bottle to Leon.

Leon took it, baring his teeth. "Keep your filthy hands off my cousin."

Alessandro smiled again, his face serene, as if Leon had just complimented him on his choice of wine. "Please forgive me, the selection in the local stores is rather limited, but I was able to find a decent variety of Grenache."

"You can take that wine and shove—" Leon started.

"Leon," Mom said.

He clicked his jaw shut and went to get the wine-glasses.

"Thank you for the wine," Mom said. "Please join us."

Alessandro stepped to my chair and held it out for me. Runa leaned on her elbow, clearly enjoying the show.

Grabbing the chair and hitting him with it was out of the question. I sat and let him scoot it closer to the table for me.

A phone flashed as Grandma took another picture. I clenched my teeth and stared straight ahead.

We passed the food around.

"You're very pretty," Matilda observed. "Are you a prince?"

"No," he told her with another dazzling smile. "Only a conte. A count."

"Hot damn," Grandma Frida said.

A quiet thud sounded. My mother had set her glass down with some force.

For a brief time, nobody spoke as everyone dug into the food.

Alessandro ate like a starving wolf. His manners were flawless, but the food disappeared off his plate with staggering speed. He finished it all and went in for seconds.

"This is delicious," Ragnar said around a mouthful of food.

"The chicken is *ottimo*," Alessandro said, looking at my mother. "*La cena migliore che abbia mai mangiato*. Absolutely wonderful. I could eat this every day until I die."

The chicken was "delicious," and it was the "best dinner he had ever eaten." Give me a break. And so much Italian too. He was laying the charm on thick. Oh, look at me, I'm Alessandro, so handsome, so refined, at such a disadvantage because I don't speak good English and have to reach for my native tongue. He probably had a better English vocabulary than I did. Ugh.

"I didn't cook it," Mom said. "Catalina did."

Alessandro froze.

Ha! Didn't expect that, did you?

"That's nothing," Runa said. "Just wait until you taste her pithivier. It's to die for."

I glared at her. She gave me a look of pure innocence and went back to eating.

Alessandro made a short cough that sounded suspiciously like choking. "There is a pithivier?"

"Yes," I said.

He put his fork down and faced me, his expression besotted.

Do not blush, do not blush . . .

Alessandro opened his mouth. "Marry me."

"If she says yes, shoot him," Bern said to Leon, his face completely serious. "She'll thank us later."

Bug stirred in his seat. "Catalina, do not marry this dickfucker. There are better birds in the sea." He turned to my mom and said, "Pardon my French."

Matilda leaned forward, looked at Alessandro, then looked at me. "Your children would be very attractive."

Alessandro winked at Matilda. "Thank you. You are most kind."

Runa covered her face with her hands and made some whimpering noises.

Okay, no. I had to nip this in the bud. "Matilda, picking a husband is more complicated than just selecting an attractive mate. He has to be smart and kind, and he has to be a good person."

Alessandro glanced at me. The sharp fire in his eyes sparked and vanished before anyone else noticed.

Runa's cell rang. She took her hands from her face and looked at my mom.

Mom sighed. "Go ahead."

Runa answered it and frowned. "Uh, Mr. Moody?"

Sigourney Etterson's financial adviser.

The table went completely silent. Bern pulled a tablet out of thin air and set it to record.

"So you want me to come to your office, right now?" Runa asked, and held the phone out at arm's length toward us.

"Yes," a distant male voice said. "It's urgent."

"I understand it's urgent, Mr. Moody. I just don't understand why. My mother has been dead for four days, and I'm the executor of the estate. Why do I have to see you in person, now?"

"I can't discuss this over the phone."

"Yes, but it's almost seven o'clock, it's dark, and your office is across town. Can you come here instead?"

"I have documents I need to show you. They're of a sensitive nature and cannot leave my office."

"Why can't I see the documents tomorrow?"

His voice spiked into exasperation. "If you want to see a cent from your mother's estate, you need to come here as soon as possible. Tomorrow may be too late."

The call cut off. Runa put the phone down. "He hung up."

Bern turned the tablet toward us. On it a white, dark-haired, middle-aged man smiled into the camera. He was the type my mom called the "good ole boy in a suit." He could have been handsome in high school in an I-love-football way, but time, indulgent diet, and money had softened and thickened his features. He looked like he wore suits to work, drove an expensive car, and practiced trustworthy smiles in the mirror to more effectively separate clients from their money.

"Dennis George Moody II," Bern announced. "Fifty years old, married twice, adult son from the first marriage, two children from the second. MBA from Baylor. Series 7 license from FINRA, which enables him to sell stocks, bonds, options and futures, in addition to the sale of packaged securities. Never declared bankruptcy. One DUI arrest in college, nothing since. Wife sells real estate. Good credit score and a two-million-dollar house, three quarters paid off."

"Wow," Ragnar said. "You found all of that in three minutes?"

"No," Bern told him. "Catalina ran a background check on Moody because he's mentioned in your mother's financial documents. I just pulled up the file."

"How well do you know him?" I asked Runa.

Runa shrugged. "I've seen him at Christmas parties once or twice."

"He was helping Mom to readjust her portfolio in response to the market slowdown and recession," Ragnar said. "He's been our financial adviser for four years. I interviewed him for my economics class essay. He doesn't belong to any House and he's proud of being a self-made man, his words."

"So, he isn't a friend of the family?" Mom asked.

"No," Ragnar said. "Mom worked with him closely, but I wouldn't call him a family friend."

"This is a trap," Runa declared.

Leon rolled his eyes. "Of course, it's a trap, Admiral Ackbar. The relevant question is, is he working for them voluntarily or do they have a gun to his head?"

Grandma Frida wrinkled her nose. "He's a money guy. They waved a check under his nose and he followed."

"I can't believe they would think I'm so gullible," Runa said.

"Not gullible," Bernard said. "Impulsive and prone to panic."

She stared at him, mortally offended. My cousin remained stoic.

"Panic?" Runa asked in the kind of voice one normally proclaimed, *Do you know who I am?*

"You did poison Conway," Leon pointed out.

"Oh my God! I poison one guy and now all of Houston thinks I'm a raging idiot."

"Wait," Ragnar said. "You poisoned somebody?"

"It's a long story, I'll tell you later."

They wanted Runa to leave the warehouse, which meant she had to stay here. But Moody just designated himself as an excellent lead. He knew something, and I wanted him to share it with me. I wished Arabella hadn't left. The safest thing to do was to wait until Heart got here, but for all we knew, someone from Diatheke had a gun to Moody's head, and if we delayed, he'd be a corpse by the time we got there.

"I need your keys," I told Runa. "It will go smoother if I drive your car."

"I'm coming with you. He asked to talk to me."

Leon tapped his plate with his fork and raised his hands like a conductor. "Three, two, one . . ."

"No," we all chorused.

I caught a glimpse of Alessandro. He leaned back in his chair with a resigned expression. He knew where this would go, and he was waiting for us to get there. He caught me looking and nodded slightly. He wanted in on the Moody thing and I would be an idiot to go there without backup.

"The rule of thumb is, do the opposite of what the bad guys want you to do," Leon said. "They want you to go to Moody's office, so you have to stay here."

"Leon is right," I said. "If I wanted to kill you, I would try to lure you out of the warehouse. And then, once I figured out that my ruse had failed, I would hit the warehouse as hard as I could. The most prudent thing would be for all of us to stay here. But somebody must either rescue him or ask him some very important questions, like who convinced him to make that phone call. Arabella is gone, so we're shorthanded until Sergeant Heart and his people get here, which should be in a couple of hours. Until then, you and Leon are our best defenses."

"Excuse me?" Grandma Frida said.

"You, Leon, Grandma Frida, Bern, Mom, and Matilda are our best defenses. There, did I leave anybody out?"

Ragnar raised his hand.

"I will instruct Zeus," Matilda promised. "He is excellent at close quarters defense."

Alessandro cleared his throat. *Yes, I know, I know.*

I looked straight at Runa. "I'm going to Moody's office and I need you to stay here and protect the kids. Please give me your keys."

Runa dug in her pocket and tossed me the rental's keychain.

 **Chapter 10**

Being brave was easy in the kitchen, surrounded by my family. But by the time I got to the back door, all of my courage had evaporated. We were about to drive to a place where people would try to kill us. While we were gone, the warehouse was very likely going to be attacked, and Arabella wasn't here to defend it. I had no doubt that my family could hold the fort. But my sister's presence guaranteed a quick victory.

I stepped into my office and grabbed a ratty trench coat off the coatrack. My hands shook.

This was ridiculous.

I moved around the office, collecting things I'd need. Let's see; chalk, spare magazine for the Beretta, phone, keys, what was I forgetting? The sword sheath. I would take the gladius again. It offered the most versatility. I took the sheath out of the cabinet. Driving with it on would be a pain in the butt, so I would buckle it on after we got there.

Alessandro leaned against the door frame and watched me. "It's very you." He gave the office an elegant sweep of his hand.

Very me? He didn't even know who I was. "How so?"

"Organized and businesslike." He said it like a condemnation.

"It's a business office. It's supposed to be organized and businesslike. This is where I work."

He strolled into the office, reached behind my monitor, and swiped his finger across the desk's surface. "No dust."

"That's a good thing," I told him. "Dust is bad for computers and people."

"Have you ever tried making a mess, Catalina?"

"I don't make messes, I clean them up." And now I was sounding like a renegade detective from some edgy cop drama.

Alessandro shuddered. "Ooh, so hardcore."

I ignored him. It was that or throw something, and the chief of police said next time it would be my badge.

I pushed past him and walked out to my car. He followed. I couldn't see him behind me, but I knew exactly how much space separated us. Sometimes Matilda and I took Zeus to her aunt's property on the edge of Houston, to walk the trails through the woods. The moment we let him out of the car, Zeus melted into the brush. He would follow us while we took the path, invisible but always there, a dangerous predatory presence gliding through the woods like a ghost, watching us. Walking with Alessandro behind me was just like that.

I took my gladius and slid it into its sheath. The holster was next. I didn't feel any need to hide it from Moody. I fitted the Beretta into its holster, locked my car, and went to Runa's Nissan.

Alessandro held out his hand. "Keys."

I made a face at him, popped the locks open with the fob, and put my coat and sword in its sheath in the backseat.

"Catalina."

I got into the driver's seat and shut the door.

Alessandro knocked on my window. I could just drive off, but then I would have to go to Moody's office by myself. It wasn't like he could follow me in his car. Oh, oh, that was good.

I rolled the window down. "I thought you'd follow in your Jeep."

Alessandro leaned his right arm on the top of the car and bent forward, so our faces were close. The urge to scoot out of the way gripped me.

"I get it," he said. "You had to put on a show for your family. But it's just us now. I'll drop you off at a coffee shop, go see Moody, and pick you up on the way back."

Who the hell did he think he was? "Amazing."

"Give me the keys," he said.

"You have two choices. You can get in the passenger seat or you can stand there looking stupid as I drive away." I rolled the window up and started the car.

He didn't move. I wiggled my fingers at him in a little bye-bye wave, put the car into reverse, and eased my foot off the brake. The Nissan rolled a bit. He stepped back to save his feet.

I let the car move back another foot.

He looked like he wanted to take the door off the Nissan with his bare hands and pull me out of it.

Another foot. Last chance, Alessandro. I really didn't want to go there without him. Thinking about it turned my insides cold. But I would if he left me no choice.

Alessandro circled around the front to the passenger side. I unlocked the door. He got in, and suddenly there wasn't enough air. He stole it all, saturating the car with menace. It rolled off him in waves.

I pulled my phone out and snapped a picture of him. Mine.

He glared at me, his eyes full of orange flames.

"For my private collection," I told him. "Seat belt, please."

Moody ran his business from an office building on Bering Drive, sandwiched between the multimillion-dollar mansions of the Villages in the west and the less luxurious but still prosperous neighborhoods of Tanglewood in the east. The traffic was decent for Houston, and the eight-mile drive to Bering took us only twenty minutes.

I turned right and continued down the street. We were almost there.

Alessandro hadn't said a word since he had buckled his seat belt.

Any other time, the prospect of spending twenty minutes in a car with Alessandro would have petrified me. He filled the vehicle, his presence much larger than his physical body, and his magic simmered just above his skin. I felt it, a volatile power ready to lash out. The faint scent of his shampoo or soap, herbal and slightly spicy, curled around me, enticing and distracting. It was just me and him, together in the car, with the night wrapping around us like a length of smoky velvet.

It would have been shockingly intimate, except that the memories of slitting a human throat with my sword cycled through my head. I saw myself kill over and over, I smelled the blood, I heard the hoarse gasp one of them made through my fingers clamped on his mouth. We weren't driving to dinner where Alessandro would be charming and clever and make me laugh while I drank my wine. We were going to do terrible things.

Alessandro reached over and touched my right hand. I jerked my hand off the wheel, the Nissan veered right, and I caught it just before it jumped the curb. I glared at him. I must have seemed a bit freaked out, because he rolled his eyes.

"The coffee shop offer is still on the table."

"What the hell was that?"

"You were gripping the wheel so tight, I thought your fingers would break."

"I wasn't." Yes, I was. My hands hurt.

"I'm good at this. I won't let you get hurt. We'll get what we need, get home, and I'll sample that mythical pithivier I've been promised. We'll have dessert, we'll have coffee, everything will be fine. You won't die there."

"That's not what I was afraid of."

"You're not scared of dying?"

"I am. And I'm scared of getting hurt. But I'm more afraid of what I'll have to do to walk out of there."

For a long moment we were both silent.

"You can always stay in the car," he offered, his voice seductive, as if he were trying to tempt me with expensive chocolate. "Or you can come inside and watch me work and tell me how good I am. I'm very susceptible to flattery."

"Not susceptible, Alessandro. More like dependent on, addicted to, live only for."

I pulled into the nearly deserted parking lot overshadowed by trees. The twelve-floor office building towered over the lot, its big black windows dark. Only the lobby was lit, a haven of warm electric light trying to push back the night.

"So judgmental," Alessandro said. His tone was light,

his mouth was smirking, but the humor didn't reach his eyes. They were hard and sharp. "First you tell your family that I'm a bad person, now you're accusing me of vanity."

"I have an idea. Why don't I go in and you can sit here in the car and look pretty?"

He heaved a dramatic sigh. "But what would I do alone for hours with no one to admire me?"

"Take selfies, kill random people, take selfies of you killing random people?"

"Is that why you think I'm not a good person?"

"No, lots of people take selfies. You just do it more than most."

I stared at the building looming in front of us. I had to get out of the car.

Alessandro turned, leaned over, and looked me in the eyes. "Catalina."

I really hated the way he said my name. It cut through the constant busy hum of my thoughts like a knife. I could never let him learn about it, because then he'd purr my name in the middle of random conversations just to mess with me.

"You don't have to go in there. Once I'm out of the car, drive away. Don't park anywhere, keep moving. I'll call you when it's done."

I opened my door and got out of the car. The cold night air bit at me. I shivered, retrieved my sword sheath, buckled it on, and put on my trench coat. The weight of the weapons inside was comforting and familiar, like hugging an old friend. I started toward the building.

He caught up with me. "Why are you so stubborn?"

"I'm here because a girl is missing. Someone killed her mother in a horrific way and took her from her bed in the middle of the night. It's wrong and I'm going to fix it. As much as it can be fixed. It's my job, Alessandro."

"Good," he said.

The doors slid open at our approach. The cavernous lobby lay empty, the grey and cream modern walls rising two stories high. A polished concrete floor, a matching shade of grey, reflected the cluster of white oval lights floating like glass jellyfish suspended from the ceiling by thin wires. At the opposite wall, a bank of elevators offered access to the top floors.

After the gloom of the parking lot, walking into a brightly lit, huge space, with its polished floor and shiny light fixtures, was like striding out of a dark passage into a sun-drenched arena. The sound of our steps sent echoes scurrying up the tall walls. In my imagination, they morphed into the beating of a drum counting heartbeats until the start of a fight. The space between my shoulders itched, expecting a bullet. I couldn't see the other fighters, but I knew they were waiting.

We passed the empty reception counter and walked to the wall opposite the entrance, to a bank of elevators. On our right a small waiting area offered ultramodern grey loveseats and a coffee table with a selection of magazines, their bright covers fanned across the wood. On the left a narrow hallway led to two doors, one marked as an exit and the other as stairs.

I checked the directory posted next to the elevators. Moody's office was on the second floor. The elevator would be a trap. All they had to do was stop it between floors and we would be sitting ducks.

"Stairs," Alessandro said.

I nodded.

We turned left, into the hallway. As we reached the end, Alessandro leaned on the metal bar of the exit door.

It didn't budge. Locked. One way in, one way out. Better and better.

I tried the door to the stairs. It swung open, revealing a concrete staircase. I held the door open and listened.

Silence.

Alessandro glided past me and went up the first flight of stairs, completely silent, like a ghost. I followed him, carefully, quietly, moving at a measured pace. A few tense breaths, and we emerged into a simple hallway, lined with a charcoal rug. A row of doors, each an identical wooden frame with frosted glass, punctuated the right wall, with small signs identifying the individual offices. We started down the hallway, Alessandro stalking next to me on quiet feet. The signs slid by.

L.M. Markham, CPA
Eunice C. Roberts, Affinity Insurance
Dennis George Moody, Moody Investments

The rapid staccato of someone typing filtered through the frosted glass. Alessandro reached for the door handle, swung the door open, and held it for me. I walked into a cozy office with a desk on the right and a couple of chairs on the left. A woman sat behind the desk, typing at the computer. She was Hispanic, in her sixties, and as I walked in, she raised her head and gave me a smile.

"Runa Etterson?"

"Yes," I lied.

She opened her mouth, saw Alessandro, and stopped for a befuddled second. "And who are you?"

"My personal assistant," I said.

My personal assistant dazzled the receptionist with one of his armada-launching smiles.

The woman finally recovered. "Mr. Moody is waiting

for you. You go on right ahead, it's the second door on your right."

We walked deeper into the office suite. The short reception area terminated in a hallway. We turned right and found the second door. It stood wide open, and we went through it.

Moody looked just like the headshot on his website: broad-shouldered, not exactly fat, but thick through the chest and middle, the way football players sometimes got thick in the offseason. He was probably strong, but he wouldn't be fast, and if he had to chase me, he would be slow to build up speed. His desk matched him, massive and solid. The pinewood had been cut against the grain and stained with waxed tobacco to imitate a rustic Old West look. The rest of the decor in the office went along with the desk; a Texas star on the wall, a huge map of Texas, cowhide rug on the floor, the client chairs upholstered in dark leather. Good Old Texas, reliable and trustworthy. The desktop was the only modern touch.

"You're not Runa Etterson," Moody observed.

"Clearly, I'm not," Alessandro said.

"Not you. Her." Moody pointed at me.

I let him see a glimpse of my feathers. "That's okay." My magic surged through my words, stretching for him. "Runa is a very good friend of mine. You can tell me whatever you wanted to tell her."

My power wrapped around him, twisting like a magical grapevine spiraling over his body. I could apply it delicately, light as gossamer. I could do it so subtly that after I was done asking my questions, Moody wouldn't even remember the conversation. But Moody didn't seem like a man who had a gun to his head. His posture showed no tension or nervousness, his eyes didn't betray any apprehension. He sat behind his desk, completely at ease except for being annoyed that Runa hadn't come herself. A man whose life depended on Runa's presence would have panicked.

There was no need to be gentle with him. He was in this up to his eyeballs.

I sank more magic into my voice. "I'll be sure to let Runa know everything you tell me."

Moody smiled at me and sat up straighter in his chair. "Well, I guess that's okay, then. Please have a seat."

I sat down. Alessandro remained standing right behind me.

"Why did you call Runa?" I asked.

"I have these papers."

My magic was all around him now. He was breathing it in, it seeped through his pores, and I shook my feathers at him one more time.

"Are these papers important?"

Moody's smile widened. "Nah, they're some bullshit I cooked up. You're a really nice girl, you know that?"

"Thank you, Mr. Moody. Why did you cook up bullshit papers?"

"I got a call from Diatheke and they asked me to do it. I mean, it's a small thing, and they pay me enough, by God."

And there it was. "How long have you worked for Diatheke?"

"About four years. They called me right after Sigourney hired me. What was I supposed to do, turn down easy money?"

You greedy asshole. "And what did Diatheke require from you in return for that easy money?"

He chuckled. "Not much. I was supposed to tell them if she made sudden large deposits."

Benedict wanted to know if Sigourney started doing jobs on her own.

"And of course, now they called me to get Runa out here."

"What do they want with Runa?"

He shrugged. "Hell if I know. Who cares about Runa, anyway? Let's talk about you."

Let's not. "Do you know who killed Sigourney?"

He shook his head. "Nope. Don't know, don't wanna know, don't need to know. She must have pissed off some powerful people and it ain't my business."

The more we talked, the more the polish of education wore off. He sounded more Texas country with every word. I needed to wrap this up, or he would chase after me, and Alessandro would shoot him. He deserved it, but I didn't want to murder anyone we didn't have to kill. Besides, there were better ways to punish.

"Do you know what happened to Halle?"

"Burned up with her momma."

"Are we done?" I asked Alessandro.

"Ask him who his contact was at Diatheke."

"Who did you talk to at Diatheke?" I asked.

"Some lady named Jocelyn."

"I'm done," Alessandro said.

I yanked my magic back. Moody gasped, throwing himself back against his chair, his spine rigid, his eyes glassy.

I got up, turning around. Alessandro had this cold look in his eyes, as if Moody wasn't a human, but some centipede that had slithered out of the drain and needed to be stepped on.

"We have to go," I told him.

He didn't move. "Wait for me in the front office. I'll catch up with you."

"Alessandro, please."

He sighed and turned to the door. "If that's what you want."

The receptionist waved at us as we passed her. "Y'all drive safe now."

We were out of the hallway and going down the stairs when I heard the scream.

Alessandro paused midway on the stairs.

"He won't come after us," I told him.

"I wasn't worried. What did you do to him?"

"He's been to Sigourney's home. He's met her children. She invited him to holiday parties. The entire time he was spying on her. And after she died, he tried to lure her daughter here knowing that nothing good would come from it. I can remove my magic gently or I can do it the way I did it to Moody. I'm told it feels like the love of your life has died in front of you. I wanted him to feel grief. It's all he can feel right now, and it will take him a long time to heal."

"So, he's suffering?"

"Yes."

Alessandro gave me a narrow smile. Just a hint of fangs. "I like your way better."

We exited the stairs into the lobby hallway and kept walking. This was too easy. Why get us all the way out here and not do anything about it? Maybe once they realized that Runa hadn't shown up, they dropped the whole thing and went to the warehouse to get her.

"We could be cutting Moody apart with a bone saw right now, and Diatheke wouldn't give a crap, would they?"

Alessandro shook his head. "Sigourney's dead. They

have no further use for him. He's a loose end. We didn't cut it, but they will."

"Who's Jocelyn?" I asked.

"A psionic. Upper-range Significant. Experienced. Strong. Dangerous."

We rounded the corner. A person stood in front of glass doors, blocking our escape. Tall, wrapped in a black coat, deep hood hiding his face. More a dark shadow than a human, a smudge of night in the lobby flooded with electric light.

Hello.

The hooded figure thrust its hands to the sides, palms up. The mage pose. A knot of black smoke burst into life above him and surged open, spiraling out like a blossoming flower, a deep indigo darkness shot through with blue lightning at its center.

A summoning portal.

Alessandro raised his arms, a gun in each hand, and fired.

Before the first shot rang out, the portal flared with blinding white and a swarm of flying creatures tore out of it. Bright psychotic green splashed with blotches of yellow and crimson, they swirled in front of the summoner, hiding him from view, each beast the size of a turkey vulture and shaped like a bloated tick with beetle wings and six long segmented legs. The swarm churned, chaotic, contracting and expanding like a flock of monstrous birds, the creatures zipping back and forth.

I pulled my Beretta out and fired into the mass of whiplike tails and big mouths lined with serrated teeth. The gun spat thunder and I counted the shots.

One, two, three . . .

A few bodies dropped, leaking nacre-colored ichor, but more kept coming, spilling out of the portal. This was beyond any summoner Prime on record without a complex, House-grade arcane circle to help them. There was no circle under the summoner's feet.

Four, five . . .

They kept coming and coming. Too many. We had to get out of the lobby.

We backed up in unison, moving toward the stairs.

Six. Seven.

The swarm built on itself, so big it filled the lobby like a storm cloud come to life.

In a single smooth move, Alessandro lowered his arms, letting the two guns clatter to the floor, and raised them again without a pause, a new firearm in each hand. He squeezed the triggers, and bullets punched into the beasts. *How?*

Metal clanged behind me, the exit door swinging open. Pressure smashed into my mind, searing hot, trying to crush my will. I lunged to the side to cover Alessandro's back and snapped my wings open, taking the brunt of the mental attack on my feathers.

The pressure battered my defenses. A psionic. At least a Significant, maybe higher.

Alessandro whipped around, looked over my shoulder, and fired a rapid burst down the hallway. Boom, boom, boom.

"Stay behind me," I ground out.

If I turned around, I'd have to engage the psionic full-on. Once two mental mages locked in combat on a mental plane, there was no moving. I couldn't fight a mental duel with flying scorpion ticks trying to rip us apart.

The first wave of creatures dived at us, screeching. Alessandro shot, quick, barely bothering to aim, the steady gunfire mixing with the shrieks of the summoned beasts into a deafening cacophony. The scorpion ticks rained on the floor. Every bullet he sent hit and killed a target.

A beast dove at me, flying low. I raised my gun and fired. The creature crashed to the floor by my feet, splitting open. Ichor spilled onto the polished floor. An acrid, salty stench washed over me. I gagged.

The pressure turned into pain, the dull battering ram of the psionic's magic splitting into sharp spikes trying to rend my defenses. Claws tore at my side, slicing across my thigh in an ice-cold burn. I fired to the side on instinct, without turning to look. A shriek answered and died.

The swarm flailed around us. I couldn't even see the walls. Claws cut my left arm, then my right.

Alessandro dropped the guns. A machete appeared in his right hand.

"Elevators!" he barked.

I had to save my bullets. I thrust the gun into its holster and pulled my gladius out. We sliced at the swarm, carving a way through it. Alessandro cut a path ahead of me, slicing, chopping, cutting in a controlled frenzy. A step. Another step. The battering ram of the psionic's magic hammered against my will. If my defenses broke, the psionic would flood my mind with fear, rage, or any of the other primal emotions, smothering all conscious thought.

I stumbled after Alessandro, hacking with my gladius on pure instinct, almost collided with the wall, and frantically pushed the call button.

A creature smacked into the wall on my right. Ichor splattered my face. Oh, gross. I pushed the button again. *Come on. Come on!*

The elevator chimed. The doors took forever to open.

"Get in!" Alessandro shouted and hurled his gun into the swarm.

I dove in, grabbed his jacket, and pulled him back into the elevator. A scorpion tick thrust in behind him, trying to claw at Alessandro's arms with its segmented legs. Alessandro chopped at it with the machete. The beast screeched, ichor and severed legs flying everywhere. I punched the panel, lighting up all floors, and mashed the close doors button.

The doors started closing, ever so slowly, the swarm surging toward us like a tsunami through a shrinking gap.

Close, close, close!

The doors shut. The cabin slid up. The pressure on my mind vanished and I exhaled.

Alessandro raised his hands, flexing his fingers. I ejected the magazine out of my Beretta and slid the full one in. I still had eight bullets left, but I might need fifteen bullets fast.

The digital display counted off the floors: 2, 3, 4 . . . I had pressed all of them. The elevator should have stopped.

"They're taking us to the roof," I guessed. On the roof there would be nowhere to hide.

"Yes." His face was grim. "Stay close to me."

"What is your Antistasi range?"

"Not far," he said.

When he'd used it on me, he'd been within touching distance. During the trials, when he was defending himself, he was about fifteen feet away. That was probably the extent of his range. He would have to get close to either mage to negate their magic, and neither the summoner nor the psionic would let him do that.

A summoner and a psionic. A far easier plan would have been to snipe us as we exited the building. Benedict had tried a strike team, and when that hadn't worked, he sent two magic users perfectly paired to pin down and capture a Prime. Benedict wanted me alive.

The elevator door slid open and delivered us into a small room. On the left was a metal door marked stairs. On the right an open doorway gaped, leading to the roof, its door missing.

Alessandro tried the stairs door, then rammed it with his shoulder. It held.

"Barred from the other side."

The elevator slid down.

A soft thud sounded from the other side of the stairs door, then another, followed by a shriek. The scorpion ticks had flooded the stairway. In a few moments they would be in the elevator shaft too.

I needed to get an arcane circle going fast. Most commercial buildings had flat concrete roofs.

I sprinted for the doorway and into the night.

A rectangular roof stretched in front of me, lit up by orange lights along its perimeter and perfectly flat except for the stubby row of AC units to the far right. Gravel crunched under my feet. A tar and gravel roof. It wasn't smooth enough for a circle. The gravel would break the lines. Damn it.

Behind me Alessandro marched out of the utility room.

A whirlwind of green spiraled up over the building's edge, directly opposite us, smashed into the roof, breaking into individual creatures, and vomited the summoner onto the gravel. He landed on his side, awkward, and staggered to his feet, his movements jerky and disjointed. The scorpion ticks circled him, whipping about. I could see glimpses of him, but I had no shot. Pumping bullets into the swarm was futile. I might as well just toss the gun over the side of the building.

To the left of me, Alessandro strode forward, putting himself into the path of the swarm. I moved to my right to get a clear shot.

The summoner focused on Alessandro, his swarm thickening to counter an attack from his direction. His coat hung open, revealing a thin body and a face that was no longer human. His skin had a sickly bluish tint, stretched too tightly over his features. His forehead protruded over his temples and the corners of his jaw were too far apart, as if someone had grafted extra bones onto a human skull.

Revulsion squirmed through me. The mix of human and insect felt wrong on a deep, primal level.

The summoner opened his mouth and hissed.

He was warped, and he was using magic. And doing a damn good job.

I reached out with my magic, trying to sense his mind. It was there, a weak, pale glow to my mind's eye. The scorpion ticks streamed over him, each a faint greenish dot of primitive sentience. They buzzed around him like bees. On their own, they wouldn't deter me, but collectively, they formed a mental veil that wrapped around him, all parts of it communicating, connected, and one.

I was looking at an alien hive mind.

This was so far out of my frame of reference, I didn't know how to go about attacking it. I couldn't even tell if he was human enough for my siren call to work.

Alessandro pulled a nail gun out of thin air, dropped it, lifted up a shovel, threw it, and came up with a tennis racket–shaped bug zapper. He hurled it at the swarm. It sparked, and one of the scorpion ticks went into a swan dive, landed a few feet from me, and lay on the ground twitching.

I can't even . . .

A small flock of scorpion ticks tore out of the utility room behind our backs and swallowed us. The creatures washed over me, scratching, biting, stinging, tearing my clothes and skin. One clamped onto my leg. I shot it. It stopped chewing on me, but hung from my jeans, dead. A scorpion tick tore at my hair. I grabbed it by its tail, yanked it off, and slammed it onto the gravel. They were shredding us. I wouldn't last much longer.

Alessandro barked a short "Ha!"

A stream of fire arched over my head and seared the swarm. Bodies plunged down, burning. The air around me was suddenly clear and I spun left. He had a small black flamethrower in each hand, the fire pouring from them in twin orange jets. A maniacal grin twisted his face, lit up by the flames. His eyes glinted. I had never seen him so happy.

The summoner screamed, an odd, guttural sound.

All around me scorpion ticks dropped out of the night sky, fell to the roof, and kept burning. The stench of chemicals, fire, and singed hair filled the air. Thick black smoke poured from the flames. It looked like a medieval painting of hell come to life, and Alessandro Sagredo was its devil.

The flamethrowers sputtered and died.

"*Ma porca puttana*," Alessandro swore, his voice ice-cold. "*Ne andasse dritta una!*"

A second swarm coiled over the edge of the building to our right, broke apart, and deposited a middle-aged black woman onto the roof. The receptionist from Diatheke. She still wore the same dark suit with a string of pearls, except now it was torn from dozens of scorpion tick claws.

Alessandro was right. Everything had gone wrong today.

I snapped my wings open and hit her with a stream of my magic. My power crashed against the solid wall of her will.

"Thank you, Lawrence," the psionic ground out.

Her defenses wrapped around her mind in layers. She'd had them up before she ever set foot on this roof and they were entrenched, their pattern old. She must have maintained them for decades and now activating them would come effortlessly to her.

Her magic was combat grade, mine wasn't. She relied on direct assault, while I beguiled and used subterfuge until my magic gained hold. If I had surprised her or if I had the time and opportunity to draw a circle, it would be a different story. I had her pinned with the blunt press of my power, but that was as much as I could do. If we had been swordsmen, I would be a large strong fighter beating my blade on the shield of a more skilled, more experienced opponent. She made no effort to parry me. She knew that once she engaged me on the mental plane, only one of us would be left standing, and I was a Prime of unknown power. She refused to commit. Instead she sat behind her shell like a turtle and bided her time.

I began to hum, sending tendrils of my magic through my voice, trying to wrap them around the mental sphere of her defenses and trying to burrow into it.

The scorpion ticks regrouped, readying for the next assault. They hung around Lawrence like a maelstrom. The summoner's jaws moved continuously, cracking invisible walnuts between his teeth. His eyes bulged out of his skull. He'd planted his feet. The muscles on his shoulders bunched, causing the sleeves of his trench coat to ride up his arms. Everything about him emanated rage.

There was no pain feedback between the summoner and the summoned. Mages like Lawrence reached into the arcane realm, pulled creatures out, and sent them to do their bidding. Alessandro's pyrotechnics hadn't injured Lawrence, but they did piss him off. He looked like he couldn't wait to tear Alessandro's head off.

It was a standoff. Lawrence wouldn't move until he knew what weapon Alessandro would conjure, and for some reason, Alessandro did nothing. Out of the corner of my eye, I saw him, his magic winding about him shining with orange fire. He watched both Lawrence and the psionic, his hands empty, a look of intense concentration on his face.

Little flashes of pain flared in random spots on my body. The adrenaline was wearing off, and I was bleeding from a dozen places.

I managed a Victoria Tremaine sneer. "If you run away now, I might not chase you until tomorrow."

"The name is Jocelyn Rake, my dear. I don't run and I don't chase. And your cheap parlor tricks won't work on me."

"You just chased me through the building."

The effort to keep her pinned wore on me. It took all my concentration to keep her where she was. Magic flowed out of me in a steady torrent. I had spent a lot of my power at Keystone and now I was deep into my reserves. Soon they would run out. I couldn't keep this up too much longer, and if Lawrence unleashed the swarm again, I would be done.

Jocelyn sneered back. "You're a talented amateur. But I'm a professional. I didn't survive this long by losing battles. I'll kill you and be home in time to watch *Out of Order* and drink a glass of wine before bed."

"You're not leaving this roof." My magic had grown

with every word, but the tendrils of my power drummed against her mental shields without doing any damage. This was about to end, one way or another.

Jocelyn bared her teeth. "Big words for a little girl. I know all about you. You were the spare and now you're the heir. You won't elbow me out of the way like you did your sister."

What?

"Look at you. You wanted to be in charge so badly, you climbed over your own flesh and blood to do it. It must have burned you that you had to follow her lead. She's married and rich and so pretty, and here you are, an ugly dark duckling." Jocelyn clicked her tongue. "You sad little thing. Couldn't match your sister in anything else, so you decided to be the Head of your sad little House, climbed over her, and now you'll die here, and your sister will laugh and laugh . . ."

The words burned. She wanted me to throw everything I had at her. I would exhaust my magic on her shell, then she would hit Alessandro, and Lawrence would finish us. I saw it in my head, me dying, curled into a fetal ball as the swarm tore at me, Alessandro running off the building, his eyes full of rage.

"Stop talking," Lawrence spat, his voice low and inhuman. The swarm subtly realigned itself to face me and Jocelyn. "Kill the bitch. Kill the asshole. Bugs eat. We get paid."

He could speak. He understood words.

"Hush, Lawrence," Jocelyn told him. "You have your orders."

"Fuck it. Kill, eat, go."

Lawrence, a man of simple pleasures.

"You take orders from her?" Alessandro asked Lawrence. "She's old and weak."

Lawrence refocused on Alessandro, the swarm around him shifting in his direction.

"Hey, Lawrence, how about this? Kill her and we'll go out for drinks. We will even find some roadkill for your friends."

"Lawrence!" Jocelyn snapped.

"Yes, Lawrence," Alessandro taunted. "Be a good boy and listen to Mommy."

Lawrence opened his mouth. "Fuck you, shithead."

"Such eloquence," Alessandro noted. "Poetry in the flesh. No wonder she has you on a leash."

Lawrence hissed at him.

"He's all talk, but you got nothing to say?" Jocelyn mocked me. "Hey, pretty boy, your girlfriend weighed the odds, and she doesn't like them. I can see it in her face. You understand, don't you, little girl? There is nothing either of you can do, except die."

"Switch," Alessandro said, the single word cracking like a whip.

A new, longer flamethrower popped into his hands, white letters on the side spelling out "Property of the Houston Fire Department." A twenty-foot jet of flame tore into the swarm and died. The scorpion ticks shied from the flame and heat, opening a gap.

I dropped my magic, spun to my left, and ran into the hole in the mass of insects. Behind me, the flamethrower roared, spitting fire at Jocelyn.

Hadn't weighed those odds, had you?

The swarm surged to me, but it was too late. I charged through them, arms crossed to shield my face, knocking the small bodies out of the way. It was like trying to fight my way through a ball of barbed wire. Lawrence loomed in front of me, his eyes surprised and burning with fury. He bared his teeth at me, all three rows of them. I threw myself at him, hugging his neck, so we were face-to-face, and exhaled two words and all of my magic. "Love me."

The surprise vanished from his eyes. His expression went slack, his features relaxing. "Hi," he said.

He was mine.

I let go of him, stroked his jaw with my fingertips, and told him, soft like I would tell a lover, "Jump for me."

He spun around and threw himself over the edge. The swarm followed the falling man. He crashed onto the pavement of the parking lot and lay still. The swarm spun about him and folded in on itself, blanketing him, a shining blanket of green mottled with red and yellow . . . I had seen this before, in a documentary on piranhas. They were devouring him.

I turned. Alessandro sat on the edge of the roof. Jocelyn slumped next to him, whispering, her eyes wild.

I ran up to them. His magic would wear off in about a minute. I had to hurry.

"It's gone," Jocelyn babbled. "My magic is gone."

"She's all yours," Alessandro said.

I crouched by the older woman and swiped away the blood that was leaking into my eyes from a gash on my head. "Jocelyn," I sang out. The world turned dim for a second. The last reserves of my magic emptied. If I took any more, I would pass out.

Her eyes widened. She stared at me.

"Where is Halle Etterson?" I asked her, keeping my voice gentle.

She strained, trying to fight me. Her will was strong, but mine was stronger.

"Magdalene has her."

"Who is Magdalene?"

She shut her eyes tight.

"Don't you want to tell me?"

She nodded like a child.

"It would make me so happy if you told me."

Tears glistened in her eyes and slid over her cheeks. "I can't. I'm trying, I'm really trying."

"What's her last name?"

Jocelyn bit into her lower lip. Blood ran down her chin. She would tell me if she could. Someone had hexed her. A mental mage, probably a Significant or a Prime, had placed a powerful compulsion in her mind that prevented her from speaking about Magdalene. Getting around the hex would take time and preparation and we didn't have either. She wanted to tell me, she was desperate to tell me, but if I pushed any harder, her mind would break, and we would be left with nothing.

I switched gears. "Who killed Sigourney?"

She opened her eyes, relieved. "I don't know. It went through Benedict."

"Why was she killed?"

"She was supposed to do a job, but the dumb bitch backed away. You don't ever do that."

"Who was the target?" I asked.

"Linus Duncan."

The name landed like a brick. Linus Duncan, former Speaker of the House Assembly, which had made him the most powerful man in Texas. Crossing him was fatal. He had also witnessed the formation of House Baylor. His name was written into the Book of Records next to my sister's request for our family to be recognized as a House.

Rage sparked in Jocelyn's eyes. Her magic stabbed me. Raw, primal fear burst inside me and exploded into panic. My vision blurred at the edges. A sharp metal taste coated my tongue. Every instinct I had screamed. I had to run away. I had to run away now or terrible things would happen. I scrambled back, away from her, trying to get to my feet. The fear whipped me into a frenzy. I had to run as fast as I could . . .

Alessandro grasped Jocelyn's head and twisted. There was a dry crunch. Jocelyn's head lolled to the side, her eyes blank.

Alessandro got up, stepped over her and held out his hand. His amber eyes were so warm and kind. "Catalina, come here."

No! Danger! Go, go, run fast!

But it was Alessandro. I swayed, not knowing what to do. My whole body shook. The world was dancing, and its leaping made me dizzy.

"It's okay." Alessandro smiled, his voice so soothing. "Hold still. I'll come to you."

He moved toward me slowly, smiling and holding his hand out.

The last shreds of panic melted. The jittery blur in my peripheral vision dissipated. A long drop down to the parking lot yawned in front of me. I was standing on the edge of the building, balancing on my toes. I froze.

"Take my hand," Alessandro said. "Don't worry. Everything will be okay."

I reached out. His hand gripped mine, his strong dry fingers hot on my skin. He pulled me back from the edge and hugged me to him. "I have you. It's over. It's over, *angelo mio*."

The heat of his body shocked me. I was still shaking, so I wrapped my arms around him. He was pure muscle, hard and strong, and when he hugged me to him, the world slowed and stopped spinning, steadying with Alessandro as its axis. I shut my eyes. He was murmuring things to me, comforting, soothing things, his arms shielding me, his hand stroking my back, and I wrapped myself in his strength.

I would deal with what it meant later. I'd rationalize and dissect it and berate myself for being stupid, but right now I just needed him to hold me, and he did.

Gradually the world stopped doing a jig. My shaking muscles relaxed.

The dry crack of a gunshot popped to the right, close.

"Did you just shoot something?" I asked him.

"One of the bugs was eating Jocelyn's face. Don't look."

He pulled me tighter to him, turning slightly to block my view. He would kill anything that came within his striking distance. Standing like this, with him holding me was the safest I had ever felt in the last three years. Something uncurled in me, happy and warm, and whispered that this was the perfect place for me to be.

I had to let go. I couldn't just stand here on the roof for the whole night. The warehouse had probably been attacked, and we needed to go back and help.

I had to let go.

I had to.

Breaking away from him actually hurt.

I took a slow, deliberate step back. "I'm good."

"Are you sure?" He was looking at me, his eyes concerned and warm. I looked away. If I didn't walk away now, I would kiss him and I wouldn't stop.

"I'm good," I said again. I stepped around him and went to Jocelyn's body.

She had nothing on her. No weapon, no identification, no wallet. Not even a tissue in her pocket. I checked her suit, and her jacket had no tags. I didn't expect to find anything useful, but cutting all the tags off really took it to the next level.

We found Lawrence on the ground where he fell. His swarm, once terrifying, now lay around him, dying slowly on the grass and asphalt. They'd stripped his carcass of every shred of flesh, and only his skeleton remained, wrapped in his tattered coat. If we could identify Lawrence, we might be able to walk the trail back to his creator. We bundled the inhuman bones into what was left of the cloth and Alessandro carried it to Runa's car, cursing the whole way.

I had no idea Italian had that many swearwords.

 **Chapter 11**

*L*awrence's bones stank. Once, I had stupidly smelled muriatic acid in a high school lab. It felt like inhaling razor blades, and the experience taught me to never stick my nose into a test tube. The skeleton reeked just like that, except worse. I had an absurd feeling that if I breathed through my mouth, it would cut my throat and I'd choke on my own blood.

Alessandro was carrying the bundle of Lawrence at arm's length. I had to hurry up before one of us started retching.

I popped open the hatchback of Runa's rental Rogue. An open suitcase tumbled out, spilling underwear and clothes onto the pavement. I jumped out of the way.

The back of the Rogue looked like an airport baggage claim after a tornado. Clothes strewn in a heap, tangled charging cords, shoes, a pack of sanitary napkins, and on top of it all a bottle of conditioner with its cap half off. The bottle had leaked pale green goo over the entire mess like the corpse of some alien creature. Arabella's room was cleaner than this.

I grabbed the suitcase and frantically stuffed the

fallen clothes and shoes into it. Alessandro waited next to me, a patient look on his face.

I just wanted to get out of this parking lot.

The suitcase was full, and half of the stuff still remained. How in the world had she packed it all in there?

"Backseat," Alessandro said.

I heaved the suitcase into the back, slammed the hatchback closed, and opened the rear passenger door. He deposited Lawrence onto the floorboard. The bones clacked, pushed against each other.

Alessandro held out his hand. "Keys."

I opened my mouth to fight with him about it and realized I had nothing left. I'd burned through every reserve I had. The world had gone soft and fuzzy, my legs refused to carry me, and the pavement of the parking lot looked very comfy and inviting. I could curl up on it, right here by the car, and sleep until morning. I was in no shape to drive.

I put the keys into his palm and climbed into the front passenger seat.

He got behind the wheel, moved the seat back, and started the car. The engine purred and we rolled out of the parking lot.

Alessandro cracked the rear windows half an inch and turned up the heat. I watched for the first few minutes, but he drove with easy confidence, comfortable behind the wheel, and merged into traffic as if he was born in Houston. Fatigue filled me, sand trickling into an hourglass. I lay back against the seat and closed my eyes.

"Catalina, are you all right?" he asked gently.

"I'm just thinking."

"What about?"

"Lawrence's hands. They didn't look anything like the hand in Sigourney's video, and his talent is completely different. I understand one warped person capable of magic. Strange things happen, and in life there are no absolutes. But two?"

He didn't answer.

"And he was strong, Alessandro. Stronger than a normal summoner Prime. You said Diatheke had rapidly expanded over the last year. Are they manufacturing warped assassins somehow? Is that what's fueling the expansion?"

"I don't know."

"Magic warped don't occur naturally in significant numbers," I recited from memory. I sounded tired even to myself. "The incidence of babies born with magic-induced birth defects is one per roughly nine hundred thousand. Almost all warped are the result of us meddling with inherent magic through experimentation. There is an Everest-size mountain of research on it, and none of it mentions them retaining any magical abilities post-transformation. Where would Diatheke get warped mages?"

"Again, I don't know."

"You can't just cook up a warped human out of thin air. It requires fundamentally altering their talent. It requires years of research, complex arcane interaction, teams of mages working together. And money. A great deal of it."

"Diatheke has the money," Alessandro said.

"What about the rest of it?"

He shook his head, his gaze distant. "Every time I get close . . ."

"Close to what?"

He didn't answer.

I should have probed deeper, but I was so tired, and thinking hurt. I wanted to feel him holding me again. I wanted him to pull over so I could climb into his seat and wrap myself in his strong arms again. I would put my head on his hard chest and let the steady pulse of his heart carry me off to sleep; safe, warm, and free of this oppressive sense of doom that hung over me like a storm cloud.

This could never happen. He and I could never happen. I was a siren. My magic would turn him into a love-sick zombie. He was an assassin. He killed people for a living. What did it say about him that he felt comfortable ending the life of a human being and getting paid for it?

What did it say about me? When he was with me, I felt alive. I had my family, I was never by myself unless I chose to be, but when he walked away, I suddenly felt alone, like someone had torn a vital part out of my life and I desperately needed it back. This wasn't who I was.

I closed my eyes. The scarred hunter's face surfaced from my memories, his eyes devoid of human emotion like the eyes of a gator. He and the man who'd put his arms around me on the roof were a world apart. The hunters had felt flat to me, as if some integral thing that made them fully human had withered and died, leaving only self-interest and bitter pragmatism. Alessandro felt vibrant and alive. When he talked about finding Halle, when he went out of his way to buy Shadow a treat, when he had asked me if I was all right a few minutes ago, he showed compassion. He had nothing to gain by doing any of these things. One couldn't be compassionate and be a hired murderer.

Bits and pieces floated through my mind, trying to string themselves into a coherent whole. The derision in his voice when he called the assassins "they," the dossier on Diatheke, the way he had explained how Sigourney hired him. *I have a certain reputation, the kind people like Sigourney make a point to note.* He wasn't a simple assassin. There had to be more there.

Or perhaps I was deluding myself. I wanted him to be something more, because I wanted him. I would settle for the mere possibility of a future, a hope. Was it making me blind? Was I deliberately twisting the facts so I wouldn't feel guilt about falling in love with a hired killer?

No, love was too strong of a word. Definitely too strong.

I had to stop thinking. Right now. "Why a shovel?"

"What?"

"On the rooftop when we fought the swarm, why did you conjure a shovel?"

He paused, obviously deciding how much to say. "It's the way my magic works."

"So it's intention-based?"

He sighed, resigned. "Yes. I imagine the action, and the magic does the rest. It's very fast. Sometimes I'm not fully aware of my intent before the item manifests."

"So if you imagine stabbing someone, your magic produces something sharp?"

"It might. A knife, an ice pick, a shard of broken glass. Whatever is in range. It's magic, not science. It takes a lot of training because thinking too broad or too narrow is useless."

"What were you thinking of on the roof?"

"A really large bug swatter."

The reek of Lawrence's bones spread through the car, diluted by the wind but still strong enough to turn my stomach.

"Tell me about Linus Duncan," he asked.

"I first met him at our trials and then again at Nevada's wedding. He is charming and intelligent and very retired. Or at least so he claims."

"Is he retired?"

"Men like Linus never truly retire. One time I asked Rogan about him, and he said Linus Duncan was the most dangerous man he knew."

Since we became a House, Linus had been a constant presence in our lives. Sometimes he stopped in for dinner without warning. Sometimes we received an invitation to his house. His magic was off the charts. Nevada thought the world of him because he helped broker a ceasefire between us and Victoria Tremaine. Rogan respected him but treated him the way one would handle a loaded gun, aware that a single mistake could lead to tragic consequences.

With us Linus was always pleasant and charming. But no matter how likeable, a man who steered the Assembly full of bickering Primes had to be ruthless.

The image of him dancing with Victoria Tremaine popped into my head. My grandmother had cut a bloody path through the country's magic elite. People were terrified of her. Just mentioning her name killed the conversation.

Who the hell dances with Victoria Tremaine?

He had to have done something for Diatheke to want him dead. I had no idea how he would react to me bringing this information to him. Did I want him to be aware that I knew someone had put a hit on him? How mad would he be when he found out that we knew about this?

I wish Nevada was here.

I wanted my big sister. I needed her advice. I wanted her to hug me and tell me the right thing to do.

No. At this point I knew more about all of this than she did. She was in Spain and I was here, on the ground. I had a front row seat to all of this. The responsibility for the decision was mine. If I called her, she would tell me the same thing. She would tell me to trust my instincts.

Jocelyn's words floated up from my memory and stung me again.

"I didn't climb over Nevada."

"I know," Alessandro said.

I glanced at him. I loved the way he looked right now, his profile etched against the light-studded night city. His expression had turned harsh, his eyes scanning the road in front of us. The wolf was out of the woods and on the prowl.

"How?"

"You hate being the Head of the House. Every bit of it."

I had to work on hiding it better.

"Why did you do it?" he asked.

"There was nobody else." I had no idea why I was even talking about this. He didn't care about my family problems, but it felt vitally important to make him understand.

"What about Nevada?"

"It's a long story."

"I have time."

I sighed. "Three years ago, several powerful Texas Houses conspired to overthrow the democratic government. The plan was to destabilize the current social order and, when everything went to hell, step forward as the saviors of the state, the heroes who stood for law and safety. They had a leader they called Caesar, and their goal was to remake our republic into an imperium, the way the original Caesar and his legions remade Rome. Rogan and my sister stopped it. We never did find out who Caesar was, but the conspiracy itself died. There were arrests and trials. My own grandmother was part of it. She's still in prison. It's a very posh prison, but it's a prison. It seemed so simple. Bad guys failed. Good guys won. We thought we won."

"Nothing is simple when it comes to Houses," Alessandro said, his voice tinted with just a hint of bitterness. He hid it well, but I still heard it.

"Yes. All those powerful Houses and Primes had friends and allies, and once the dust settled, they attacked. They couldn't touch us because we were an emerging House, but they came after Rogan full force. They attempted a hostile takeover of his businesses, they accused him of illegal trade practices, they manufactured evidence that he was involved in human trafficking. He had known all along it would happen, but none of us anticipated it, and it hit Nevada the hardest. She was trying to do everything at once: help Rogan, build goodwill to make sure we were safe once the grace period was over, and earn money for us. Our business was mortgaged. We were in debt. The Houses didn't have to attack us. They just didn't hire us. We had to fight for every dollar."

He was listening to me and the words just kept coming out.

"Nevada didn't ask for help. She was going to fix it all herself. She'd been fixing things herself since she was seventeen, when she took over the business. She lost weight. She looked sick. We asked her to slow down. She said she would, but she didn't. We went to Rogan. He asked her to stop. She promised she would but kept on going. She was trying desperately to make sure that all of us were okay."

My heart was speeding up. Talking about it was like jumping into an ice-cold well full of anxiety and fear. You would think time would have dulled it, but no.

"What happened?" he asked.

"Arabella and I came home and found her facedown on the floor." The memory slashed across reality, raw and charged with pure panic: Nevada prone in the hallway and Arabella's bloodless face and the terrifying sound of her screaming.

"It was just like when we found out my father had cancer. Mom, Arabella, and I had gone school supply shopping and when we came back, he was passed out on the floor in the home office."

"I'm sorry," he said quietly. "What did you do?"

"We freaked out and called an ambulance."

There was so much there that couldn't be explained. The single thought running through my head on a loop, "Cancer, cancer, cancer . . ." Mom's glassy eyes as she stared straight ahead, driving the car behind the ambulance; Arabella rocking back and forth in the hospital waiting room, hugging herself and mumbling, "My sister's going to die. My sister's going to die"; the waiting for the doctor; my cousins running into the waiting room, Leon freaked out and stuttering, Bern lost and somehow small; and finally, Rogan tearing through the hospital hallway like he was going to take the building down. That was the only time I'd ever seen fear on my brother-in-law's face.

"Was she sick?"

"Yes. She had the flu. She hadn't eaten in two days, she was dehydrated and running a fever, and she'd spent the night in the rain doing some bullshit surveillance."

Violence didn't come naturally to me, but at that moment I had wanted to grab Nevada by her shoulders and shake her until her head popped off.

"I'm glad you found her. I know it was terrible for you to see her that way, but you found her that way because you were supposed to. If you hadn't, she would've done permanent damage to herself."

Who are you, Alessandro Sagredo? Why did you walk into my life?

"We all told her she had to stop. She said she would take two weeks off. The hospital released her. Rogan carried her out to his car. It was terribly romantic."

Alessandro raised his eyebrows. "How long?"

"Fourteen hours. I found her in the office going through case files the next morning. It's like she was stuck in a hamster wheel and couldn't get out. Talking to her was pointless. Everything I said just bounced off."

"She knew you were right, but she didn't think she was wrong."

"Yes." I sighed. "I realized that we had to act. Arabella had turned eighteen a couple of months before this happened. When our dad died, he was the sole owner of the agency and he split his shares equally between the three of us."

"You voted her out of the business?" He glanced at me, the disbelief clear on his face.

"No! Of course not. Nevada took the agency over from Dad at its lowest point and built it back up. She's the reason our bills were paid and there was food on the table. We could never lock her out."

"Then what?"

"We took away her ability to financially contribute to the business."

He laughed under his breath.

"She could take all the cases she wanted, she could use all of our resources, but instead of getting a set salary and letting the bulk of the fee go toward our debt, she had to keep everything she earned. I told her that if she wanted to work herself to death, there was nothing we could do about it, but we wouldn't be complicit in her slow suicide."

He smiled.

"What?"

"An elegant solution. It's very you. Was she mad?"

"Livid. She tried to force us to rescind the provision, but we wouldn't do it. Then she got this strange look on her face and said, 'I can't be the head of a family that doesn't trust me.' And then she walked out."

The hurt on her face would stay with me forever.

"She didn't speak to me for three weeks. She wouldn't take my calls, she didn't respond to my texts . . . Nevada gave me my first case, she taught me how to drive, she stayed up and talked to me when I would cry in my room over some teenage catastrophe. Once, she drove all over the city for hours looking for me when I used my magic accidentally and had to run away from a kid . . ."

"What?"

I shook my head. "It was stupid. I was fifteen, he was paying attention to me, and I went on a date with him. It got out of hand. I wanted him to like me, and my magic leaked. It was just a trickle, but it was enough. Everything was going well until I had to go home, and he grabbed me by my hair and tried to drag me into his car. I ran away and hid, and Nevada searched for hours until she found me."

He had an odd look on his face.

"Anyway, Nevada was always there for me and I had hurt her. It was my idea. I had ripped a hole in our family."

"Arabella went along with it. I assume the rest of the family did too."

"Yes, but I was the mastermind."

"Did she call you that?"

"Leon did."

"Your cousin is a hotheaded idiot."

"Leon is impulsive, but he wasn't wrong." I shrugged. "Nevada came to see me eventually. She told me she understood where I was coming from, but she couldn't be the Head of the House anymore. As far as she was concerned, that was a vote of no confidence. Somebody had to be her replacement. I was the next oldest Prime. I had engineered the coup. There was nobody else."

"What happened to the agency?" he asked.

"It belongs to all of us. Nevada is still a shareholder. I run the House Baylor part of it, and she's in charge of Baylor Investigative Agency. She takes complicated cases, mostly pro bono, usually to help people who have nowhere else to go. A lot of her work revolves around Rogan too. They're still dealing with the fallout from three years ago."

"It had to happen," Alessandro said. "You can't belong to two Houses at the same time, Catalina. Eventually you have to choose. No matter how close of an alliance you have with your family, once you're married, your loyalty belongs to your spouse."

"Is that why you never went through with any of your engagements?" I was really brave. Or maybe it was the blood loss. I was bleeding from a dozen shallow gashes, and the stench of Lawrence's bones made me feel woozy.

"It was part of it," he said.

We turned onto our street.

The burnt-out shell of a Guardian lay on its side on the left. Black, greasy smoke rose from it. Next to it a charred body in urban fatigues sprawled on the ground.

The spike barriers were up, blocking access from the sides. Ahead, a Howitzer sat by the guard shack. Sergeant Heart had arrived.

Alessandro raised his eyebrows.

A huge, shaggy shadow charged from behind the shack.

"Stop!" I grabbed Alessandro's arm. "Don't hurt him."

He slammed on the brakes.

An enormous grizzly sprinted toward our car. I unbuckled my seat belt and jumped out. The massive bear reared up on his hind legs and loomed over me, blocking the floodlight at the top of the guard booth.

I held out my arms. The grizzly leaned over and hugged me to him.

I caught a glimpse of Alessandro, halfway to us, a chain saw in his hands.

"This is Sergeant Teddy," I told him, leaning my head against the soft fur. "He won't hurt me. He's a pacifist."

"*Che gabbia di matti!*" Alessandro said.

We might be a bunch of lunatics, but it didn't matter. I was finally home.

The street in front of the warehouse was strewn with bodies. The streetlamps, which we turned on in an emergency, flooded the scene with bright electric light, and every detail of the corpses was clearly visible. Some had simply fallen, their expressions blank, neat bullet holes in their skulls. Those had to belong to Leon and my mother. They were the lucky ones. They died fast. The others lay contorted, their faces twisted into hideous masks by fear and pain. It took them a while to die and they knew it was happening. They felt it.

Ex-soldiers in the dark uniforms of Rogan's private army moved around them, quick and efficient, all wearing hoods, gas masks, and gloves up to their elbows.

Runa sat in front of the motor pool on a huge tire,

watching as Heart's people hooked the bodies and pulled them onto plastic, vacuum sealing them like pieces of meat to be stored in the freezer. There was an odd look on her face, not exactly blank but tired and sort of satisfied.

She saw me. "I told them to just burn the bodies, but they didn't listen to me."

I came and sat next to her on the tire. Across from us at the other end of the motor pool Ragnar sat at the wooden table, his head tilted up. He was looking at the moon.

"I told him to stay inside." Runa shook her head at her brother. "He didn't. Those three bodies over there"—she pointed at the far right, where three fallen bodies formed a clump of arms and legs—"they're his. He asked me if that meant he was now a werewolf, and now he's staring at the moon and won't talk to me."

Alessandro walked over to Ragnar and sat down by him.

Runa looked at me. "Nobody listens to me. What the hell happened to you?"

"Flying scorpion ticks."

Runa raised her eyebrows.

"Never mind that," I told her. "What happened here?"

Runa took a deep breath, puffed her cheeks out like a chipmunk and let the air out. "Let's see . . . You left. Your security dude, the one with the A name . . ."

"Abarca?"

"Yes, him. He came in to talk to your mom. He wanted to hire somebody, she said no, he got all upset and started ranting about authority issues and how he was in charge of security, and your mom lost her patience and told him he was being replaced. He freaked out. He actually screamed at her. And she got this weird look on her face."

Oh no, oh please no. "Is he alive?"

"He was when he stormed out. Leon got between the two of them and told Abarca to start walking. Abarca said, 'If that's the way you want it, I'm walking and taking my people with me.' Leon told him that if he did that, he shouldn't count on severance pay. That the job wasn't over until they were relieved. And then your mom said that deserters didn't get severance pay. Abarca spat on the floor and took off."

"I left for two hours. Two hours."

"I know, right? Then your security guards rolled out, quick too. Fifteen minutes and they were gone."

He left us defenseless. They wouldn't have been able to leave so quickly unless they'd prepared in advance. Abarca must have made up his mind that if he didn't get what he wanted, he'd be gone. The entire team must have been packed and ready to go.

They knew we were in danger. They knew there were children in the warehouse, and they just left us to die. I wanted to punch something.

"Then Montgomery showed up."

"Augustine? Why?"

"Apparently Matilda's aunt asked him to pick her up. Your mom wouldn't let her go until Matilda called her aunt and confirmed it."

Well, MII did have a division specializing in private security. Matilda would be safe with Augustine.

"Half an hour after that, two teams attacked in four of those things."

Runa pointed inside the motor pool, where Grandma Frida was elbow-deep in the engine of a dented Guardian and humming softly. Two others waited on the left, in addition to the two she and Arabella brought from Keystone. The entire side wall of the motor pool was black with soot.

Grandma saw me looking, gave me a big smile, and went back to singing lullabies to the personnel carrier.

"Bug warned us when he spotted them, so we had time to set up. Leon took that street, on the left, and I took this one. Your mom was up there, in the attic thingy. She had wanted your grandma to take the tank out, but your grandma said, 'Penelope, once you hit them with a tank, there isn't much left, is there?'"

I can't even.

"And then your mom said that all those vehicles would make a lovely funeral procession when we bury the children. She said maybe your grandma could paint them black to match the coffins."

God.

"Then your grandma went to get the tank. There isn't much else to tell. She shot the first car. It exploded, which was kinda cool. Then she knocked it out of the way with her tank and started chasing the other three cars with it. They made a circle around the warehouse. Whoever was driving the cars was pretty good, because I've never seen anyone drive backward that fast before. She banged another one with the tank, and then the bad guys decided to get out of the armored SUV things, and we started killing them. They had a pyrokinetic mage with them. That's his corpse over there. He fireballed the warehouse. It caught on fire, which was exciting. Then I killed him. And then the cavalry showed up. Some of the bad guys ran away."

Judging by the carnage in the street, most of them didn't.

"I don't know if you know, but Leon is psycho. I heard him talking to himself when shooting people. He used funny voices, Catalina."

"Your brother thinks he's a werewolf."

"Good point." Runa looked at the moon. "You didn't tell me your mom was a sniper."

"It didn't seem important."

"Of course, it is important. We both have moms who kill people for a living. Well, had, in my case, but still important. We have a lot in common, actually. Our dads are gone. We're both the Head of our Houses. We both have younger male brothers or cousins who are crazy. We're both murderers."

Okay then. "Are you all right?"

"I'm great," Runa said. "I can't decide if I should start screaming because I killed nine people or celebrate because I avenged my mom. It felt good to kill them, but now I feel really guilty about it. I'm probably going to have a nervous breakdown once I process all of this." She paused. "Yes, that sounds really nice. I think I'll do that."

"Okay, let's go inside." I got up and pulled her off the tire to her feet.

"But the dead people . . ."

"I think you've had enough dead people for today. Come on, let's go inside, I'll make you a nice cup of tea, you'll cry and you'll feel better."

I was dragging her inside when my sister pulled up in her armored Mercedes.

"Where were you?" I growled as soon as Arabella jumped out.

"I drove to Austin to our insurance company HQ. They had no right to cancel our policy."

"Did you get anywhere?"

"They called the cops and threw me out."

"Did you get arrested?" If she had, I would deal with it. Her expression turned bitter. "No. They didn't have the balls."

"Don't leave my brother alone with Alessandro," Runa said. She tried to turn around. "He's a killer. Don't leave them alone!"

"I've got this," Arabella told me.

"I'll go and get Ragnar," I promised.

Arabella took Runa's other arm and led her into the warehouse.

I turned around and walked over to where Ragnar and Alessandro sat at the table. Ragnar watched me approach.

"Your sister is worried about you," I told him.

"He'll be fine," Alessandro said.

"He asked her if he was a werewolf."

Ragnar sighed. "It's a quote from a book. 'When war knocks on your door, bringing suffering and death, good men turn into savage wolves.' Am I a wolf now?"

"It depends on your definition of a wolf." I sat on the bench. "Sometimes wolves go rabid. They slaughter everything they see just because they can. But most wolves kill only to eat or to defend their pack. You seem like more of the second type to me."

"It's my fault." Ragnar turned to me, his eyes clear and lucid. "If I hadn't tried to kill myself, none of this would've happened."

His memories had come back. Hell of a timing.

"That's ridiculous," I told him. "None of this is your fault in any way."

"If I didn't collapse like some stupid baby, Runa wouldn't have asked you for help. People wouldn't have attacked your home. They wouldn't have tried to kill your family because of us."

"You're being a dramatic fifteen-year-old," Alessandro said, his voice harsh.

Ragnar drew back as if slapped.

"Guilt is a luxury and right now you can't afford it," Alessandro continued. "Do you want to be an adult or a child? Children require comfort even in a crisis, because they can't understand how urgent things are. In a child's world, it's all about them: how this affects me, how this makes me feel, why is life so unfair? An adult sees a problem and tries to fix it. They think of other people and they plan their actions aware of the consequences. They understand that there will be time to deal with grief and loss after the danger is over."

"So how do I fix this?" Ragnar asked, his face grim.

"Survive," Alessandro said. "The enemy is trying to kill you and your sister. If you live, you win."

Ragnar shook his head. "That's not enough."

"It's plenty for now," I told him.

"What do you want to do?" Alessandro leaned closer to the boy. "Do you want to go over and kill the people who murdered your mother?"

"Yes!"

"You can't. Not yet. You'd die and they would win. That's also part of adulthood—adults understand their limitations."

"I did fine," Ragnar squeezed through clenched teeth.

Alessandro looked at the bodies. "Their faces tell me that your sister is too caught up in making her enemies suffer. And that trail of vomit over there tells me you hesitated. You made them sick first. Was it hard to kill them?"

A tear swelled in Ragnar's left eye. He swiped at it, his face a rigid mask.

"Don't be ashamed," Alessandro told him. "That's good. That's what separates us from them. It should be hard. Killing another human being is the hardest thing you will ever do. But to fight in this war, your kills must be instantaneous. Any hesitation gives your enemy an opening to end you. You die, they win. Acknowledge to yourself that you hesitate. Don't engage unless you must. Remember your job. You must live through this."

"To do what?" Ragnar stared at the corpses.

"To train and practice to make sure that the next time someone comes for your family, you will be ready. Your sisters will need you."

Ragnar jumped off the table and went inside.

"Harsh," I told him.

"That's what he needs right now. Trust me," Alessandro said. "If he has a goal, it will keep him looking forward. Thinking about what already happened and what he could've done about it will just drive him mad."

He got up and walked away. I took in the street full of corpses one last time and went into the warehouse, to the warm light and sounds of my family.

It took us half an hour to settle Runa down. In the end, Mom gave her a sleeping pill. Runa took it with her tea and then fell asleep at the kitchen table. Bern carried her to her room. Leon took Ragnar and two beers to the Hut of Evil to check out his gaming setup. I hadn't seen Heart. He was definitely around, supervising, examining the lay of the land, and giving orders, and Mom had spoken to him. I would see him tomorrow. The last thing he needed right now was me underfoot.

Shadow had acted like I was gone for a century. She stood on her hind legs and scratched at my thigh. She made small, happy doggy noises and wagged her tail so much, it was a wonder it didn't break off. She also trailed me wherever I went. I had gotten Lawrence's bones out of the car, put them into a plastic bin, and carried the bin into the motor pool, and she'd managed to trip me twice.

Grandma Frida turned at our approach. Her eyes narrowed. "Girl, you're all beat up."

I'd counted on everyone being too busy to notice. Leave it to Grandma to zero in on my scratches like a homing missile. "It's just torn clothes."

Grandma Frida raised her finger and pointed. "Laceration. Abrasion. Puncture. Several punctures. Chunk of hair missing."

I dropped the bin and grabbed my hair. "Where?"

Grandma reached out and touched the left side of my head. "Right there. You're bleeding and you look like you've gone through a shredder." She wrinkled her nose and sniffed. "And you stink like accelerant and smoke. Has your mother seen you?"

"Mom has her hands full. I'll just take a shower . . ."

"Take off that rag and sit." Grandma Frida pointed to a stool.

I dropped the torn trench coat to the floor and sat. Grandma Frida took one look at me and reached for the first aid kit.

There were times in life when alcohol really hurt.

"Actually, it's been proven—ow—that treating wounds with—ow—rubbing alcohol slows the healing. A saline wash is so much better. Ow, ow, ow!"

"Saline wash is for your eyes. Alcohol is for getting arcane goo out of holes in your skin. Be a big girl and deal."

Ow.

By the time I told her the story and my wounds were treated, it felt like I had no skin left. Or rather I had skin, but it was on fire.

"Where's your Italian now?"

"In the old fire station building. He isn't mine."

Grandma Frida chuckled. "I think boatneck."

"What?"

"For your wedding dress. It would be very flattering on you."

"Grandma!"

Grandma Frida rubbed her hands together in anticipation. "I never canceled my subscription to *Brides* magazine."

I jumped off the stool. "I'm not going to sit here and listen to this."

Grandma Frida hugged me. The familiar scent of engine oil and gunpowder enveloped me.

"You're doing great, sweetheart. I know you think nobody notices, but we all do. You go take that shower now."

I hugged her back and went to the door.

"What do you want me to do with your bin?" She pointed at Lawrence's plastic coffin.

"Could you lock it in the cage for safekeeping. Don't open it."

"Will do," Grandma promised.

I snuck upstairs into my room before my mom also noticed my punctures, went to the bathroom, stripped off my torn clothes, and stepped into the shower. I didn't even look at myself in the mirror. The sharp sting of open cuts let me know exactly where I was hurt.

Shadow assumed a devoted vigil outside the shower door.

The hot water hit me, sending a fresh pulse of pain through my wounds. I cried out and cringed. Body wash was going to suck.

Gobs of translucent bug ichor splatted on to the tiles of the shower floor. I reached up and touched my hair. It was like sticking my fingers into half-set Jell-O. Ugh. I poured way too much shampoo into my hand and started working it into my hair.

Tomorrow I would have to meet with Heart and figure out how much our new security was going to cost us and where we were going to get the money for it. I had a pretty good idea of how to get some quick cash for the deposit but I knew Grandma Frida wasn't going to like it.

Finally, the water ran clear. I stepped out, smelling of lemon and lavender, dried my hair with a towel, and carefully wrapped another big, soft, fluffy white towel around myself. I only whimpered twice as I did it. I was a big girl and I dealt.

My dog was gone. Well, her devotion was short-lived.

I dragged my brush through my hair. It got stuck. Great. This would take a while.

I walked out of the bathroom, keeping my movements small to prevent the towel from rubbing me too much and trying to not rip all my hair out with my brush.

Alessandro lay on my bed, petting Shadow.

I squeaked and hurled the brush at his head.

He snatched it out of the air. "Stop throwing things at me."

"Stop being in my room. Stop being on my bed. I'm wearing a towel!" And why had I just pointed that out?

He took a slow look from my feet all the way to my eyes. "Yes, you are."

All of my thoughts derailed. My body recalled how it felt to be held by him in every vivid detail. Safe, and warm, and exciting. His carved chest under my cheek, his washboard stomach, the heat of his body, his arms around me . . .

I clamped the towel to my chest and pointed at the window. "Get out."

He sat up, unhurried, confident, like a big cat stretching, and got up to his feet. If I could have recorded it in slow motion and then posted it online, I'd break Instagram.

"We need to decide what to do about Linus Duncan," he said.

"We have to tell him," I said. "His life might be in danger. Also, he might have a reasonably good idea why Diatheke is trying to kill him."

"Do you think he'll answer our questions?"

"I don't know. He's sort of a family friend, so he might. I'll call him first thing tomorrow. Alessandro, do you know who Magdalene is?"

"No."

"More for tomorrow."

He was looking at me like he was thinking of stealing my towel. And I wanted him to.

No. Bad idea. Really, really bad idea.

A hint of a smile played at his lips. He looked evil. "What are you thinking right now?"

"Nothing."

He tilted his head to the side. "Thinking about wearing nothing?"

"Out."

Alessandro sighed. "I'm so tired. Are you sure I can't just rest right here? I promise to behave. Unless you don't want me to."

Yes. No!

"Alessandro," I pronounced each word as firmly as I could. "Leave my room. My mother has informed Heart that you are permitted on the premises, so there is no reason for you to hide here. You won't get shot or evicted."

"You think that's why I'm here? You think I'm afraid of your new army?"

"I think you enjoy mocking me, why I have no idea. Don't mistake Heart for Abarca. These are the people who take down Primes."

He bared his teeth. "Now you've made it into a challenge."

I met his stare. "Are you really contemplating killing people who have done nothing to you and who are here to protect my family?"

He sighed. "No."

"Good night, Alessandro."

He turned and walked to the window. My magic pulsed in appreciation, recognizing another swordsman in the sure, easy grace of his movements. I could never spar with him. If we ever tried it, I would end up having sex with him right there, on the spot.

He picked up an object wrapped in tinfoil from the windowsill. "If you scream, I'll hear you. So if something bad happens, scream, Catalina."

"That's great, but there won't be any screaming."

His eyes lit up. "Wait for it. Three, two . . ."

"Damn it all to hell!" Leon roared downstairs.

I sprinted out of the room onto my landing. "What is it?"

"Someone took the damn pie!"

"What?"

"He wanted a piece of the pithivier," Bern called up. "He already had a piece, but he said he was a great defender and deserved more."

I spun around. A blast of cold air hit me. At the open window, Alessandro winked, grabbed his tinfoil loot, and vanished into the night.

"I just wanted some pie." The despair in Leon's voice was overwhelming. "That Italian bastard took it! I know he took it. It's the kind of rat dick move he would do. I'm going to find him and . . ."

"And what?" Bern demanded. "Shoot him over the pie?"

I closed the door. Leon kept yelling, but I couldn't make it out. I went to the window, shut it, locked it, and lowered the shades. I slipped on underwear and an oversize T-shirt and crawled into my bed.

The covers smelled like Alessandro.

It had been such a long day and now finally I was safe and cozy. My little dog snuggled into the crook of my knees. I closed my eyes and willed myself to go to sleep.

Chapter 12

Abarca's corpse hung from a telephone pole at the entrance to our street.

In the light of the early morning, his face was unrecognizable, a swollen purplish mass of flesh. The sun had just risen, painting pink light onto the buildings around the warehouse. The world looked bright and cheery. Abarca's body swayed slightly in the breeze against this backdrop, his intestines hanging like grotesque garlands from a gaping wound in his stomach. They'd gutted him like a hog.

I hugged myself. It wasn't that cold, but I couldn't get warm despite a thick sweatshirt. Five minutes ago, I'd been sleeping in my bed, blissfully wrapped in a soft warm blanket, with Shadow curled against me. And then Mom knocked on my door and told me Heart needed to see me and it couldn't wait. I knew it had to be bad, but I didn't expect this.

Next to me Heart waited. He stood like he was ready to repel an assault, his feet planted, his broad shoulders straight, his muscular frame solid. Of Japanese ancestry, he was about my mother's age or slightly older.

Time didn't apply to him, the way it didn't apply to a granite crag. He was always battle-ready. His eyes, dark and smart, radiated calm. He had seen worse. I hadn't. He knew that and he positioned himself to provide support. If I cried, he would offer me a shoulder. If I asked questions, he would answer them. And if I tried to do something rash, he would stop me.

"He was killed elsewhere," Heart said. "They slit his throat with a serrated blade. Everything else was done postmortem. He was still using the cell phone you had issued to him, and the record shows a call from an unlisted number last night, at ten o'clock. His cell pinged from three towers north of Houston and then stopped. I sent a team to the origin of the signal and they've recovered his vehicle and possessions. They're on the way back."

"Do you think they lured him out of his house?"

"Yes. It appears he left to meet someone voluntarily."

I hugged myself tighter. Yesterday, Abarca talked to me. He had opinions and if you asked him a question, he would answer. He was moving around, he was breathing. He was alive. He was a person. Now there was nothing.

"Why would they do this? He was out. He quit, he took his people and left."

"Someone is trying to send a message." Heart said.

"There is no escape?"

Heart nodded.

It didn't matter if you quit, ran away, or got fired. Everyone associated with us was a target. Diatheke offered no mercy.

"What about the rest of his people?"

"As of now, everyone is accounted for. Abarca was the only casualty."

I let out a breath. Diatheke must have considered the

others beneath notice. They were grunts, none of them had magic, and a rash of sudden civilian murders would draw attention. Since they were no longer employed by us, killing them wouldn't count as House warfare, and the Houston PD took civilian homicides seriously.

"You have two choices," Heart said. "We can treat this as a civilian matter. He deserted. His employment ended the moment he left his post. We can notify Houston PD and let them take it from there. There will be questions, but ultimately this absolves your House of any further responsibility."

"What's the second option?"

"You can treat it as House warfare."

If we pretended that Abarca died in the line of duty, it would save his reputation. While he worked for us, we maintained a two-hundred-and-fifty-thousand-dollar life insurance policy in case of his death. That policy ended when he chose to terminate his employment with House Baylor.

Abarca had two children and a wife.

"He's dead because of us," I said.

"No." Heart's eyes held no mercy. "He's dead because he ran."

There was really nothing to say to that. "We'll treat it as House warfare. Please notify his next of kin. I'll authorize an insurance payout today."

It wouldn't fix anything. It wouldn't give them back a husband or father, but it would help a little.

"Do I have your permission to take him down?" Heart asked.

"Yes. Please do."

Heart nodded and pointed up at the corpse. Two of his soldiers, a man and a woman, jogged over, carrying a ladder. Heart turned and gestured for me to follow him.

"I need your help," I told Heart.

He nodded.

"We've always made an effort to treat our security people well. We gave them good gear, good benefits, and we tried to accommodate their wishes, but they still ran. I want to make sure we don't repeat the same mistake twice."

"The only mistake you made was hiring George Abarca." Heart stopped and turned to me. "Do you know why Abarca resigned his commission?"

"He told us that he wasn't making enough money to support his family."

Heart smiled. It was slightly unsettling.

"I've worked with some excellent officers. I've also worked with some officers like Abarca. They put in the time, they do an acceptable job, they get promoted, but they don't serve. Their primary motivation is ticking enough boxes to earn the next promotion. They miss the point. It's simple: you're assigned a job, you learn that job, you strive to excel at that job, and then you train the person under you to do that job. You set standards. New job comes along, you do it all again. That's it."

"Abarca wasn't like that?"

"No. When I met him, George Abarca was assigned to a schoolhouse, training new officers. He was comfortable. About that time, the Army had started an initiative to actively recruit Significants and Primes. Because of their unique abilities and needs it was decided that the easiest way to integrate them was to build a small unit around each such officer, complementing their strengths and compensating for their weaknesses."

"Like they did for Rogan?"

"Just like that. Rogan served as a test case for the program and I was assigned as his NCO. Abarca wanted badly to work with Rogan, but Rogan was a crucial asset and access to him was tightly controlled. At the end of Rogan's training, command staff announced the formation of a new section within the schoolhouse dedicated to working with high-caliber magic users. Abarca wanted that command. He'd decided it would be very good for his career. He had put in his time schmoozing the colonel in charge, he'd made sure he was well liked, and he felt it entitled him to the post."

"He didn't get it?"

"No. They brought in Captain Swan, a Significant with a lot of combat experience. He shared a common background with the trainees, and he'd put in more time in combat. Abarca blew up in the colonel's office. I was in Sergeant Major's office at the other end of the building and I heard it. We all heard it. Enlisted, officers, students. The next day he resigned his commission."

The light dawned. "It was never about us, was it? We were a stepping-stone to Rogan."

"I suspect so. I don't know if he was motivated by money or if it was the prestige, but Abarca wanted into Rogan's inner circle. He had sent his résumé to us three times. I imagine he thought working with you would be the doorway to Rogan's confidence."

"Except we hired him specifically to keep our independence from Rogan." It all made sense now. "So, when Mom told him he would be let go for doing a bad job and that the people he wanted to impress would be replacing him, he couldn't handle it."

"Now you understand." Heart fixed me with his direct stare. I felt a strong urge to stand straight and very still. "A unit is only as good as its leader. That's why a good leader holds herself to the highest standard. It's not about being liked or being fair. It's about deciding what your goal is and doing what is necessary to achieve it. Especially when it's difficult. What happened to Abarca wasn't the result of your actions. He made his choices. Don't let it cripple you. You still have a job to do."

"Thank you," I said.

"Don't mention it. We will build a new security team around a strong leader. I have someone in mind. With your permission, I'll extend an invitation to interview to her and her wife. She's a talented soldier, but she comes with some baggage."

"Everyone comes with baggage," I told him. "Please invite her to interview."

"Good," Heart said, and smiled.

I was in the kitchen, chopping up a mango, when Alessandro sauntered in and parked himself by the kitchen island. He wore a dark suit with a crisp white shirt and a conservative black tie. His jaw was clean-shaven, his hair tamed. His shoes cost more than the rest of his outfit combined. A long cashmere scarf, snow white and unadorned, hung from his neck, thrown up there almost as an afterthought. A Prime; successful, elegant, confident. Someone to be taken seriously. He would give Augustine a run for his money.

At the kitchen table Arabella raised her eyebrows and elbowed Runa. Prime Etterson raised her head from her laptop and did a double take.

I kept chopping. "Is that your I'm-going-to-see-Linus-Duncan outfit?"

He took a long look at me, inspecting my award-winning ensemble of sweatpants and an oversized T-shirt covered by a pink apron with a frilly ruffle. "Is that yours?"

I rolled my eyes, slid the chopped-up mango into a plastic bowl already containing minced onion, garlic, cumin, ginger and other spices, and picked up plastic gloves.

Alessandro eyed the assortment of cooking ingredients in front of me, taking in honey, apple cider vinegar, and small orange peppers. "What are you doing?"

"I'm waiting until 8:00 a.m. before I call him."

"Why are you doing this?"

"Because he's Linus Duncan. I have no idea when he gets up." I put the gloves on and began slicing the peppers. "Maybe he does yoga in the morning, maybe he swims, maybe he sleeps in. Eight o'clock seems like a reasonable time to call out of the blue demanding that he drops everything and sees us. Seven forty-five, not as much."

"I understand that. I'm asking why you're chopping little bell peppers first thing in the morning."

Because my cousins pitched a fit when we ran out of their favorite taco sauce.

"She cooks when she's nervous," Arabella volunteered.

I stopped chopping and looked at her. My sister giggled. "You look just like Mom."

"Are you afraid of Linus Duncan?" Alessandro frowned.

"No. I told you, he's a family friend." Of course I was afraid of Linus. Who wouldn't be?

Alessandro leaned forward, invading my space, and hit me with a seductive smile. "So why are you nervous?"

"I'm not nervous."

"Do I make you nervous?" Alessandro purred.

My sister choked on her coffee.

"No."

Leon walked into the kitchen, saw Alessandro, growled "For fuck's sake!" and walked out.

Alessandro laughed, reached over, and stole a piece of one of the little orange peppers.

Arabella's eyes got big. Runa opened her mouth and Arabella clamped her hand over it.

I gave Alessandro a sweet smile. "That's not yours."

Take the bait. You know you want to.

"Give me back my pepper. I mean it, Alessandro. You can't have it."

Three, two, one . . .

Alessandro winked at me and popped the pepper into his mouth. His gorgeous jaw moved.

He froze. His expression locked into a harsh mask.

"Don't you want to say something suave?" I asked. "Go ahead. Flirt with me."

A red flush washed over his face.

"What's the matter, Alessandro? Do I make you nervous?"

His eyes teared.

I took pity on him. "Welcome to Texas. That 'little bell pepper' on fire in your mouth is called a habanero. The bathroom is down the hall, first door on the left. Don't be a hero, Alessandro. Spit it out. I don't have time to take you to the hospital."

"Dibs on holding his hair while he pukes," Runa announced.

"Fine," Arabella said. "But I get to rub his back and make 'there, there' noises."

Clearly, she and Runa were the same person.

Alessandro turned on his heel and marched out of the kitchen.

I held it together until I heard the bathroom door

close and laughed. Runa put her head down on the table and squeaked. My sister giggled, making snorting noises.

"That was evil, Catalina," Runa managed between howls of laughter.

"I told him to give it back. He saw me put on gloves."

"He did," Arabella moaned.

"Did you see the look on his face?" I laughed so hard, I cried a little. Some of it was probably a hysterical reaction to everything that had happened since Augustine dragged me out of bed three days ago, but I didn't care. It felt so nice.

Leon walked back into the kitchen and slid a piece of paper on the island. "While you're in a good mood."

I swiped at my tears with my forearm and focused on the words. *The purpose of this letter is to request full reimbursement for my personal property destroyed on January 6th by an employee of House Baylor Investigative Agency . . .* Blah, blah, blah . . .

"Twenty-three thousand dollars?!"

Leon took a step back. "Remember, I'm your favorite cousin and you love me."

"We only got paid seven thousand for the Yarrow job. You put us sixteen thousand in the hole. How, Leon?"

"I can explain. I got to the house to confront the accountant lady, and her husband ran out in his pajamas and started screaming that she locked herself in the panic room with their baby."

"And you called the cops. Because that's what we do when we find ourselves with a hostage situation. We defer to law enforcement, don't we? Because they have authority and jurisdiction and experienced hostage negotiators, right, Leon? Because we can't assume responsibility for resolving a hostage crisis since we don't know what we're doing. Because we don't want anyone to die, and we don't want to be sued."

Leon raised his hands. "Who hasn't been sued?"

"Us! We haven't been sued. And we aren't getting sued if I can help it. Did you call the cops?"

Alessandro chose that moment to wander back into the kitchen. He looked pale, his eyes were bloodshot, and his hands shook a little.

"You had to be there," Leon said. "I made an executive decision. Time was of the essence."

"Bullshit. It takes twenty minutes to drive from our house to that subdivision. You called here, convinced Grandma and Arabella to bring Brick over, and waited for twenty minutes for them to arrive. And then the three of you thought it would be a grand idea to drive Brick through the house. Literally!"

"It sounds bad when you put it that way," Leon said. "But we saved a hostage."

"No, you put the life of a child in danger."

Arabella stirred. "Technically, it wasn't exactly a child."

I turned to Leon. He sighed, looking resigned, and held up his phone. On it a middle-aged white man clutched a giant orange cat.

"What is that?"

Leon visibly braced himself. "It's Tuna. Also known as Baby."

"I'm going to kill you."

Leon backed away.

I dropped the knife and grabbed a habanero. "Come here."

"What has gotten into you?" Leon backed away, keeping the island between us. "You're always so calm and reasonable . . ."

I chased him around the island. "I'm trying to solve a murder and a kidnapping, a consortium of assassins is targeting us, we had to hire the most expensive private army in the country to keep us alive, I have no idea how to pay for any of it, and instead of making money, you decided to put us deeper in the hole. For a cat in a domestic dispute."

"I didn't know it was a cat until we busted down the door. He said baby, not fur baby."

We made a full circle around the island. I stuck my hand out at Arabella. "Hold him."

My sister shook her head. "I'm not involved."

"You rode in Brick. You're involved. I'm the Head of the House and I'm ordering you to hold him down so I can stuff this pepper up his nose."

Alessandro moved into my path, put his hands around my waist, and picked me up. Everything stopped. He was holding me effortlessly five inches above the floor. He was touching me.

Leon made a break for the doorway.

"Put me down," I growled.

"No, you've gone mad with power."

"Alessandro!"

"It's eight fifteen," he said. "We have bigger fish to fry. Call Linus. Or I can keep holding you just like this. I don't mind."

Runa put her hands to her mouth, making a funnel with her fingers, and dramatically whispered. "Door number two."

The fight went out of me. "I'll make the call."

Alessandro lowered me back to the floor. He held on to me for another long breath and slowly let go. I marched to the cutting board, dumped the chopped habaneros into the bowl, and pulled my gloves off. "Arabella, please put this into the food processor, pulse on high for three minutes, pour it in a pan, and simmer it for ten. Don't let it burn. Also, I'm taking your Mercedes for this trip."

"Yes, Your Highness."

I made a face at her and reached for the phone.

The moment we got into the car, Alessandro morphed back into a killer. The slick veneer of polish he projected in the kitchen dissolved into calm alertness. He wasn't on edge, but he was ready, his magic coiled and simmering just under the surface. Right now, he was lying back in the passenger seat, his eyes closed. We were making our way west, to Cat Spring, a tiny town about an hour out of Houston.

Alessandro could look like multiple people. There was Instagram Alessandro, meeting my family, charming and harmless. There was sexy Alessandro, flirting and too hot for real life, posing on my bed and petting my dog. There was Alessandro the Count, in an expensive tailored suit, and Alessandro the Prime, frighteningly competent, his power an impenetrable wall wrapping around him at the trials. None of them was a lie. He put them on like clothes to match the occasion.

But his default was this, a relaxed but ready killer. Assassin in repose. That's what he was when he didn't have to be anything else. I wondered if anyone besides me ever saw him like this.

They probably did. Just before he killed them.

"How many people have you killed?"

He glanced at me. "Why is that important?"

"I just want to know."

"There is no upside to this conversation. How do you

quantify it? What's the right number? More than ten? More than twenty? When do I become a monster, banished from family meals?"

What brought that on? "Do you even know how many people you've killed?"

"Do you?"

"Three with my sword in Keystone. Three more upstairs on my orders, so I didn't do it myself, but I was there. Another two at the escalator. And Lawrence. So, nine."

"Impressive. If you keep going like this, in a couple of years you might catch up to me."

"Is that based on the average number of people killed per week?"

He looked at me.

"I'm just asking because an average year has roughly fifty-two weeks, two years would have a hundred and four and at a rate of nine murders a week, it would amount to nine hundred and thirty-six . . ."

"Does your brain ever take a break?" he asked.

It did every time he said my name, or he touched me. Or propositioned me in my bedroom while I was wearing a towel, but he didn't need to know that. "Do you ever answer a direct question?"

"Yes."

Touché.

A ranch-to-market road wound its way through copses of oaks. We took a smooth turn and the trees on the left parted to reveal a picturesque lake, perfectly smooth like the surface of a mirror.

My phone chimed a triumphant little note. I knew that sound. That was Alessandro's Instagram alert chime. I reached for the phone, but he grabbed it first. He really was ridiculously fast.

"Give me back my phone."

"I thought so. You have an alert that tells you when I post." He looked unbearably smug, like a cat who had just licked the steak left to rest on the counter and gotten away with it.

"I have many accounts on alert."

"You follow your sisters, your cousins, your grandmother, and me."

I really hated technology. "How did you even find my profile?" I'd made sure to not post pictures of myself or link it anywhere.

"I looked at Nevada's friend list."

The road forked, and I took a left onto a small private drive. An iron gate seated into a stone wall blocked access. Usually wrought-iron letters announced the name of the property, but there was nothing above the gate except a sign that said private property. The gate swung open and I maneuvered the Mercedes through.

"So let me get this straight, the great Alessandro Sagredo took the time to look for me on Instagram, and when you couldn't find me, you looked up my sister and went through her friend list one by one until you figured out which of her three hundred–odd followers belonged to me?"

"Yes."

People in glass villas shouldn't throw boulders, Signor Sagredo. "And why would you do that?"

He gave me his wolfish grin. "I wanted a picture for the frame on my nightstand."

I opened my mouth. Nothing came out.

Alessandro shook the phone at me. "Don't you want to see what I posted?"

When I got my hands on that damn phone, I would throw it out the window. Then I would stop the car and go look for it, because all my contacts and business things were on there, but throwing it would make me feel so much better.

The road turned. A grand driveway rolled out in front of us, flanked on both sides by enormous mature live oaks. Their branches, green despite winter, braided above the road into a beautiful canopy. At the end of that long green tunnel a giant house waited.

Built with beige stone, Duncan's mansion sprawled at the top of a very low hill like a medieval fortress. Its lines managed a nod to both a Spanish *castillo* and a Mediterranean villa, but it was unmistakably Texas. Thick walls, terracotta tile roof, circular driveway, enormous mission-style doors; everything about it said Southwest and wealth. One look at the house and you knew it was custom built to match one person's vision. There was no other house like it.

Alessandro blinked. "What did he call it on the phone?"

"His little ranch."

He swore.

"Before we go in there, I need to warn you. Linus Duncan is a Hephaestus Prime," I said. "Named after the Greek God of weapon smithing."

"I've dealt with Hephaestus Primes before."

"Not like him. He can make an antitank grenade launcher out of scrap metal in seconds and explode our car with it. You have to be on your best behavior. There are weapons everywhere in that compound."

Alessandro smiled.

"I mean it, Alessandro. You're too vain to die."

He reached over and grasped my left hand, his face solemn, his eyes earnest. "*Tesoro mio*, I'm always on my best behavior." He brushed his lips against my fingers.

"Stop that! I'm serious."

"Fine, fine. I'll mind my manners."

We reached the driveway and passed through a second set of gates, standing wide open. I parked and we got out.

The tops of two short towers rising from the second story split and twin turrets slid out, bristling with barrels. Behind us identical turrets emerged from the wall.

Alessandro arched his eyebrows, a calculating look in his eyes.

"No," I told him.

The tall mahogany and wrought-iron doors swung open. An older man strode out wearing jeans, a sweater, and a black cook's apron. Tall and still athletic, with a Texas tan and a wealth of wavy hair that used to be black and now was mostly silver, he cut a striking figure. His features were bold and handsome: square jaw, large nose, lively hazel eyes under the sweep of wide brows. He saw me and smiled, his teeth even and white. The warmth from that smile sparked all the way to his eyes, making the crow's feet at their corners stand out. His whole face lit up, as if I had brought him a gift he'd always wanted.

Linus Duncan raised his arms. "My dear, finally. I made fajitas. I used your guacamole recipe. I think I've got it, but it might need a pinch of salt."

"You said he was sort of a friend," Alessandro murmured.

"I might have understated. He's more like a favorite uncle we're all scared of. Best behavior. You promised."

I ran up the three steps to the front doors and hugged Linus.

Linus' Houston mansion was elegant and refined, with exquisite molding, frescos, and ten-thousand-dollar chandeliers. At the ranch, however, Linus went full Texas. Everything was stone and mahogany and huge fireplaces.

Alessandro squinted at the deer antler chandelier and drawled in a perfect imitation of a local, "Teeeksus."

I elbowed him and hissed, "Stop it."

Ahead of us, Linus turned. "People expect it."

We followed him through the great room and a sunroom to the outside, to a massive patio of Oklahoma stone and a state-of-the-art outdoor kitchen. Padded chairs ringed a table filled with all the things fajitas required, shredded cheese in a pretty bowl, grilled peppers, guacamole, sliced tomatoes, chips, salsa, and queso. An enormous chiminea outdoor fireplace lorded over it all, the fire blazing in its hearth.

Linus headed for the grill, opened it, hooked a skirt steak with tongs, and flipped it over. "Almost there."

An odd-looking turret slid out of the chimenea's side and pointed itself at Alessandro with a soft whirl. He took a step to the right. The turret turned, tracking him.

"Is that really necessary?" I dipped a chip into the guacamole. He was right. It did need a pinch of salt.

"It is. He's a dangerous man and it greatly distresses me to find him in your company."

Alessandro gave him his wolf grin.

"The turret is fully automated. Nullifying me or it will have no effect on its ability to explode your handsome head." Linus brushed some marinade over the meat.

I added some salt to the guacamole and mixed it.

"Yes," Alessandro said, his voice breezy. "But it's just one turret."

"Do you see what he's doing?" Linus turned to me and waved his tongs. "He's goading me into revealing my weapon placement."

A loud clang echoed as two dozen assorted turrets

and automated guns slid from the walls of the house, the roof, and the ground. A dozen red dots danced over Alessandro's chest and back. He stopped moving.

"I never understood why you have laser sights on automated turrets," I said, arranging chips in a bowl.

"It's a warning. It communicates that standing still is the wisest course of action."

The turrets slid back, all except the one in the chiminea.

"Catalina is very dear to me." Linus moved the steak onto a cutting board. "I think of her as family. Should you harm her in any way, I'll skin you alive and roll you in salt."

"And lime?" Alessandro asked.

"If you wish."

"She has nothing to fear from me, but I do wish you would try."

"Ahh, the arrogance of youth."

"Ahh, the overconfidence of old age."

"Are the two of you finished?" I asked.

"My dear," Linus said, "we're just getting started."

Linus pulled three frosted bottles of Corona out of the mini fridge built into the outdoor kitchen and brought them over. "The steak needs to rest."

I opened my beer and sat down.

Linus passed a bottle to Alessandro, took a wedge of lime from the table, and squirted the juice into his beer. "What are you doing in my city?"

"I didn't see your name on it when I landed."

"That's because I have no need to announce it. You arrive, you don't introduce yourself, and now you're here in the company of this bright, capable young woman who is entirely too intelligent to risk being involved with you." He gave me a pointed look. I knew that look. It said that he wasn't mad, just disappointed.

How did I get myself into these things?

"I'm here on business, the young lady and I have a professional arrangement, and what happens between us outside of it is none of your concern."

My beer went down the wrong way. I coughed, and the two of them turned to look at me with identical concerned expressions on their faces. I waved my arm at them. "Please carry on with your manly posturing. It's very entertaining."

Linus rolled his eyes and took a swallow from his beer. "It's not about posturing. It's about courtesy. Manners matter. They separate us from savagery and cut down on unnecessary violence."

"You're being a bit harsh with him. He's a guest."

"No, you're a guest. He's a guided missile and I want to know where he'll explode."

I had to defuse this before it turned ugly. Experience said that Alessandro would do anything to avoid answering questions about himself. I turned to Alessandro. "How is it that he knows what you are, and I don't?"

Alessandro saluted Linus with his beer. "My apologies. I should have come by. It was rude of me."

Ta-da. It worked.

"Apology accepted. What's done is done."

Linus rose and began carving the steak.

"You're not an assassin, are you?" I asked him.

"No."

"Just checking. Lately it seems like everybody is an assassin."

"Is that why you're here?"

"Yes." I had to do it quick, like ripping off a wax strip. "Is there a reason why Diatheke would try to hire Sigourney Etterson to kill you?"

Linus stopped cutting.

A long moment passed.

"There are certain things in life that are just not done," he said, his tone measured. "Abandoning a wife and three children after soiling the family name is one of them. I was always fond of Sigourney. She had been dealt a lousy hand and she handled it with grace."

"Is that why you chose her as the Gold Staff?"

"Yes. It was a small thing I could do for her. So, to answer your question, Diatheke tried to hire her because if she came to visit me, I would let her in. I might share food with her, like we're doing now. I would not suspect her. She was my friend. I take it she refused?"

"She did," Alessandro said.

"Did she hire you?" Linus asked.

"Yes."

Linus turned to me. "And your part in this?"

"Halle is missing. Someone, probably Diatheke, killed Sigourney and planted a second corpse at the scene before burning the house to the ground. I suspect Diatheke is holding Halle hostage, for whatever reason. Runa hired me to get her back."

Linus shook his head. "Sigourney should've come to me . . ."

"She had a history with Diatheke," Alessandro said. "Years ago."

She might not have wanted Linus to know about it.

Linus threw the knife on the table and stepped away from it. An odd expression claimed his face, a mix of sadness and rage. He stared at the knife for a long breath, not really seeing it, then his face relaxed into his familiar friendly expression. He imposed it over his grief like a mask. The effort of will it had required must have been staggering.

"Have you made any progress?" he asked.

"We know that someone called Magdalene is involved and possibly holding Halle."

"The name doesn't ring a bell. What else?"

"Diatheke tried to kill you," Alessandro said. "There is that."

"We were hoping you could tell us why."

Linus smiled. "My dear, on any given day there may be a number of people trying to kill me. I didn't just put together my arsenal for your visit. It's a necessity."

Alessandro leaned forward, his expression harsh, his gaze focused. "Benedict operates in your city. You know him. He's calculating and careful. Trying to eliminate you is a risky move. If he failed, it would put the firm into your crosshairs, and they bend over backward to avoid drawing official attention. The reward must have outweighed the risk. This is more than just money. What would he have to gain from your death?"

"That is the question. I'll have to think on it. Let's eat. The food is getting cold."

He brought the meat to the table. We passed things around, putting together our fajitas.

"By the way," I said, sprinkling cheese on top of the meat. "Have you ever heard of warped mages?"

Affable Linus vanished in a blink. His gaze pinned me, his eyes iced over and focused. Fear punched through my spine in an electrifying jolt. He was looking at me like he was about to hurt me. I sat very still.

"Did you kill one?" Linus' voice snapped, harsh and commanding.

I looked into his eyes and knew with absolute certainty that I had to answer the question. "Yes."

Magic flared around Alessandro. His eyes sparked with orange. "Don't take that tone with her."

"Did you take pictures?"

"No."

Linus looked at me as if I had been unforgivably stupid.

"It was running around in 'your city' and we killed it." Alessandro leaned forward, the Italian Count forgotten. "A thank-you is in order."

We could never do this again. Putting Linus and Alessandro into the same room was like throwing a mongoose and a cobra into a pit.

"How could you not have taken pictures? Your generation takes pictures of everything." The cold hardness in Linus' eyes didn't ease. It was like being face-to-face with an attack dog, expecting a charge but not knowing what would set him off. One wrong word and we would meet a hail of bullets.

"There wasn't time. Besides, we kept his bones." I braced myself.

Linus paused. "Where are they?"

"In the warehouse."

"Where in the warehouse?"

"They're in a plastic bin, locked in the weapons cage."

"Who else knows?" Linus asked.

"Just the two of us. Well, the three of us, now."

Some of the tension eased from his face. Linus pulled out a cell phone and dialed a number.

"Go to the Baylor warehouse. There will be a plastic bin with bones waiting for you. I need you to identify them. Don't wait, do it there. Call me when you're done. Once identified, transport the bones and secure them in the Scroll vault. On my authority."

Linus ended the call. "Catalina, call your family and tell them that Mr. Fullerton from Scroll is coming to pick up the bones. He'll need complete privacy."

I let out a breath, took out my phone, and called Bern.

"Yes?" my cousin said.

"There is a plastic bin in the cage. Please get it and take it to the conference room. Mr. Fullerton from Scroll is on his way to you. Please show him the bones when he arrives. Please don't tell anyone and don't ask any questions."

"Will do."

The conference room had an excellent security camera concealed in the smoke alarm. Whatever Fullerton did with the bones, I wanted to know about it.

I put the phone down and looked at Linus. "What's going on?"

"The proverbial shit has hit the fan and now we're all getting splattered with it. Let's eat. We will know more once Fullerton calls. While we're eating, tell me everything about the warped mage. Don't leave anything out."

$\mathfrak{F}$ullerton called twenty minutes later. By this point, we had finished eating. Linus answered the call and walked away to the house.

While he was on the phone, Arabella, Runa, and Leon simultaneously texted me three different pictures of the same helicopter landing in front of our warehouse followed by their versions of "What the hell is going on and why wasn't I told about it?"

If I had told them about it, Fullerton would find them playing beer pong with Lawrence's bones. There was no better way to prank my sister than to hand her a box with a glitter bomb inside and tell her to not open it. She never met a secret she could resist.

I didn't even know Scroll had a helicopter. Scroll was an independent entity that worked for everyone but answered to no one. Why was Fullerton obeying Linus without question? Why did I have a feeling that everything had just gotten dramatically worse?

We already had an assassin firm gunning for us. How much worse could it get?

"What exactly is your relationship with Linus Duncan?" Alessandro asked.

That was an excellent question. I got the plastic lids for the bowls from their spot in the outdoor kitchen cupboard and began putting the food up.

"He served as a witness to the formation of our House. There is an old tradition among the Houses that a witness also acts as a guide and adviser. Like a godfather or godmother but for the entire family. Linus takes it seriously." I hadn't realized until ten minutes ago how seriously.

"It's more than that."

"What are you implying?" Because if he was implying what I thought he was implying, he needed to backpedal real fast or I would stuff his head into that chiminea.

"Not that." Alessandro looked at Linus, then looked at me, then looked at Linus again, opened his mouth . . .

"What is it?"

Alessandro started to speak and clamped his mouth shut, staring behind me. I turned around. At the house, Linus was looking straight at us. He shook his head once with deliberate precision and went back to his phone call.

"*Sono un idiota*," Alessandro muttered.

And he'd just called himself an idiot. While I agreed in principle, he hadn't done anything particularly stupid right this second. Something obvious must've occurred to him and I wanted to know what it was.

"Do you want to enlighten me?"

"Never mind," he said. "Your godfather is walking over, and he looks unhappy."

At least unhappy was an improvement over homicidal.

Linus marched toward us. "Come with me." It didn't sound like a request.

"Do you want me to bring the food to the kitchen?"

"Leave it, please."

We followed him into the study, a place of floor-to-ceiling mahogany shelves, leather chairs, and original art on the walls. The air smelled of aromatic cigars. Linus shut the doors. A metallic click announced the lock engaging. Great. Now we were locked in.

Next to me, Alessandro was still, but ready, his magic coiled like a python about to strike.

Linus strode to his desk and placed a palm on the glass plate within it. A drawer slid open from the wall. Linus walked to it and retrieved a wooden box about a foot long and half as wide. He set the box on the desk.

"Do you want to find Halle?"

What kind of question was that? "Yes."

"And you, do you want to find Sigourney's killer?"

"That's why I'm here," Alessandro said.

"You two have stumbled onto a uniquely dangerous secret. There are three types of people who have this knowledge: the soon-to-be-dead, the criminals, and the Wardens. The only way for you to avoid the first two categories is to accept my authority."

Alessandro bared his teeth.

"I'm trying to keep you alive, you young idiot," Linus snapped.

He picked up the box and opened it. Inside on black velvet lay a simple dagger with a wooden grip and a wooden crest with a staff carved in its surface. A tiny clear jewel marked the top of the staff. Above it, a banner reading *In ministerium hominis* curled along the edge. In the service of man. And that wasn't ominous. Not at all.

"Catalina, place your hand on the seal," Linus ordered.

I hesitated. He was about to swear me in, and I had no idea to what. I wanted to call Rogan, or Arrosa, or someone to ask them for advice. If I asked him for a lifeline, he would probably explode.

"Catalina," Linus said, "I have your best interests at heart."

I met his gaze. "And if I don't do this, will I walk out of this house?"

"Of course. But if you don't do this, I cannot protect you from what follows."

"Protect me from what?"

"The combined might of the National Assembly."

Cold shot through me. Nobody could take on the entire National Assembly, not Rogan, not Linus, no one.

What do I do?

"Your safety is very important to me," Linus said. "I'll do everything in my power to shield you; however, my power has limits."

"He really does have your best interests at heart," Alessandro said. "He's invested in your survival."

"Be quiet," Linus told him.

"I'm trying to help."

Things were moving way too fast and there was no time to acclimate. There was no opportunity to make an informed decision. I just had to do the best I could and hope I didn't screw it up.

"If it wasn't for you, she wouldn't be in this mess," Linus said.

Alessandro raised his eyebrows. "I'm curious, have you ever attempted to prevent her from doing what she wanted to do? I'd be delighted to hear how it went."

"If you had kept Sigourney from dying, none of this would be necessary," Linus growled.

"She died while I was in the air over the ocean. Perhaps, if you had been a better friend, she wouldn't feel the need to hire—"

"Enough." I put my hand on the seal. I didn't really have a choice.

"By the power vested in me by the National Assembly of the United States, I, Linus Duncan of House Duncan, Warden of the State of Texas, hereby appoint you, Catalina Baylor, to the office and responsibilities of Deputy Warden of the State of Texas. Do you swear to give your loyalty to and obey the orders of the National Assembly and its appointed representatives?"

He paused.

"Yes." That seemed like the only reasonable answer.

"Do you swear to faithfully and honestly fulfill your duties to the best of your ability?"

"Yes. I swear." To fulfill the "I don't know what duties" by "I have no idea which means."

"Do you swear to never directly or indirectly reveal matters pertaining to the Office of the Warden and any investigation or inquiry undertaken by it unless questioned by a Warden or testifying before the National Assembly?"

"What if I'm subpoenaed by a court of law?"

"You'll have to plead the Fifth."

"I could lose my license."

"You could lose your life."

"Would the National Assembly provide me with legal representation?"

Linus smiled. "In the two hundred years the Office of the Warden has existed, no Warden or Deputy has ever been called to testify about matters of the office in a civil court. But, should such a thing occur, yes, the Assembly will provide you with defense and you can be assured it will be vigorous."

"I swear."

Linus took the dagger out and held it to me. "Cut the thumb of your right hand. Not a deep cut. We just need a drop of blood."

I took the dagger and pricked my thumb. A drop of blood swelled.

"Place it on the gem."

I put my bloody thumb onto the jewel crowning the staff. Magic swirled from the seal. The wood cracked and a glowing gold tendril slipped out of the gap, curling and growing like a grapevine. It hovered over my forearm, spiraling. So beautiful.

The vine dived at my forearm and pierced the skin. I yelped and dropped the dagger. Agony gripped my arm, scorching me. The world went dark, and against that midnight blackness the glowing vine burned in a fiery ring . . .

My eyes snapped open. I blinked away the tears.

I tried to stand. The floor wasn't there. Also, there was a metal robot arm clutching me. Was I still passed out and hallucinating?

"There, she's awake," Linus said. "I told you."

I twisted to look over my right shoulder. Alessandro wore a reinforced exosuit. The power armor towered above me, bristling with weapons. He was holding me with one armored arm and pointing the other at Linus. Four laser sights lit up Linus' chest with a raspberry glow.

"Are you all right?" Alessandro asked, his voice deepened by the armor.

"Yes. How?"

"He won't tell me how, but this is one of my suits," Linus said. "They're stored fifty feet under us in an armored vault and taken out only for special occasions. Quite remarkable, really."

Alessandro gently set me down. The power armor whirred, split along the seams, and hydraulics lowered Alessandro to the floor. He stepped out and brushed imaginary dust off his suit sleeve.

He'd tried to save me from Linus. I was unconscious for barely a minute, maybe two, and the two of them had nearly murdered each other.

"It's not polite to play with other people's toys," Linus told him. I couldn't tell if he was upset or amused. Either way, it wasn't good.

Alessandro shrugged. "Sometimes it's necessary."

"This wasn't one of those times."

"I'll make that determination for myself."

My arm hurt like hell. I rubbed it, expecting a brand or a burn, but no blemishes marked my skin.

"Normally you would undergo weeks of training, but there's no time." Linus stood next to me and raised his arm. "Think of your magic as a bubbling fountain and use it to push the vine to the surface."

A double circle appeared on his forearm, formed by a vine with tiny leaves. In the middle of the ring a five-point star glowed, outlined with vine shoots.

I raised my arm and concentrated. Slowly, hesitantly, the vine shifted within my arm, a dense elastic ring. It was an odd feeling, not pain exactly, but discomfort and a sense of wrongness. I wanted to claw at my arm until I got that thing out of me.

"Push harder. You are a Deputy Warden. You now outrank every law enforcement officer in Texas, except for me. You can take over any investigation at will. You can compel testimony from all members of the Texas Assembly. This is your badge. This is authority. Believe in your right to wield it."

I focused on the vine within my arm, sending a current of magic underneath it. It shone through my skin, a single ring containing a star within. I held it for a long second and let it fade.

Linus turned to Alessandro and held out a tablet. Alessandro took it and scanned the contents. He glanced at Linus and pressed his thumb to the screen. The tablet chimed.

"I just hired him as your bodyguard until this investigation is complete. He doesn't have the same power as you do, but it should shield him from most of the ramifications."

Linus poured himself a couple of fingers' worth of whiskey from a decanter, drank it, and stared at the exosuit. "Well, that's settled. The real question now is how am I going to get it back into the vault without damaging the floors."

Chapter 13

$\mathcal{L}$eave it," Alessandro said. "It will disappear once I'm out of range."

"By disappear do you mean it will teleport back?" Linus asked.

"No, I mean it will cease to be." Judging by the set of his jaw, disclosing the details of his magic brought Alessandro actual pain.

"Is this a copy of my suit or the original? I don't wish it to disappear, if it's the latter."

Alessandro unclenched his teeth and waved his hand. "It's a copy."

Linus stroked his beard. "How peculiar. You see, the suit is keyed to my biometrics. You shouldn't have been able to use it. How exactly did you manage that?"

Alessandro gave him his dazzling smile. "It's magic." Smartass.

"Where did you find this charmer?" Linus asked me.

"In an abandoned mall. He followed me home. Could we please stop talking about the exosuit?" I asked.

"Why don't we sit down?" Linus said.

I landed in the nearest chair. My head felt woozy and

the room kept trying to crawl sideways. Linus poured two more glasses of whiskey and handed them to us. Alessandro sat in the chair next to me and inspected the amber liquid.

"Thirty-year-old Scotch whisky," I warned him.

As hilarious as watching eight-hundred-dollar whiskey come out of Arabella's nose had been, I didn't want him to repeat her experience. Linus was offended enough as it was, and I didn't savor the prospect of listening to another lecture about the unsuitability of aged Scotch spirits for shot taking.

"Single malt." Linus held his glass up to the light and smiled.

Alessandro sipped from his glass. His face took on an appreciative expression. "Exquisite."

"There may be hope for you yet. A very slim hope." Linus leaned back. "The Office of the Warden was founded with the singular purpose of protecting and preserving the integrity of the Osiris serum. Over the years, its role has been expanded to respond to the most egregious crimes committed by the members of the magic public. We do not concern ourselves with run-of-the-mill House feuds, murders, kidnappings, and such. A crime comes to our attention only when it puts the survival of humanity or the National Assembly at risk."

He paused to take another sip.

"I'm not qualified for this position," I told him.

"Actually, you are, which is ironic considering the situation. You have power and investigative experience, and your House has very few ties to the rest of the families, which makes you impartial."

"Is this going to cause difficulties for you?" I asked. I should have brought this up earlier. Now it was too late. Not my brightest moment.

"On the contrary. The selection of a deputy is left to my discretion. They've been after me for years to train someone. In my defense, I did offer the position years ago to a certain telekinetic you know quite well. He declined. So I do believe the National Assembly will be overjoyed and I won't have to endure any more questions about whether or not I plan to live forever."

Rogan had passed on the job. Should I have passed on it too? "Why did he turn it down?"

"He didn't want to be accountable to anyone but himself. Which conveniently brings us to my next point: rules and limitations. You are subject to my orders. You will *not* undertake any investigations, follow any leads, or make any decisions in your official capacity without consulting me. Please bear in mind that every action you take means I'll have to explain or defend it before the National Assembly. Do not reveal your position as Deputy Warden without my permission to anyone."

"Can she breathe without asking you?" Alessandro asked.

"A more important question is can you keep her breathing in the immediate future?"

"I'm going to leave the room," I said. "You two can brawl and settle this. Would five minutes be long enough?"

Alessandro rolled his eyes. "I won't need five minutes."

Linus shrugged. "Good, because you won't last five minutes."

They stared at each other.

I sighed. "Can we get to the warped, please?"

"Each sample of the Osiris serum is synthesized using DNA from an actual human being," Linus said. "It follows that each strain bears a particular genetic marker.

Eighteen months ago, the Northern Vault was breached. Five samples of the Osiris serum were stolen."

I hadn't heard anything about it. It wasn't reported online or in the news.

"The recovery of the serum is our highest priority. Our society functions because we all agreed that the serum must be locked away. If it were to become widely available again, the world would drown in violence. It's the Pandora's box of our age. War, political upheaval, crime, pandemics; every sin a civilized society sought to eradicate would be released."

"Have you recovered any of it?" Alessandro asked.

"No." Linus grimaced. "About twenty years ago a sample of the serum was stolen from China and used in experimentations by a private laboratory connected to a temporary alliance of three French Houses. They sought to bolster their magic abilities. They succeeded in refining the serum to produce a new variant, 971, as it came to be known. The 971 serum strengthens weaker inherent magic but warps the subject beyond the limits of humanity."

"So the human subjects went from duds to magic-capable monsters?" I asked.

"In essence, yes. The lab was destroyed by the combined actions of the international Assemblies, and all of the research was eradicated."

"Clearly not all of it," Alessandro said.

Linus grimaced. "It would appear to be so. The 971 serum contained DNA from a powerful magic user. Everyone altered by it exhibits the same genetic marker. Fullerton informs me that the bones in your plastic bin have that marker and the marker from one of our stolen samples."

"Explains the jump."

The two of them looked at me.

"Diatheke rapidly expanded over the past year, probably by using overpowered warped magic users. Biomagical research takes time, and the information related to the serum is strictly controlled. Analysis of the serum alone could take years, never mind synthesis of a new variant or clinical trials. Eighteen months isn't enough time to go from zero to viable warped mages. However, if Diatheke gained access to the 971 serum and the underlying research, they could springboard from it. They likely used a pure sample of the Osiris serum and the 971 serum to create their own new variant."

The wheels in my head turned faster. "Did the 971 serum have a high mortality rate?"

Linus nodded. "Yes, higher than pure Osiris serum. It's stronger but deadlier."

"What are you thinking?" Alessandro asked.

"Runa mentioned that Halle specialized in purification. She excels in removing toxins from the human body. They may be using her to cut down on their fatality rate."

"None of this explains why Diatheke decided to murder you," Alessandro said.

Linus tapped some keys on his tablet. A screen slid from the wall and came to life, showing an empty parking lot lit by a single lamp that barely held back the night. A woman with long dark hair sprinted across it, little more than a silhouette. A swarm of familiar flying ticks tore into the woman. Lightning burst from her, arching over the pavement. Ticks rained to the ground, but the swarm kept coming, a black cloud wrapping around her. A piercing scream rang out and died. The swarm boiled, folding in on itself, as the ticks tore into the body in a feeding frenzy. Behind them Lawrence strode into the frame, the light of the lamp playing over his warped features. The video ended. Linus pressed pause. The image froze, showing a dark computer screen and in it a faint reflection, a hint of a silhouette with glasses and familiar sharp hair.

"Augustine," I breathed out.

Linus nodded. "It was sent to my business office a month ago from an anonymous source."

Alessandro smiled. "He let you know that he's aware that you're the Warden and he wants credit for bringing the matter to your attention, but nothing in that recording is strong enough to tie him to it. Clever."

"Benedict knows," I said. "When he was menacing me in his office, he told me to say hello to Augustine. He thought I was working for him."

"MII is a mammoth beast," Linus said. "And Augustine is entrenched in the state's power grid."

"Benedict couldn't go after Augustine," Alessandro surmised. "Too loud and too dangerous, but he couldn't take the chance that the recording reached the Wardens, so he tried to eliminate you instead. One man versus a corporation."

Benedict had badly miscalculated. I would rather take on Augustine with all his resources than Linus any day.

Linus studied the whiskey in his glass. "This Magdalene the psionic mentioned. She's likely the brain of this warped factory. What do we know about her?"

"Nothing," I said. "A cursory search of the Prime database didn't reveal any Primes with related specialties. There are four Magdalenes currently in US Houses, of which two are under the age of twelve, one is eighty-two, and the fourth is a telepath and unlikely to be involved." I tapped the armrest of my chair. "We would be looking for a mage with chemistry or biological specialization."

"It's a code name," Alessandro said. "Everyone in Diatheke takes a new professional name. It's the firm's policy."

Selecting a code name would be personal. It would carry meaning to the person. Very few people chose an alias at random.

"Then here's your first order," Linus said. "Identify Magdalene. Nothing else matters. You may use Fullerton to assist you if necessary. If you need money or access, let me know. You'll tell nobody about what happened here today or about what you've learned. Not your sisters, not your cousins, not your mother or grandmothers. Are we clear?"

"Yes," I said. "But that's not realistic. I'm not a tyrant, I'm in charge of a family. They'll want explanations. They know that I came to see you. The moment I start accessing government databases, they will put two and two together."

Linus took a heavy leather binder from his desk and passed it to me. "Congratulations. House Baylor has been hired as a subcontractor for an unspecified government agency."

I opened the binder. Nondisclosure agreements, contract, lots of scary language, . . . generous compensation.

"And if I tell them the truth, I would have to kill them?"

"Quite literally."

My insides turned cold. He wasn't joking.

"Your mother and your grandmother are both veterans. They understand how it works. Get them on your side and the rest of the family will fall in line."

"What about the Ettersons?"

"What about them?"

"They're victims in this case. I don't want to involve them in this."

Linus' face was merciless. "Runa Etterson is the Head of her House. She could've collected her brother and flown back to California. Instead she chose to stay here and take care of her family business. She involved herself. Every action carries a consequence."

He was leveraging my family and friends against my cooperation. I finally understood why Rogan watched him the way he did. Except it was too late.

I forced my shoulders to relax, leaned back, and let Victoria Tremaine's granddaughter rise to the surface. "Very well. We'll view the Ettersons as part of my House for the duration of this investigation. Since you mentioned access, I'll need entry to all the crime databases; the Assembly Prime criminal list, the FBI's Mages of Interest, the Department of Motor Vehicles, the whole thing."

Linus took the seal from the table and turned it over. On the back was a username and password. "With this you will be able to log into the Warden Network, which pulls data from every government network you mentioned. Everything you look at will be recorded and examined by me. Do not use it outside the scope of this investigation."

"Understood." My fairy godfather had just waved a magic wand and granted me top-secret clearance.

"My dear, I've been doing this for a while. Do give me some credit." Linus pinned me with his stare again. "I want to be crystal clear in regards to what's at stake. If means of manufacturing the 971 serum became public, every unscrupulous House in the world would jump at the chance to have it."

"They would breed magic monsters for their private armies," Alessandro said.

"Exactly. Eventually, there would be more monsters

than people." Linus' face turned hard and unyielding. "And that, children, I will not permit."

Alessandro and I didn't speak on the drive back. He seemed lost in thought, and I felt like I had signed my soul away and sealed the contract with my blood. What had I gained? Was it anything at all?

Just before I reached the warehouse, I took a detour to a coffee shop. Alessandro didn't want anything, but I bought a huge latte full of sugar and whipped cream and all the things that were bad for me. And then I drank it in the parking lot.

Alessandro stared at the giant cup with a mix of horror and morbid curiosity. "What is that?"

"Coffee-flavored sugar and cream."

"I thought you only drank tea."

"Why would you think that?"

"You post pictures of your tea on Instagram. It's really very exciting. Will it be English Breakfast or Earl Grey?"

I should just delete my account. "Well, right now I need coffee." I aggressively sucked the latte through a straw and nearly choked.

"It will be fine," Alessandro told me.

"No, it really won't."

By the time Linus had gotten through the first half of the explanations about the 971 serum, half a dozen terrifying scenarios unfolded in my head and they kept spawning others, each more disturbing than the last. The weight of responsibility crashed on me like an anvil falling from a great height. It was Alessandro, me, and Linus between my family and the total collapse of our society.

"Of course it will be fine. You're smart, resilient, and don't forget conniving. Now you have the authority to be all those things in the service of humanity."

I shut my eyes.

"If you keep doing that, someone will kill you. Or kiss you."

My eyes snapped open.

"Ah, missed my chance." Alessandro's wolf eyes laughed at me.

"Is everything a joke to you?"

He thought about it. "Yes."

I slumped against the car's seat.

"He was right, you know," Alessandro said. "Unless we stop this, it's the beginning of the end. Dangle enough money and people will line up on the street to get warped. At first only a few Houses will have them, then others will have to match them and will get their own pet monsters, and then it won't be if you have them but who has more of them, and who can breed the best strain, the most vicious, the most durable, with the greatest magic."

"It's wrong. All of it."

"Yes, it's very wrong. I never take more than one contract at a time, but I took this one. It's bigger than Sigourney or Halle or me and you."

"I know. I'm scared for my family. What if I fail?"

He dipped his head to catch my gaze. "'We.' What if 'we' fail. I'm not going anywhere. I'll stay here with you until we see this through."

He would, I realized. I wasn't alone. It didn't undo the weight that settled on my shoulders, but it made it lighter. Alessandro would stay with me.

I started the car and headed home.

If we did fail and die, my sisters and cousins would

inherit a nightmare world. In human history whenever one social group enslaved another, the slaves suffered until they could take no more, and it always ended in an explosion of violence. And the warped would be enslaved as living weapons, I had no doubt of it. They were too dangerous, and they operated at a diminished mental capacity. Without Jocelyn, Lawrence would have killed the first person who pissed him off and eaten their face.

Atrocities would be committed to keep the warped in line and then more atrocities would follow when the warped were deployed. My stomach lurched, sending acid into my throat. Failing to contain the 971 serum would spark a biological arms race, while well-meaning politicians debated if it was more ethical to destroy the new monsters or heavily regulate their use.

By all reasonable projections, our system of individuals with remarkable powers who existed parallel to the rest of society should have collapsed. What kept it stable was the deep-seated human urge of self-preservation. The Primes tempered their feuds and minded the safety of the general population because they were afraid to die.

I didn't even know if the warped had a sense of self-preservation. Cherry, the woman to whom Nevada used to bring chicken, didn't. She stayed in the Pit, the flooded area of Houston, because she liked it, not because it was safe. The one time she had gotten out, because she wanted to eat a little dog running along the highway, she walked straight into traffic, oblivious to the oncoming cars, and a semi hit her so hard, she flew almost twenty feet. She was dead before she had landed.

Lawrence knew Benedict ordered me to be captured alive. But during the fight, he just wanted to kill me and eat me. The idea that Benedict, scary, scary Benedict, would be angry with him didn't even cross his mind.

There wouldn't be enough Jocelyns in the world to keep the Lawrences from setting it on fire.

We passed through a now heavily-fortified entry point, stopped by the security booth, where Alessandro and I were examined and questioned by two stone-faced guards, and then allowed to park in front of the warehouse.

Alessandro went to change. I went into the conference room and called a family meeting.

The room filled. I looked at the faces of my family, and I was so scared for them I couldn't even breathe.

"As of this moment, all of us are working for the US Government." I placed the leather binder on the table. *Victoria Tremaine's granddaughter. Project strength. Radiate confidence. Reassure.* "We've been retained by an unnamed governmental agency to perform a specific task. I can't tell you anything more. You know where I went this morning and whom I met. Draw your own conclusions."

Nobody said anything. I looked to the left where Mom and Grandma Frida sat next to each other.

"We've been drafted," Arabella said.

"We've been retained. We will be generously compensated."

"What if we say no?" Leon asked.

"No isn't an option. We have no choice in this matter. It's decided and done. That's the only way we can survive right now."

"What do they want?" Mom asked, her voice calm.

"They want us to find someone. Sign the NDAs please so I can tell you more. Runa, House Etterson's participation is optional. If you want out, you and Ragnar have to leave this room right now."

Runa drummed her fingernails on the table. "If we

assist in this research, will anyone with real power remember it?"

"Yes." I would remember it and so would Linus.

"Then we are in. We need friends in high places."

I waited until all of the NDAs were signed and returned to me. "We are looking for someone named Magdalene. She's a monster maker."

Arabella was the one who found it. An old account on Herald, abandoned for six years. The user's name was Magdalin and the posts consisted of House snark. Making fun of this Prime celebrity's hair, that singer's nose, calling a young darling of the Houston elite a "skank" because she slept with more than one guy. The sort of snark a teenager might post, but the voice was older. She read more like a woman in her twenties, playing to a younger crowd. Once in a while she posted a piece of juicy gossip, proving that she was "in" with the local House scene, and her adoring teenage mob went crazy.

Eventually the posts slacked off and stopped altogether. Bern read through the last fifty, getting a feel for her voice patterns. The rest of us scoured the feed for any clues. Magdalin was careful to never mention names, other than the people she made fun of, and her pics were coy. A sparkly shoe, a designer bag, a half-smoked joint. No obvious clues to her identity. A search of the other social networks didn't uncover any relevant Magdalins, so we went after her followers.

Of those, Killer Bee was the most frequent contributor. She liked all of Magdalin's posts even after most of her fans had abandoned ship, and their banter referenced particular restaurants and clubs. On one of her later posts, Magdalin seemed dejected. Killer Bee had replied, "You're brilliant as fuck! Can't wait to have our lunch tomorrow. BFF forever."

Which was redundant, because BFF already stood for Best Friends Forever.

Magdalin and Killer Bee knew each other in real life. Leon found a Killer B Twitter account, and Bern confirmed that the vocabulary and sentence patterns matched Killer Bee on Herald.

We sifted through her images until we found a picture of five women, all drunk, wearing party hats and screaming. The hashtags said #DoctorBitch and #BFF-Forever. Three other accounts were tagged. Of those two were dormant. We went through them to other networks until we found Lillie Padilla, an Herbamagos mage from a small House. Her Facebook account was set to private, but her education was left public. Lillie Padilla was a Ph.D. and she got it from Baylor.

At this point, Runa rubbed her hands together and got on the phone to the Baylor Alumni Association. The rest of us worked Lillie Padilla until we determined that her Ph.D. was in ecology and she was not our Magdalin.

Following a reverse image search uncovered two more women, one of whom, Shondra Contreras, turned out to be our Killer Bee. She had earned a master's in entomology and had abandoned her quest for a Ph.D. in favor of charitable work in Africa. Last year she had been honored for her humanitarian work restoring bee populations and promoting the revival of bee farming.

Runa's phone calls gave us two more names, Noriko McCord and Cristal Ferrer. Noriko had died in House warfare three years ago. Cristal Ferrer was a prodigy. She graduated from high school at fifteen, earned her bachelor's two years later, and three years later successfully defended a dissertation in molecular biology followed by a second in genetics. She would have been a scientific savant, if it wasn't for her magic. She was a Magister Examplaria, like Bern, but her specialization wasn't computers and code, it was the microbiology of the human body.

I logged into the Warden Network. In five minutes, I had everything the government and the Assembly knew about Cristal, from her SSN and DL to the particulars of her magic and the family scandal of her grandmother running away with a Chinese businessman. House Ferrer was well connected, with half a dozen active alliances and an MCI badge by their name, which stood for Military Contractor Inactive.

Cristal ticked all the boxes. She was a Prime from House Ferrer, which specialized in genetic research and treatment. She ran her own lab, Biocine Laboratories. She had a reason to resent her parents, who had likely pushed her out of her peer group and into college. And after Bern read three of her scientific papers, he declared that her written voice pattern matched Magdalin's posts.

I stared at her picture. She didn't look like a monster. Twenty-six, average height, average build, pale, with dark blond hair and golden highlights. Pleasant features, a heart-shaped face, large blue eyes. She seemed brittle in her images, likely half upbringing and half deliberate effect. Cristal was clearly trying to fit into the fragile flower category of high society; lovely yet delicate and looking for someone to shield her from the harsh world.

I could have been a version of her, if I'd wanted to. I'd had Arrosa and three years of education on how to look, what to say, what not to say, and how to say it. Cristal spent that time earning her degrees. The fragile flower pose allowed her to fit neatly into an established niche.

She blended in, but she was still broken. Somehow Cristal never learned that it was wrong to rob people of their humanity.

It took us half an hour to assemble Cristal's dossier. It took me less than five minutes to tie her to Diatheke. Cristal was a member of the Houston Opera Admiration Society. Randall Baker, Diatheke's figurehead founder, was also a member. A picture of last year's gala had run in the newspaper, gushing about the money the society had raised for charity by selling invitation-only tickets at one hundred thousand dollars a pop. In it, Cristal sat at a round table. To her left, four seats down, Benedict De Lacy raised a champagne flute to his lips.

This was as close to a smoking gun as we could get. It would never stand up in court, but it didn't need to. I went into my office, shut the door, and emailed the dossier to Linus. I could see straight through the glass door into the conference room. The entire family was watching me, silent. Runa's face turned white again.

My phone rang. I picked it up.

"What's your assessment of access?" Linus asked.

"Extremely limited. Her family is well connected and has a history of cooperation with military forces."

All of which I had put into our report. Getting an interview with her would be difficult, getting her House's permission for me to magic her would be impossible, and if we used brute force and demanded she submit to interrogation and I was wrong, there would be hell to pay.

"I can compel her testimony, but we will need verification," Linus said.

"Cristal rarely leaves the House Ferrer compound," I continued.

"But she does enjoy the opera," Linus said.

"Yes, but the next HOAS gala is tonight, in less than

three hours. The tickets for the Crystal Ball are invitation-only and have been sold out for months—"

"I'll pick you and Alessandro up at seven."

He hung up.

No good job, no thumbs up. Just pick you up at seven.

Arabella jumped up, ran across the hallway, and opened my door. "What did he say?"

"He wants me to go with him and Alessandro to the gala. Tonight. At seven."

I stared at my phone. 5:37 p.m. There was no way. The hair alone . . .

"Up!" Arabella snapped at me. "You have less than an hour and a half. You need a shower."

I texted Alessandro, **Opera, 7:00 p.m., tuxedo,** and ran upstairs, thanking Arrosa in my head for insisting that I buy a small but expensive wardrobe.

I had three evening dresses: a white sheath, a red dress the color of blood, and a flowing blue gown that hugged my breasts and waist, spilling into a flowing skirt. The sheath was too tight to allow any sort of running, the red dress drew too much attention, so the blue gown was it.

It had taken a miracle, but at 6:58 p.m. Arabella herded everyone into the kitchen, so I could go into Runa's bedroom and change, because there was no way I could make it down the stairs in the gown.

I stepped into a pair of small silver heels, slipped the dress on, and examined myself in the mirror. My dark hair fell on my shoulders in wide waves, combed back behind one ear in a deep side part. It framed my face, showing off the diamond earrings glittering in my ears. The diamonds were lab made. Arrosa had insisted on the real thing, but I'd refused. Nobody had died digging my earrings out of the ground, and that mattered more to me than what Houston's elite would think.

My makeup was light for the evening. I never looked good wearing bright lipstick, so I opted for a lighter pink and smoky eyes. Given another half an hour, I would have done a better job contouring my face, but it would have to do. I looked appropriate for the evening, and nobody would laugh in my face. Most of it was in your poise anyway. As long as you looked like you belonged at the venue, people assumed you were supposed to be there, and being escorted by Alessandro Sagredo and Linus Duncan meant most of the attention would be on them.

I took a deep breath and walked out of the room. Voices drifted from the kitchen, and I headed in that direction.

". . . a dignified pleasant gentleman," Alessandro was saying. "I was honored to make Mr. Duncan's acquaintance."

Honored my ass.

"We shared a drink. It was perfectly cordial—"

I walked into the kitchen. Alessandro stopped in mid-sentence.

He was wearing a tuxedo. It fit him like a glove. He looked like he was born in it, every inch a Prime.

I had seen him in a tuxedo a dozen times on his Instagram, but nothing could've prepared me for the real thing. My pulse sped up. I felt slightly light-headed. I wanted to reach out and touch him to make sure he wasn't a hallucination. People weren't that handsome in real life. It just didn't work that way.

It dawned on me that he was staring at me with a slightly bewildered expression.

My sister opened her mouth. Runa elbowed her.

Silence stretched.

I waited for him to speak, but he seemed content to just stare at me.

And this wasn't awkward. Not at all.

Everyone's phone chimed, announcing someone at our front door. The most beautiful assassin in the world blinked. It was enough to snap me out of my trance.

"That's probably Linus. We should go." I slid my phone into a small, glittering Edie Parker clutch.

Alessandro came back to life. "Yes, we should."

Grandma Frida blocked the way. "Neither of you are going anywhere until I get a pic for my Insta."

"Grandma, they're not going to the prom," Arabella protested.

"Shush. They're going to a high society shindig and I'm getting at least one good picture of them together."

If we didn't do it, I'd never hear the end of it. "He's supposed to be in Hawaii right now."

"I won't post it until next week."

I turned to Alessandro. "She's lying."

Alessandro graced her with his brilliant smile. "I'd be delighted to pose for a picture."

"Smile, Catalina," Grandma commanded.

I arranged my face into a carefree smile.

Grandma took the pic and checked it.

"Good enough?" I asked.

"It will do."

Alessandro offered me his arm, I put my hand on his wrist, and we walked down the hallway. He smelled of sandalwood, vanilla, and a hint of citrus. I felt completely ridiculous. I was Cinderella going with my prince to a ball. Where I would beguile and interrogate a woman who made monsters for an assassin consortium, and I had to do a very good job so the National Assembly wouldn't murder the lot of us.

We reached the door to the office, he held it open for me, and we headed to the front door. Every step was an effort, like someone had put a rubber band around my legs.

"You look very beautiful," Alessandro said.

When given a compliment, always respond, Arrosa's voice murmured in my head. "Thank you. You look very handsome."

He opened the door and I walked out into the street, where Linus' armored Escalade waited under the light of the streetlamp.

"Weapons?" Linus asked.

"No," I said. I had checked the security requirements for the gala. Ever since Baranovsky, one of the richest Primes in the country, was murdered at his own charity dinner, the safety measures for high society events had risen to ridiculous levels.

Alessandro shrugged. "No need. There will be plenty of security people around."

And they would be carrying weapons he could copy.

"How wide is your range?" Linus asked.

Alessandro gave him his wolfish smile.

"I ask, because I brought a full trunk. How close does the vehicle need to be to the building?"

"How far away will the car be parked?"

Linus shook his head. "If it's parked 0.14 miles away, would that be close enough?"

"Yes."

The car turned onto Texas Avenue and pulled up in front of the Wortham Theater Center, joining the line of other luxury vehicles dropping off their passengers, as if we all were elementary school kids. Night had fallen, but the entire street was bathed in bright electric light.

"All right, children," Linus said. "We're going to walk inside, mingle briefly, and be seated at our table. The ball will consist of five acts with twenty-minute intermissions. Dinner will be served in courses during the intermissions. It is customary to dance and socialize between the acts. Catalina, you're going to find Cristal, and when an opportunity presents itself, become her best friend in the whole world. We need definitive proof of her involvement, the location of the facility, and an admission of guilt, if you can get it. Record everything she tells you. Alessandro, under no circumstances is Catalina to be harmed. Avoid violence, but if you have no choice, try to take care of it quietly. Do you understand?"

"Yes," I said.

Count Sagredo didn't dignify the question with an answer.

The Escalade slid to a stop. The usher opened my door and offered me his hand. I leaned on it and stepped out of the vehicle into the night.

A hundred and fifty feet of red carpet stretched across the narrow plaza, bordered by lush oaks and lit by globe streetlights. At the end of it, the glass entry archway glowed with golden light. People in evening attire strolled toward it, women in glittering gowns and men in suits, pausing at the topiary to have their pictures taken against the red-carpet backdrop. Onlookers waited on the edges of the path, eager for a glimpse of the rich and famous. A TV crew lurked in the distance, by the entrance, the correspondent interviewing the guests. Cameras flashed, ushers hurried back and forth, jewels sparkled on skin and hair . . .

The urge to crawl back into the Escalade gripped me.

I raised my chin. I wasn't some Cinderella with a magic dress from my fairy godmother. I bought my own dress with money I earned, I bought my shoes and my bag, and nothing was going to turn into a pumpkin at midnight. I didn't like this fake world of glamour and excess, but nobody had the right to question my presence here. I had a job to do, and I would do it.

Alessandro came around the car and offered me his arm again. A few heads turned our way.

Linus exited the Escalade. A subtle change came over the crowd. They didn't exactly gape, but the Primes of Houston paused. Every single one of them knew Linus was there.

Linus flashed a thousand-watt smile. When he was young, he might have given Alessandro a run for his money. He waved at no one in particular, and the on-lookers went wild.

Linus strode up the red carpet. We followed. Ahead, the TV crew realized that a Big Name Prime had landed, and the correspondent was desperately trying to wrap up her current interview.

Alessandro walked next to me, beautiful and slightly aloof, a prince just a touch above it all, while Linus grinned and played up to the crowd. Ahead, the walls of the Wortham Theater glowed with colored projections of acrobats and rings of fire. The Houston Opera Admiration Society was celebrating the opening of *Madame Trapeze*, a new hybrid show that blended elements of the circus and opera. It had sold out in London and New York, and somehow Houston was the next to get it. We wouldn't be getting the entire performance, just a few chosen acts before the real thing was open to the general public, but it was exciting being one of the first people to see it.

A woman shrieked from the left, "Alessandro! Look at me!"

He turned without breaking his stride and winked. The group of girls on our left erupted.

"Oh my God!"

"Marry me!"

"Who's the girl?"

"My number is 830 . . ."

We resumed our march toward the entrance.

"Enjoying yourself?" I murmured.

"Jealous?"

"Of your many admirers? No."

"You never say anything nice to me," he said, his voice low and slipping into an intimate tone that brushed against my skin like velvet. We were on display in front of hundreds of people and he was speaking to me as if we were about to make out in my bedroom. "It's always 'Stop driving so fast, Alessandro.' 'You have to leave, Alessandro.'"

"What would you rather hear?"

"I could think of a few things." His face took on a wistful expression. It looked good on him. Like everything else. "I missed you, Alessandro."

Why did I ask?

"Hold me, Alessandro." His seductive voice wove around me. All my senses came to attention. The crowd was fading and only his voice mattered.

"Kiss me, Alessandro."

Heat warmed my face. I was blushing. Damn it.

"Will you stop?"

We were almost to the TV crew. Maybe we could slip by them unnoticed while they pounced on Linus.

"Don't go, Alessandro. Don't stop, Alessandro . . ."

"Stop lying about who you are, Alessandro."

His face shut down as if someone slammed a door closed. I hit a nerve. Good.

The correspondent pounced on Linus. Alessandro

smoothly passed by him and we joined the throng of overdressed people walking through the wide-open glass doors. Nobody asked us for our invitations. Apparently just arriving with Linus Duncan was good enough.

Six armed security guards in black suits lined the sides of the short lobby. We passed through the arch of the metal detector, then the airport-style bio scanner, and took the escalator up.

The Grand Foyer had been transformed. An enormous wagon wheel chandelier supporting stage lamps hung suspended fifty feet in the air. Above it yards and yards of midnight-blue fabric stretched from the ceiling to the walls and dripped to the floor, imitating the inside of a big-top tent. Strings of golden lights curved from the chandelier to the sides of the room where the walls met the ceiling, glittering like summer stars against the night sky. Colored lamps tinted the fabric with splashes of lavender and turquoise. Soft music played from hidden speakers, a complex modern interpretation of the circus theme performed with a full orchestra.

A round stage dominated the center of the room, level with the floor, smooth, and shimmering with flecks of gold. Rings of round tables surrounded the stage, each covered with a golden tablecloth and set for ten.

A pair of tall metal golden supports towered on the opposite sides of the foyer. A high wire stretched between them. Two female acrobats twisted in the air, suspended by lengths of blue ribbons. To the left, on a small raised platform, a contortionist in a black bodysuit ripped in strategic places bent backward, touching his elbows to the floor. To the right an animal trainer strolled through the crowd, two lions in tow on absurdly thin silver chains. The lions followed him, oblivious of the onlookers. He had to be an animal mage.

The sights, the sounds, the colors, and the hum of the crowd combined into a fairy-tale opulent circus. Reality ceased to exist. If I turned, I could still catch a glimpse of it through the giant window, the dark winter street, but here only fantasy existed. I could wander through it for hours, making up stories and watching people.

"It's beautiful," I murmured, as the current of people carried us to the right.

"Eh." Alessandro shrugged. "The Melbourne Christmas Gala was better."

I punched him in the arm. I didn't punch him hard, it was more of a tap, but his eyes sparked with orange. "Careful. I'm a bad man, remember? Who knows what I might do when provoked?"

"If you decide to get provoked, let me know, and I will bring you back to Earth with the rest of us mere mortals."

He lifted his hand and a waiter appeared as if by magic, wearing a blue vest over a black shirt, black pants, and a red clown nose, and carrying a tray with champagne flutes. Alessandro took two glasses off the tray and held one out to me. "Champagne, *tesoro mio*?"

My tolerance for champagne was about two sips. Any more, and I lost coordination. If I finished two glasses, I would fall asleep in my chair. But he was holding it out to me and I didn't want to cause a scene.

I took the flute and sipped. Linus materialized next to us. "Children, work now, bicker later. Follow me."

We trailed him to a table in the outer row. We didn't have the best view of the stage, but we had an excellent perspective of the room and the crowd. Alessandro held my chair out. I sat. Alessandro was a touch slow to take the chair next to me. I glanced in the direction of his gaze.

Benedict De Lacy raised his glass at me from across the room. He sat in the back row almost directly opposite us. I raised my glass and offered him a pleasant smile. Alessandro laughed next to me.

I scanned the crowd. Cristal sat to our left in the front row on the opposite side of the stage. An older woman in a silver-green dress with blue-black hair and harsh features sat on her left. I remembered her from Alessandro's hired killer gallery. The woman had an Armenian first name, Yeraz, and Alessandro's database had listed her as a Magus Sagittarius, which meant she never missed. It was highly unlikely that she could have smuggled a gun through security, but MS magic came in many forms, my own included. Maybe she would throw forks at us.

The white man in the chair to the right of Cristal looked like he had jumped out of a pro wrestling match. Sitting down, he still towered over everyone else at the table. His impossibly broad shoulders strained his tuxedo jacket, and when he raised his glass, I thought his sleeve would rip. He had the face of a street brawler: a misshapen nose that had been broken too many times, scar tissue chewing up the skin around his eyes, and a heavy square jaw that would break your hand if you punched it. His haircut, a short, blond stubble, did nothing to soften his impact. His eyes, sunken deep under heavy brows, scanned the crowd, looking for someone to hit.

"Of all the idiotic things," Linus growled.

"Yes, you'd think Benedict would have more brains," I murmured.

Alessandro had caught us looking at the giant. "Who is that?"

I leaned toward him, keeping my voice low. "Frank Madero."

House Madero included five brothers, and of those five, the oldest two looked so alike, they could be twins. But Dave Madero had a permanent scar on his left cheek.

"And what does Frank do?"

"His skin and bones harden, his muscles swell up, he grows to seven and a half feet tall, and then he punches through furniture. Or walls. Or people. Whatever is in his way."

"House Madero is what happens when you breed for strength instead of brains," Linus said, his voice dry. "In a couple of generations, they'll have to hire handlers to help them put their pants on in the morning."

"There are more like him?" Alessandro asked.

"There are five brothers total and a grandfather," I explained. "They're mean, stupid, and they hold grudges. And they're for hire."

In theory, hiring one of the Maderos as a bodyguard made sense: they were huge and scary even before they used their magic and they served as an excellent deterrent. But the Maderos had a temper. Bringing Frank here was like dragging an enraged bull to a toddler's birthday party.

Alessandro pondered Frank. "Do your families have a history?"

"His brother, Dave, tried to kidnap Nevada, and Rogan broke both of his arms. Frank also tried to kidnap Nevada and ended up in the ER. If Frank turns, bullets and knives won't work on him and the only way to fight him is to dodge and hope his body gives out from the strain before he gets his hands on you. The Maderos can't sustain the combat form for too long. They overheat and pass out."

Alessandro narrowed his eyes. "Does he still have to breathe in combat form?"

"As far as I know."

"Excellent," he said.

"Remember, be discreet," Linus warned.

"We may not have a choice. Benedict brought friends."

I surveyed the crowd, trying to pick out faces I had seen on Alessandro's laptop.

"How many Diatheke employees are here?" Linus asked casually.

"Seven," Alessandro said. "The dark-haired man to the left of Benedict is an aegis Significant."

I glanced in Benedict's direction. A lean, pale-skinned man in his late forties sat by Benedict, picking at the appetizer with his fork. Aegis mages specialized in protection. They could throw a barrier in front of themselves that would absorb physical impact and block elemental magical assaults. An aegis Prime could walk through a modern battle with everything from snipers to artillery shooting at him and emerge unscathed. A Significant would be considerably less powerful, but still, shooting at Benedict would do no good.

"Catalina, lean toward me again," Alessandro asked.

I turned slightly and tilted my head closer to him.

Alessandro smiled. "Benedict is having a fit."

Looking at Benedict would be entirely too obvious.

Alessandro's eyes narrowed. "Let's see what happens if I do this."

He reached over, took my hand, gently rubbed his fingers on mine, and kissed my knuckles.

All my hormones stood up and gave him a standing ovation. Damn it, Alessandro.

"Careful," Linus said, raising his wineglass to his lips. "He might explode."

I finally glanced in Benedict's direction. He was staring at me with a kind of possessive hatred. If I were in range, he would have hit me.

"What is his deal with women?"

"He's a half phobic with sadistic tendencies," Linus said. "He finds pleasure in inflicting torture and fear, and the more exquisite the woman, the more he wants her."

"He prefers mental mages for his amusement," Alessandro added. "Maximum satisfaction."

I turned to Linus. "Why has he been allowed to operate?"

Linus grimaced. "I could give you a long explanation about magical checks and balances, but the short answer is that powerful people find him useful. He's a known quantity; he's reliable and rarely unpleasantly surprising. There are a great many things I wish I had the ability to change."

There were nine other people at Benedict's table and nine at Cristal's. Most of the tables around us had filled. Several women were looking in our direction, some at me, but most at Alessandro. Our table remained empty except for the three of us.

"Will we be joined by anyone?" I asked.

"No," Linus said. "The Society maintains a table for me to use as I see fit."

If Linus wasn't here tonight, nobody would have sat at this table. For some reason, I found that more disturbing than all of his turrets, guns, and exosuits.

A handsome older Hispanic man in a ringmaster's suit of blue velvet strode to the middle of the stage, a top hat in one hand and a cane in the other.

The opening act began.

Chapter 14

$\mathcal{T}$he beautiful acrobats in silver bodysuits cartwheeled off the stage to enthusiastic applause. The clowns, the animal trainers in pink, the magician, and the rest followed. The baritone in the ringmaster's suit took a bow and strode off. The first act was over, and the intermission began.

Soft music filtered in. People got up and began mingling, some drifting to the tables, others to the stage. Half of them could kill me, and the rest would put up a serious effort.

Avoid Benedict, get to Cristal, get her to confess, and go home. Don't screw this up or we would never find Halle.

A stunningly attractive woman jumped to her feet and crossed the stage, heading straight for us. Petite, with a perfect figure, golden skin, and a wave of glossy black hair, she seemed almost elflike, otherworldly, as if she had stepped out of some fantasy painting. I caught sight of her face. It was perfect. Too perfect, with the same flawless coldness as Augustine.

I knew her. Natasha Popova, Illusion Prime from the Russian Empire. Alessandro's fiancée number three.

"Do we have a problem?" Linus asked.

Alessandro put his fork down. "No."

Natasha crashed to a halt at our table, her eyes blazing. "You! How dare you show your face?"

Alessandro smiled.

Natasha spun to me. "Are you with him? You shouldn't be with him. He's a liar. Everything that comes out of his mouth is a lie. He isn't who he says he is. His family is—"

"Do I need to remind you why you ended our engagement?" Alessandro asked, his voice carefree. "Perhaps you would care for another demonstration, right here?"

Natasha froze for a furious second. Fear flickered in her eyes. She spun on her heel and walked away.

Alessandro's expression turned dark. "See? No problem."

And that wasn't weird. Not at all.

I rose to my feet. Both Linus and Alessandro stood up.

"Where are you going?" Alessandro asked.

"Cristal is on her third glass of wine and they refilled her water. She's going to have to visit the bathroom and I want to get there first."

"I'll escort you," Alessandro said.

"Play nice," Linus warned.

We strolled through the stage toward the back of the Grand Foyer, where a hallway led to the women's restroom. We turned a corner, and suddenly the hum of the crowd and the lights receded. We walked side by side. The women's bathroom was almost halfway down the hall, past a couple of doors presumably leading to other smaller rooms. We were completely alone.

I leaned against the wall by the bathroom. I would step inside as soon as we saw her coming.

We waited.

Minutes ticked by. My skin was on too tight.

Maybe I had miscalculated, and Cristal had a bigger bladder.

Another minute. Two . . .

She wasn't coming. I started back to the Grand Foyer. At least I could see where she was.

"So, about this business of me lying," he said.

You've got to be kidding me. "What about it?"

"Care to explain what you meant?"

"I don't want to talk about it right now." I felt like I was running on the edge of a sword as it was.

Alessandro fixed me with his stare. Magic flared around him, flashing with orange for a fraction of a moment. "I'm afraid I have to insist."

I stopped and crossed my arms on my chest. "Or what?"

"You're just going to throw it out there and walk away?" The stalking killer was back in all his glory. "A bit cowardly, don't you think?"

"Fine, let's talk about it. When Benedict's goons chased me into that mall, I beguiled four of them. As they cheerfully murdered their friends for me, they told me this charming story about how they killed a lawyer in his own home. They put a gun in his mouth, pulled the trigger, and left him for his wife and daughters to find. They killed him with no remorse, collected their payment, and then went about their lives, fishing, saving for their kids' college, and doing whatever else hired killers do in their off time."

"And you think I'm just like them."

"That's precisely my point. You're nothing like them. At first, I thought you might be, but it made no sense. You were born with a silver spoon in your mouth. You're a Prime from one of the oldest and most respected Houses. You have a noble title. You're smart, funny, handsome, charming, and rich. If you see a fast car you want to drive, you buy it. If you find a woman you like, you seduce her. You could be anything. Every door is open to you. The world is your playground."

He winced.

I should've stopped, but he'd started it and now I was on a roll like a runaway train. "So I thought to myself, why would a man with your opportunities become a hired killer? It could happen if you were an adrenaline junkie. There probably comes a point when the cars, yachts, and women no longer provide enough of a thrill. Perhaps taking the life of another human being is the only way you feel alive."

His expression was flat, but his eyes were drowned in orange fire. "So that's how you see me?"

"A man like that would be fundamentally selfish, Alessandro. He would put his enjoyment above the lives of other people. He wouldn't give a half-starved dog a treat. He wouldn't pose for a picture for an elderly woman just to make her happy or comfort a teenager lost in guilt and grief. He wouldn't fight his way through an assault team to save a girl he barely knows. He wouldn't promise her that he would stay with her to see things through. Because a man like that only cares about himself. Why are you doing this, Alessandro? What is it you want?"

He just looked at me.

"Will you answer the question for once in your life?"

His face was resolute. "You have family obligations. I do too."

"What does that mean?"

He didn't answer.

"I hate you." The emotional dam broke and words

tumbled out. "You walked into my life and screwed it all up. I've wanted you for so long, and now you show up, and you flirt with me, and you hold me to protect me, and you tell me things like 'I'll stay with you as long as it takes,' and all the while I have to constantly check myself because I'm scared to death that if my control slips, I'll turn you into a lovesick zombie. I know you're trapped somehow, and all I want is for you to be happy, Alessandro. Tell me what's going on, and I swear I'll do everything I can to help you. Tell me. It's driving me insane . . ."

His big body braced mine against the wall. I saw his eyes, amber and heated from within, he bent his head, his lips touched mine, and I tasted the faint hint of champagne . . .

He kissed me.

It felt like lightning. It tore through me in one blinding jolt and then I was on fire. There was nothing hesitant or gentle about it. He kissed me like he needed me to breathe. I grabbed his jacket and pulled him closer, fierce and desperate, my body screaming for more of him. It was reckless and stupid, and I knew we had to stop, but nothing in this world could make me let go.

His tongue licked mine, his strong arms gripped me to him, his hand slid into my hair, and it felt so good, all of it. So impossibly good.

His magic boiled around him, the searing flashes of orange dancing, the power churning and twisting. There was no going back. There was life before this kiss and there would be one after, but they wouldn't be the same.

He broke away and looked at me, his amber eyes full of lust and a searing need. That hint of the terrifying edge I'd glimpsed in him before was out now, dangerous and glaring right back at me from deep inside him. It took my breath away.

He should've never kissed me. He was mine now and I wanted him.

I threw my arms around his neck and sealed my mouth to his. Touching him was like coming home. I'd wanted to do that since the moment he put his arms around me on that roof. I tasted his mouth, trying to feed the howling need. He growled low in his throat.

His hands slid over my back. The wall behind me gave. I stumbled back, but he caught me, and then we were in a small room and he shut the door behind him. He kissed my lips, my neck, my throat. It felt like I had shattered, and he was putting me back together with every touch of his lips.

There were too many layers between us. I clawed at his jacket and he let me go for a torturous second to shrug it off and toss it to the side. We came back together like two fighters about to grapple. He cupped my butt, picked me up, and hoisted me onto something, a counter, a sink? I didn't care. I threaded my fingers through his hair, knotting my fingers in it, and kissed that gorgeous jaw, tasting his skin. I was burning up.

He yanked the straps of my dress down my shoulders, trapping my arms, and buried his face in my bare breasts. I gasped and arched my back. His lips found my nipple. I closed my eyes, savoring each delicious moment. His teeth grazed the sensitive bundle of nerves, his hot tongue tasted me, and he sucked, sending a tiny electric shock through me. I moaned. I wanted to make love to him, and I wanted it to be amazing, so he would stay with me forever.

"*Angelo mio*," Alessandro whispered, his words ragged and rough. "So beautiful."

I opened my eyes and saw the edge of my feathers glowing as his magic roiled around us. I was sitting on a counter, gloriously half naked, and my wings were out, spread wide above my shoulders, each luminescent feather deep green at the base then brightening, like the water of the Aegean growing lighter as one rose from a deep dive, turning emerald, then grass-green, then turquoise until finally at the tips, they shone with radiant gold.

My wings were out.

Reality punched me with a cold hard fist. I jerked away and shoved him back.

"What is it?" Alessandro spun, alert, looking for threats.

My magic was all around him. I had lost it. It made sense now. Why else would he suddenly want to make love to me in the hallway and then kiss me like his life depended on it? Oh my God, what had I done?

"I'm sorry. I'm so sorry . . ."

"What are you sorry about?"

"We have to go." Panic clawed at me, ripping me apart from the inside. I'd destroyed his life. "I have to drain you. We have to . . ."

"I don't have to drain."

"You don't understand. I didn't mean to. We have to fix it."

He grabbed my shoulders and looked into my eyes. "Look at me. Look me in the eyes. Your witchery doesn't work on me. I'm already obsessed with you."

He was too far gone. He was saying nonsense. "Of course you are."

I turned around. Where the hell did it go? "It's okay, it will be okay, I'll fix this."

"What are you looking for?"

"My clutch. I have chalk in it." Even if I drew a circle, it would take forever to drain him. He was a ridiculously powerful Prime. I could run out of magic before he did, and then it wouldn't work.

"What should I do?" he asked. "Should I stay right here, out of the way, and not go anywhere? Would it make you happy?"

"Yes, stand right here and don't move. It will make me very happy."

"Don't move. Got it."

He grabbed his jacket off the tiled floor and walked out. My magic wailed in mourning.

I was alone in the bathroom. Sitting on the sink counter. The sound of rushing water came from the pipes.

He had walked away from me. No person I'd beguiled could've done that.

This was too much. I couldn't process it.

I looked at myself in the mirror. My neck was red. Lipstick smears stretched across my skin from my lips.

In the distance a loud chime announced the end of the intermission. I pulled my dress back up over my breasts, jumped off, and frantically looked for my clutch. I'd put a compact and lipstick into it, and I had to make myself presentable again.

I slipped out of the bathroom. My neck was back to a neutral color, my hair was fixed, and my lipstick tinted my lips and nothing else. Alessandro was fully dressed. We rushed down the hallway to the foyer.

"This did not happen," I told him.

"Oh, it happened. Stopping felt like the hardest fucking thing I had to do in my life. Fighting Benedict now would be a breeze."

"No, it didn't happen and we're not talking about this."

"We are going to talk about it. Tonight. My room, your room, wherever we can find some privacy."

Privacy was the last thing we needed.

We reached the end of the hallway. The second performance was about to start. Alessandro walked me to the table. Cristal was at her table with another glass of champagne.

"I was getting ready to send out a search party," Linus said.

"That's all right," Alessandro told him, "we found our way back."

Pairs of acrobats in silver suits took to the trapeze to the sound of haunting music. The soprano stepped onto the stage. She was about my mother's age, a beautiful black woman wearing a shimmering gold suit that set off her brown skin. Her glossy dark hair fell on her back in a cascade of locks and golden jewels. She tilted her face up and began to sing, her voice rising to the ceiling, clear, pure, and tugging on some deeply buried emotion I couldn't identify. Everything stopped. Madame Trapeze sang her heart out, pouring out emotion as if she had torn herself open for us. I had to fight to keep from crying.

Alessandro covered my hand with his. I should have pulled away, but I didn't. I would get to the bottom of this. I didn't know if I could pry him loose from whatever forced him into murder. I would try as hard as I could. But there was nothing to be done about it right now. We had a job to do, so I listened to the best singer I had ever heard in my life, while the only man I wanted in the entire universe sat next to me and held my hand. Whatever came after, I would always have this moment.

The last notes of the aria died. The song was over. An overwhelming sadness settled over me. We all applauded, Madame Trapeze bowed, and the lights came on.

A waiter came to clear our plates and faltered, perplexed because I hadn't eaten anything. A new lively melody filtered through the speakers.

"Dance with me," Alessandro said.

I put my hand in his and we made our way to the stage. He rested his hand on my back and we swayed among other couples. I had taken enough dancing lessons to not embarrass myself, but nobody around us was doing anything identifiable or complicated. Drifting in pairs seemed to be perfectly acceptable.

Alessandro drifted with a purpose, moving us slowly but inevitably to Cristal's table.

"What are you doing?" I murmured.

"I don't know yet."

"That's great."

"It probably will be."

Humility, thy name is Alessandro. "Were you always immune?"

"No. You sucker-punched me at your trials. Your magic was unfamiliar. But I recovered. If you're asking whether I pretended for your sake, I didn't. I would never falsify the test of a Prime."

"What about when you came to see me after?"

"Back then I just wanted to get to know you better. After I received the invitation to your trials, I looked you up on Instagram. I thought you were cute. I followed you and you deleted your account. I was intrigued. Then I came to invite you for a drive, and you called the cops on me."

"I thought you were besotted."

"I know. You tried to save me from yourself. It was

adorable. Almost as adorable as seeing you chase Conway down the hall."

I quashed the urge to growl.

"You're right, you know." He raised my hand to his lips and kissed my fingers. "I am besotted."

My face was on fire. "Stop."

"Never."

We were nearly to Cristal's table. A pink flush tinted her cheeks. Her eyes were glistening, and her movements, as she leaned in to listen to a young, attractive aquakinetic Prime, were very deliberate. It was the most animated I had seen her all evening. Cristal seemed to suffer from crippling social anxiety and she dealt with it by getting drunk. It was easy to be the queen of snark online. Real life was a whole different war.

A young, dark-haired woman stepped into our way. We had two choices, to stop or to collide with her. We settled on stopping.

"Alessandro Sagredo," she purred.

Alessandro gave her a polite smile. "I don't believe I've had the pleasure."

"Mira Fiore, House Fiore. The American branch of the family. You dated my cousin last spring, Constantia."

Was there anyone he hadn't dated?

The expression on Alessandro's face cooled by several degrees. He didn't respond, he just waited.

His silence and cold stare took some wind out of Mira's sails, but she bravely sailed on. "My friends and I were wondering about your date."

She wasn't even looking at me.

"She's basically a nobody," she continued. "Her House is five minutes old." Her voice rose. Other nearby couples had stopped dancing and watched us. "Her sister marrying Mad Rogan is the only thing that her family is known for. So, you could have had my cousin, but here you are with Catalina Baylor. I'd like to know why."

Okay, that's about enough. I didn't even have to reach for Victoria's granddaughter. I was already there. I looked at her, and Mira wilted.

"Go back to your table." My voice was icy. "You've embarrassed yourself enough for tonight."

Mira opened her mouth and saw the people around us. *That's right, you look rude and stupid. Run away while you can.*

"Baylor?" a deep voice rumbled.

Oh crap.

Mira scooted off to the side. Behind her Frank Madero lumbered to his feet.

"What are you doing?" Cristal squeaked. "Sit down." She put her hand on his forearm as if to restrain him and he pushed it off.

"Your sister put me in the hospital." Madero peered at me, pure rage in his eyes.

I stared him down. Maderos understood strength, nothing else. "You tried to kidnap her."

"Well, I've got just one word to say to you. Rematch!"

He flexed and his suit exploded. His skin turned red, his muscles swelled. He grabbed a table and hurled it at me.

I dodged left, Alessandro dodged right. The table flew between us and froze in mid-air. An older black man next to us turned and fixed Frank with a hard stare. Shelton Woods, Head of House Woods. "That's enough. Sit down."

"I didn't ask you shit, old man!" Frank bellowed, and charged.

The telekinetic swung the table with his magic and smashed it against Frank. The table shattered into splinters. Frank didn't even slow down. Lilian Woods, Shelton's wife of nearly fifty years, grabbed her husband and yanked him out of Madero's way. The pieces of the table and silverware rose in the air and pelted Frank. It didn't stop him, but he had built up too much speed to turn. He tore past us and crashed into the row of tables.

Yeraz, the Armenian Magus Sagittarius, jumped to her feet, grabbed a knife off the neighboring table, and hurled it at Lilian. The knife stopped, reversed, and sank into the table an inch from Yeraz's hand.

"Don't do that again!" Lilian snapped.

Yeraz hissed at her like a snake, grabbed a handful of silverware, and launched it into the air.

Frank rolled to his feet, grabbed two tables like they weighed nothing, and slammed them together, screaming obscenities. Shelton Woods waved his hand. A third table slammed into Frank, slapping him down like a fly-swatter coming down on an annoying insect.

Yeraz's barrage of knives and forks fell harmlessly on the floor. The glass next to Yeraz shot into the air and splashed water into her face.

"Cool off," Lilian told her.

"Kill the old bitch!" Yeraz howled.

Everything happened at once: Diatheke's killers zeroed in on Yeraz's target; the guests realized this was not part of the performance and half of them headed for the exit, while the others stayed to watch or fight; security rushed through the staff entrance and stopped, not sure who to target, and Frank Madero screamed and hurled tables into the air. Magic crackled, furniture flew, and to the left a table burst into flames.

Where the hell was Cristal?

I spun to look behind me. Linus pounded his fist on the table. The silverware flew to his arm, melting, twisting, and snapping together into a barrel. Linus swung his new hand cannon and fired at Frank, who was rampaging in the middle of the floor. Frank's head jerked as the bullet bounced off his skull. He spun around, roaring. I caught sight of Benedict, his face twisted with rage, standing in the middle of the melee, the dark-haired aegis directly behind him. A stray chair hurtled at Benedict's head hit the translucent blue screen of magic and bounced off.

Across the Grand Foyer, Cristal ducked into the hallway leading to the bathrooms.

Frank finally saw me. His beady dark eyes lit up. He barreled at me through the crowd, enormous, brick red, and breathing like a charging bull.

Crap.

Alessandro thrust himself into Frank's path.

"Go!" Alessandro yelled to me. "I've got this."

I ran after Cristal. The last thing I saw before I turned the corner was Alessandro on Frank's shoulders, choking him with a plastic bag.

The hallway stretched in front of me, empty. I sprinted, checking the doors with my hand as I ran.

Locked, locked, locked, empty, bathroom. Nobody in the stalls.

I kept running. The hallway turned, ending in a big round room. A stack of tables waited at the opposite side, where two other hallways branched off. Next to the tables, Cristal had halted, obviously trying to choose an escape route.

"Cristal," I sang out, sending my magic her way.

She turned, a panicked look on her face.

"I'm so glad you're safe," I said in a cheerful, singsong way.

Her mind fluoresced in my magic's eye, a pale glowing smudge. She had a lot of power. It burned bright, but her will was weak and she wasn't a mental mage. My magic wrapped around her, cushioning her from the world and reality. It was almost too easy.

Cristal turned to me.

If I pumped too much magic into her, she would do anything to keep me happy. I needed her to be honest and answer my questions, but not so far gone that she started lying. Linus would have to defend this interrogation, and I didn't want to give anyone ammunition to question it. It had to be evident that Cristal still had some control over herself.

"You know what helps me when I'm scared? I like to sing a little song. Twinkle, twinkle, little star . . ."

"How I wonder what you are," Cristal finished. "It's a baby song. It's stupid."

Perfect. "Do you feel better?"

"I do. But I'm still scared." She knotted the fabric of her skirt in her hands. "Big events are difficult for me. This was supposed to be safe. It was supposed to be nice. There are only nice people here and I have two bodyguards."

I had no idea how much time I would have with her. "It's okay. You're safe with me."

"I know. You seem like a nice person."

I turned my phone on and started Bern's app. He'd written the custom piece of software specifically for times like this. With one tap, I turned on recording, encrypted it, and uploaded it to our cloud. Even if I lost the phone, the conversation would be saved.

"Tell me about Lawrence. Was he a good subject for your research?"

Cristal frowned. "He survived. In terms of compatibility, we could have done better. The goal of the process is to enhance magical talent without the warping side effect."

"What did you use to enhance him?"

"The 1012 variant."

No good. "Variant of what?"

Cristal gave me a look like I was stupid. Even besotted, she still kept her natural disdain for people below her level of expertise. That was some deep personality flaw.

"Variant of the Osiris serum."

"Is 1012 a derivative of 971?"

Cristal gave me a bright smile. "Of course it is."

"Why are you experimenting with the secondary application of the Osiris serum on human subjects? Do you know that it's illegal?"

"Throughout human history a great many things have been illegal. There are always people who stand in the way of progress. There is no difference between Galileo and me. He was the first to discover that the Earth revolved around the sun. I'll be the first to cure a failing vector." She paused, looked at me, and added, "A person born into a magical family whose talent is weaker than their parents' magic."

She had dumbed it down for me. How nice. I wondered what she would say if I told her that the model of heliocentrism was first developed by Aristarchus in the third century BC, eighteen centuries before the birth of Galileo. "That's so interesting, Cristal. Who is financing this important research?"

"Diatheke. Benedict isn't a scientist, but he understands the value of scientific discovery."

"Do you know what Diatheke does?"

"Of course. They're assassins."

And that didn't bother her at all. "How many warped assassins have you supplied to Diatheke?"

"Three."

"How many test subjects died?"

"Seventeen."

"How were these people selected?"

"They were homeless and addicts. They would do anything for their next hit."

That had to be enough. She admitted to doing the research, she acknowledged that it was illegal, and she specified that an assassin firm was paying her bills in return for her supplying them with warped killers. Linus couldn't ask for anything more. It was time for my questions. "Why do you need Halle?"

Cristal frowned again. "Why are you interested in Halle? Halle doesn't matter. You should be interested in me. I'm the important one. Halle is a tool."

She saw Halle as a rival for some reason. I fed more of my magic into our bond. This part wouldn't have to be presented to the National Assembly.

A happy smile stretched Cristal's lips. She linked her arm with mine and stared at me with adoration.

"Tell me about Halle. It would make me happy."

"She's a stupid girl. I'm using her to counteract the toxicity of the serum. You would think a person in her circumstances would figure out that she was trapped and try to please the people who have power over her. If I tell Benedict that she's not useful, she'll just disappear, and nobody will ever find her. I'm keeping her alive. She should be grateful. Instead, everything is a fight with her. I actually had to threaten to have her sister and brother killed to get her to do the simplest things. I mean, does that seem rational to you?"

"Clearly she isn't as smart as you."

Cristal nodded enthusiastically. "I'm very smart. I'm not a failing vector. I'm smarter than my parents."

That's great. "Where is Halle now?"

"At my lab."

"House Ferrer lab? Biocine?"

"No, my personal lab. The real lab. Biocine is where my parents work."

"Where is the real lab? Can you give me the address?"

Cristal's mouth gaped open. Her eyes widened, her eyebrows rose, pulled together, her lips stretched, baring the edge of her teeth. Horror stamped her face, and she stood petrified, locked in place, but shaking. I turned around. Behind us, at the mouth of the hallway leading back to the Grand Foyer, Benedict stood, his face twisted by pure rage. The aegis waited two feet behind him, his face flat. He had seen it all before and none of it bothered him.

Cristal fell to the floor and scrambled up on all fours. A high-pitched animal shriek broke free from her mouth. She spun and dashed down the nearest hallway, sprinting away like she was running for her life.

"Well." Benedict raised his arms. "Here we are. She's an expensive asset. It will take me weeks to undo what I did. Stupid bitch."

I didn't ask which one of us he was referring to. He was a combat Prime and he had an aegis. My best bet was to make it past him and run back to the Grand Foyer, where I'd have the combined firepower of Alessandro and Linus and hundreds of witnesses. Problem was, Benedict stood between me and that hallway.

"I'll need that phone," Benedict ordered.

"You can have it. Let me go and I'll give it to you."

"Let you go?" Benedict tilted his head. "Do you have

any idea how difficult it is to recruit a Prime from an active House? I cultivated Cristal like a priceless orchid. I flattered her, I did her favors, I consoled her when she failed, I rewarded her when she succeeded. I have eighty million and four years wrapped up in this project, and you almost fucked it up for chump change and a dead woman."

I could run into the hallway behind me, but I wasn't a fast runner. If he didn't catch me, his magic would.

Benedict shook his head. "Until now I stayed my hand, because I thought you were working for Montgomery, following that mishap. But now I have confirmation that you're on your own. So, let me break it down for you, Ms. Baylor. You're not going anywhere. You will hand me that phone and walk with me out of this theater. You will get into my car and you will smile the whole time, because if you don't, I'll murder your entire family and I'll make sure they suffer."

You arrogant asshole. I slid the phone into my clutch and gave him a tepid golf clap.

His magic slithered out of him, splaying out like a black thundercloud. The ghostly serpents snapped, demonic mouths forming and melting.

The more I delayed him, the higher the chances were that either Alessandro or Linus would get here. I stalled.

"At first I thought you were creepy, but intelligent. Sadly, I was mistaken. Only an utter moron would bring a Madero into this setting. You've offended two hundred of Houston's most powerful Primes. Yeraz, one of your employees, attacked Lilian Woods in public, in front of witnesses. Do you really think you're coming back from this?"

"Nothing that can't be fixed." Benedict stared at me,

his gaze cold and hungry. "Last chance. Come with me or die here."

Behind him, the aegis looked bored.

Benedict's arrogance had curdled his brain. He killed people without remorse. He kidnapped women just like me. They were scared just like me. He tortured them, squeezing out every drop of fear for his perverse pleasure until there was none left, and then he threw them away like trash. I wanted so much to rip into him. For the first time in my life I wished for Arabella's magic. If only I could grow huge and strong, I'd grab his bodyguard and beat Benedict to death with him. I'd kick him and bounce him off the walls, while his pitiful little snakes bit at my hands. The sight of his terrified face before I stomped him into human pulp would mean everything.

"Fine," Benedict said. "I would have rather done this in private, but why wait?"

The ghostly serpents rose around Benedict. He was about to strike.

My wings snapped open, every feather visible, glowing, radiant with power. Emerald fire danced across their width, flowing into dazzling gold at the tips. My magic erupted and soared, free from being constrained for so long.

Benedict halted in mid-step, his face shocked. Behind him the aegis gaped at me, his face slack.

"Beautiful . . ." Benedict whispered.

I opened my mouth and sang out a high, powerful note, born of pure magic. There was no need to calibrate it. It was utter power made into sound. Madame Trapeze would've been proud.

Benedict jerked his serpent swarm to him, wrapping it around his mind to shield himself.

The note resonated and died, tiny echoes of it traveling into the hallways. I fell silent.

The ghost serpents uncoiled, melting and twisting. Benedict smiled, emerging from the dark storm of his power. "You missed."

I looked past him at the aegis and said, "Save me."

With a primal scream, the aegis tackled Benedict from behind. They went down in a tangle of limbs. I sprinted to my right toward the hallway leading back to the Grand Foyer.

Behind me, the aegis howled, a sound of sheer terror, cut short. I didn't look back. I knew what I would see—Benedict's demonic snakes ripping into the aegis' mind.

The walls of the hallway flashed past.

I turned the corner and almost collided with Alessandro. He caught me. "Hurt?"

"No."

"Benedict?"

"Behind me."

Alessandro sprinted back in the direction I'd come from. I followed. The reasonable thing to do would be to go back to the Grand Foyer, get Linus, get backup, security, other pissed-off Primes, instead of dramatically running toward danger to have a duel with a deranged megalomaniac with snakes growing out of his soul. But if he left the building, he would go straight for my family. And I was done. I was done listening to him, I was done with him killing people and everyone else acting like it wasn't a big deal, I was just done. Someone had to step on that cockroach. Combat mage or no, I could block Benedict's magic enough to give Alessandro the edge, and two Primes were always better than one.

Ahead of me Alessandro slowed and walked into

the round room. The body of the aegis lay crumpled against the wall, his face a twisted, terrified mask. His eyes had rolled back in his head, the milky whites staring up unseeing, as if he had looked his death in the face before it devoured him, and the sight of it had struck him blind.

At the opposite wall, Benedict paused at the mouth of a hallway leading deeper into the building. His jacket hung on his body, one sleeve ripped. Blood stained his pale blue shirt. He saw us and bared his teeth. "You're back. How fortunate for me. You could have run away. Who is an utter moron now?"

Magic flashed with orange, pulsing from Alessandro. A shoulder cannon flashed into existence on his shoulder. He raised his right hand, and an oddly shaped sword popped into it, resembling a violinist's bow, except that the stick was an amalgam of metal parts and the ribbon was a metal cord, thin and razor sharp.

Linus made some weird stuff.

Shock slapped Benedict's face. He recovered almost instantly and raised his eyebrows, his voice mocking. "The artisan graces us with his presence. I'm flattered."

The sword in Alessandro's hand let out a high-pitched metallic whine. The metal shuddered, spinning into the sword, turning it into a weaponized buzz saw.

Benedict's magic lashed out. Orange pulsed from Alessandro. The black serpents fell short.

Benedict turned and sprinted into the hallway. Alessandro's cannon spun and fired, spitting bullets into the corridor. Alessandro marched after him.

I moved to follow.

"Stop." Linus' voice snapped like a whip.

I froze.

Linus strode into the room, still the picture of elegance. If he had gotten into a brawl in the Grand Foyer, he'd come through it undamaged.

"Did you get it?" Linus asked.

"Yes."

"Come with me."

"But—"

"That isn't your fight. He can handle himself. He took the contract as your bodyguard. Let him do his job while we go and do ours. Follow me."

"But—"

"Now."

I gritted my teeth and followed Linus back to the Grand Foyer.

Chapter 15

I sat on the opulent sofa in Linus' Houston mansion and watched him scrutinize my video testimony.

After the opera, Linus and I drove here. He reviewed the recording of Cristal, told me I did well, then interrogated me about it. I wanted to run and find Alessandro. I wanted to kill Benedict. I wanted to search for Cristal's lab so I could rescue Halle. Instead, I had to patiently recount everything that happened, several times over. Once I was done answering questions, Linus instructed me to write an account of what happened, which he then spent half an hour editing, then he had me recite the statement in front of the camera. He wasn't satisfied with my first try, so I'd had to do it again. And again. He was reviewing attempt number three now.

"What happens now?" I asked.

"We wait for authorization. Once granted, we will dismantle House Ferrer until someone tells us where the lab is."

"How long will that take?"

"Does he mean so much to you?" Linus asked.

He was asking about Alessandro. "It's not just him. Halle's life is on the line."

Linus pivoted to me in his chair. "That's not what I asked."

"He means something."

"Why him instead of all the others?"

"What others?"

"You've had opportunities, Catalina. I've watched you come in contact with several young men in the past three years. Four months ago, at the Mercier Exhibit, Justin Pine followed you around like a tail for the entire hour you were there. He is also handsome, wealthy, and a Prime."

I'd barely noticed. I only attended because Arrosa wanted someone to go with her and Nevada couldn't disentangle herself.

"Alessandro Sagredo is dangerous. You could do better. Is it a teenager crush?"

Linus waited.

"I like him," I said. It seemed completely inadequate to describe what I felt. "He's immune to me."

Linus leaned forward, his face serious. "When I was asked to witness the birth of your House, I researched your talent."

How exactly had he done that? I was the only siren in existence. There was another family somewhere in Greece, but they claimed to have lost the magic generations ago.

"Have you ever wondered why your family is immune?"

"They already love me."

"Exactly. Your talent is a survival mechanism, like all magic. It seeks to keep you alive. It activates when it senses someone is a threat. Think back to your childhood. Some adults succumbed to your magic, but others didn't. Do you understand me? Any man who truly falls in love with you and is invested in your survival will be immune. Alessandro isn't your only chance at happiness."

"Even if that's true, I still like him."

"Why?"

I spread my arms. "I don't know. Half of the time I'm with him, he makes me grind my teeth. But I know that if I were in danger, he wouldn't stop until I was safe. He looks at me like I'm beautiful. And he makes me laugh."

Linus put his hand over his face. "God help us all."

What did I say now?

He waved his hand. "Go. Go save Halle and help that young idiot. I'll have the car ready for you."

The little dog stirred on my bed and let out a quiet woof. I opened my eyes. My bedroom was dark, gloom pooling in the corners. The clock on my nightstand said 3:21 a.m. All was quiet.

When I'd gotten home, everyone had swarmed me. I'd kept the explanation short, omitting anything to do with the Osiris serum. I'd told them that Cristal was doing illegal research to make super assassins for Diatheke. They'd bought it, probably because it was mostly true. I told them about Benedict. We made plans for tonight with Heart. We had to get the location of that lab no matter the cost. Every minute we delayed, Halle was in danger.

Alessandro hadn't responded to my text messages. I asked Bug to track him down, but he couldn't find him. I scoured Cristal's background and her family, looking for any scrap of information about the location of the lab until the words on the screen blurred. Finally, I went up to my room and collapsed. That was two hours ago.

Shadow looked at the window. *Woof.*

Woof.

An intruder was coming.

I sat up, scooped Shadow into my arms, and carried her to the bathroom. I set her on the floor and shut the door. I didn't want her to get hurt.

A long-clawed hand hooked my window and slid it up.

I leaned against the wall in the corner.

A dark figure slipped through the open window and into my room. Tall and gangly, he wore a black bodysuit painted with swirls of grey. It clung to him like second skin, highlighting every imperfection of his odd, disjointed body. His shoulders and thighs were too short, while his forearms and shins ran disproportionately long, ending in huge clawed hands and feet. His neck, long and flexible, supported a round head, and as he crawled through my window, he swiveled it like an owl to glance back at the street.

He stepped on the floor and straightened, a bogeyman born from childhood nightmares.

I held very still.

He turned, scanning the room, and the moonlight caught his eyes, big and white, reflecting the light with an eerie green glow.

In the bathroom, Shadow broke down into a cacophony of barks and snarls, digging at the door.

He pivoted to the bathroom door. Step. Another step. Another.

Far enough. I stepped into the soap circle on the floor and sank my magic into it. The arcane lines ignited with sapphire flames in a complex, dazzling array. The assassin froze, startled, his face clear in the glow of the glyphs. Bald, with thick glossy skin mottled with a patina of green, brown, and orange, like the carapace of some strange beetle, he didn't look even remotely human. The typical contours of a man's face, the cheekbones, the nose ridge, the brow, were thickened, as if someone had injected fat under his skin in all the wrong places. The nose had no tip, reduced to a broad, flattened bulge. His chin receded, almost delicate by comparison. The eyes, unnaturally large, stretched toward his ears. Only the mouth was somewhat normal.

Revulsion slithered through me. The urge to flee was so strong, I almost took a step back. I couldn't even tell if it was his magic or just intense xenophobia, triggered by encountering a thing humanlike but not human enough.

Benedict had sent his butcher. He must've given up on taking me alive.

The lines around the assassin pulsed with yellow. The feedback jolted me. He'd struck at me and the circle dispersed it. A wave of emotion washed over me, disgust, hate, and anger, and underneath it all, a sucking vortex of bloodlust. The circle had lobbed his feelings at me. There was no way around this feedback.

The assassin leaped to the side. The circle pulsed in response, and he landed back where he started.

I had designed the circle by modifying an Acubens Exemplar spell to incapacitate an intruder, no matter what brand of magic he or she wielded. It was an all-purpose trap created to contain and interrogate. From above it looked like a large circle filled with a maze of lines and glyphs, with a double circle inside it at one end. Five smaller circles, each filled with progressively smaller rings, touched the outer rim of the main circle.

I stood within the smaller double circle, while the assassin was trapped in the larger ring. The complex pattern around the butcher imprisoned him. He couldn't attack me. He couldn't leave the circle either. His own magic interacting with the boundary held him back. However, he could still attempt to strike at the circle itself, and when he did, his magic would surge through the lines and run off into the five smaller magic sinks.

The assassin crouched on all fours, looking around. The circle fluoresced brighter under his feet. His big, misshapen eyes found me. "Die."

A bright yellow flash exploded from him and ran through the lines of the circle. The five magic sinks spun, absorbing it and became still.

"Die. Die, die, die."

Each burst sent a fresh spike of fury and hate through me. I waited until the sinks stopped spinning. I had all the time in the world.

The assassin stared at me. "Release me."

"Tell me your name."

"Release me or I'll eat your family."

That's what I liked about warped assassins. They were reasonable, pleasant people. Such deep thinkers.

"Tell me your name."

"I'll kill you and eat your guts while you scream."

"Not in that order, you won't."

He charged my circle, clawing at it, his mouth gaping, his small, sharp teeth trying to scrape at the wall of magic. We were barely six inches apart, yet we might as well have been on different continents.

Outside, the emergency streetlamps came on.

The assassin had worn himself out and crouched on the floor again.

"You're here because I let you come here," I told him. "I told the soldiers outside to stay out of your way. I knew Benedict would send you or someone like you. I hoped he would come himself, but he doesn't like to get his hands dirty, does he?"

The assassin bared his teeth. "Whore."

"Answer my questions and it will hurt less."

The assassin grinned. "You sound like him."

"But I'm not him. I didn't look for you. I didn't force you into the circle. You came here to kill me, my friends, and my family. You are a murderer."

"Self-righteous bitch."

He had retained more IQ points than Lawrence. He had a good vocabulary, and his reasoning ran deeper than the summoner's "Kill that bitch because my bugs are hungry." Explained why this one didn't have a handler.

I raised my arms and concentrated. The circle around me began to spin, sending hair-thin chalk lines spiraling through the larger ring. The lines collided with the pattern around the warped, forming a new design in the circle's matrix.

The assassin swiveled his head side to side, trying to keep track.

I sank a burst of power into the circle. The magic shot through the new lines like a spark running down a detonation cord. The assassin's mind flared before me, a bright hot target. I zeroed in on it and struck.

With the right circle, even a weak mental mage could put pressure onto the target's mind, and I was not weak.

The assassin shrieked. I gripped his consciousness with my power and squeezed.

To be beguiled, a person had to be capable of love, and no matter how deep that spark was buried, my magic would coax it into a bonfire. This inhuman creature was knitted from deep-seated hatred, and rage, and contempt for humans. For all of his regression, Lawrence had loved his swarm. The butcher loved nothing. Guilt, fear, or doubt never troubled him, and regret wasn't a concept he understood. I couldn't wrench him open by pulling one of the usual levers present in a human mind. He had none. His will was an impenetrable shell and his inhumanity gave him an extra layer of protection.

I wasn't at my strongest. I was tired, but I didn't need to beguile him. I just had to squeeze his mind open. The circle would do most of the work and it didn't ask for anything complicated. It required raw power, so I reached deep inside myself and found some.

In the ring, the killer raged. Yellow radiance drenched the lines, saturating them. The magic sinks spun, siphoning it off. He had an insane reservoir of magic. His loathing battered me, wave after wave, relentless, his mind churning with rage. Wading through it was like trying to swim through waves carrying razor-sharp rocks. My emotional defenses shook. I gritted my teeth and squeezed him harder.

The two sinks closest to the butcher turned yellow, then orange, saturated to the brink. A normal mage would have stopped out of sheer self-preservation. Spending too much magic too quickly taxed the body, and if a mage exhausted all of their reserves, they lost consciousness. Some never woke up. But he had no capacity for self-preservation. He pounded and pounded against the circle, trying to shatter it, driven by pure rage.

The tide of psychic hatred drowned me. I could no longer keep my head above the water. His emotions coursed through me, threatening to tear me apart. My own reserves were running dry.

A faint crack appeared in the assassin's will. Fear of being trapped and helpless. Finally.

Another magic sink turned orange and stopped spinning.

I gripped at the edges of the crack with my will and pushed.

The fourth sink froze. We were down to one.

He howled, throwing all of his power against the circle in a frenzied barrage.

The final magic sink stopped, saturated. The tide of his emotions swallowed me whole and I hung suspended, no longer sure where I ended and his fury began.

I couldn't quit now. Runa deserved answers. Her brother deserved answers. Halle deserved a life. I would give them that.

The first two sinks collapsed. Magic tore out in twin geysers. My room cracked like a broken mirror. Chunks of wall and window hung motionless for a tortured moment and exploded outward. The roof vanished and the stars stared down at us, cold and indifferent. The entire wall facing the street collapsed. I glimpsed people running below.

The crack in the butcher's mind widened. I could almost sense the creature beneath, a hateful, evil ball of spite.

The third sink burst. The floor under us fell apart. We hung in mid-air, held up by the power of the circle alone. In the bathroom, still safe behind the door, Shadow howled.

He would not win. He crawled into innocent people's houses in the night and he murdered and took them from their beds. He would not take anyone else. He would not kill another mother, another daughter or sister. I would not let him.

I tore myself open and fed the last of my magic into the circle. His will cracked open like a walnut. Darkness clutched at the corners of my eyes. I fought it off and stared at the assassin cowering in the middle of the circle.

"Tell me your name."

"Louie Graham."

"Did you kill Sigourney Etterson?"

"Yes."

"Why?"

"Because Benedict De Lacy ordered it."

"Did you kidnap Halle Etterson?"

"Yes."

"Where did you take her?"

"To Diatheke."

"Where is she now?"

"I don't know."

"Where is the lab where Cristal made you?"

"I don't know."

Damn it. He truly didn't know.

This was why I had let him in. That was all I wanted, and I wouldn't get it. Damn it!

"Do you know that what you did was wrong?"

"Yes."

"Why did you keep doing it? Did you ever think about leaving? Running away?"

He raised his head to look at me. "Why? Benedict doesn't force me to do things. He *lets* me do things. I like to kill. I like to feed. I would kill you if I could and I would enjoy it."

That was it. There was nothing more to ask. I pulled my power out of the circle. The last remaining sink—the fourth one must have shattered while I interrogated him—vomited magic to the sky. The circle faded slowly, collapsing. We fell to the ground, softly at first, then faster. I landed in a blanket stretched under me. The people who held it gently lowered me to the ground.

Louie crashed on the hard pavement ten yards from me. A ring of people surrounded us, Heart's soldiers,

Mom, Grandma Frida, Arabella . . . The familiar faces were turning fuzzy. I'd overextended.

Someone pushed through the crowd and walked over to Louie. Red hair—Runa.

"You killed my mother," she told him.

Louie bared his teeth at her. Magic lashed from him, but the butcher had nothing left. His strike cut Runa's cheek. She touched the cut, looked at the red staining her fingers, and smiled.

I would remember that smile till the day I died.

Deep green magic flared like a glowing ribbon between Runa's bloody fingers. It snaked out and kissed Louie's cheek.

The assassin screamed.

I sat on the curb, wrapped in a blanket and drinking a cup of hot tea, Shadow curled by my feet chewing on a stick. Arabella had found my phone among the rubble and brought it to me. A big crack split the screen, but miraculously the phone still worked. Alessandro still hadn't replied to any of my messages.

The warehouse was wrecked. The entire corner where my room used to be and everything under it was gone, as if a giant had looked at the warehouse from above, decided it was cake, and carved himself out a piece. I could see straight into our house. Heart's soldiers had declared it unsafe and made us stay back fifty feet.

To the right, across the street, Bern stood with a despondent look on his face gazing at the collapsed floor between him and the Hut of Evil inside. We had no idea if any of our servers survived. On his left, Bug tentatively touched his shoulder, the way you would do to comfort someone at a funeral. On his right Runa was talking. I couldn't make it out, but I understood her expression. *It's not that bad. I'm sure it will be fine, you'll see.*

It would not be fine. Before all of our modifications and insulation, the warehouse was a single steel building. The integrity of the structure was likely compromised. The electric wires, the pipes, and the walls themselves looked neatly cut. A stream had formed on our street, where water had fountained out of the severed pipes before someone shut it off.

Our water bill is going to be huge.

I didn't know why, but that thought almost pushed me over the edge. If I had any strength left, I would have cried, Head of the House or no, but I was too tired.

Where would we find the money to repair this? Where would we live? Theoretically, we could split up and move into other buildings we owned, but the warehouse had been our home and now it was gone.

A chunk of the roof the size of a garage moaned with a metallic screech and plunged to the street.

I couldn't even. I wasn't sure I could ever even again.

On the bright side, we had no insurance to pay for any of this.

I had gambled everything on finding Halle and I lost. I was so sure that Benedict would send another warped assassin after me and it seemed so logical that they would know where they had been altered. I was wrong.

Mom came over and sat next to me.

"I destroyed the house," I told her.

"Don't be ridiculous. You tried to save a child. We all went along with it. Nobody could have anticipated this."

My cell rang. I looked at it. Nevada.

"Hello?"

"Hi! How's everything?"

Next to me, Mom shook her head, her eyes really big.

"Everything is great," I lied. "We're doing great. The warehouse is great."

"Umm, Catalina?"

Another chunk of the roof collapsed. "We're having a thunderstorm." It was good her magic didn't work over the phone.

"Okay," Nevada said. She wasn't buying a word of what I was selling. "I have big news."

"Oh good. Mom is here. I'll put you on speaker." I pushed the icon. "Go."

"I'm pregnant!"

I raised my voice. "Hey everybody, Nevada is pregnant."

Everybody made cheering noises.

"Catalina," Nevada said. "I can hear water running. I can tell by the sound that you're outside. If it's raining, why are all of you outside in the storm?"

"Love you, got to go." I hung up.

A van pulled up to the curb. Shadow dashed toward it, barking. The windows rolled down and four heads stuck out, one human and blond, and the other three belonging to boxer dogs.

Cornelius stared at the warehouse. "What did I miss?"

I'd laugh, but again, no strength left.

Mom and I looked at the warehouse some more.

"Sorry," I said.

"It will be okay," Mom said. "It was time to let it go, anyway."

Runa looked at her phone and jerked it to her ear, her eyes wild. "No! Don't do it, please don't do it!"

Oh, what the hell now?

Runa hurled the phone to the ground, then dived down, grabbed it, turned, and ran to us.

Mom and I looked at her. Arabella dropped what she was doing and sprinted over to us.

"It's Ragnar." Tears wet Runa's eyes. "He just walked into Diatheke."

"Why?" The word fell out of me.

"He said that he was done surviving. He couldn't let them hurt anybody else." Desperation skewed her face. "I need a car. A fast one."

"I've got you," Arabella said.

"I'm coming with you," I said.

"Can I talk to you for a second?" Arabella looked at everyone around us. "Can we have some privacy?"

"I'll meet you at your car." Runa spun on her foot and walked away.

Arabella crouched by me. "You're in charge and if you order me, I'll take you. But you're tapped out. You can't even stand. My car sits four. I'll take Runa, Leon, and Mom."

She was right. I hated it but she was right. Every second counted, and they needed to pack as much firepower as they could into four seats.

"Go," I said. "I'll come with the second wave."

She hugged me and took off at a run. Mom followed her.

My phone rang again. Alessandro. Alive. Oh my God, he was alive. Relief drowned me.

"Are you okay?" I whispered.

"Yes," he said. "Are you?"

"Yes."

"I didn't get Benedict." Frustration sharpened his voice. "I'll be at the warehouse in half an hour."

"I won't be here. Ragnar just attacked Diatheke. We're going to get him."

"What the hell is he doing?" Alessandro snarled.

"Trying to kill everyone by himself."

"I'll get him. I'm closer."

"Don't! It's suicide."

He growled something fast in Italian and hung up.

Ten minutes later I strapped myself into the safety harness inside Heart's APC. Next to me Bug fiddled with a tablet, his hand flying over the onscreen keyboard.

The APC rumbled and lurched forward. All around me Heart's soldiers rode, their faces relaxed.

Bug thrust the tablet in front of me. On it, Alessandro walked into Diatheke.

What the hell was he doing? My heart squeezed itself into a tight, painful ball in my chest. *Please, please let it be okay. Let it all be okay.*

The sound of gunfire emanated from the building on the tablet, tearing the silence. Everyone looked at us.

"That's all I got," Bug said.

The doors of Diatheke were gone. Glass shards littered the sidewalk. The metal grate hung crumpled to one side. Heart's people streamed into the building past me. I wanted to run, but walking was the best I could manage, and the two bodyguards Heart assigned to me refused to move faster.

Bodies sprawled in the lobby, two men and a woman. Black fuzz sheathed the corpses. Runa or Ragnar had been through here.

A soldier waited by the elevator. He swiped a bloody keycard and the doors swung open. "Your mother and sister are on the top floor," he said. "Leon is sweeping the building with a team."

We stepped into the cabin and the elevator carried us up. I couldn't even worry anymore. I was just numb.

The elevator opened to the aftermath of a slaughter. Bodies lay on the expensive carpet, some slashed, some shot, others sprouting the same black fuzz from downstairs. The door to Benedict's office had exploded and broken shards protruded from the walls. Inside, the butchery continued. Blood soaked the carpet. Corpses stared with unseeing eyes as we passed. Priceless art lay discarded like trash, ripped from the walls.

We turned into the Ottoman room. The massive rug had disappeared. The remnants of an arcane circle smoked, etched into the floor. To the right, my mother slumped in a chair, Arabella kneeling by her. To the left, Runa wrapped her arms around a sobbing Ragnar. Blood drenched him from head to toe, dripping from his hair and clothes.

A heap of clothes smoked slightly in the center of the circle. I had seen this before. Someone had used an arcane circle to teleport out. Unless the teleporting mage was a Prime, teleporting killed almost as many people as it transported safely. It was a desperate last resort, it required a high-caliber teleport mage, and it couldn't transport anything inorganic. When someone teleported a human, clothes, breast implants, and pacemakers stayed behind.

Mom saw me.

"Is anybody hurt?"

"No," she said. "This wasn't us. The place was like this when we got here. The boy and Alessandro turned this place into a graveyard."

Panic punched me. "Where is he?"

Mom shook her head.

What does that mean?

"Is he dead?" *Oh my God, oh my God, oh my God . . .*

"He saved me," Ragnar said through his sobs.

"Where is he?" I barked.

"They teleported him." Arabella stood up. "They contained Ragnar and were going to take him to the lab, and then Alessandro showed up and murdered everyone in the damn building. When he broke into this room, the teleport mage panicked and teleported herself and Alessandro out."

The teleport circle took forever to set up and it corresponded to a marker at the destination. You couldn't just change the arrival point on the fly.

I turned to Ragnar. "Were they going to teleport you?"

"Yes."

The teleporter had to point to the lab. If Alessandro survived, he would arrive naked, dazed, and without weapons. He had already taken on a building full of killers. He had to be near his limit.

We had no time. We had to find the lab now.

If they tried to magic warp him . . .

I shoved that thought aside. "Ragnar, did they say where the lab was?"

"No. I'm sorry, this is all my fault . . ."

I tuned him out, scouring my memories. There had to be something, something I heard, something I saw, something that would point me in the direction of that damn lab.

Going to Linus was out of the question. He told me to wait. I didn't wait. I would have to answer for that. There was no way to predict how he would react.

Benedict would know. Benedict—

It hit me like a freight train. I spun to Arabella. "I need you to drive me."

She didn't ask where. She jumped to her feet and followed me to the elevator.

"You are out of your mind," Arabella said.

The Shenandoah State Correctional Facility, nicknamed the Spa, rose in front of us. About an hour and a half north of Houston, the Spa knew it was a prison, but it really wanted to be a luxury resort. Wrapped in a picturesque stone wall ten feet high, it was built in the style of the Spanish masonry star forts, a four-story-high pentagon with bastions at the corners of the walls. A luxurious park occupied the space between the wall and the citadel, complete with a track, a driving range, and a tennis court. As we drove past the guard at the gate to the main parking lot, elderly people on the track waved at us.

When the Texas magical elite chose to serve time, they did it at the Spa. The residents were predominantly older, not necessarily nonviolent, but shrewd enough to recognize that spending a few months at the Spa for their transgressions was much more pleasant than pitching a fit and being shipped off to the Ice Box in Alaska or the Iron Locker in Kansas. This was the place our grandmother chose to pay her debt to society.

Arabella parked. "She's not going to help you. Even if she wanted to, she's locked up here. What do you think she can do?"

"I have a plan." I got out of the car and headed for the arched doors. My body ached, and my legs shook a little. I had passed out two minutes into the drive and didn't wake up until Arabella turned the music all the way up about two miles back.

My sister followed me. "Your plan involves making a deal with a rabid shark."

"Sharks cannot get rabies. They're fish."

My sister waved her hands. "You know what I mean. Don't do this. We'll find him another way. We can go to Linus. He likes us."

I looked her in the eye to make sure I had her attention. "Linus forbade me from attacking Diatheke. Right now we have to stay away from him. If he calls, don't answer the phone and don't tell him where we are."

"What the hell happened at Linus' ranch?"

"I can't tell you."

"What will he do when he finds out you disobeyed?"

I put my hand on the door handle and pushed. "One problem at a time."

We walked into the lobby. Two surveillance cameras and an automated turret mounted on the ceiling registered our presence. The Spa seemed old but looks were deceiving. It was a state-of-the-art facility. By now our faces had been scanned and run through their database.

"Please don't do this. Nothing good will come from it."

She was right, but I had no choice. "Please wait for me. Don't go anywhere."

"No, I'm going to drive off and have ice cream." Arabella rolled her eyes and headed for the elegant reception area equipped with its own coffee bar.

I walked to the officer trapped in a round cage of bulletproof glass.

"Catalina Baylor, Head of House Baylor," I spoke into the small window covered by a grate. "I'm here to see Victoria Tremaine. It's urgent."

"Visitor hours begin at eleven," the officer behind the glass told me.

"Did you not hear me? I'm here to see my grand-mother."

The officer took a step back, spoke into her headset, and then said to me, "Proceed. Follow the blue line."

As I passed by the booth, an older white woman sipping her coffee leaned to her visitor, a dark-haired man about my age, and murmured, "Apple didn't fall far from the tree."

Ugh.

I followed the blue line, which consisted of a beautiful glass mosaic built into the travertine floor. It brought me to a heavy door, which swung open at my approach, releasing me into the inner garden. Roses bloomed on both sides of the brick and gravel path, behind a row of boxwood. I stopped and waited.

A door opened somewhere. A few seconds later my grandmother walked onto the path from the side. She'd lost weight. Six inches taller than me and two shades paler, my grandmother wore a white blouse of tiny hexagons defined by silver thread, soft grey slacks, and a brocade coat with silver and mother-of-pearl embroidery tracing a pattern over cream fabric. Her silver hair was twisted into an elegant coil on the back of her head. Her makeup was understated but flawless. The only concession to prison she had allowed were her shoes, light grey, expensive, but with a short heel. The type Grandma Frida would have called sensible.

Victoria Tremaine looked at me. Everything about her, from the way she stood to the way she stared, communicated unapologetic power. She turned and walked down the path.

I chased after her, caught up, and fell in step. I had demanded an audience, and now she put me in my place.

"What can I do for you, Head of House Baylor?"

I had rehearsed this speech in the car on the way over, after Arabella woke me up. Looking at her now, I knew none of it would work. She was a truthseeker and she would know if I lied. "I need your help."

"Obviously. Be more specific."

"Runa Etterson came to me for help because Diatheke killed her mother and kidnapped her sister. Diatheke had recruited Cristal Ferrer to produce warped killers capable of magic manipulation. Cristal Ferrer has a secret lab, where she's holding Runa's sister. Runa's brother attacked Diatheke. Alessandro Sagredo, who has been working with me, went in to save him, and was teleported to that same lab."

I paused for a breath.

"So far I fail to see how any of this is my problem."

"I have to get Alessandro and Halle out of the lab."

Victoria narrowed her eyes. "This Alessandro, what is he to you?"

"I love him."

Alarm dashed down my spine. I had admitted it.

"I see. Where do I fit in?"

"Before I took the case, Augustine warned me away from it. His exact words were 'I know exactly what you're up against. Sometimes when you search the night, you'll find monsters in the dark.' I discovered later that Augustine's agents caught one of Diatheke's warped assassins in action. By now Augustine's people would have extensively surveilled Diatheke. That's how he operates. He knows where the lab is."

"Most likely. Has Montgomery approached you with an offer? House to House?"

"Yes. I regretfully declined."

Victoria raised her eyebrows. "Why?"

"Because House Baylor will not be a vassal House."

She didn't say anything.

I kept going, trying to stuff my desperation deep inside to keep it from showing on my face.

"Augustine never shares. He trades. When I rejected his offer, I told him that if I came seeking information, I would bring valuable information in return. I have to give him an item in trade."

Victoria tilted her head. "You could just accept his offer."

"I can't do that."

"But what about Alessandro?"

I closed my eyes for a second. It felt like I was being ripped apart. "I can't. Not for him, not for Halle. This is about our survival as a House. If I put on Augustine's leash, he would force us to compromise everything we stand for."

"So you come to me, because you think I have information to trade?"

"I know you do. You approached Augustine when you were looking for Nevada. You would not have gone to that meeting empty-handed. Please help me."

"Why?"

"Because I'm your granddaughter. Our House doesn't bear your name, but we have your blood. We're the only family you have. You don't want to see us fail."

I held my breath.

She stopped and pondered the delicate golden roses. "Your older sister failed me. She has my magic, but she's too set in her ways. She's inflexible and incapable of cruelty, and sometimes survival requires it. Arabella, adorable as she is, is too young and impulsive, and her magic makes her think she's invulnerable. She's rarely afraid, and the Head of the House needs to know fear. Failure is the best teacher, and fear is the best motivator. Of the three of you, you're the most like me. You're smart like me. You're sensitive like me. The world cuts you deeply, and it will either kill you, or you will grow armor the way I did."

When I thought of my father's mother, *sensitive* was not a word that came to mind.

Victoria studied me. "I can work with you. But it will cost you."

I raised my chin and waited.

"And that's the difference between the three of you. Nevada would have told me she would give me nothing and stormed off to fight the war on her own. Arabella would have promised me anything. And you are . . . just waiting."

I kept waiting. It seemed to be working for me.

"For the House to survive, the family needs someone to steer it. You can't belong to two Houses at once; you have to choose. If you marry into a powerful House, you'll choose your husband over your House the way Nevada did."

I opened my mouth to argue.

"I'm not finished. My deal is this: I'll give you information to trade to Augustine. And I'll help you in the future with advice, knowledge, and influence. In return, you'll dedicate yourself to House Baylor. You won't dilute your bloodline. If you marry, your husband must be a Prime and he must join your House and renounce all ties to his other family."

That was impossible.

"So, you can save your pretty Italian, you can fuck him, but you can't marry into his House. I know that family; they're old nobility, so wrapped up in their own blue blood, they can't see past their noses. They'll never let him go. You won't be a countess. You will never go to Italy. Your place is here. Think very carefully before you say yes, because you might get out of a deal with the devil, but you won't bargain out of a deal with me."

With one hit she ripped my future away from me. I stood there frozen while my mind feverishly sorted through it all.

What did I want from my future? I'd never asked myself that before, but I always knew the answer. I wanted to find someone who made me happy and whom I made happy. I wanted to marry him. I wanted kids. I wanted a family. And most of all, I wanted to be myself, to be open instead of clenching myself into the tight fist of my will every waking moment. I wanted to be loved for who I was, and I wanted to love in return.

There would never be another Alessandro for me. Having sex with him wouldn't be enough. She'd shattered the little fragile hope that I could pry him loose from whatever trap he was caught in and we could be together.

Even if I found another Prime immune to my magic the way he was, even if that Prime agreed to abandon his House—which would never happen—that Prime would not be Alessandro.

My life was over. In fifty years, I might end up just like her, alone, abandoned by everyone because of the things I had to do to keep them alive. If I somehow managed to have a child, would my grandchild stand before me fifty years from now and pass judgment on my life? Would he or she think I was horrible and didn't understand what it meant to be young and in love?

This was the first step onto the path of my new life. There would always be hard choices, hard decisions to make, but none would be harder than this.

My future versus Alessandro's life. Halle's life.

I had to look my reflection in the eye at the end of the day.

"We have a deal," I said.

"Ten years ago, another House attacked House Montgomery and murdered Augustine's father and his younger sister."

I knew everything there was publicly to know about House Montgomery. There was no record of that attack anywhere. Public record said Augustine's father died after a long battle with pancreatic cancer.

"The attackers were killed, but the identity of their employer was never discovered. The hit was arranged through a middleman, Melvin Rider. Before the attack he disappeared. Hand me your phone."

I unlocked my phone and passed it to her. She grimaced and showed me the crack in the screen. She typed exactly the same way my mom did, holding the phone in her left hand and pecking at the letters with her right index finger. Grandma Victoria handed the phone back to me.

"This is Melvin Rider's new name and his current address. Make sure Augustine gives you the information first. Always make it seem like you are negotiating from a position of strength. Remember, you are my granddaughter. Chin up, shoulders back. Look them in the eye and make them cower."

I walked back to reception. Arabella saw me and hurried over.

"Are you okay?"

"Yes."

"You're crying."

I swiped at my eyes. My cheeks were wet. Weird. I hadn't even noticed.

"I've got what I need," I told her. "Let's go."

𝔐ontgomery International Investigations owned an entire building downtown. An asymmetric structure of blue glass and steel, it rose above its neighbors like a shark fin whose owner was about to surface.

Augustine's office took up an entire corner of the seventeenth floor. I had walked on my own power across the lobby to the elevators and now to the office. I had fallen asleep again in the car. When I reached for my magic, I no longer felt a void. I wouldn't be at full strength for another forty-eight hours or so, but it was coming back slowly. Sleep helped.

Augustine's receptionist, a young woman with pale brown skin and lavender hair, saw us and picked up the phone.

"He'll see you now, Ms. Baylor."

"Thank you."

I headed toward Augustine's desk behind a wall of frosted glass. Behind me, Arabella chirped, "I love your makeup."

"Thank you!" The receptionist's voice warmed by at least ten degrees. "It's the new Oksana palette."

"The limited edition one?"

A section of the frosted glass slid aside with a soft whisper and I walked into Augustine's office. He sat at a modern white desk in an ergonomic chair. Behind him two walls of cobalt glass met at a sharp angle, presenting a panorama of the city below.

Augustine looked up from his computer, a god in his palace of crystal and ice. The door slid shut behind me.

"Do you have anything for me?"

He knew I did. "Yes. Before we trade, I need to know if you have the information I require. The matter is urgent. A yes or no answer will be fine."

"Please sit."

I sat. "I need to know the location of the lab Cristal Ferrer uses to produce warped mages for Diatheke."

Augustine's eyebrows rose. "I have it."

Of course he did.

"How good is your information?" he asked.

"It comes courtesy of my grandmother. She sends her regards." I had weighed this answer very carefully. I could have taken credit for the information or left him wondering where I got it, but I couldn't give him any reason to doubt its authenticity. Victoria's name was an iron-clad guarantee.

He considered it. "Very well, I'll play."

He took a pad of paper from his desk, wrote on it, tore off a page, and slid it across the desk to me. I picked it up. An address northeast of Houston, in Williams, a small town along I-69. I could be there in less than two hours. He could've texted it to me, but then I would have proof it came from him.

Hold on, Alessandro. I'm coming. I would get him and Halle out of there, if they were alive.

"Thank you." I took a picture of the page with my phone and sent it to Bern. "You may want to write this down. Bradley Lynton, 12703 Mistie Valle Drive, Houston, Texas 77066."

Augustine wrote it down. "And why is this important?"

"Because Bradley Lynton is his new name. He was previously known as Melvin Rider."

All the color bled from Augustine's face. The illusion fractured for a moment and I saw his real eyes, shocked and triumphant. His face snapped back into perfection. "Thank you, Ms. Baylor. I look forward to our cooperation in the future. Now, if you'll excuse me, I have someplace to be."

So did I. I rose. "Good luck."

"You too. You're going to need it."

Arabella shook me. "We're here."

I opened my eyes. The inside of Brick was surprisingly comfortable and the narrow side windows let in just enough light to make it cozy. Across from me, Runa grinned from the bench. Arabella slid back into her seat to her right.

Next to me, Leon was checking two P320-M17 Sig Sauers. Same model as the official sidearm of the US Army, they were his favorites. Each came with a seventeen-round magazine, which meant he could fire thirty-four 9mm rounds before he had to reload. He rarely had to reload. Leon was a one-shot, one-kill shooter.

In the front passenger seat Mom patted the rifle case resting against her shoulder. Her Barrett sniper rifle was inside. She'd also taken her favorite.

Grandma Frida brought Brick to a stop. I peered through the windshield. We had left the road behind and parked on top of a low hill. Below, sheltered by a concrete wall topped by razor wire, sat a fourteen-story tower. Unlike most modern buildings of glass and steel, this structure looked older, made of rings of concrete interrupted by rows of narrow, dark windows.

I unbuckled my harness and opened the back hatch. We filed out. I checked my face in the side mirror.

If I'd had an extra day, I would have spent it in a charging circle trying to regain my magic. But I had no time, and you couldn't draw a circle on the floor of Brick. There wasn't enough space. So, instead, I drew the glyphs on myself. My face, my neck and most of my body where I could reach it were covered with arcane patterns in henna. I'd turned myself into a walking arcane circle absorbing magic at an accelerated rate. It would give me back my power, but in another hour, maybe two, I would collapse.

Had anybody in my family known how dangerous this was, they would have never let me do it. I was lucky Nevada was in Spain.

The lab building rose, so close. Somewhere in that tower Alessandro and Halle waited, hopefully still alive. I checked the Beretta on my hip and the gladius in its sheath on the other hip.

"Are you sure about this?" Mom asked.

"Yes."

"You will have to tell Duncan," she said.

I took out my phone.

Linus picked up on the second ring.

When in trouble, go for the good news first. "I have learned the location of Cristal's lab," I said.

"Delightful." He did not sound delighted. "Where are you right now?"

"May I have authorization to assault the lab?"

"Are you at the lab?"

"Technically, no. But I'm looking at it."

The steady rumble of a helicopter echoed from above. A large chopper passed overhead, carrying a container on steel cables. The cables snapped free, and the container plummeted to the ground and landed in the field with a loud thud.

"Oh," Grandma Frida said. "A present."

The sides of the container collapsed outward, revealing a strange-looking block of metal parts. With a loud metal clang, the block rose, unfolding into a nine-foot-tall exosuit on two sturdy legs. Massive turrets protruded from its arms. Its shoulders bristled with weapons.

Great.

The exosuit turned, zeroed in on us, and stomped in our direction. Runa raised her hand, aiming for it.

"No," I told her.

The exosuit treaded over, each step of the heavy metal legs like a blow of a giant hammer, and towered over me. Its facial shield turned clear, and Linus stared down at me from the inside.

Perfect. Just perfect.

Linus' voice spilled out of the loudspeaker. "When this is over, you and I are going to have a long conversation about the nature of orders and the meaning of the word *wait*."

I winced.

Grandma Frida wiggled her fingers at him. "Hello, Linus."

Mom put her hand over her face.

"I promise to sit through the entire lecture quietly," I said. "May I please have authorization to rescue Alessandro and Halle Etterson?"

"Authorization granted. You are authorized to go down there, gain entry to the facility, neutralize any hostiles you encounter, and retrieve any civilians you find. Do not screw with anything in the labs. Don't touch anything, don't drink anything, don't put anything in your mouth."

Leon looked like he was about to speak. I made the *no* face at him.

"Follow me," Linus ordered. "And cheer up. We're about to embark on a killing spree accompanied by massive property damage. Try to have fun."

The facial shield darkened. Leon grinned and gave Linus two thumbs-up.

The exosuit started down the hill. Mom climbed onto

Brick's roof with her sniper rifle. Grandma Frida took a picnic basket out of the vehicle and perched on a grassy spot. The rest of us followed Linus.

"So, do we have a plan?" Runa asked.

"We go inside, Leon and I try to find your sister and Alessandro, and you and Arabella kill everyone you see. Try not to die."

"That's it?"

"The best plans are simple," Leon said.

Ahead of us a barrel on the exosuit's right shoulder spat out thunder. A missile streaked through the air and smashed into the wall. Concrete exploded, huge chunks hurtling into the air. Sirens wailed, reaching a hysterical pitch.

Linus continued his advance, the exosuit stomping forward, *boom, boom, boom.*

"Well, I'm off," Arabella said.

"Give me a few minutes before you start on the building," I told her.

"It's not my first time."

Leon grinned. "Remember, try to have fun."

My sister smiled. "I always do."

She sprinted after the exosuit. Her body tore, the transformation so fast, it seemed almost instant. An enormous shaggy beast spilled out of my sister, towering sixty feet above us. Arabella raised her head with two curved horns, opened her maw, baring a forest of fangs, and bellowed.

Runa jumped back. "That's the Beast of Cologne!"

"Yes, it is," I told her.

"How?"

"Long story," I told her.

The monster that was Arabella charged to the left, circling the lab, and cleared the wall in a single leap.

Gunfire erupted. She screamed in rage, grabbed a vehicle, and threw it at the building.

In front of us Linus broke into a run. The barrels on his shoulders spat more missiles, trailing smoke in their wake, and for a moment he had wings of smoke. The missiles flew through the gap in the wall. Explosions blossomed, yellow and orange. Linus charged into the gap, the turrets on his arms sending death into the air.

I stopped. Leon sat on the grass next to me and whistled. Runa stared at the two of us. "Shouldn't we go in?"

"Not yet."

"You have to let the big kids have their fun," Leon said.

Arabella had gotten ahold of a semi-truck and was pummeling something with it.

Seconds ticked by, dragging minutes behind them. Waiting was torture.

Please stay alive. I'm almost there.

The sound of explosions receded, moving deeper toward the building and into it.

"Now we go in." I ran for the gap.

The inside of the wall was chaos. People ran back and forth, equipment and vehicles burned, broken bodies slumped everywhere. Thick, oily smoke poured out of what once might have been a truck and was now an unrecognizable clump of metal. Small firearms crackled. Somewhere a turret was going, spitting out a staccato of bullets. I turned toward the tower.

The doors no longer existed. I jogged inside, Runa and Leon following me. The inside of the tower was hollow. A bank of glass elevators waited in the center of the room. Each floor resembled a wheel with a central narrow hallway and individual rooms radiating from it like spokes. If I rode that transparent elevator, I could see the entirety of the lab.

A woman with a gun stepped out from behind the elevator. Leon's gun barked and she collapsed.

"Don't shoot the next one," I said. "We need a guide."

"No promises," Leon said.

I closed my eyes, looking for the nearest mind. Someone was hiding behind the counter to our right. I turned and started humming. "Mary had a little lamb; its fleece was white as snow . . ."

The mind under the counter responded to the tendrils of my power. A chair rolled to the side, and an older white man in a lab coat stood up and smiled at me. His name tag said "Chad Rawlins."

"Hello, Chad," I said, sinking power into my voice.

"Hi." He waved at me.

"Come stand by me."

Chad moved over on trembling legs. "I'm very scared right now."

"I'm sorry to hear that."

An explosion burst above our heads. The building shook. Chad cringed.

"Do you know where they're holding Halle Etterson?" I asked. "She's my friend. I want to find her. It would make me very happy."

He nodded. "She's on the seventh floor. Room 713. Can we go? We shouldn't be here. It's very dangerous."

Runa ran to the elevator and mashed the call button. Stairs would be safer, but I wasn't sure I could make it. My magic was replenishing, but my body was still exhausted and getting more so by the minute.

"What about the prisoner they teleported in this morning? Where is he?"

Chad blinked. "I don't know about a prisoner."

Leon nudged me. "Ask him where Benedict is."

"Is Benedict De Lacy here?"

Chad nodded. "He's on the top floor."

Of course he was. Benedict would never pass up a chance for a penthouse. If Alessandro was here, Benedict would keep him close. They hated each other, and Alessandro made a valuable hostage.

"Tell me about the top floor where Benedict stays."

"I don't go up there. I don't know what's up there, except that you can't bring any weapons up there. He's got an automated turret pointed at the elevator. The elevator opens in this little room that scans you and he won't let you exit it with a gun."

Fuck.

"You can go," I told Chad.

He started toward the hole where the doors used to be, then turned. "But what about you?"

"I'll be fine."

"I think I should stay with you. Just in case."

Leon sighed and reached for his gun. I put my hand over his. "Chad, do me a favor. Go outside and check to see if it's safe for me to escape."

"I'll do that. Don't go anywhere. I'll be right back."

He took off for the door and the three of us ducked into the elevator. Runa had pressed the button for the seventh floor. I reached over and pushed the top button.

"What are you doing?" Runa asked.

"Leon will go with you. He'll get you and Halle out."

"That wasn't the deal," Runa growled. "You can't go up against Benedict by yourself."

"That was always the deal," Leon said. "You're the client. We're here to save your sister."

The elevator doors opened. Leon thrust his arm out to keep them open.

"We get Halle and we go after Benedict together," Runa said.

"No," I told her. "That would put you and her into additional danger. Save your sister, Runa. Please."

"Come on," Leon said. "Halle is waiting."

He took Runa's arm and pulled her out of the elevator. The doors shut and the cabin sped upward. The elevator climbed through what I had thought to be the ceiling and kept going, the shaft no longer transparent, but dark.

Linus' priority was the research and retrieving the serum. Runa's priority was her sister. In the grand scheme of things both Alessandro and Benedict mattered very little. But Alessandro meant everything to me.

I took out my Beretta and placed it on the floor of the elevator. I would never get through that room with it.

The doors whispered open. A small room waited for me, complete with an X-ray arch. A security camera stared at me from the ceiling just above a turret facing me.

I pulled out my gladius and jammed it in the elevator door.

"Entertaining but futile," Benedict's voice said.

I stepped out of the elevator. The door behind me tried to close but my sword kept it open. I stepped into the X-ray, letting the beam of the scanner dance over me.

There was a pause, then the door in front of me opened. A big room lay past the doorway, the entirety of it taken up by an arcane circle of dizzying complexity, its lines glowing with pale light. In the center of the circle Alessandro paced, nude, his face furious.

"Welcome to my parlor," Benedict said.

I took the chalk out of my pocket, palmed it, and walked through the doorway.

Time slowed and I saw everything at once, as if my mind was a camera flashing to capture the details: Alessandro, his magic flaring around him; Benedict to the side standing in a separate circle connected to the larger one; a windowless round room, a cupola above us; a large screen on the wall showing the elevator still trying to close; the body of a woman, crumpled at the far wall; and the bigger circle itself, a seemingly chaotic array of circles and lines.

The glowing patterns snapped together in my head. Alessandro was trapped in the center, able to use his magic, but cut off from the rest of the room and the building by the power of the circle. He couldn't manifest any weapons because his magic didn't work past the arcane boundary. Benedict, on the other hand, was free to use his magic, and the circle allowed him to attack at will. The lines would channel his power and unleash it on whoever was trapped in the center.

It was eerily similar to the trap I had created in my bedroom, but my trap was designed to contain and inflict mental pressure. This circle was designed to contain and amplify Benedict's power. Old blood smears and scratch marks scarred the wooden floor under Alessandro's feet. The kind of scratch marks human nails made.

This was Benedict's fun room. He brought women here and tortured them in that circle. This was what Alessandro had saved me from with that shot shattering the elephant. The teleport spell had been less than thirty feet away from that window. I had crossed the rug that covered it to talk to Benedict.

Benedict must have tried it with Alessandro, but Alessandro's magic worked within the small space allowed to him. He would have nullified Benedict's attack. The moment Benedict left the smaller circle, the power of the bigger one would dissipate, and Alessandro would be free. They had trapped each other.

Benedict's suit coat lay discarded on the floor. His tie was missing, his shirt open at the collar. Sweat drenched his face, darkening his hairline. They must have been at this for hours.

All I had to do was knock Benedict out of his point of power. There were forty feet between us.

"Get out," Alessandro snapped, his voice harsh.

"Let me guess," I said to Benedict. "You were packing, getting ready to disappear, and then, poof, Alessandro lands in your trap, and a terrified teleport mage appears in the room. You had no time to do anything except step into the circle to activate it and contain Alessandro before he killed you. Did you murder the teleport mage?"

"Catalina, run!"

Benedict smiled. It looked a bit deranged. "Unlike our friend, I'm genuinely happy you're here."

He would try to force me to walk to him. The magic of my body could power the circle even if I was unconscious. If he managed to knock me out, he could drop me into the circle under his feet and walk away, while Alessandro remained trapped. He must have tried it with the teleport mage, but she died before he could get his hands on her.

I had to let Benedict think he was winning. If he thought I retained my will, he would kill me.

"Come here," Benedict ordered.

"Walk away," Alessandro called out. "His magic is line-of-sight only."

The dark cloud erupted out of Benedict. I snapped my wings up, shielding my mind. The ghostly serpents struck. Fangs tore into my feathers, ripping lesions in my defenses. I let them slither in. Panic burst in my mind, a gaping, bottomless hole filled with darkness and fear. I collapsed into it, curling into a ball to keep from unraveling.

The void melted away. I blinked my eyes open. The boundary of the circle shone only inches away. I had collapsed on the floor in a fetal ball.

"Dear God," Benedict squeezed out.

He shook in the circle, his face slack with euphoria.

"You taste like nothing else," he whispered. "Come here."

I leaned on my hands, drawing a tiny line with my chalk from the boundary out, and struggled to my feet. He didn't notice. He was too focused on getting another hit.

"No." I turned.

The serpents struck again. Pain ripped through me. Before it dragged me down, I let my magic wind about them. They took it back to Benedict, carrying my power in their phantom mouths.

Darkness melted away. Benedict moaned.

"It hurts . . ." I murmured. I was out of breath. My mind burned, writhing from hundreds of needles stabbing it. I drew another line.

"Come here. Come to me and it won't hurt anymore." His voice was almost tender.

In the circle Alessandro was screaming.

I needed one more. I almost had him. I turned, trying to crawl away.

The serpent swarm engulfed me. This time I couldn't escape into the darkness. They wrapped around me, biting, striking, pulling me to Benedict, as my power wound around their bodies. It hurt. It hurt worse than anything I'd ever felt. The agony pierced my mind again and again.

I crawled forward, striking small lines along the boundary with every move of my hand.

In the circle Benedict crouched, waiting for me. "That's it, you're almost there. A little more. I want more. I need more."

I collapsed a foot from his circle. He reached for me, pulling me up to my feet, and as he dragged me upright, I struck the last line, long and sharp against the boundary of the larger ring.

Benedict pulled me to him, hugging me to his chest, his eyes insane, the pupils tiny specks of black in the pale blue irises. The serpents wrapped around us, shredding my wings. My feathers bled.

"Mine," Benedict said. "Mine . . ."

"Hit him now!" I barked.

Magic detonated around Alessandro. The lines of the larger circle flashed with orange. The outer boundary cracked along the faults I had added. The circle exploded, melting into nothing.

A single gunshot cracked. A bright red dot blossomed between Benedict's eyes. His deadweight hit me. I dropped him, and then Alessandro caught me, my Beretta smoking in his hand.

"You're crazy," he snarled, and kissed me.

The cupola above us groaned, tilted, and was lifted up, like the lid off a jar. Arabella peered down into the room and saw us hugging, me draped over a nude Alessandro with dead Benedict at our feet.

Silence reigned.

My sister opened her nightmarish mouth and laughed.

I walked up the iron steps to Alessandro's lair. Shadow bounded ahead of me, no doubt expecting a treat.

Three days had passed since we raided the lab. I slept for two of them. I had dim memories of being moved and

Alessandro sitting next to me, but I couldn't tell if it had been real or wishful thinking.

Today was the first day I was up and moving around. While I slept, the rest of the wall near my former room had collapsed. The warehouse resembled a crushed shoebox, with one side still up, and the opposite wall in shambles. We had to move into the nearest building while we figured out what to do. At least we managed to save the servers.

Runa did rescue her sister. I met Halle this morning. She was just like her sister and her brother. Ragnar wouldn't stop touching her to reassure himself that she was really alive, and she finally told him to knock it off or else.

Linus left a cryptic email for me, consisting of exactly two sentences: "One down, four to go. To be continued." I assumed it meant the National Assembly wouldn't be coming for our heads.

Nevada would be on her way home in four days.

Ahead, Shadow barked.

I climbed the last of the steps and walked into the old fire station rec room. Alessandro turned and my world stopped.

"Hey," I said. An intelligent human being, that's me.

"Hey," he said.

So far this conversation was going splendidly.

It dawned on me that the folding tables in the middle of the room were gone and so were all his weapons. Two suitcases and a duffel bag waited in the corner.

"You're leaving," I said.

"I have to go."

He said something else, but I couldn't hear it over the sound of my heart breaking.

Embarrassment flooded me in a hot rush. I was an

idiot. I loved him, so I thought he loved me and wanted to be with me, and he had never considered it. The job was over, and he was leaving.

He was leaving.

I had this whole speech planned. I was going to tell him that I loved him, but I could never join him in Italy. I planned to explain that a fling with him wouldn't be enough for me, that I knew it was presumptuous because we hadn't even gone on a date, but I'd made a deal with my grandmother and I had responsibilities to my House. I wanted to tell him that I would help him break free of whatever forced him to do what he was doing now no matter how he felt about me. I wanted to get it all out in the open, so if he wanted to try to be with me, he would know everything before we even started.

I had built a fantasy in my head again, and the sight of his packed suitcases shattered it. He wasn't even thinking about introducing me to his family or taking me with him. If he had, I couldn't, but I still thought . . . I wanted . . .

I was a moron.

"Catalina?" he asked.

I forced myself to look up and meet his eyes. "Are you going back to Italy to your family?" My voice didn't shake. It was a small miracle.

"No," he said.

"Too bad. I'm sure you must miss them." The words came out on autopilot. I was babbling but it was better than crying. "If they are ever in the States, I would be happy to meet them."

He crossed the floor and put his hands on my shoulders. "I'll never take you to meet my family. They wouldn't understand. They don't deserve it."

Of course. Who was I to meet House Sagredo?

"I have to go," he said.

He looked like he was about to kiss me. I waited for another breath, but he didn't move.

"Let me help you, Alessandro." The words escaped before I caught them.

Alessandro let go of my shoulders and stepped back. "You can't."

"Are you coming back?" *Tell me you're coming back. Tell me you'll move mountains to get back here to me and I'll wait for you, no matter how long it takes.*

"I won't lie to you."

And just like that it was over. I turned around and walked down the stairs, out of the building and all the way back to our makeshift house.

He did not come after me.

Arabella stepped out of the doorway and saw my face. "What happened?"

"He's leaving."

"What? He can't leave! You fed him the pepper! You joked. You were happy!" She spun toward the fire station. "I'll make him stay. I'll bring him back here…"

I held up my hand. "No. I don't want anyone to force him. It's for the best."

"Catalina!"

"It's for the best," I repeated, my voice wooden.

She hugged me and we walked into the house together.

 **Epilogue**

He sat on the roof and watched her through the window. She was trying to cook with a hot plate and utensils she'd salvaged from her ruined kitchen. That was just like her. Instead of buying a new pan and knife set, she had dug in the rubble and fished them out. They meant something to her. She never left things she cared about behind. Or people, no matter what it cost her.

The look on her face when he said he was leaving nearly broke him. He thought of walking away from it right then and there. He'd almost kissed her, but if he had, he couldn't have torn himself away. But he didn't leave things unfinished and he'd sunk too much of his life into this hunt to abandon it now.

A soft chime sounded in his headset.

"Go ahead," he murmured in Italian.

"I looked through the files you got from Diatheke," a familiar feminine voice said. "You're right. He was last seen in Montreal."

"Then Montreal it is."

"Did you get to see her?"

"I did."

In the window she was chopping vegetables. He wondered if it was one of those hell peppers.

"And? Was she everything you expected?"

"She was nothing like I expected. You'd love her."

"You could stay with her. I know you want to."

"It's not about what I want."

She huffed into the headset. "You've done enough. Eventually, it has to be about what you want. Otherwise, what's the point?"

Right now he didn't need the extra doubt. "Did the wire clear?"

"Of course, it did. I can't do this for too much longer. I can't sleep at night. I have nightmares, I wake up thinking you died. You are my only brother. Walk away, Alessandro. Please."

"I will after I kill him."

He pushed the button on the headset and ended the call before she said anything else.

The ticket was already booked. He looked one last time at his angel and jumped off the roof.

*Next month, don't miss these exciting
new love stories only from
Avon Books*

How The Dukes Stole Christmas by Tessa Dare,
   Sarah MacLean, Sophie Jordan, and Joanna Shupe
From the ballrooms of London, to abandoned Scottish
castles, to the snowy streets of Gilded Age New York,
four bestselling authors whip up some unforgettable
holiday romance complete with stranding snowstorms,
Christmas miracles, arrogant dukes, and New York
newspapermen.

Heiress Gone Wild by Laura Lee Guhrke
When Jonathan Deverill promised a dying friend that
he'd be guardian to the man's daughter, he never
envisioned his ward would be Marjorie McGann, a fully-
grown, defiant beauty. Under his watchful, protective
eye, Marjorie has no chance at romance . . .until one
fateful night when Jonathan's devastating kisses makes
her wonder if love might be right in front of her.

When The Marquess Was Mine by Caroline Linden
Georgiana Lucas despised the cruel Marquess of
Westmorland even before learning that he's won the deed
to her friend's home. But when he shows up, bloody and
unconscious, she makes a plan: say he's her fiancé, nurse
him back to health, and make sure he never returns. The
man who wakes up, though, is nothing like the heartless
rogue Georgiana thought she knew.

REL 0919